THE REQUEST FOR LAMBENCY

ileso DMC

The Request for Lambency
Published in Jan 2019 by WMS PRESS

For any ordering information or special discounts for bulk purchases, please contact ilesodmc@yahoo.com

The Request for Lambency
Copyright © 2019 All rights reserved.

By WMS PRESS

ISBN 978-1-7323425-1-4

1st edition, Jan 2019
Printed in Boston, MA

Dedication

Glory of the poet, glow O' the humorist who
castigates his kind,
Suave summer-lightning lambency which
plays On stag-horned tree,
misshapen crag askew,
Then vanishes with unvindictive smile
After a moment's laying black earth bare.
— Clarke, Helen Archibald

Dedicated to my Mams. You sacrificed so much for me and
my sister. I now know what that sacrifice feels like. When the
parent becomes the child and the child becomes the parent. If
we all lose our minds, we might as well do it while laughing.

Thank You

To my family: I am sorry for keeping you all in the dark about this project. But that is where I am at my brightest.

Special Hi-5s to:

The wife: thank you for the support. I know it wasn't easy or convenient, but it is recognized and appreciated.

My son who I call my brother: keep PTG. I am proud of the things you are learning from life's lessons. Remember who rules the world.

My daughter: You DO NOT have me wrapped around your little finger, but you keep getting close to brainwashing me. Stop it.

Table of Contents

Cast Of Characters

Powa: 16-year-old Latina who is 5'6" thin build, unnatural dirty blond. Not much of Spanish accent yet speaks broken Spanish.

Nhim: 9-year-old Costa Rican migrant. Strong Spanish accent.

Koonzo: 16-year-old Latino who goes to the same high school as Powa. 'A' student. No Spanish accent but speaks it fluently. Leader of his Comic-Con group.

Sung-Suu: Koonzo's Korean friend. 17-year-old boy that has been Koonzo's friend since grade school. Has a Korean accent. Large chin, tan complexion medium to pudgy build.

Cliffster: 16-year-old African American athlete. Tallest of the group who does not act nerdish but has a strong connection to this group.

Shaboomba: 17-year-old New Zealander with tropical tan and long curly hair. Oversees Noni and Goji.

Noni and Goji: Twin 15-year-old boys from Russia. They are a rambunctious pair.

Munch: Friend of Koonzo and Sung-Suu

DeadRick: 9Lock staff

Mac: Shaboomba's close friend

Mrs. Bellows: 67-year-old Caucasian who is very demure and always classy in her delivery.

Pendleton: 69-year-old scientist.

Jerry: 55-year-old sibling.

Carter: Mrs. Bellows' chief of her personal security detail.

Rilo: Carter's driver and one of the security personnel assigned to Mrs. Bellows. African American. Muscular yet thin build.

Everest: Government Agent.

Rutherford: scientist-African with a thick accent. Well groomed.

Somewhere in the Jungle, Somewhere in the Night

1	2	3	4	5	6	7	8	9	10	11	12	13	14	15
0918	1864	8204	8123	404	44.8	8364	8240	7318	8109	8.980	4868	10.24	11189	1800
16	17	18	19	20	21	22	23	24	25	26	27	28	29	30

€

A large and extremely bright explosion tears the midnight hour into complete havoc. The once slumbering tropical landscape is smashed with a concussion from the blast. The clear vision of the moon is tarnished by chunks of mud and rock spearing through the cool tropical air. Every nocturnal creature that was sounding off scurries to safety while the remaining startled species screech from panic. This explosion is different than the others within the past two weeks. The earth quakes much longer and with more intensity as the rural landscape suddenly changes in a small region of French Guiana.

Along the Maroni river is the fast-growing town of Apatou. There, a team of 13 individuals emerge from the jungle to get a clear look at what has taken place. They are dressed in orange biohazard type suits that encloses their entire body, including their faces. In the Maroni River is a considerably large crater. As the river water fills the crater, a thick white cloud spews from within as if it had been under extreme pressure for many centuries. The white plume skyrockets about 100-feet in the air until it calms down to just a slow gush like lava slowly flowing down a trail. The slight breeze from the Atlantic Ocean provides certain guidance for this cloud as it pushes it towards the small town of Apatou. One of the biohazard suits removes his head gear. He looks to the white cloud through a set of night vision binoculars. An alert goes off on his gauntlet device. He raises his left hand with the device on it and pushes a red light on its slick black screen. The gauntlet's screen lights up. The man reads the information from the gauntlet to himself. Another person removes his head gear as well and asks, "Ruthe, what is it?" Laboring to put a sentence together, Ruthe looks over at the gentleman. He looks back at the town. The gentleman lifts Ruthe's gauntlet and reads the information aloud, "Hydrogen chloride 10,000 parts per million. Hydrogen chloride?! Ruthe, that's hydrogen chloride! It is heading straight for Apatou!"

Ruthe whispers to himself, "My little girl is in there." His eyes and his mind realize what his mouth is saying. Ruthe quickly puts on his head gear and starts to sprint towards the town. The other team members follow him. The gas cloud engulfs the town along with the 13-member crew. The only difference is that they happened to be wearing the right gear. Unfortunately, the Apatou people did not.

Inside a tree line, flimsy huts had collapsed with ease. A three-year old little Guiana girl uncovers herself from the wooden planks that used to be the side of her home. Other family members do the same as they look around attempting to recover from the strange event. The little girl sees a faint glow beyond the trees. She heads to the light as her family helps the other villagers come out from their collapsed huts.

The little girl quietly and gingerly walks beyond the tree line until the riverbed stops her. On the other side of the river, she sees the small town of Apatou covered in a thick white cloud reflecting from the moon's rays. Some structures have crumbled due to their primitive engineering, but the newly developed areas of the town still remain. The screams from afar echo into the night but quickly mutate into ragged coughing and choking. The little girl climbs a tree until she can get a clearer view. With a better vantage point, she scans the town and notices several glowing lights. The screams, coughing, and choking all grow silent. The thick cloud is dissipating which helps the little girl get a better look at what is going on. Several minutes later, more circular lights are seen. These lights are of various colors and sizes. No one light contains just one color and no one light acts exactly like the other. The thin cloud is now more like a fog which amplifies their illumination yet conceals their specific detail. The lights come on spontaneously. They linger for a short while and then disappear individually.

The mother comes for the little girl. She sees what is taking place across the river. Her face changes from concern to fear. The mother makes a statement that catches the little girl's ear. She calls for her mom's attention as she points to the glowing lights. The little girl smiles as she says in her native tongue, "Maman, Nous sommes autorises a les voir maintenant." (Mom, we are allowed to see them now.) The mother does not reply as she is shocked by what she sees.

A small boat manages to escape the fog. It appears no one is on the boat. What cargo is making its way to this little village? Three of the other villagers come for the little girl when the boat nears their shore. They jump in the river and complete the boat's journey. One of them hops in it and lifts up a middle-aged lady native to Apatou. She is shaking uncontrollably; her lips, hands, and feet. The right side of her face has marks on it. Those same marks are on her forearms, hands, neck and chest. Visibly shaken, the lady begins to speak. She turns to stare at the glow from her recently silenced town and says, "Voleurs. Les voleurs sontVenus prendre tout." (Thieves. The thieves came to take everything.)

HyD

Subterranean Slip, Pressure PoP

ENCRYPTION AUTHORIZATION 438-908A

+97 minutes from time of incident-Date and Time Stamp follow
HyD encryption protocol
Location: Apatou, French Guiana
Injuries: Mass Casualties due to toxic chemical exposure
Employees affected: 48 unaffected survivors; 107 affected-all
critical condition; 562 deaths
Accompanied/family members affected: Unknown number of
accompanied and family member deaths
Local population affected: Unknown number of local residents/
hospitality staff affected/deaths
Equipment damage: Unknown if any equipment was destroyed
or damaged due to chemical exposure
Status: Open; Sensors reflect all airborne toxins are no longer
present in the town of Apatou. Currently, the region is under
internal field level investigation. HyD area of operation
is currently under protocol (see below for details). Local
government not informed, yet. Private intervention has not
been approached.

Summary: Satellite deployed Experimental Spectrum Analyzer
(ESA) ANXO-619 field tested to detect oil deposits for POLR
(Path of Least Resistance) drilling activity. Following ESA
procedures, in order to confirm the precision and accuracy of
the sensor, field technicians had to blast immediately into the

site to confirm the integrity of the data validating the spectrum analyzer's operability. The detonation at the POLR site resulted in the release of a highly pressurized hydrogen chloride gas pocket that created a toxic cloud. This cloud swept through the town of Apatou which houses HyD employees, their accompanied/family members as well as the local hospitality staff and residents. This incident is classified as a Mass Casualty Event hMCE) due to HyD activity.

Additional information: The town of Apatou has been authorized by the government of French Guiana to be gentrified in order to accommodate HyD employees without relocating any local residents or businesses. HyD has been obedient to this demand from the French Guiana government.

FLASH!!! Unexplainable occurrence (UXO). 13 POLR field technicians observed certain artifacts enveloped by various light probes hovering over each recently deceased resident of Apatou. Light phenomenon only lasted less than 60 seconds before both the object and the light probe disappearing from the deceased. Each technician's video interview is attached and encrypted with this report.

Containment Requirement: Initiate Protocol Nine thru 13. See below for details.
Protocol 9a-Request limited media exposure directed towards assigned corporate spokesman.
Protocol 9b-Initiate dialogue with regional government officials once representatives are on site.
Protocol 10-Activate HyD regional journalists to receive instructions on release of information activities.
Protocol 11-Exhaust all measures to incorporate jamming sequence to limit media exposure.
Protocol 12-Request Geosynchronous Orbit of Satellite 213 for surveillance activity and COIN (Counter-Intelligence) operations.
Protocol 13-Conduct covert electromagnetic pulse drops of

the Apatou region in order to prevent unauthorized release of media and communication.
Protocol 14-Investigate UXO.

Immediate Action already initiated:
Protocol 4-Quarantine site Plus 10 miles.
Protocol 5-Canopy Bird's Eye of affected areas.
Protocol 6a-Containment of employees.
Protocol 6b-Containment of accompanied members, hospitality staff and local population.
Protocol 7a-River City: Temporary Black out on all communication systems.
Protocol 7b-Temporary EMP blasts of region until response from Echelon representative conducts on site assessment.
Protocol 8a-Stand up Field Hospital and staff.
Protocol 8b-Place the deceased in stand up field mortuary.
Protocol 1-3=Not Applicable-Used only for physical plant.

Distribution: Senior Executive Level Echelon (SELE) only
Report Originator: RE-9-213-9

INCIDENT REPORT/FORMAT 6

Subterranean Slip, Pressure PoP

Senior Executive Level Echelon ORS-9i890 Field Correspondence

ENCRYPTION AUTHORIZATION 908A-438ORS
+33 minutes from receiving Incident Report 438-908A
-Confirm Protocols 4-8 initiated as per policy.
-Protocols 9-14 will be initiated once SELE representative conducts site assessment.
-SELE representative will be at Apatou within six hours. Prepare to present detailed analysis to include UXO.
-Set up general purpose tents for 250 additional employees. Must be completed within 12 hours.
-Segregate all 13 eyewitness technicians. Detention standards are not required.
-Prepare to transfer all 13 technicians to other HyD facilities after questioning is completed.
-No further access to the affected areas to include your field investigators.
-Cease current investigative efforts and consolidate all findings and present to SELE.
-Initiate a patrol on field mortuary. Zero activity allowed on those bodies.
-You have no authority to provide your analysis from your last statement in the summary. You will recant that statement and submit new summary to SELE.

Report reply by: SELE BL-0317

Chapter 1

Three months later

It's typical. The sterile smell in the air, the flowers, the used tissues, and the rhythmic beeping noise are part of the norm now. Pictures and cards drape the walls and the nightstands. The news on the television is not loud enough to draw anyone's attention. The weeping in the background comes in waves, but sometimes it is intense. You know the type, the grunting and painful crying as if you were trying to force all the sorrow out of your body?

The contraption everyone is clawing for sits on the right nightstand near the window. I cannot believe how the entire world changed because of this thing. It looks like a skinny, dark tinted crystal vase with an LCD touch screen in the middle. These things have evolved into an app. What is funny is that this is no longer the center of attention anymore even though they are in higher demand now than when they were first introduced a year ago. But I will get into that later.

At the center of all this activity is Nhim. A nine-year old boy that will make you cry during times like this. He is so kind to everyone. Nhim has the amazing ability to carry on a conversation with a child or adult. He always expresses his perspective but never without an intelligent argument or defense. At such an early age, he has developed a passion for life and how he views it. Last year, he created his most fantastic of gadgets. It was a moment of awakening for him. He pieced together a camera from scraps found in multiple areas throughout his hometown of Colon, Costa Rica. It was the first time he found a passion for something.

I remember his story well; his family migrated to the United States soon after. The immigration officials almost did not allow the camera through Customs as it appeared more unusual than the standard camera. Nhim used his charisma to convince the customs folks to allow it through. It was another triumphant success for him.

There is only one issue, Nhim has leukemia. That is the only reason why his family moved to America, to get him the best medical care available. His family knows how incredibly special he is. Sure, his older brother and sister would be worth the pilgrimage to America as well but in this case Nhim happens to be the one to bring them to the USA. The local hospital was looking for children with leukemia to perform an experimental process to battle the cancer and of course Nhim's parents jumped on the opportunity. The hospital made all the arrangements for them; the proper documentation to get them to the country and keep them here permanently. Anything that involved the hospital was free for them – even their evening meals were included - They hooked them up with a rental home that is near the hospital, too. But part of the deal is that they would have to get a job to take care of the rent as well as their expenses.

Nhim underwent treatment every day which happened to be pretty intense from what he told me. Lasers, radiation, sweet drinks, vibration techniques, and horse pills; all of it made him sick. But after five-months he was getting better. He got healthy enough to be discharged but with daily check-ups. It was then that I first saw the little guy. Six-weeks ago he passed out in school. His doctor told his parents the sad news, his cancer was no longer in remission.

It is a Sunday afternoon. Both his siblings are busy doing their own thing. His older brother plays basketball while his older sister travels with the school's debate club. I did not even know that was a thing. Nhim made a really big deal and actually insisted that his family continue doing their regular activities.

Trust me, I saw a different side of him the day they explained to me his type of cancer. They honored his request and try to lead normal lives. As for me, well I just do school and that is it. I am not interested in any after school activities. My after-school activities are homework and then my online life. In there, I am an amateur virtual reality artist. I love it and so does Nhim. We have often gotten lost in the mazes and cities I create. But once I got word of Nhim's deteriorating health, I put all that aside and headed straight for the hospital. I have been coming after school ever since. I know, it is weird. Having school on a Sunday is not the norm. But then again, lately a lot of things have not been business as usual.

The government has even dipped into Sunday, nothing is sacred anymore. It is some new restructuring process that has been met with heavy opposition. Every religious congregation has been fighting against this, calling it a blasphemous spit in the face on their beliefs. They are accusing capitalists of forcing the change to get more productivity out of workers. Unions, lobbyists, and multiple affiliations of the education system are also enraged.

I feel their pain. It is bad enough they are grossly underpaid, overworked and now they will not have a day off. Like they were not already tired of dealing with the likes of us. My goodness talk about cruel and unusual punishment! From what I understand, the government is somehow going to add two extra days to the week.

Yup, I did not get it at first either, let me break it down. In the near future, whenever the government decides, we will have a nine-day week which will turn our calendar from 12-months to 10-months. The monthly breakdown is as follows: five 36-day months and five 37-day months. I know, it sounds bananas, but I did the math and we will still have a 365- day year. Talk about redoing a calendar. Think about how significant that is. Our current calendar has been in use since when, the 1500s? And now the government is going to change all of that?!

Everyone is arguing about how this will affect birthdays and certain dated documents that will require some crossover matrix or equivalency chart that is beyond my intellect. And it does not stop there. Check this out. Other countries are talking about how we tell time will also be reconfigured. No more 24-hours in a day. I read somewhere that they are going to break it down to 100-seconds versus the standard 60-seconds we have been using since humans have started keeping track of time. We are going to start messing with time! Talk about history changing.

There is a lot of chatter on the web that it has something to do with a recent discovery or an experiment. Many are saying it has to do with 'the requests.' Do not worry, I will get into 'the requests' in a bit. The government is not going to implement the new calendar system just yet, but it appears to be inevitable. For now, they just want to mess with people's Sundays. Alright, back to my little buddy, Nhim.

Nhim's treatment requires a regimented schedule and lots of attention from the staff. But right now, I get Nhim all to myself. His mother and father are still at work. They work several blue-collar jobs to afford the cost of living. They offset their work hours so that one of them is always here with him but that doesn't always work out for them. Today happens to be one of them.

Nhim's parents are fortunate to have made friends that help take his brother and sister to their school and sports commitments. It must be a difficult situation for Nhim's parents. Living a life that is all about work and nothing else in order to give their children a life worth living is something I never thought about until I met Nhim. Enough of that before it gets soggy in here. Right now, is the half hour I get to mess with my little buddy. I am not here by myself today. Some of his older friends are here too. They are adults who are acquainted with longevity. I wait outside until I sense it is an appropriate time to enter his room. My dad always told me to enter a room at an opportune time because timing is the identical twin of luck. I have found his advice to be very helpful. In the past, I got to hear a little more than I should, and by entering the room during those awkward moments that make you wish you never should have walked in. Nhim just wrapped up a conversation which made some of them laugh and some others cry. They are probably crying out of joy. There are two ladies inside that are constantly crying every time they are there. Right now, I can hear the remnants of whimpering. They must be tired. That is my cue. As I walk in, I smile, and the gesture is reciprocated by the audience. They recede from his bed as I step up. I almost begin talking about my day but Nhim looks different. I pause from my normal greeting of the day to examine him. He looks pale and fragile. One of the elders informed me that the first alarm has sounded off already. My heart pounds through my chest as my mind processes this difficult information.

Nhim still having a great attitude says, "Hey freak show! Are you going to keep staring at my hotness or are you going to hit on me?"

His Spanish accent is thicker than mine. I snap out of it, "Pff, no I am not going to hit on a boy that cannot even make me a quesadilla. You are lucky I got here in time. These folks here were about to go backyard wrestling on you."

We both laugh at each other. I add, "Besides, my threat of telling them how we met is still on the table."

Nhim makes his comeback, "You keep threatening me with that. I am just going to tell them, so you have nothing left to use against me."

"No need to do that. Your storytelling skills will put them to sleep." Nhim playfully scoffs at me. I know it is unusual for a 16-year old to be close friends with a nine-year old boy. But like I said, he is not an ordinary boy. Unlike him, I am plenty ordinary though. I am not totally invisible, but it is not like I am the most popular girl in Klamath Union High either. I just fit in.

Back to Nhim. He brings me in closer, "Powa, I want to be recorded like the others. And I want you to upload it for me. I want the world to pay attention to this Costa Rican boy even if it is for a short moment."

I was already planning on recording him. But it is different now that he has asked me. I tell him, "Do you really believe people are going to pay attention to a scrawny kid from Puerto Rico? Do you even know one Costa Rican dish?"

Nhim replies, "Ha ha! You are lucky I don't get butthurt when you call me Puerto Rican. I love my Boricua brothers and sisters. And for your information I do have a Costa Rican dish that you can help me with."

"What is that?" I said laughing.

"I like Ropa Sucia with a side of flat buns. Can you hand me the two you have stuffed in your back pockets?"

I break out laughing, "What did I tell you about talking about my butt?! I get self-conscious about it."

Nhim laughs along, "I make myself laugh. It is like you got this long back and then you have legs! Do some butt squats or something."

"Shut up, Nhim!"

As I smile at my friend, he points to an object on the end table, "Before I forget or pass out, there is my camera. We should practice because as my dad says, 'opportunity is like a good woman, the hardest part is knowing what to do when you meet her.' That is why my dad calls my mom Oppie, short for... you know."

"Enough already, you sappy Sapo. What I am going to do is record you with this hideous contraption right now since I am being forced to do it against my will. And try to look pretty. Oops, I forgot. That face is tattooed to your head. Ha ha!"

"Okay, okay. You got me. But you cannot record on it. The SIM card slot is busted. I already have it paired with my tablet."

So, I grab the camera and make sure the tablet is picking up the video feed. Everything is paired. I begin recording.

Nhim directs, "Do not do it like the other videos, Powa. I want you to move about. I have multiple pretty sides I want the world to cherish. Be a great camerawoman."

"Okay, Mr. Demanding. I will get up and get some close ups so that everyone will know that is your real face and not some cheap special effect." We both get a good snicker out of that one. Nhim is distracted by the television. I tell him, "Hey there movie star, you going to do this or are you making this the most boring of all the videos?"

I hear the news anchor say, "Due to the toxic situation in this small village of Apatou, it has taken the rescue crew three-months to finally reach it. The death toll for the Apatou event has reached over 4,000. It is devastating that something like this could happen in what scientists suspect was an unforeseen tragedy for so many people. Scientists are speculating that this was a two-headed manmade disaster. As we can see on the satellite imagery, it appears an explosion took place judging by the crater seen underneath the river, and somehow that triggered the release of a poisonous gas. This poison gas found its way to the citizens of Apatou in the middle of the night. Some of the nearby villagers witnessed the catastrophe. Here is what one of them has to say…"

Nhim looks back at me, "Can you imagine how many families have been lost? The destruction and the people it has impacted? It is an extremely sad situation."

I tell him, "Turn that off, Nhim, and tell the world what you want them to know!" As he turns off the television, he smiles at the camera. He clears his throat. Then he clears it again. He adds a few coughs. The smile is no longer present.

Something intense happens, the beeping noise begins to increase in tempo. The vase blinks inconveniently with its touchscreen flashing a special pattern possibly requesting its attention. I look over at Nhim. He looks even more pale. His hand signals for me to keep recording. I push the medical response button. Then I raise the camera to my face. I keep in mind how he wants me to move about the room. Two nurses respond to the beeping devices. They do not clear the room as it is now normal practice to allow family members and friends during this special moment. Instead, they wait in the doorway as they review his vitals from their tablet. One of them looks over at the vase contraption. It is blinking a blue light which she relays to the other nurse. The nurse puts the tablet away and pushes a few more buttons on the other side of the wall. The lights dim gently. The nurses wait quietly in the doorway again. Nhim looks scared now.

I yell out, "I love you, freak show!" I see a tear run down his face. I take that as a sign he heard me and feels the same way.

"We love you, too, Nhim." I had lost track of the elders behind me. They have been so quiet all this time. One of the nurses calls out to one of the elderly ladies, "Please put away your recording device. Respect the no recording orders of the hospital." The embarrassed woman places her phone back in her purse.

It is amazing how everything has to do with money. More on this later. Nhim could tell the strict nurse was coming after me next and says, "Please let my special friend keep recording. She does not want to forget me, and I always want to stay with her. This is my special gift to her. You would not deny the wish of a dying boy, would you?"

Nice one, Nhim! Even dying you manage to outsmart grownups. The nurse is disarmed by Nhim's whit and cute face and lets me be. Almost immediately the tempo of the beat goes quietly flat. I lower the camera. Nhim is gone. I start to cry but remember his camera is still in my hand. I have an obligation to my friend. As I raise the camera to my face, I pan over to the pictures on the wall. Surely one of these will be the one. I zoom back out. The time is near. I can feel the warm tears softly flow down my cheeks. As I try and focus on every item in the room, the camera begins to get hot. The battery must be getting low or something. I keep looking through the view panel. The camera is not as heavy as before. The heat has now dissipated. Then something I will never forget takes place. Flickers of light spring from the camera. These lights pop out like embers from a fire and take on an orbit around the camera. They start off slow and begin to pick up pace. There is no noise, just lights. Before I know it, the camera had partially disappeared. More lights of all colors spring from the camera now and their orbital rings make for a beautiful ceremony. I could have removed my hand, but

I did not want to risk messing up this special moment. I knew from watching other request videos not to interfere with the request process unless I wanted to end up with more lines than a tiger. The faster the rings of light spin, the faster the camera disappeared. Then my hand became empty just like that. The lights are now gone. Eventually my eyes adjust to the dimly lit room again. I look over at Nhim as he lays there in silence. I sink my head into his little belly and join the weeping crowd.

I do not know how much time went by. Everyone clears the room as the hospital staff begins to care for his body. They let me stay for a bit longer. As I look around, I realize all the pictures and flowers are where they were before Nhim passed. I put myself together and grab all my gear and head out. Before I leave the room, I reach out for Nhim's tablet. I look at the image on the screen and get upset with myself. The video is playing nothing relating to Nhim's hospital room. At first, I think it is one of Nhim's home videos or something he downloaded before. But then I look closer and realize the red recording light is still on. The live feed is still going. "No way is this possible. No one is going to believe me," is the thought that keeps running through my head. But it does not matter. I realize this video is something different as I keep examining it in detail. Then it cuts off. Just like that, it stops. After so many minutes, the live feed finally ends. I am weary about looking at the full recording. There is always the possibility nothing was recorded. You know, like something you always see in the movies when something crazy, fantastic, or unexplainable happens yet the recording device never records it. I decide not to flirt with cinematic superstition and choose to not review its contents right away. But I still have to keep my promise to him.

The reality of my little friend's passing begins to catch up with me again. I bite hard on the inside of my cheek to keep the tears from spilling. It works. I have to go. I kiss Nhim's forehead which is cold on my lips. I want to cry again. I hear my dad's voice, "Bite hard, Powa. No need to cry now. If at all possible, do it when you are alone for a while. That way you can calmly let it out with no distractions and be at peace with yourself." It works. I leave the room thinking about Nhim's family. Are they on their way here? Were they allowed to leave work? Were they notified that he has already passed? No, I cannot deal with these questions. I bite down on both cheeks to keep me calm as I exit the hospital.

I am home after a long walk down memory lane. My eyes are red, and I am exhausted. But I have to upload this video. The worst that can happen is that I upload a blank video. Well here I go. The site is up and all I have to do is push a button. "Ok, Nhim, the world is about to see what you have to offer." "Should I leave the comment section on or off," I ask myself? Eh, I will leave it on. If the video is blank, then no one will really care that much. But if it is uploaded then Nhim gets the recognition he so deserved. Click. And it is now available to the masses. It is late, and tomorrow is a school day. I am going to fill the rest of my day in my 3D universe; I need the distraction.

Chapter 2

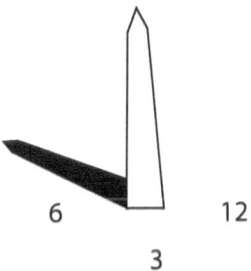

6   12

3

Monday morning

I feel I have been sleeping for far too long. I finally persuade myself to check the time. What in the…? Is that daylight creeping through my curtains? As I jump out of bed, I check my phone. Sure enough, the time says it is close to seven along with too many push notifications.

I yell out, "Mom, we are late!" I hear her stumble out of bed, "How did that happen?!" "I will meet you in the car in about five minutes." Getting dressed is not an art for me. I usually pick out an outfit the night before, so I do not have to guess what looks good. Make-up and hair, I can do in the car. My dad taught me to be time efficient when things change. The poor guy is always working odd hours.

Mom finally gets in the car. She is not a morning person. She stopped working a couple of months ago. I never found out why though. All I remember is that her and my dad were arguing one night. They do their squabbles in the car with the radio on blast, so we cannot hear them. They do their best to never fight around us. Ever since then, she has been home. My dad has been working extra hours probably to cover the income my mother no longer provides. And because of that I do not get to see my dad as much. I blame my mom for that, of course. I have not confronted her about it. I can tell she feels bad that she has put a strain on Dad. But I am sure the next argument we have, I will give her a piece of what has been bugging me. She drops me off. I still show my respect and give her a peck on the cheek, "Love you." I close the door as she repeats my words. I make it to school with some time to get my mind ready for the day. I still cannot bring myself to think about Nhim, if I do I will not be able to function.

Why are school mornings so difficult to adjust to? I get to my first class, Language Arts. This class does not work for me. I just cannot get it. Anyway, other students are doing their pre-class routine of web scrubbing. You know you got a winner when you get a group huddled around you. Sometimes I think it is a competition to see who can find the most interesting thing on the web. I do not pay too much attention to it today. Whatever it is will eventually make its way to my phone. I take my seat with several minutes to spare. As I allow myself to begin thinking about Nhim, I catch the attention of two girls sitting to my left, Roxanne and Josephine.

Roxanne says, "Hurry up before the bell rings!"

An excited Josephine replies, "Ok, give me a second."

"Remember, the blue strip goes under your tongue and the red goes on top. Do not mess it up or else you will have to wait two months before doing it again," explains Roxanne.

Josephine replies, "Are you sure this is better than using the Gevity vase?" Roxanne replies, "Listen, the Gevity vase is first-generation old school technology. You are not going to be carrying around that thing everywhere you go. It is like carrying a medium size baseball bat everywhere. Not a good look for you, girl. And having to push all those buttons on that touchscreen is not as user friendly as the mobile app." Josephine nods confirming her confidence.

She follows the simple instructions and closes her mouth.

Josephine slowly closes her eyes and provides a description of what she feels, "You are right, girl. It really does give you a real nice lift. Wow, that is pretty groovy."

Roxanne laughs out loud, "Okay little hipster. Enjoy it because it is the only euphoria you get out of it. Trust me. I tried it three other times and it just gave me the runs. Not a pretty look. Okay open your mouth. Is it all gone?"

"I cannot tell. What do you think?"

Roxanne looks inside, "All gone. Oh crap, did you register on the site?! If not, then this may be a problem."

"I am good. I did it. I added the family and you, Boo Boo, to my trust fall list."

Roxanne gives her an, "Awe. Thanks BFF. Now check your phone and see if you are synced."

Josephine unlocks her phone and pushes on an app. Then she says, "Wow, this really works. All of this info is really me."

"Pretty cool tech, huh? My parents wanted me to have it for other lame reasons. I like it just to figure out what my body looks like when I am in a certain mood. Like when I am pissed off or when I am crushing on Josh Devin," as Roxanne growls a seductive laugh.

"Oh, my goodness, you still stuck on him? Anyway, how do you see what your body looks like on the app?" Josephine asks looking at her phone.

The teacher walks in as the bell sounds. Roxanne replies in a whisper, "Just look it up."

Such a common answer these days. No one needs to know the answer anymore. They just need to know where to find it. It makes me wonder why the education system has not adjusted to this new form of learning. Why do they test us on what we retain as opposed to how we can locate the information? I mean is this not how the real-world works? I see Josephine hide behind the student in front of her; I have a clear vantage point. She plays around with the app. Then she finds the video that explains its function. Josephine conceals her earbuds in the cloak of her burgundy hair. The video explains the standard functions such as medical awareness and automatic contacts. Then it illustrates the two alarms. This is what made this company mega rich. The video shows a visual of a cellphone sounding off and has displayed 'First Alert.' A cute little animated skit with a person on a hospital bed and the family in the room. There is a little doctor there with a comic bubble saying, "Death is highly probable."

Then it displays 'Second Alert.' Another animated skit shows the same person in the hospital bed, but this time the family is crying. The doctor has the comic bubble saying, "Second alert means death is imminent."

From what I have read, these alarms are pretty accurate. And because of that, this company is probably one of the fastest growing companies ever. I open the app on my phone constantly looking up to make sure I do not get caught by the teacher. Kind of like how my dad looks around for policecops when he is on his phone. Yes, I did say policecops. It is a childhood saying I never let go of. My app displays my biological data as advertised while it churns out all kinds of numbers next to a thermal image of my body.

Class begins, and I hear the whispers of the recent internet discovery from some other students behind me. One of them tries to capture my attention but I shrug it off. I do not like to have the oracle distract me from my school work. Today, those gnats are bugging me more than usual. Language arts class wraps up and it turns out Summer school really does suck. Too bad I cannot be like Nhim's siblings. They go to summer school to get ahead in their classes while I am here trying to play mustard. Yes, mustard, as in the friendly condiment to ketchup. Get it? Ketchup which sounds exactly like 'catch up.' You can blame Nhim for that corny joke.

One class down. One more to go. I am heading to my Algebra 2 class when my friend Willow approaches me. She is a little more excited than her normal perky self, "So what do you think?"

I reply, "Let me see if my phonetics knowledge is working. Your pants spell H-A-N-A-S That spells 'Heinous,' right?"

"Very funny. You know my fashion skills are much more advanced than yours...anyway. I am talking about the video, Powa! Is that really you?" I immediately go into my recall mode. I go out of my way to ensure I never put myself in any compromising positions. Sure, I will have a little fun at a party, but I do not let myself get carried away. One thing my dad taught me was to know my limits and be smart enough to push them with minimal risk or stay within them. In this case, I choose the latter. The last thing I need are my parents coming to school or lecturing me on how to make smart decisions.

So, I reply, "No. I have stayed away from boys, girls, and parties in the past two weeks."

"I am talking about the video of your little friend passing away. That video is getting crazy attention."

I am stunned, "You got to see it?"

"Of course, I did. Most of the school has seen it. But we all want to know how or who you got to do the special effects. The computer graphics are convincing."

"Willow, that was my friend dying. You know I would not joke about a thing as sensitive as that. I would not be fake like that."

Willow places her hand on my shoulder, "I know you, Powa. I figured you would not do something like that. Which makes this even more exciting. But you only uploaded a part of the video. It stops in the middle of its travel."

"What are you talking about? What stops in the middle of its travel? Look, I have not had a chance to review the video. I just uploaded it and moved on."

Willow, "Well everyone wants to see the rest of it. Finish uploading the rest, muchacha."

"Alright, I will check it out when I get home. What time is it? Let me check my phone. I am going to be late for…Wait, what?! I have over 100 emails."

Willow replies, "It is probably junk mail. You need to put your filter on."

"It is not only that. I also have 78 texts, 87 missed calls and 64 voicemails. Most of them are from unknown numbers."

Willow shrugs off a cold chill, "That sounds creepy. Maybe it is one of those nerds that found a way to hack into your phone and wants to take you on a date." She gives me this devilish laugh as if it is something I would be into. Sorry but the nerds I see are nothing like those cute folks with glasses and great skin on television.

Willow interrupts my nerd imagery, "How did you manage to miss that many phone calls, anyway?"

I show her my phone, "I have a scrubber app that places any unknown or unrecognized incoming calls, texts, emails, or social media notes in a special folder. It keeps them in there until the scrubber app gives it a green light to open it."

Willow replies in amazement, "I could not believe there was an app for that. Oh, dang! I need to get one of those. My cousin's phone got hacked through a phone call. How crazy is that?"

I point to the app log, "Look at this. All of my notifications are all still red." Says Powa.

As Willow heads to her class, "Alright girlfriend, I am off to get schooled on Geometry. Bang, bang." I give her a wave and make my way to my class.

So Algebra 2 was awkward as the teacher discussed a little about how the new time structure would affect some of the current formulas we are working on. I still do not understand why they are changing it which tuned me out.

School is over for today. But these notification pings have drained my phone. I only have thirteen percent of battery juice left. You think someone would invent a battery that can last longer than a day.

During my walk home, I look over my shoulder just to see a white car with tinted windows is slowly creeping behind me. Another thing my dad taught me is to always be aware of my surroundings. He always said where there is one, there are more. And sure enough, I see a second car. It is silver with tinted windows. There are no bumper stickers, no scratches or dents. It looks like a leased car moving at stalker speed. And my growing little lady intuition tells me I should be concerned. My dad always told me to act when I feel I should. The human mind has a sixth sense that people always want to ignore. So, with that, I sprint and take a few shortcuts through the neighborhood as I cut through a couple of alleys and a brisk jog through a neighbor's backyard. I do not see them anymore, but I anticipate they are probably still around. And to be honest with myself, they probably already know where I live. The ten-thousand-dollar question is 'Why?'

I reach the backsliding door. I grab two rocks and rub them together really hard. After about 30-seconds it should be good. I hold one of the rocks to the bottom part of the glass. Clip. The metal bar securing the sliding door is lifted. Magnetized rocks; you guessed that right. Dad's idea.

I enter through the back door which leads right into the dining room. Ow! I run into the dining table which provides an optical illusion that I can easily pass by without colliding into it. As I rub the pain away from my hip, I breathe a nice sigh of relief. Alas, nothing feels better than being in the one place I can retreat to and feel secure. I love being home. For the most part, it is serene. Not a lot of drama goes on here. And my room is my safe space. I know where everything is and why it is there.

No boy band posters either. I have artwork from artists I admire. They encourage me to be a better virtual reality artist. I love their work. I just started working on a project that I put on pause for Nhim, as a matter of fact. It is taking me a total of three weeks so far. But before I get too comfortable, I better check out that request video.

My Computer is on and the website is up. As I sit down at my desk, never mind that I outgrew it several years ago; I get a little apprehensive because I do not know what I am about to see. Is it something about a horrible past Nhim experienced? Could it be part of a movie he was watching that got mashed into his video? If it is outlandish then hackers may be the culprits. I click the play arrow. The video starts off as I remember with Nhim on his hospital bed and me busting his chops about not being a boring director. I hear myself say, "Okay, Mr. Demanding. I will get up and get some close ups so that everyone will know that is your real face and not some cheap special effects." I absolutely cannot stand how I sound; too nasal, I think. But that does not distract me from smiling at the comment while the tears start to prevent me from seeing the video clearly. As I wipe my eyes, I focus back on the video. And there is Nhim looking at the television. He is talking about the Apatou event. I shake my head in agreement; it was a terrible and mysterious disaster. And here is where Nhim starts coughing. I look away. This part is too difficult to relive. I even mute the video to avoid any emotional reaction. It does not work. I lose it anyway.

With my hands over my face, my tears find their way down to my chin. At least I am successful at not crying out loud. My dad always told me crying is part of an emotional release. But crying without all the dramatics, meaning the ability to cry in silence or speak clearly while crying, is the most difficult request to ask the soul. I guess the amount of people that can do this must be small because I still have not met anyone that can do it. He calls it Posh Rah. No idea what it means but every time I cry, I tell myself, "Posh Rah, please." It never works for me. Even with my hands over my face, my eyes are able to sense the illumination from my computer screen. I turn to face it as I wipe my eyes clean of my recent memory.

I am still amazed and confused at what was captured. It is very difficult to describe. The camera is hovering at this point. However, the way it is recording is different. It looks as though the lens has a flakey glitter or shimmer to it as everything looks a little brighter and glossy, if that makes sense. I can see the rings that I saw when all this occurred. Even parts of the camera can be seen in the video in short instances before it turns into a ring of light. Everything gets brighter as the rings accelerate in their orbit. The bright flash bounces its illumination off my walls and face. Several seconds go by and the camera comes back on like someone purposely powered it up. Now here is where it gets weird. What I can see is a landscape with either snow or a mixture of snow and some other mineral or soil. What I mean is the snow is not as white but if it is ash it is not as dark. The camera is moving forward at a speed slow enough to take in all the detail. There are two large snow-covered mountains on both sides while the ground in front is snow packed. I can see patches of dark rock beneath the snow from the two mountains. There are other rock structures bulging through the snow. I must be getting tired. It looks like there are sparks of light within these rock formations. It may be a reflection from a light source somewhere above the camera. The sky looks like the sun has set several hours already and the warm orange glow no longer presents itself. The camera is moving up the landscape as the camera angle would indicate. It is heading towards a cliff. As it reaches the edge of this cliff, something flashes in front of it. The camera is not fast enough to make out the details. I rewind the video and can barely identify what it is. It looks like the silhouette of a person. I magnify the image, but it does not help. And that is the point where the video cuts off. Where is this place? Is this heaven? Is Nhim there as well? Or is all this a bad joke from a hacker?

After reviewing the video several times, I finally decide to give my phone the attention it requires. I grab my recharging blade and connect it to my phone before it dies on me. Let me see. Too many missed calls, text messages, and emails. All of them are still red. I will just read what I can in the dialogue box instead of opening them. How about we start with the text messages? The first one reads, "Would like to speak with you about your video." Okay, not a big deal. The next one reads, "This is amazing work. We should talk about a possible future with our company." Hey a job offer! Maybe this video is going to take me places. A third reads, "You may need our help. Your video will attract a lot of attention." Now that gives me the willies. I really do not like that. The next ten or so messages read almost the same as the first three. I do not bother reading them all.

Delete. Next.

Onto my missed calls. As I have figured, the numbers are blocked. I am not going to bother with checking the voicemails. The last thing I want to do is get creeped out while I am here by myself. It is close to high noon. I have some time, so I head back into my alternate reality.

I put on my headset and power up my devices. And here we are in my world. To the left is the sunrise, and on the right is the moon setting. The sky is tapered into a battle between day and night and all the warriors of light fighting for their dominance. Below them is the city. My buildings are not the standard ones you are used to seeing. My buildings reach for the sky and then bend back down to the earth forming large arches. Some of them twist and branch out like a tree. I do have streets and even a double decker freeway. I have a subterranean world that has its own light source below. It is unique as the shadows are always cast on the ceiling. I even have my own house. It is a floating house. Everyone wants a floating home. Right now, I have it anchored. It is not a very big house, but it is perfect for me. It is a one story, one-bedroom home with windows all around. I love this place. I have decorated the inside as detailed as I can make it. The drawers are nicely organized, and I even allow myself a junk drawer. Oh, and check this out over here. In my bedroom, I have a safety box. And the safe is legit. A passcode is required and everything. I punch in the code and pull out some documents. I have written a lot of my secrets here. I also have two other places where I lock away my other secrets. I lock up the documents that hold some special part of me hostage. What may that be?

Chapter 3

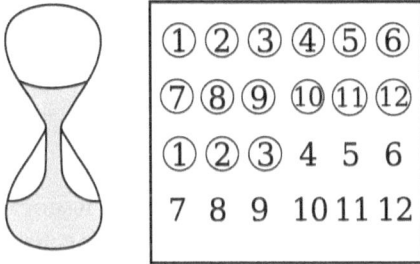

Monday mid afternoon

The doorbell rings. It startles me as I was deep in my world. It is mid-afternoon, and my phone is still pinging me for attention. I take off my headpiece and walk up to the door as the doorbell chimes impatiently several more times. What is this guy's problem? Can he not wait a little bit? As I open the door, a slender, well-groomed man dressed in a dark suit and yellow tie introduces himself, "Hello, my name is Charles. Are you Ms. Powa?" I stand like a statue and offer no expression except for how upset I am at having to waste my time telling this guy no to whatever he wants to sell me. My dad always told me to talk less and people will talk for you. Charles begins to look uncomfortable as his fake smile crumbles while he fills the void, "I would like to speak with you about a possible summer job we are scouting. I am with the local news team and we are initiating a new project in search of prospecting young journalists. All we have to do is take a quick 30-second clip of you reporting on whatever you feel is necessary. Usually our prospects pick something inside their home, a current event, or sports. I will be your cameraman and you will be the journalist. Are you ready?"

Now how can this guy know I want to be a journalist? Oh yeah, it is posted on my social media accounts. It is a bogus career description. I just put that there to throw people off. Alright, I will play along. I adjust my voice to sound a bit more innocent, "Sure, I am ready. But my dad says not to let strangers inside my house." I tell the guy.

"I totally understand. We can do this right here. Your microphone and three, two, one."

I think of something quick, "We are here at the house of a young victim. It appears the little girl is home but does not want to be harassed. Before she ran crying back to her room, she informed me that someone has been taking advantage of her. The perpetrator is described as being anorexic looking and is wearing a creepy yellow tie. Tune in next time to see what happens to the neighborhood child molester."

The man behind the camera lowers it with a forced grin and a poker face that tells me he has not done this very often. His lips quiver for the words, "Okay, that was quick and intense. You show a lot of promise. Now let me get this uploaded to the station."

I have to admit that was pretty good on my part. I know how to improvise. Charles fiddles with his camera. His face telegraphs a story that something seems to not be functioning properly. He looks back at me, "The video is not uploading. It always happens to me at the worst time." "I hate it when things work against you." Charles cracks a more comforting grin. I can tell he is ready to expose his real purpose as he says, "May I use your Wi-Fi? It will get your video straight to the station and they will see your newscast today."

Now my woman's intuition is going off again. Why would he not make his news truck a hotspot and be done with it? Why is this guy still here? Oh, that is right, he is trying to coerce me into something. I tell him, "Well, I probably should not. My dad told me never to give away our Wi-Fi password."

"That is great advice. But remember, this is for your future, Ms. Powa. And the news people are the good guys. We are where you want to be."

"You know what, you are correct. I agree. Did your camera discover my Wi-Fi?"

"Is it jfhg4568zsw?" He asks me.

"No, it is 'sleeper creeper.' My dad is a weird-o."

Charles keeps his smile, "I see it. What is the password?"

I keep my smile going as well, "It is capital M and everything else is lower case u, s, t, n, o, t, b, e, the number 2, s, m, a, r, t." I hold in my laughter.

He does not get it right away, "That does not seem to work." I can see the frustration on his face.

"Try it again. My friends have a hard time with it as well."

He gives it another try, and it fails again. My phone goes off and I use it as my crutch to pull away, "Sorry Charles, I have to go."

"I will let you get that. I will keep trying right here."

I see his play. Time to break out the teenage girl in me, "I understand. Well good luck. I am going to my room now. Sometimes child molesters like to wait on the porch of their future victims. That is when my neighbors videotape them and call the cops." I close the door slowly to see if he has another comeback. Charles keeps his grin as he disappears behind my door. I hear his footsteps while he walks away. Another moral victory for yours truly.

But something is up. I do not know what it is, but these folks generally do not get too close unless they are desperate or comfortable. Either way is not a good thing for me. I grab Nhim's tablet and stuff it in my bag. My parents will be home soon. I have a little more time to myself. My mind wanders. I cannot believe how things have changed in just three months.

I remember where I was when I first saw a video of 'a request.' It was the last Friday before spring break. The lunch bell had rung, and I noticed my friends were huddled up around their phones and tablets. I saw Claire and asked, "A new movie trailer coming out or a new product for you girls to buy?"

She looked up at me and said, "You really need to check your phone more often. The world as we know it has changed forever."

Now in my defense, during that time my dad removed the data on my phone since I went over the allotted amount. It was my first time, so he only dropped it for a week. Anyway, she hands me her phone. I am looking at a video of an old man lying in a hospital bed. He has a dark weathered complexion. There are no flowers, cards, nor the beeping noise of monitoring machines. The hospital room looks quite bare and dirty. From what I can tell, it looks like it just finished raining from the water drops on the window and the muddy tracks on the floor. His family is crammed inside. They all look uncomfortable. The cameraman is speaking in a foreign language. And it is definitely not Spanish. I would guess it is either Arabic or maybe from somewhere in Europe. Normally, I am pretty good with different languages because my family and I have been around the block once or twice but there are dialects that make it difficult for me to translate in my head.

Anyway, in the old man's hand is a photo of his family. He speaks to the camera pointing out each family member. All of a sudden, the man begins to go through convulsions. It is a horrible sight that I have never seen before. His entire family crowds around him. The crying commences as well as the praying. The nurse comes in and moves them away from the man. With her stethoscope against his chest, she provides some water to his now quivering lips. She tells the family something and their cries increase in volume. The old man begins to convulse again. Cries and prayers are heard, and they crowd the bed as before. The family is almost on top of this man as the nurses attempt to reach him. During all the commotion, the old man must have died because all of the sudden they begin to cry hysterically.

The cameraman finds an angle to catch the man's face. Sure enough, his eyes say it all. Several minutes go by. As each of the family members peel away from the bed, the photo the old man was showing us was no longer in his hands. The oldest son is holding on to it. Then something unusual takes place. Small lights begin to flicker on the photo. They look like little sprinkles of glitter popping from it. Startled, the middle-aged son drops the picture which lands on the dead man's bed. The glittering lights continue to fizz off the photo like a recently opened soda pop bottle. The fizz increases as the intensity of the lights accelerate.

This video looks different than Nhim's request. It reaches the point where the fizzing lights become one bright light. The cameraman pans away from the light and displays the family shielding their eyes. The light disappears instantly. The family open their eyes and immediately realize the photo is gone. They each question each other trying to figure out who took it. The children are the first to take the blame thinking they pulled an insensitive prank. The parents' scolding is harsh and more violent than what we would expect from parents. This begins the chaos in the room. The yelling and screaming continues as each parent begins to defend their child. Then the adults begin to accuse each other. An object strikes the camera and the video stops.

This thing goes viral. It creates the expected criticism. Everyone gives their explanation. Honestly, we heard of the video but did not pay too much attention to it because it looked like a hoax. But then something else happens. The next day, two more videos like it pop up. The first has a newscaster interviewing a family. The video shows one of the villagers showing the newscaster what he recorded. This time it was a little girl who had just died. A hair brush was levitating as it pulsates into a glow. The pulse and glow intensify and accelerate. Eventually, the brush disappears. The camera catches the hair that was on the brush floating downward to the floor. The video then pans to a flock of children who were watching outside. They yell out something multiple times. The newscaster asks her interpreter what they are saying. And with a thick Spanish accent he translates, "They are saying it was God. He allowed our sister to be granted one last wish." Their hands are up in the air as they look up and yell out what I would presume is a celebratory prayer. The senior spiritual leader of the community tells the newscaster, "This family has been blessed. They are all automatically welcomed in the afterlife. You see? We have entered a new beginning."

The third video is of a middle-aged lady like my mother. She must have just been struck with an object as she lay face down on the ground gasping for air. We can tell she is bleeding somewhere on her head. I see the dust flowing in and out of her mouth. She is with a film crew that was investigating paranormal activities in Moldova sometime in the middle of the night. The infrared light is on. The cameraman reaches her first and manages to turn her over, cautiously. The lady labors in both speech and breathing as she asks for her prayer beads. The cameraman retrieves it out of her bag while he is screaming for help in his native tongue of Moldovan. Ask me how I know that next time around. She holds the prayer beads in her trembling hands as she starts praying. The cameraman tries to stop the bleeding on the side of her head. Moments later, the lady dies.

A few minutes pass when the prayer beads levitate slightly above the lady's hand and begin to glow with this soft yellow color. Then these hair-thin strings of lights pop out in all directions several at a time about six inches and land back on the prayer beads. Each little impact makes that area disappear. The cameraman gets freaked out but gets a little curious at the same time. He reaches out to touch the prayer beads. It reacts to the impact like a pen in space. It moves away softly and slowly. Nothing like a normal swat on earth. The strings of light make contact with the cameraman's fingers. Small, dark marks appear. He comments, "These lights are very warm like a blanket right out of the dryer." He withdraws his fingers and reacts, "Wow, the inside of my fingers just got ice cold. I can feel the cold blood running through my veins." He dares not make another attempt. The prayer beads disappear before the other crew members arrive. The cameraman hysterically tries to explain what happened. The look of confusion is pronounced on their faces as they attempt to provide medical attention to the lady. The man picks up his camera and walks over to one of the crew members. The subtitles read, 'I will show you. It is recorded right here.' And that is when the video stops. I would guess once the cameraman reviewed the video, he realized he recorded the request. Then he uploads it under the show's paranormal moniker. The world goes crazy over his video. And ever since then, a frenzy of videos has been popping up with people dying and their requests being taken with them.

I remember there was a video of a big prison riot that only had several prisoner requests glowing in the cafeteria. The rest of the prisoner requests took place in the prisoner's respective cells. Another one was of royalty. A queen or princess was on her deathbed when her request appeared from her daughter's room. I forgot exactly what it was. Even a nun was caught on camera with her request not being what everyone would think. It turns out she requested a pair of shower shoes that she had been wearing since she was a child. The list goes on and it does not stop. If these videos could talk, they would tell us that there is no discrimination when it comes to the requests. I mean this will be a part of our lives. These requests make the process of death more pleasant to think about.

Yea, that is what everyone is calling it, 'the request.' The request videos are taking over and have everyone's attention. There are several websites that are strictly dedicated to only playing request videos and vlogs on these requests. From what I know, the request happens in different forms. Some happen like the ones I described while others have been like a silent explosion of light, a random burst of light, even some where the object would light up and fly right into the ceiling or wall and disappear. I mean the request would leave no sign of the impact or destruction. And yes, people have torn up ceilings and walls to verify the objects were not there.

One of the first videos I will never forget was of an old lady in the slums of Rio de Janeiro. After the lady's death, an old handheld mirror began to rattle on her nightstand. The vibration of the mirror should have cracked the mirror but did not. Then the mirror flipped onto its other side. Everyone in the room was perfectly still. It flipped one more time, spun counterclockwise. Sparks like those coming from a firecracker fuse flowed straight into the air gently before it disappeared. It was one of the creepiest request videos I have ever seen. The people in the room started to yell. But it was not an angry yell. They were all joyful. It was like the happiest moment of their lives. One of them went to the camera and said, "Deus tinhamudado as regras!" (God changed the rules.)

Another kid jumps in front of the camera and yells out in English, "Our souls will no longer go to heaven alone!" It was a powerful thing to say to the world. That statement, in my opinion, changed all of humankind.

Just like everything, there appears to be rules for the requests. Some videos would have the dying with their dog in their arms, or even one of their family members close by with his or her bags all packed up. Some have tried requesting plants, fish, and even a peach tree. But they all died not taking any of those things. But they did leave with something. Some of those requests were near their proximity. Photos, trinkets, and other memorabilia went through the ceremonial disappearance. On some occasions, the request is taken from long distance. And by long distance I mean the other side of the world. There is a video out there on it. But the things that are not allowed are living beings. No humans, animals, vegetation can be requested. Things that were once alive are not allowed either. And yes, someone actually tried to take their dead husband with her. And since videos of the requests have been popping up, there are those that try to circumvent the situation. People would tape a worm to a photo. I know. Who picks a worm to be the first live test subject? For larger requests like a car, someone would put a pet in there. That does not work. The car is taken but the pet remains with the rest of us. I forgot what type of a car that was. But it was one of those classic cars. Needless to say, people have been carrying a lot of their highly favored belongings with them these days. Backpacks are a big hit. A lot of people are carrying them everywhere for that one final moment in hopes that their request is somewhere inside that bag. For the most part, everyone has their most sentimental objects inside those bags. Others go overboard and lug around a wagon or travel case. The remainder of the world has decided to fill all their pockets and take their chances.

No wonder the number of criminals that are bag snatching and holding that bag for ransom knowing people will pay for that bag of potential requests has gone up.

Now with all this hype going on in the cyber world as well as the real world, guess who has to jump in? You guessed it, the money people. There is always a dollar to be made out of every bad and good situation. Thanks to me and the request video I uploaded, I am sure camera sales will skyrocket. Home indoor surveillance cameras with mobile access become an even bigger hit as you do not need someone present to catch the request taking place. The bigger companies think way outside the box. They go as far as placing trackers on potential request candidates. Here is where everything gets twisted. These Bigs, short for big companies, will pay off families to add these trackers to all of the potential requests. The families of the poor are easier to bribe. I mean the person is dying and no moral or legal crime is being committed. I do not fault these families for that. But the Bigs, on the other hand, they are taking it too far. They are infringing on the privacy of these families for the simple rule of greed, to be the first to track the request. So far, none of those items that have those trackers have been requested. And now that I have uploaded a video of something no one can explain, how much do you want to bet the Bigs want to know how I did it? As a matter of fact, let me turn off the Wi-Fi before anything else happens.

Literature also gets a bump. Articles are written on what these requests mean. Other articles discuss a how-to plan on getting the request you really want. These how-to videos on getting the request you want become ridiculously expensive. All of a sudden everyone is an expert. Insurance companies also sell protection insurance on any potential request. Come on, you knew the insurance companies were going to find their way in. All these scams eventually get reported. So, the government does the honorable thing and steps in. They are overwhelmed by the cutthroat culture we have created. Thus...who uses the word 'thus' when talking to the audience? Anyway, the government has been searching for a new approach. A different way to stop the scam artists. So far they have not found an answer. Wait. I can hear the garage door open. My mom and dad are home. And those footsteps are Tyler's. He must have had a bad practice. Mom and dad must be in another argument. They did not enter the same time Tyler did. And I bet my mom comes in crying while my dad walks quietly. I just want them to get along. More for my dad since he works so much. Well, we are all here and I am going to hit the rack. I will see you guys tomorrow.

Chapter 4

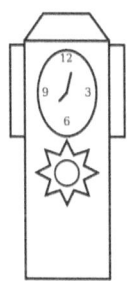

Tuesday morning

Here I am dressed not to impress but at least I am not still in my PJs. I never liked that 'too lazy to put on some clothes' look. My scrubber app is hitting higher numbers than yesterday. What is going on here? On the way to school, I notice two different cars following us. Once we reach school, I deuce my mom to get on campus to find my friends. I am a little colder towards my mom this morning. I do not mean to be. It just inadvertently happens to come across this way right now. As I exit her car, I am distracted again by the phone notifications. My mother says something, but I am too busy scrolling through my phone. As I walk towards the school, I see my friends huddled near the cafeteria door.

Wendy is the first one to tell me, "Powa, we have been trying to reach you since yesterday." I show her my scrubber app that has about 200 total pings. Celeste joins in, "There are people asking us about you. Things like who are you friends with and who does not like you. Is this about your video?" Gina tells me, "Some of our teachers are being questioned by this kind of folks. But it is all off campus type questions which makes it weird." I am a little freaked out, "I have been followed by these cars that I have no clue who they are. After hearing this, I feel like I am going to be kidnapped. Hey, I am going to class before I start to get paranoid about all this."

As I walk off Wendy tells me, "Stay away from those suits. I think they have different intentions for you." I do not bother to look back or acknowledge her warning. There is too much on my mind and it is making me feel sick. I get to my language arts class. I sit in a different seat than what I am used to. I know we do not have assigned seats but since the beginning of class I have been sitting next to the window in the back. So how come this doofus wants to sit in my spot? Anyway, before the teacher starts her class, she calls me up and whispers for me to go to the vice principal's office. I immediately think of what my friends told me. As I reach the administration office, the secretary tells me to have a seat. The secretary's aid who is a student looks me over as if I were some kind of convicted felon as her eyes look me over with a scowl on her face. For some reason it makes me feel insecure and oddly uncomfortable. It is probably because I have never been in this part of the school before.

I can see a firmly fit woman in a pant suit speaking with the veep. Since it is summer school, our principal has given the reigns to the next guy down. There is a conversation taking place between the two adults. I know I have not done anything wrong or illegal. If these folks want to question me, it is not like they can take me to jail or to an interrogation room. Unless they are the government, they can make any excuse to get away with anything. If it is one of the Bigs, well those guys can do anything and pay the government to hide the body. Oh, my mind is starting to reach the boundaries of insanity. Let me take a chill pill. So, I bypass the secretary and enter the veep's office. He greets me, "Ms. Powa, good morning. This is Special Agent Cross."

Special agent, huh? This is more of a big deal than I thought. "Hello Powa. It is a pleasure to meet you. I would like to speak with you about your recently uploaded video. I am sure you know it has received a lot of attention. It is even being broadcasted on television."

I forgot what her name is temporarily. My dad taught me to remember people's names. It is quite difficult, but he said it is a great way to keep communication open. Did she just say my video is being broadcasted on television? I have to admit, I am cheesing pretty big right now, "I am unaware of this, Ms. Cross." I keep the answers short but respectful. It keeps them polite.

"The video was cut short. We would like to see the original video. It will help us understand what we are looking at. May we have it?"

Okay, so the tablet is in my bag, but I do not feel comfortable giving it to them. I do not understand what they will find by reviewing the entire video. The special agent must be experienced. She answers my unvocalized question, "We are looking for clues as to where this unusual place may be. Please understand, Powa, we are here to help. People are in a frenzy about this. Do you understand?"

"Yes, Ms. Cross. It is in my locker. I will go get it." "No worries, I will go with you." Think Powa. You do not want her to follow you. How do you ditch her?

"Ms. Cross, in any other situation I would not mind, but I need you to understand where we are at. We are at my high school. A place where rumors grow like a virus and reputations are more important than grades. If I am seen walking next to you then the word is going to get out that I am working with a special agent or I am in trouble with the law."

"How will your friends know I am a special agent? All I have to do is cover my shield."

"Well you see, Ms. Cross, that teenage girl at the computer next to the secretary, the secretary's aid? She told me you are a special agent. So already I am in a tight spot because she is one of those girls that specializes in spreading rumors. And we both know threatening her not to say anything is counterproductive."

And right then the secretary's aid looks over at us. Perfect timing. What did I tell you about timing? I do not even know the girl, but I use her for my benefit.

Special Agent Cross replies, "I remember high school. I get it. Just do not take too long." I break out of there before more questions are asked. I head straight for my locker which is two buildings over. I am speed walking as my adrenaline is getting the best of me. What am I going to do? How much of a big deal is it to just hand the tablet over to her? I think it is a sentimental issue. It is Nhim's last hooray and I did not make a copy of it. The only full-length video is the original and I do not want to give that up without making my own copy. Ok so that is the play. I get home and make a copy for myself and give them either the tablet or the copy. It will not matter at that point. I walk past my locker and exit the campus. As I am leaving the campus, I rush home as discreetly as possible. I see two cars following me. I take my shortcuts and get home through the back door again. This time I remember to miss the dinner table. I look through one of the front windows and see a swarm of cars outside. Most of them are news vans. Why would they want to speak with me? I did nothing.

Dang it. I am spotted. They rush to the edge of my front yard and begin their harassment by yelling out my name as well as their questions. My anxiety level rises a bit. My parents probably do not know what is going on. If my dad was here, I would not be in such freak out mode.

The back door opens, and I grab the bat my dad has stored in the umbrella case. Why is the news coming through the back door? Is that not against the law? Or is it Ms. Cross coming for Nhim's video? My anxiety level is on overload right now. I can tell my senses are hyper-sensitive. I hear the back door slide all the way shut. The footsteps are light as the intruder knows what he is doing is illegal. I re-grip my bat at the ready. This is a real-life situation I never expected to confront. I hear the dinner table screech from collision as the intruder quietly utters, "Crap that hurt!" That is my cue. I jump around the corner and see an unrecognizable face and swing. Bam! I hit him square on the arm. I hear him yell in pain, but he does not fall. I go to hit him again, but he moves out of the way.

He puts his hands up, "Wait, wait, wait! I am not with them! I am here to help! Please, do not hit me again! I need to stay healthy for Hall H!" The adrenaline is still high, so I swing at him again. He grabs the nearby paper towel holder and shields himself with it as he crouches in the corner. I can see him shaking as the paper towel rattles in its holder. In any other situation, I would laugh at how comical this looks. Who is this guy? He looks too young to be a special agent. There is no way he is a newscaster. I lower my weapon slightly, "What are you doing in my house?! How are you going to walk in my house and not think you would be attacked? How did you get in?!"

"I am sorry. I could not come in through the front door. You would never have let me in. And I used the rocks to get in. Magnetized rocks, right?"

"How do you know which rocks to use? There are a lot of them."

"Easy, they are heavier and much cooler than the other rocks. It was a no brainer." I lower my bat which makes him stand up straight.

The stranger gathers himself and says, "I did not picture you as a fighter." Did he just say what I thought he said? I raise my weapon of choice, "And what is that supposed to mean?!"

The stranger crouches once again and yelps, "At school you seem to be the pretty fragile type!"

"You have been stalking me in school?"

"Well if you call sitting in the same three classes and sharing the same lunch period as stalking, then yes. I am a creepy stalker. Just listen. I know you do not know me. My name is Koonzo. I stalk you in chemistry, P.E., and history class last year. In summer school, I only stalk you in language arts."

I kind of recognize him. He is one of the invisible kids. Not like that is a bad thing. I like to be invisible, too. But if I cannot see him then he is extra invisible. He is about six more inches taller than me. A Latino like me but without the accent. He is probably a coconut. You know, brown on the outside and white on the inside. I can tell he is the nerd type. And by nerd I am not talking about those people that wear glasses and claim to do nerd things. No, this guy looks the part. And real nerds are not that attractive. So, I ask him, "Koonzo, what unsecured website did your parents find that name?"

Koonzo peeks out the front window and chuckles, "Speaking of names, it seems to me your parents do not know how to spell basic words, Powa."

"So, you want to start talking about my parents while convincing me I need your help. Is that right? Well Koonzo, you are about to get your health bashed in unless you tell me what you are doing here, right now! And you better not tell me you want to ask me out."

"Well, for your information you are not close to being my type. I only like pretty girls." I crack a sarcastic laugh. He continues, "I am here to help you. Those people outside are here to cause you more problems."

I interrupt him only because my plan to solve all this is simple. Besides, I hope he does not think he is going to play hero on me. I do not think he could fight his way out of a wet paper bag. So, I tell him, "Listen, Koonzo, I appreciate you thinking of my welfare, but I already know what I am going to do. I am going to make a copy of the video and give it to them. This way they will leave me alone. You see, there is no need to exaggerate this."

Koonzo looks at me as if that is the dumbest answer he ever heard. "Are you serious? Do you think all they will do is just take your video and walk away? Not asking any questions, not wondering what you did prior to and after the video? Do you think they will not ask about your relationship with Nhim and his family?"

Oh no, I did not even think of what his family maybe going through. They must be suffering through more of the chaos than I am. So, I tell Koonzo, "Then what is your plan, genius? We walk out there and tell them my nerd companion recommends I be left alone?"

Koonzo replies, "I have an even better idea. We walk out the back door and lose any tails."

"And where would we go?"

"I have a few friends we can reach. We would not be going to my parents' house. I would not want them to deal with all this too."

I begin to get anxious, "And then what? I hang out there for a week, a month, or the rest of the year? I am not going to do that. I want to be home. I want to be with my parents and my friends."

Koonzo tries to calm me down, "I understand. But you need to know, those guys out there are paying folks to hack into your Wi-Fi, your phone, your computer, your parents' phones and their work computers right now! Emails and phone numbers are being tracked and tacked. Nothing of yours is private anymore. As a matter of fact, any hidden secrets your family has will be exposed. The government will somehow leak this information and if you think high school sucks now, well you are going to want to get a transfer. But by that time every high school student who has a good data stream will know who you are."

And that, ladies and gentlemen, is what my dad calls a power check. I have to admit Koonzo is making some sense right now. It is reasonable to believe all of our devices have been hacked. My dad, I have to protect him. He has done his best to keep out of the spotlight and to protect us. I did this, and I have to fix this. But what would I do if I leave here? How would I fix all this?

Koonzo continues, "This is what we do. We head to one of my friend's house. From there we drive to San Diego."

"Wait a second. Why would we have to go to San Diego?"

Koonzo looks me dead in the eyes, "All my friends will be there, and they have been braining out this enter 'request' phenomenon. They will be able to help you."

My sixth sense tells me there is more to it than just that. So I asked, "Why help me, Koonzo? We never talked in class, we do not know anything about each other but all of a sudden you feel the heroic need to save me. And why is that?"

At that moment, one of the front windows is smashed in. It startles me. Koonzo grabs my hand and whisper yells at me, "You have 30-seconds to write a small message to your parents! At that point, either you come with me or you stand alone. I am no good to you if they identify my face."

I can hear the clock ticking in my head. I grab a pen and a sticky note. My mind goes blank. What do I write? Koonzo jumps on my laptop and pulls up a map. He opens up several other websites. I jot down 'Find me in my world' and put on my headpiece. Koonzo sees me doing my hand gestures as I dive into my virtual reality universe trying to reach my digital destination. There, I see it. I start my message.

He grabs my hand, "Time to go. No cells." Dang it! I did not get to finish. He covers his head with a black balaclava and a black baseball cap.

"Of course, that is not going to attract any attention," I whisper to him sarcastically. He looks over at me wanting to repeat his prior statement about remaining anonymous, but he remains quiet. We escape out the back door. Some of the news stations are peeking into my backyard from my neighbors that live directly behind me. Thank goodness there are laws in place to keep the news from trespassing onto private property. Koonzo leads me through the neighbor's backyard and pretty much everyone else's backyard as some of the media are on the chase. We reach someone's backyard and stop for some reason. The media stops, knowing they cannot enter.

Koonzo tells me as he pulls out a metal device, "Do not worry. This is one of my friend's house." There is an old truck. He crawls underneath it. I hear a grinding noise. He comes back out, "We must keep moving." I take that as a signal to get underneath the truck. I sure do hope there is a secret compartment down here. As I crawl underneath, I realize there is a manhole along with the contraption that Koonzo used to move the manhole cover. I look into it and see a ladder with Koonzo at the bottom. He whispers, "Pull the handle to replace the manhole cover."

"I do not know how to use this piece of junk. You get up here and do it." Koonzo does not waste any time arguing. He does not wait for me to finish coming down the ladder. I can sense he is a bit upset at me. But that is not my fault. We do not have the time for him to teach me how to use his rinky dink lever. I look up and see him grab the device and ease the manhole cover in its place. He hops down and leads the way without making eye contact with me. I give him credit for thinking about replacing the cover. Make it tough for anyone to track you. But he is pretty pissed at me right now. I never knew nerds to be so impatient. The sewers are exactly what I would have imagined them to be. They are dirty, smelly, and wet. And with the summer hear sizzling the vapors, well I can only say that I am gagging right now. At least Koonzo gave me a flashlight to avoid the floating whatever those are.

Chapter 5

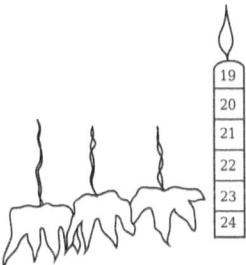

Tuesday evening

We finally reach the other end. Man did that take such a long time. We actually stopped several times along the way. None of those newscasters were smart enough to follow us down here and I do not blame them. Or maybe they are smart for not following us. This was no walk in the park. I am a hot mess. There is probably half a pound of human feces inside my shoes. I puked so much I am dry heaving to the point where my abs are sore. At this point, I am tired and in deep need of a shower. I have been walking hunched over because this sewer system is not tall enough for me to stand upright. And I have been following this guy's flat butt and what looks like a homemade backpack. At least I know this guy is not going to be talking smack about my posterior.

So, no, there was nothing entertaining or enticing about this long dismal escape plan. Koonzo goes up a ladder and uses his lever to remove the manhole cover. He exits first, and I follow. We are in a field behind a neighborhood. The sun just set. He replaces the manhole cover and we head off to the nearby neighborhood. It feels good to breathe fresh air. The mud, that is what I am calling it, is beginning to dry on my legs. A few houses in and we reach his friend's house. We head directly to the backyard. There is a flat that looks pretty rundown. We step to the door and he provides a secret knock. Oh man, I thought that only happens in the movies! But right now, I feel grimy and hungry. And this has put me in a very bad mood, "I need a shower." Koonzo fails to acknowledge my request. This time my tone is a little more representative of my mood, "Hey, I need a shower and some food!" Koonzo provides another nerdy knock without replying. As I am about to raise my voice, lo and behold, the door opens, and a nerd pops up.

The first thing I notice is his chin. This guy has the largest chin I have seen in real life. As I see him smiling, his chin gets that much larger. He is a bit husky and has a thick neck that is probably used to support his chin. From my point of view, he is about two inches shorter than Koonzo which still makes him a little taller than me. And the next obvious description is that he is of oriental descent. I see them salute each other and do their nerd handshake. As they continue with their manual greeting, I inappropriately make my way inside. I look around and the place is not in complete shambles. It is a little cluttered with comic books, DVDs, and cartoon posters. The clutter is in part because this is pretty much a studio. It is an open floor plan with the exception of three doors. I start walking to the nearest door in hopes of finding the bathroom.

Koonzo's friend comes up to me, "Excuse me, Miss." I realize his voice has an Asian accent.

I interrupt him with the same grumpy attitude I was about to flare at Koonzo, "I do not want to wait outside while you two do your nerd bromance. I need to shower and could care less about your cartoon collection." His friend replies with a bit of a shock, "Sorry but I do not respond well to daddy's snobby little princess."

My eyes grow wide as my eyebrows frown. "You see? Anyone can judge someone the wrong or right way. My guess is that I am wrong. If you are willing to walk through the sewer for about six hours with that guy in the middle of the day in the Summer, then you are one tough chick in my book. I would rather judge you that way." I say nothing in return, but I feel better about the guy.

He continues, "Sure we are labeled. Everyone in this world is labeled. We are who we are, and we are good with it. The problem is some folks forget how to peel off the labels."

After calming myself I finally open up, "That was pretty deep. And thank you for the compliment. You are right, six hours with that guy was not fun at all. And he has no junk in that trunk but who am I to judge? I have been called flat booty Judy." We both laugh as Koonzo glares.

He replies, "Yea, we call him Pancake Hank whenever he needs to be reminded. And I am Sung-Suu. This loser's best friend until we fight about something and then we are just good friends. Over here is the shower." I do not bother asking any more questions. Whatever is on my skin is drying and it feels gross.

Sung-Suu turns to Koonzo and asks, "Does she know what they are doing?"

Koonzo replies, "I did not bother to ask. The paparazzi was stalking us."

And I chime in, "Yea, six hours in a sewer and there was so much to talk about. He overlooked it."

Sung-Suu grins knowing Koonzo is not capable of running his mouth for that long. He tells me, "Koonzo talk for six hours? Ha. The only time he ever talks a lot is when…"

"Shut up, Sung-Suu! We need to get ready unless you want to talk about your phone addiction... or something even more personal."

Sung-Suu replies as he laughs, "First off, it is not an addiction. It is me continuing my quest for knowledge. Besides, my phone is more valuable than everything in my room. And there is no need to get personal, sucka! Hey Powa, here is a towel. Oh, and the shower is busted. You are going to have to cat-bath it."

My face asks without me saying it out loud. Sung-Suu answers, "It is when you grab a washcloth and clean yourself off. You never had your water shut off before, huh? You can borrow my sister's clothes in the room next door. They may or may not fit. She is a little skinnier than you."

Oh, this guy got jokes. I do not bother with a reply, but I do give him a grin.

Koonzo has something to say, "You have ten minutes. We will finish packing up." As I walk to the bathroom, I give him a lazy wave for acknowledgment. I close the door and finally get the chance to take this grime away.

Alright, so I finally cleaned myself as best as I could. It feels good to get freshened up. It is not like having a hot bath but good enough. At least I do not stink. I hope I do not stink. I pick out the best outfit that fits. Sung-Suu was not playing. His sister is skinnier than me. But I did find these black jeans and a white shirt with some print on it. It will do for now. As I walk back into the living room, Koonzo and Sung-Suu are on his computer chatting it up in Spanish. And I do mean fluent Spanish. It catches me off guard to see someone not Hispanic speak my native tongue better than me. I mean I get jealous when I see a Caucasian lady speaking it. I do Spanglish but that is as far as I get. And Koonzo speaks fluent Spanish?! Now I really feel out of place. I would rather not ask them about their Spanish speaking skills. It will only uncover my regrettable rebellious decision to go against my mother's wishes.

Sung-Suu sees me and signals for me to sit next to them. Koonzo leans in close, "Powa, there has been a lot of chatter on what the government is doing."

Oh, hell no, this guy is going to tell me the government has something to do with the request! He must be one of those conspiracy theorists. Koonzo continues as Sung-Suu pulls up certain images, "You know how there is a lot of business flowing out there. The hospitals are charging extra to record your request if a family member is not present or you happen to be asleep. I mean they are raking in big bucks. The insurance companies are not covering that because it is not a medical benefit. I bet the insurance lobbyists and the hospital lobbyists are in on it. I am talking about over $4,000 to record a 60-second light show. Small businesses break out with the cameraman rental packages. You can rent a person to be with you in case you die. That way your request is recorded. He is not to perform CPR or stop the bleeding. You cannot even ask for him to help you. That dude is only supposed to record you dying in front of him."

Sung-Suu pulls up an ad for this type of service. I never paid attention to the request services. I figured it was something old people would be more interested in. Koonzo adds, "Apps are out there that will automatically turn on the camera on your phone to record your request. The problem is you do not always die in the selfie pose. There is a lot more changing in the world and money is a large motivator for this push. Listen, there are victims that are suffering from all this. People are cashing in their fortunes to put their confidence on those scam artists. But the government is stepping in because people are putting themselves in a vulnerable position for a paid false sense of security. To think there is now an insurance policy in case you get scammed on your request service. It goes on and on."

Koonzo keeps my interest, "The government has initiated an agenda on these requests. One of their strategies is to reach out to the originators of certain request videos. Usually they are the ones that drum up a lot of attention. We actually took bets on whether you were going to get pinched by them." Sung-Suu pulls out a board that has the names of all the bettors. They are all probably more nerd friends that appear to think the same because they all bet I would be contacted by the government.

Koonzo keeps talking, "The government is doing double duty here. In one part, those scamming services are getting magnified real hard. The other part is they are to debunk all videos relating to these requests. If they can calm the frenzy over these requests, then they would not have to work so hard squashing the scammers out there. That is why they are so interested in you. You are the originator."

I begin to feel overwhelmed by everything that is going on. I think today's events are now catching up to me. So, I lean in and tell him, "Let me get this straight. You are telling me the government is after me because they want to make sure what I recorded is not a fake because it is going to lead to some small-time crooks in ripping people off. Is that right? Because there is a lot more going on in the world the government could be doing than to interrogate a small-time high school student. Have you seen what happened at Apatou?! So, go back into your girlfriend of a computer and try it again!" Oh man am I so disappointed in myself. I am capable of unleashing more than that pathetic display of frustration. Koonzo jumps out of his seat knocking it over. He is a little fidgety. Probably one of those that never was yelled at as a kid.

Sung-Suu steps in with a more persuasive tone, "Hey! We are on your side here. He did not have to get you. I did not have to let you in. He did not have to tell you what is going on. If you do not believe us, then you are free to leave. But like I said before, we are here to help, Powa. Besides, this is my computer which makes it my girlfriend. Not his." I give Sung-Suu credit for trying to make a funny.

I look over at Koonzo. Poor kid is pissed off. I do not blame him. I know the feeling. "Hey, Koonzo, I am sorry, man. I was out of line. Everything just hit me all at once."

Koonzo nods his head acknowledging the apology but remains quiet. After a few quiet seconds he calls me over, "Look here. All these videos are of people from around the world that have been scammed. All these windows are articles on people being scammed. These are folks that put their hard-earned money into a piece of hope. These scammers are destroying that hope and robbing them with a smile. My family went through this. I know how it feels. My family no longer has a life insurance policy, money for our college, or an emergency fund. So, if you are questioning my intentions then I hope this answers them."

He is for real. I can tell. I dare not ask who it was that passed away. I reciprocate the nod. I feel bad for jumping to conclusions. I wind up sticking my foot in my mouth. I hate feeling like a jerk.

Koonzo picks up the fallen chair, "We are still sticking to the plan. Powa, the invite to San Diego is still open. Most of my friends will be there. They will help."

Again, I do not understand, "What is in San Diego that all your nerd friends will be clumped into one spot?"

"Comic-Con! We make the pilgrimage every year," Sung-Suu interjects with his excitement.

That is one nerd question I will never ask again. But the more important question, "What are you all going to do that will help me?"

Sung-Suu answers as Koonzo stuffs some items in a duffle bag, "We have been talking amongst each other on what we would do in your situation. To be honest, Koonzo is the one that brought up the topic because he said you guys share a class. But for the record, you and I also share a class, lunch." I laugh out loud. He is pretty serious, "Lunchtime is a quintessential part of the high school experience that studies have reported reflect how a student will interact with society."

I have to say something, "So you are telling me how I act during lunchtime is how I will act in the real world?" Sung-Suu nods. This guy just added himself to the nut-so clan.

Sung-Suu continues, "Before we talk about how lunch will uncover who we really are let me finish what I have to say. We would find a way to simulate everything about your video and share it with the world. This way the government will no longer focus on you but rather they will focus on us. Does that make sense?"

I think about it. There is no guarantee they will not come after me but there is a strong likelihood they will focus on them as they will be willing to talk. Even more, if they tell them they spoke with me on recreating those conditions of the video it may draw more attention away from me. But I do not make it easy for them, "No, that does not make sense. Why not do all of this here in Klamath Falls?"

Koonzo knew this question was going to be asked, "Because right now we are all heading to San Diego. It is where we all will be putting our minds together. You see those names on that bettor board. That is your rescue team. We leave in five minutes."

I look back over at the board. My rescue team is made up of a bunch of nerds. Are the bad guys nerds, too? "I go on several conditions."

The room goes silent. Koonzo speaks, "Go on."

"We first need to stop by Nhim's house."

I know what his reply is, "Powa, you know they are already there. They were probably there before they came to your house. No longer an option."

I knew it, "Then we can drive by their house."

Sung-Suu steps in, "Koonzo, this might be a good idea. We can validate if there are any folks at the house. We can see what cars are there, get license plates, and even see a face or two. Where is Nhim's house?"

I answer, "Three blocks from mine. Here is the address."

Sung-Suu replies, "I will go on my bike and record what is going on out there. We should still be good for time."

I interrupt, "Hold on. It took us six hours to get here. You are not going to make that in just a few minutes even on a bike."

Sung-Suu replies, "No, we are only about ten minutes away by bike. I am pretty fast."

My head tilts like a dog trying to understand a command. Koonzo takes notice and answers, "The sewer system webs in multiple directions. I had to make sure we were not being followed or that we were not going to get snatched as soon as I opened the manhole cover."

I can feel my face getting warm, "You mean to tell me we walked around in circles for six freaking hours?!"

Sung-Suu steps into my line of sight, "We can discuss this on the road because right now this is not adding to our timeline."

I step back and snatch some bags to load in the vehicle. I am hot, fuming hot.

Koonzo makes one final statement, "Oh and we are Daedalus."

I look at Sung-Suu since I am in no mood for Koonzo right now and ask, "Daedalus because we are going to leave a complex maze, so they cannot find us?" They both look at me like I have a horn growing from my forehead.

Sung-Suu smiles with his chin, "No, Powa, Daedalus sounds like data-less meaning do not bring any devices that take on data. Who is the nerd now?"

I give a little grin, "Got it, Daedalus. You probably do not know who that is anyway." They both look at each other once again and smile nonverbally telling me that I am wrong. I keep quiet. Sung-Suu takes off. Koonzo hands me some bags to load in the car. What did I get myself into? I know I am going to ask myself this question several more times. I do not know these guys, but I am putting my trust in them and a nerdfest that is in another state. I should be scared or concerned. But the truth is I only have one other option. That is to go back and deal with the chaos. It will be bad enough with the media and the government swarming my house harassing my family. If they find out I am not there, then maybe they will lay off a little bit. Koonzo comes back with two more bags for me to haul. These things are heavy. It is food. I can smell the Twinkies.

Here we are in a green Ford Expedition. It is not the newer version either. At least it is clean inside. I never would have thought that looking at the faded paint on the outside. But this is our chariot to San Diego. I am in the backseat while Koonzo sits up front to provide navigation.

Koonzo trying to ease the tension from the sewer system dialogue asks, "So what are the others?" I sure do not know what he is talking about so my face asks the question. He replies, "You said you have several conditions. So, what are they?"

That is right. I forgot about that. I play it cool, "I will tell you if and when the moment presents itself."

Koonzo looks at me like I just made that answer up. And he is right, but I am not going to admit that. Sung-Suu returns. He is breathing heavy as he ditches the bike and jumps in the driver's seat. I ask, "Are you ok? Were you followed?"

Sung-Suu turns on the truck and hands Koonzo the camera. Koonzo plays the video as Sung-Suu drives. First, we see him struggling to peddle that flimsy bike as he is heaving through each peddle stroke. He reaches Nhim's house. Everyone is there. The news crew, the police, a small crowd, and an ambulance was there. Some folks already put up a memorial wall with candles, flowers, and notes. The image of that wall complimented the dusk horizon hitting the neighborhood. Several of those cars that followed me were there as well. Large camera lights were on the lawn highlighting Nhim's house. The front door was open, and a small group of people were inside. One of the newscasters was broadcasting at the time Sung-Suu rode by. It looks like an intense and frightening moment over there. I hope they are ok. I begin to feel bad for putting Nhim's family through this. I had no idea all this would happen. Several tears escape. I wipe them away and sink into the backseat.

I can tell they have made this journey plenty of times. Their bags are all labeled. They marked their timelines. They ration their food. We even left just eight minutes past their mark. I give them credit for being organized. I feel a little better about who I am riding with. Still, I do not know how the plan is going to work. But that is their problem. I just need the suit and tie people to go away. We stay on the road. I keep a lookout for anyone following us. The road is clear. I am turning in. It has been a long day for me. I am going to sleep.

Chapter 6

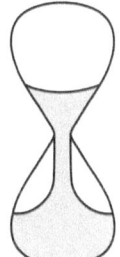

(1) 2 3 4 5
7 8 9 10 11
1 2 3 4 5
7 8 9 10 11

Wednesday dawn

K oonzo wakes me. It is early morning and we are still on the road. The sun is giving the coast a hint it is about to stop by. "Here, take this.

It is a breakfast burrito." Still groggy I ask, "You guys should have woken me up. I would have ordered something else."

Koonzo looks at Sung-Suu with this grin and then looks back at me, "No, spoiled one, we made these for the trip. And by the way, nothing that we have is vegan or gluten free. It is all high in fat and fun."

Sung-Suu greets me with a snicker. Whatever. I just do not like the smart-ass statement of him calling me spoiled. I am definitely not spoiled. One thing my dad taught me was if I can do it by myself then do it. But be smart enough to know when you need a helping hand. I do not think that is the definition of a spoiled person. Besides, where did they get that perception from anyway? You know what, "Hey, where did you get the perception I am spoiled?"

"Koonzo biting into his burrito says, "I did not. I just wanted to mess with you this morning."

Sung-Suu speaks to me through the rearview mirror, "You see, Powa? He only talks like this when…"

Koonzo yells, "Hey watch the road, man! The last thing we want is to go to jail."

Red star clusters are going off in my head, "Jail?! Why would we be worried about jail?"

Koonzo turns around to face me, "Because the almighty bright one here failed his driver's test three times."

Sung-Suu defends himself, "But the last time I should have passed. A car almost hit us."

That does not make sense to me, "So? What does that have to do with failing the test?"

Sung-Suu's head tilts slightly to the floor as he mumbles something. "What did you say? Speak up please," I ask in order to get to the bottom of this mystery.

Koonzo speaks for him, "He crapped his pants last year." Sung-Suu looks at Koonzo like he just told the most forbidden secret. That look from Sung-Suu proves it happened. There is a brief silence in the car. Then from nowhere, my childish behavior exposes me. I start laughing so much I fall back into my seat.

Sung-Suu reacts to my reaction as he is trying to talk over my laughing, "We were on Crater Lake Parkway and I had a stomach flu from the night before! I think it was my mom's Kimche!" His explanation makes me laugh even harder. Koonzo looks over at me and then at Sung-Suu. He cannot quarantine himself from my laughing frenzy as he even joins in on the laughter.

After a couple of minutes, I finally wipe the tears away and ask him, "But how does crapping your pants make you fail the test?" I still have the aftershock of the giggles.

Sung-Suu hesitantly replies, "I tried to hold it in but I had to let it out. So I tried to be quiet about it. So as I made a left turn, I raised my right butt cheek up just enough to let one out. It was like a ninja. Next thing I know I hear her sniffing. Then she blows it out her mouth trying to eliminate the odor from her lungs while pushing the rest of it away from her face. I could tell it was not working. It made the test lady nauseous. She tried to roll down her window but all the windows on the car do not roll down, so she starts to gag. She winds up vomiting on the floorboard. This made me jerk the wheel which makes her puke in my lap."

Koonzo and I start to laugh again as Sung-Suu keeps with his story, "Sure enough that makes me sick so I am puking on the back of this lady's head. I accidentally use the back of her head to place my elbows on because this is helping me from hunching over and not look at the road. The examiner lady is trying to pull herself out, but she is still puking. And I can feel the warmth of the vomit running down my seat, through my pants, and onto my butt cheeks. I mean I am doing my best to keep my eyes open while throwing up! And then it happened. As I was puking, I felt a squirt. It was one of those that I knew I gave birth to. I tried to gaff it off, but I threw up some more which made me push out another one. I am a proud mother of two liquid turds swimming around in my butthole with this lady's vomit."

Oh, my goodness, I am laughing so hard I think I am going to crap in my own pants.

Sung-Suu still defending himself, "I am able to pull off the freeway onto a side road. As Lady Luck would have it, I wind up rear ending a Driver's Ed car with students in it."

This story cannot be real. Sung-Suu tells me more, "And to make it worse, they all get out of their car to see if we are ok. I, and the test lady are in a daze. The test lady sits up and I can see half of the puke on the back of her head made its way to her face. And the other half is clumping off into the passenger seat. They pull us out as the pungent scent of trapped vomit and feces slaps them in the face. I can hear some of them gagging. I plop out of the car exhausted and lay face first on the road thankful we finally stopped. And sure enough, these student drivers see this big brown and yellow spot on the back of my pants."

As I am still laughing, I tell Sung-Suu, "Well at least they helped you guys."

"I rather they did not. You see those students go to our high school. So, of course, they felt obligated to share their heroism with their friends."

My eyes grow wide, "Wait a second! Are you the dookie doo driver?! I heard about that!"

Sung-Suu responds, "Listen, I would appreciate if you guys keep that to yourselves. Most of the school has moved on from that incident."

I laugh to the point where I do not make a sound. I am almost suffocating from it. But the feeling is stress relieving. Koonzo is getting a rise out of it as well as he imitates the vomiting facial expression. Poor Sung-Suu. The rest of the drive I remain mostly quiet except for the intermittent giggle flare ups.

After about two hours, we reach another house in Redding. The road is still clear of any tails. This house looks like the other track homes here. I can tell this used to be a really nice neighborhood back in its day. Some of the houses have really impressive front yards. Too bad the rest of the neighborhood does not follow suit, especially this one. We go around back, and you guessed it. Another secret squirrel knock. It is another nerd that answers. Who would have guessed that? He is African American with a wrestler's body. You know, the thick neck, big chest, broad shoulders and decent size arms. He is about three inches taller than Koonzo with a pretty cool hairstyle. How is this guy a nerd? He does not look the part. Oh, I get it. He is their bodyguard to fend off the bullies. Or he is one of those so-called nerds but is just a poser. He reaches out with his arms extended. Ok, I am not going to hug this guy. I cautiously extend my hand and then he bear hugs me! As a defensive reaction, I knee him in the nuts. He screams as he falls to the floor. Koonzo pulls me back and Sung-Suu tends to his friend in need.

"My balls! She kicked me in my balls!"

I realize what I did, "I am so sorry! You took me by surprise. I thought I was going to be in a fight." I kneel down to help him up.

Sung-Suu comforts his friend, "It is ok Torin. She has a way of making a great first impression. She wants your vote for homecoming queen."

I can hear Sung-Suu chuckle as we help him up. This guy extends his hand out. This time, without question, I reach in and grab it. Bzzzzz! I get electrocuted. Another gut reaction as I kick him in the balls. Again. He falls to the floor wincing from the pain. All those drills with my dad actually paid off. I am rubbing my hands to get the feeling back.

As Sung-Suu helps his friend up one more time, I notice the device on his hand. His friend gets up and walks to his closet. Uh, oh. I think he is going to pull out a bat. Even Koonzo and Sung-Suu look worried. He finds what he is looking for as he turns around. He walks towards me as he places a groin protector down his pants, "Ok, now I think I am ready to meet you." He holds out his hand with the device still on it. What to do? Ah screw it, my body will know. I shake his hand. Bzzzzz! No matter how much I braced myself for it, it still shocks me. No pun intended. I reactively kick him just above the groin. I get the response I am looking for. He takes me down with him as I purposely hold on to his hand. I squeeze it so tight the device no longer works. I keep my eyes locked on him as he is hunched into the fetal position. Koonzo and Sung-Suu stay back.

Their friend speaks up, "Ok, ok! You are not like other girls! Good. Now you can stop kicking me in the babymakers." We help each other up as he labors to introduce himself, "Hey Powa, my name is Clifford. But you have to call me Torin. Clifford is too adult, and Cliff is just horrible. And do not even think about calling me Cliffster. My grandma calls me that every time I get in trouble."

I smile, "Well Cliffster, number one rule, never tell me your pet peeves."

Cliffster looks over at Koonzo, "If she calls me Cliffster I am going to...."

Koonzo laughs with his hands up in a defensive posture, "Hey man, I am just here to help. That is beef you have to deal with. Do not get butthurt at me, man. Anyway, so you know, we have been on black out mode. What is the buzz?"

Cliffster removes the groin protector as he takes his seat and starts typing away. He looks over at Sung-Suu, "Hey man, how is my hair? Did she mess it up?"

Sung-Suu smiles as he replies, "Naw, brother, your fro looks pretty as ever except for that bald spot in the back."

Cliffster responds with, "Yo momma," as he records the back of his head.

I look at Sung-Suu with a question mark. With the same large chinned smile, he answers, "Cliffster has a hair complex. He had a bad cornrow experience that left him temporarily bald."

Cliffster interrupts while examining the recent video and the back of his head possibly in search of a bald spot, "Listen, let me get it out the way before these guys twist it several different ways."

He smiles at his phone in what appears to be no visual signs of balding. Cliffster plugs it in and continues, "I used to be one of the popular students in Klamath Union High. Got me a letter jacket, also played football and basketball. Life was good. Well, last year I had a wrestling tournament, so I had my cousin hook me up with some rows, right? I also wanted my hair color changed to red and white for our school colors. So, he colored the sides white and a thick red stripe down the middle. Well once he started making the cornrows, he realized the roots were still black. So, he repainted them. The paint was not taking so he added more bleach. It really did not work. He told me to add this applicator after I shower at night and then wash it off in the morning. Well I woke up late in the morning and did not wash the applicator off. I just rinsed it off.

I finally get on the mat and start my match. I am getting the best of my opponent when I see some red lint on the mat. Seconds later I see white lint. The more we go at it the more I realize this is my hair. I hear the crowd start to laugh as my opponent and me are wrestling around my hair. I mean the sweat has this stuff sticking to us. It gets to me and I wind up losing. The spectators are still laughing. We both look like patchy wooly mammoths. I take my seat on the bench and realize most of my red hair has ripped off and patches of my white hair were missing. In the end, I looked like a kid with an inverted Mohawk with patchy white cornrows. It was not a pretty sight. Social media gets the word out and I wind up getting clowned on. I could have handled it better, but I have to live with it now. Thankfully, my parents got jobs here in Redding at the end of the school year. So, I do not have to worry about seeing my former classmates anymore. So Powa, I am the prime example of a popular teen falling from the top of the mountain."

His story is nowhere near as funny as Sung-Suu's. Cliffster is about to retreat back into his mind when Sung-Suu puts him in a headlock, "Looks like I am finally gonna get my chance to make this guy tap."

Cliffster laughs as he stands up with Sung-Suu on his back. "You do not have your forearm deep enough. Just let go before I atomic drop you."

Sung-Suu remains in his position. Cliffster somehow manages to undo the choke and shoulder presses him over his head. Sung-Suu yells, "Ok, Ok! You got me, bro!"

Cliffster demands, "Say it!"

Sung-Suu yells, "Tio, tio!"

"No. Say it in Korean."

"Samchon, samchon, man!"

Cliffster lowers the Korean to the floor.

Sung-Suu looks at Cliffster, "I am going to figure you out one day, Torin."

Cliffster shakes his hand as they take their seats as he says, "Just to let you know, yo momma has much stronger forearm strength than you."

Sung-Suu thinks for a bit as he says, "You are lucky I am not as good at Yo Momma jokes as you. Wait, I got it. Well the only reason my forearms are weak is because yo momma does everything for me. Can you say hands free?"

Cliffster battles back with, "Yo momma is so fat..."

Koonzo steps in the middle of them, "Knock it off! We have a lot to do." Koonzo shakes his head giving the impression those two do this all too often.

Now that the hot-dogging is over, Cliffster brings up a website and logs in. Within this web page several windows pop up. He comments, "Ok, here we are. As you all know it is crazy out there. This page here is talking about what they are going to name the nine new days."

Sung-Suu interrupts, "You mean they are getting rid of the original names of the seven days? They just cannot come up with two new names?"

Cliffster nods his head and continues, "Yea, I would have named one of those days after yo momma. That way I know when she is coming over."

I laugh at that one; that one was funny.

Sung-Suu smiles trying to think of something but Cliffster shuts him down by continuing, "This page here shows me people are definitely looking for her. As we anticipated, they broke into every device they can hack into. They are probing into her family's government files and found a few things."

Koonzo asks, "Like what?" Cliffster looks over at me. I know that look. That is the look of juicy gossip they are trying to keep from me. I take a seat next to them since I hate having someone talk about me when I am in the same room.

Cliffster turns to me, "Oh hey there. How is your hand?"

"Almost as good as your balls. What are they saying out there?"

Cliffster grins at my quick comeback. He wants to retaliate but the look on my face tells him this is not the right time. He focuses back on his computer, "Well, whatever your father does it must be a big deal because they are breaking into his three work computers which happen to be in three different states. Nothing much on your mom and brother."

How can my dad have computers in three places? What is the point if he is never there to use them? If my dad is a government spy, then that would be pretty cool. But then he would have been able to help get me out of this mess. It must be a case of mistaken identity.

Cliffster and Koonzo can sense I am having a battle of words within myself. Cliffster adds, "And they are hitting up your extended family as well as your friends. Pretty much everyone in your contacts list is getting pinged."

I have to say it, "Well here is a good time for my ex-boyfriends to get their revenge."

Cliffster comes back, "I used to have a girlfriend once. When I was lighter. I dumped her, though."

"And what does that have to do with this situation?" I ask.

"What do your ex-boyfriends have to do with this situation?!"

"I get it. This must be some form of machismo you are doing, right?"

Cliffster returns, "No, I just wanted to give you crap since my balls are still swollen."

I am going to shut up right now because I am tired of hearing this guy remind me of his balls.

Sung-Suu seizes the opportunity, "That is how small they are when they are swollen?! I am going to have to talk to my momma about her itty-bitty standards."

Cliffster laughs out loud and gives Sung-Suu a well-deserved hi-5.

I am beginning to like their chemistry.

Koonzo remains focused as he asks, "What else has been happening?"

"Well the government hackers took the bait. Those websites and maps you pulled up at her house have them heading east. That should buy us enough time to make it down to San Dieg-oooooooo!" He drags out the name San Diego like it is a party song he is singing to a crowd during a pep rally. And of course, his nerd friends join in on the last syllable, "Ooooooooooh!"

My current life situation has me burying my head in my hands as I am stuck between this nerd lifestyle and my crisis.

Once the celebration dies out, Cliffster continues with his briefing. He pulls up a few documents that he scrolls through as he is explaining what is going on, "Guys, the world is still going crazy over this video. Check this out. New propaganda on future cameras are to have request filters from Singapore. I do not know what a request filter is. The hospitals even get in on the action as they sell request packages such as indoor surveillance cameras that are light sensitive and added fees for overnight family members. Selfie-sticks get popular with the wide-angle option. One company even created a miniature printer that attaches to your phone and will print your favorite photo prior to your death just so you can request it. Everyone is jumping on board."

I am astonished at how quickly all this is escalating. It is like the world is looking for an excuse to make money. I have to say it, "Look at how fast we are to make a dollar. We are willing to spend it on the dying, but we cannot give a dollar to the living. Technology has advanced incredibly fast to attempt to identify the request but people dying from starvation take a backseat!" I become disgusted by this topic.

Koonzo comes over, "It is a crummy situation. Some people would say it is this same technology that we use to link with our friends and family from far off places. Those folks that find hope in these requests, well, I do not believe anyone should get in their way. But these scam artists really take things to a pathetic level. They lower the human standard. We have spoken of this topic plenty of times before. At least here we can do something about it."

Cliffster adds, "Did you guys know that attendance at religious services has increased exponentially since these requests have taken place?! I mean talk about a way to make amends with the big guy upstairs."

This seems like a fair question to ask, "What do you mean 'make amends?'"

Cliffster begins to explain, "From what I gathered on the web and the chatter boxes out there, everyone is calling this a religious divinity. This means a higher power is granting us this privilege or right. The question they all have is not what it means but how long is this supposed to last. And that is what is driving every dialogue at these establishments. People are actually willing to change their ways for the better because they believe what is requested is a reflection of the type of person you lived to be."

Koonzo interrupts, "Listen, if we are going to get this done then we need to go now. Talk about it on the ride down. Cliffster, time to roll out."

Cliffster grabs his bags and heads to the truck. He looks down at the bags and immediately drops them. Cliffster wipes his hands on a t-shirt as he says, "I hope your pranks stop when we get in the road, Sung-Suu."

Sung-Suu grabs a few other things from the refrigerator as he laughs while talking, "Not a chance, my big balding brother."

Koonzo is tapping away on the computer. I figured this is the best time to ask, "Are your parents ok with you traveling the western seaboard without adult supervision?"

Koonzo grins, "When you are a nerd, a certain stigma is associated with that label. I do my homework, pass all my tests, and go out of my way to speak respectfully to all adults. Just by doing that, I manage to get what I want. And when I do go on a train ride to nowhere and come back safely and on time, well that trust is wrapped in confidence served hot. So, I can confidently say they know I can handle the coast. Now this may not be true for all nerds, but we capitalize on it when we can. How about you?"

"I would not say all of you are that innocent and witty. Besides, some nerds look like they are incapable of walking down a flight of stairs. For me, my parents trust me. Probably not enough to have me come out here alone. We all know there are a lot of whackos out there."

Koonzo stops typing and looks at me with a blank stare. A very odd silence comes between us. I cannot tell if I am supposed to say something else or if I should wait for him since it is his turn to speak. Was it the whacko comment that stunned him?

Koonzo breaks the silence, "You know that weird silence we just experienced? I was wondering if that was the time for me to lean in and kiss you."

Oh man does this guy not know how to read the signals? "That weird silence was not even close to being a signal, a sign, or even Morse code. What did I do to make you think I wanted that because I will make sure I never do that again!"

A withdrawn Koonzo answers, "Well it was how you were staring into my eyes."

"That was me looking at your face because it was your turn to talk!"

A voice outside yells, "We need to get on the road or we are going to miss our next hack time. And remember, Daedalus."

Koonzo takes the given opportunity to remove himself as he grabs some gear and jets out the door. I feel bad. He actually thought I was into him. In reality, I am just not thinking about that right now. My mind is on home and how to get my life back.

I take some vittles from the fridge and act like a baby and head out. As I take my seat in the third row of the truck, I ask the curious question, "Hey Cliffster, how did you manage to join these guys? I mean you do not seem to fit the nerd profile."

Cliffster and Sung-Suu lower the map they have in their hand. He turns all the way around to look at me, "Well have you ever heard of the dookie doo driver?"

I snicker at the story. Sung-Suu's face turns red. Cliffster gets it, "So you have. Well when these punk kids were squirting brown food coloring on his pants in home economics class, Sung-Suu did not know what they were doing. He just thought they were laughing at him because of the story every high schooler was passing around as it was still fresh in their minds. I could not take them doing that anymore. Even the other nerds in class were getting involved. And when there is nerd on nerd crime, I am going to fight for the underdog. So, I decided to get even. Our class project was to cook up a dish for our little potluck. After class I stayed behind and poured laxatives in everyone's food trays. Needless to say, the next day when we all sampled each other's meal, everyone was running to the restroom."

I interrupt, "Wait. You tainted everyone's dish? Why?"

"Well, each tray was marked only with the student's ID number. So, I decided to douse everyone's tray; including my own."

Sung-Suu livens up, "Yea, everyone running to the restroom was hilarious! Some of them did not make it in time. I mean chunks of chocolate left a trail to both the girls' and boys' restrooms."

Sung-Suu and Cliffster start laughing. I am mildly disgusted, but I see their humor. Cliffster lets Sung-Suu take over the story, "Me and Cliffster had a stall next to each other. We were laughing at all the fart noises coming from the other stalls."

Cliffster has to add while laughing, "You said their buttholes were puking like your driving lady."

"That is completely gross," I tell them which only makes them laugh harder.

Sung-Suu continues as his laughter calms down a bit, "Some guys even used the pissers and sinks because they could not hold it. From our laughing, the class reported us to the teacher. I tried to take the fall but Cliffster kept insisting it was his idea. I did not want him to pay the consequences. In the end, we both got suspended."

Cliffster laughs, "Yea, during that break he invited me to Comic-Con. That is how I met the rest of the clan. I have been hooked on it ever since."

"Well that is some love affair you guys have. It looks like you were meant to be a nerd."

Cliffster continues laughing, "Thank you for judging."

I changed the subject because I do not want to ruin the image of chocolate, "What are you doing with that ancient thing? I know we are Daedalus, but you guys have made this trip plenty of times, right?"

Sung-Suu gives me a fist pump which makes me feel welcomed into their jargon and replies, "Since we are Daedalus, we have to make sure we don't get lost."

Cliffster quickly hand irons the map of San Diego, "No need to worry about the visor plate. It is outdated. What is the address?"

Sung-Suu points out, "We go over this every time. I do not memorize the address. I use landmarks to find the location. It is just like remembering a phone number. No one remembers a phone number these days. But when you need it, you are dead in the water. That is why you have to find a reference point."

Cliffster laughs, "Yo momma referenced me last night.

Sung-Suu smiles, "You are so childish. Some of us are talented at being a nerd as opposed to me being a gifted one. Okay, so remember the name of the body of water?"

Cliffster replies, "Something about being a cholo, right?"

"Close. Just remember female gangster like her," informs Sung-Suu.

Like 'her?' I know they are not calling me a chola. I am nothing of the sort. I do not dress, talk, nor act like one. Plus, those girls can really fight.

Sung-Suu keeps explaining, "The place is called Chollas Creek. Right here. All you have to do is find it which is south of downtown San Diego. On the map, you just have to follow it east until you see a little green patch which happens to be the park nearest to her house. And once we get near the area, we go by memory on getting the rest of the way there. Nerd 301."

Cliffster pings the park Sung-Suu is focused on. I lose interest after that point. I actually thought they were going to start arguing but I guess nerds argue about more important things like comic book heroes or something nerdy like that. The rest of the day is spent talking about Comic-Con. They have this elaborate schedule. I decide not to partake in that discussion. And since I refused to walk down that road, I do what any other real teenager would do to avoid a boring situation. I think of something else. I bring Nhim into my mind. No thoughts of his final moments. I take it back to our beginning. Eventually, I fall asleep.

CHAPTER 7

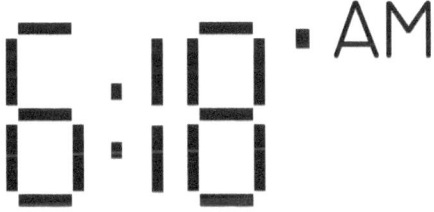 **·AM**

Wednesday late night or Thursday Pre-Dawn

It is still dark out. I am wondering where we are but hesitate to ask. We are parked at a rest stop. A decent number of cars are also parked here. Are they heading to Comic-Con as well? None of the nerds are inside the truck. Maybe they are taking a dump together? I laugh to myself at how ridiculous that would be yet very probable with this crowd.

Well now is as good of a time for a pee break. The sky is dark. There are several clouds but not an overcast. The temperature is Goldilocks. A slight breeze makes it just right to break out a long sleeve shirt; I love these types of nights. They remind me of my youth when I would spend it with my family while camping. I miss them now. Before I get all mopey, I better go pee. I go inside the restroom and do my business. While there, I can hear some folks talking outside. It does not sound like the nerds. From what I can tell, it sounds more like adults. According to their audible expressions, whatever they are doing they seem very excited at times and then in disbelief. It is probably some more Comic-Con folks. I am sure the nerd group is with them. I finish up and head over to this mysterious group.

As I exit the restroom, I walk around the corner and see a group of about ten people huddled around the new tablet. You know, the ones that you can attach other tablets to in order to pretty much make a larger touchscreen? I mean any tablet simply has to make contact with it and it will work. And this guy has three of them propped together on a stand. Techies call it the mosaic rather than a tablet. Moving on. There are no lights in this part of the rest stop. I can see some of their faces from the light reflecting off the mosaic. I walk behind them to catch a glimpse of the action. No luck. I ask one of them what all the commotion is about. He tells me they are watching some request videos. I inform him, "You guys are going to be here all night if you are going to do that."

Someone else replies, "Oh no. Just the recent ones from the last several days." He makes room for me to watch. Do not worry. I do not easily snuggle with older men. I made sure our legs were not touching. As I watch the video, the man tells me they have seen all these videos at least three times and it never gets old. These folks need to get out more, even though they are on the road. You know what I mean?

The video is of a dying young boy about Nhim's age. They are in a room that is not well illuminated. The usual sightings of family and friends are present. Cards and flowers are also found. This time I recognize the language. That is Spanish for a fact. From the family's accent, they are much further south than Mexico. There is another cameraman recording as well. The camera he is using is an older generation. It is the type that has the viewfinder rather than the flip panels that are common these days. Then the boy goes into a seizure. You can hear the mother panicking as she cries aloud. But no one comes to the aid of the boy. I get it. They are at someone's house and they are extremely poor. But not even the mother is at her son's bedside. Looks like her husband is holding her down. They all remain seated against the walls like spectators watching their team lose. What kind of strange ritual is taking place here? I can see the struggle for life from this kid and no one is around to help him through it. It is an awful sight to see. The boy stops moving. I can hear him gasping for air.

A couple of minutes later, the suffering boy dies. The crying from everyone erupts so loud it crackles the speakers on the mosaic. And then the background begins to reflect flickering lights. I cannot tell the origin as the camera seeks for the source. I can see the flickering reflecting off the walls. Some of the cries go silent while other family members begin to shout and point.

The cameraman pans the camera to where they are pointing. He cannot find the source. "You idiot. Just lower the camera and look with your face!" I want to yell at this guy. I find myself moving my head to one side and the other for whatever reason trying to locate the source of light myself. The flickering comes in front of the camera, but I cannot tell where because it stops immediately. Then a bright light pops in and out to the left of the camera. The camera moves. The chatter picks back up and they all point to an empty spot on a table. As one of the ladies holds up a photo of the boy, three children point to the little toy he is holding.

I tell myself that was some horrible videography. But the video is not over. The other cameraman steps in front of the camera. He flips the panel and replays what he caught. I put my hand over my mouth. I cannot believe what I am seeing. No way is this possible. No way. It turns out the first light source our esteemed cameraman could not find was coming from the camera he was holding. But somehow the request went from the camera to the toy. I have never ever heard of that happening, but my mind is on freeze mode. Then our cameraman flips the camera around. Guess what? It is a teenage girl. And then the camera pans around and a gentleman in a dark suit is handing an envelope with the impression of a large amount of money to the mother who has finally come to the aid of her dead son's bedside.

Wait one minute? Did what I think just happened? Did some organization just bribe the family of this dying boy to recreate my video of Nhim? Oh man, I do not know if this is going to increase the attention on me or take it away. I have the feeling there are going to be more people wanting to do this. Which means the government or corporate folks are really going to want to get a hold of me. Ok, I better stop thinking of this right now or else I am going to start freaking out. And if that happens, these curious people here are going to recognize this gorgeous face and then I am really screwed. I keep my head down and gently slip away.

My goodness, that poor boy died alone. He had to have been scared. No final comfort from his family. No farewells. I know his mother paid a hard price to allow that. She missed out on her last moment to sooth her son's pain. She will carry that nightmare with her until she dies. I feel for her. It is a mortal wound she will never allow to heal. Walking towards the truck, I hear two ladies talking about a specific issue. Thinking this would take my mind off the video, I decide to eavesdrop. I will call them shadow one and shadow two. These women are around their 30s or 40s. I only know that because of an aunt I have around that age who sounds just like them. Shadow One says, "Did you know there are companies now that make their products with cameras and GPS tracking devices in them?"

Shadow Two replies in shock, "No way! What type of items are they putting this inside of?"

"Well I know they have trackers inside photo albums. They also have them for kids like toy robots and dolls. There is even a focus on teenagers with guitars and video game controllers."

Shadow Two, "That is amazing how these companies would think of every age group to accommodate. I am really interested to know where all the requests go. Naturally, they must go with the deceased to heaven. Has any of them been requested?"

Shadow One comes back with, "I do not know. They just started up. It is a growing company with some great ideas. I plan on investing in their stock as soon as they go public. Because once they show everyone their stuff works, they are going to be big time."

Shadow Two adds her story, "When my time comes, I am going to hire a Request Advisor." Shadow One leans in closer. Shadow Two continues, "The request advisor would come over when you are about to die. He or she will use certain devices to help get the dying their request into heaven. They kind of act like palm readers. And they are quite expensive."

Shadow One asks, "Has anyone used them?" "I have not heard of anyone using them but then again it is a fairly new occupation." Shadow One has another question, "Now you said they will show up when you are about to die. How do they know you are about to die? I mean that is unpredictable. And if you are paying them by the hour then there is no possibility, I will be able to afford that."

Shadow Two has the answer, "Oh dear, have you not heard of the Gevity Alert? I do not know too much about it. From what I know, it is an app or device that will send you two alerts…"

Shadow One, "Now I remember. I heard of that app before but not the device. I need to get that for my smartphone."

"Well you better hurry. I hear it is not going to be free next month. Hold on, my phone is pushing another request note." Shadow two looks at the message and pushes the touch screen, "Looks like we got a new one." She tilts her phone, so her friend can see.

I circle around behind them for a better view. I hear a lot of scrambling as the video is still searching for a place to focus. It is night time and these people are in some abandoned building. A young boy about my age walks in front. He begins to speak in Russian. There are other teenage boys and girls present. Something odd going on here. There is no crying or sobbing. Someone is on the floor which I would guess is the deceased. Then the request begins to shine through the dead person's left front pant pocket. It burns through the pocket leaving an exact burn silhouette. The request is a pocket knife. The lights zigzag out and away until they disappear.

Another boy in a red shirt makes a remark as he grabs for the request. Immediately upon making contact with it, he experienced some pain. He was wincing with pain but did not let go. There is no smoke coming from his hand. He attempts to pull it towards him but fails. He places his other hand around it for a second attempt and still fails. All of a sudden, a bright pulse of light from the request illuminated bright enough to show the inside of his hands. The teenager opens his hands and the request has vanished. One of the boys asks a question. He replies as the camera light is turned on. Everyone starts laughing. Red shirt has his hands cupped around his mouth huffing into them. He rubs them together viciously. Another teenage girl asks a question. Red shirt provides an explanation. Then another boy makes a statement, and everyone laughs a lot harder as the camera focuses back on the star of this video. The cameraman reaches out and lowers the red shirt's hands. Just as we are astonished so are these teenagers. This boy has burn marks on the inside of his hands. But these are not like second or third-degree burns. They mimic the exact pattern of the lights from the request. The hands are not blistered or charred anywhere. Red shirt presents his hands to the cameraman as the detail of these burns is recorded. His friends rub their fingers along the marks. One of them makes a remark and they all laugh out loud. Then a loud and authoritative voice stalls their celebration. The cameraman finds a police officer yelling at them. Then they take off and the video ends there.

Shadow Two starts, "Looks like now there is something else everyone is going to want to do. I know I am not going to be doing that. That is their request. They should be respecting it and leaving it alone."

Shadow One replies, "I do not believe it is a sign of disrespect. Think about it. This would mean getting one everlasting reminder of your loved ones' final moment. You get the request on video which the world gets to see. But the marks on your hands stay with you from what I would hope to be until the day you die. It is almost like a tattoo except one of heaven's angels gets to do the honors."

Shadow Two laughs, "Now you done it, girl! I have heard it all! I would like to know what they said before we go thinking about our guardian angels giving us..." I sneezed from the cold. It catches their attention as their silhouettes shift to my direction. I gently walk away before they involve me in their conversation.

I return to the truck and find the boys sitting inside looking at the little boy's video. I do not know what to think of the Russian video. It may be a hoax. Those guys were convincing though. This is the second video I have seen about the marks. How would the world react to that? The light emanating from Sung-Suu's camera distracts me from that thought. They recorded the first video. It is a smart move. This way they can examine it without internet access later.

Sung-Suu asks, "Powa, have you seen the latest request video? It is amazing!"

"Which one? They are all far from amazing." My voice expresses my disbelief. They look back at me and then face each other.

Sung-Suu tells Koonzo, "I knew we should have stuck around some more. I feel so outdated."

Koonzo replies, "Hey, we are almost there. Then you can geek out on those other videos. But for now, see what details you can pick. We got to hit the road." Koonzo starts up the truck. I hear them talking about it some more. I do not want to hear anymore. I put on my headphones and listen to some blues, but I cannot fall asleep. The first video winds up on replay in my head for the rest of the night. That sucks for me. I keep thinking of the family of that little boy. Why would the father allow this? That is his son. His bloodline, and he wanted to put a price on his son's final breath? Was this his idea or the mother's? And his brothers and sisters, what did they have to say? Was the black suit that convincing or was the bribe amount that high? The crying in the room only sends the message that they regretted not holding their dying child one last time.

I want to blame the government or the Bigs for all of this but logically I cannot. It is these families that are allowing them to prosper from this. Then again, these families are extremely poor. The decision to do this must have been difficult. An opportunity presented itself and there must have been several large arguments between family members. An argument I would love to be a fly on the wall for but am thankful I never had to personally experience. It is hard to not be judgmental about this, but I already picked a side. It is true. The entire concept of death has changed. Will we die alone for the sake of money? Is the value of a lifetime of experience and emotion worth money to sustain those you love for the rest of their lives? When is it right to feel selfish enough to want your family and friends to be as close to you in your final moment as possible? Will this be the new norm? Eventually this has to level off. Eventually, the viewers will become bored of their excitement and these entities will hopefully leave the dying alone. I hope this happens.

When my time comes, I would not want to be sold out for the sake of next month's rent. Now that is a thought. We should want to make a strong effort to be successful in life so that we are not desperate enough to need this type of handout.

But the dying can only control that. There is no control for the diseases of memory loss, daily functions or when a power of attorney takes over your lifelong efforts for success. To have a family member take over for you and neglect the primary reason you worked so hard for is a possibility I cannot grasp, yet. To ultimately lose what you have gained has to be the kiss of death. And it is done by your loved ones who are doing all of this in the name of endearment.

Yes, it is a slippery slope indeed.

I notice a paper bag next to me, "What is this?"

Cliffster answers, "They are media sticks. Since we are technically off the grid, figured this would keep us in the loop without detection." Media sticks are a new and cheap technology, liquid technology to be exact. I have not seen one in person, but we were introduced to them in my media class earlier in the year. They look similar to a glow stick but are a little thicker in circumference. Like a glow stick, you have to crack the stick and that is when the magic happens. So, I do just that. I shake it up. I do not know exactly how this works but all I know is the chemical reaction creates an electrical charge which powers up this creative device. It is similar to how the nanites are created when the red and blue strips melt inside your mouth. After a few shakes, I look at the long end of the media stick. That is where the media is viewed. It is kind of like the recently retired newspaper except you are reading through a cylinder. Some law was passed to keep the newspaper business open and this happens to be the most economical and eco-friendly replacement.

The tube is biodegradable as well as the liquid contents inside. The font is very clear but can only be magnified two times over. The farsighted will not be fans. There are no images on the media stick which makes sense. You can only store a limited amount of data at one time as it streams for a relatively short period. Media sticks only last about five minutes. Right now, they are free in order to get some buy in from the public. I scroll past several articles until I reach one about the requests. It provides a recap of my video. Then it discusses how companies are trying to recreate this phenomenon. The problem is trying to find people that genuinely want to spend their only request on an item they are most likely not interested in taking with them. My glow stick is about to go out so there is not much time remaining. I read about how some of these request companies are leaving their footprint on as many services and gadgets as they can to include the medical field. The media stick's illumination fades. I want to grab another one but there are only three sticks left. It does not matter. My mind runs in a loop over this information as the stick ends its light. I have to let that go but it keeps me awake. My mind wanders even more, and I finally fall asleep somewhere in the middle of all the haze.

Chapter 8

Thursday just after dawn

I wake up to some hollering. It startles me to where I instinctively kick what is in front of me. In this case, it happens to be the back of the second-row bench. I quickly look out the window to see if we are getting pulled over. It feels like first light. The sun is orange and bright, and we are still on the freeway. The hollering still continues.

Koonzo looks back at me, "Did you see it?! The sign says San Diego 35-miles. We are almost there!"

Cliffster looks at me, "We always do this when we pass that sign. We consider it a ceremonial event." Sung-Suu is behind the wheel doing a little jig that I hope I never remember.

Cliffster pulls out a sandwich, "Here, take it. We will not be stopping until we get there. You are going to need all the nutrition you can get."

I look at the sandwich, "Cliffster, this is a bologna sandwich with chips inside. What nutrition chart are you using? The one from the fast food menu?" I deny his kind offer.

Cliffster bites into his sandwich when he rolls down the window and spits it out, "You dirt bag! You put...what is that? Protein powder?!"

Sung-Suu laughs, "It is strawberry flavored. Your favorite. At least that is what yo momma told me last night."

A slightly upset Cliffster throws out the sandwich when he says, "Thanks for ruining breakfast. You are almost as bad a cook as yo momma."

I give Sung-Suu the win in that exchange.

Cliffster opens a bottle of water and plays the video from last night. He asks me, "How do you think it happened?"

I give him the gas face, "What do you mean? We all saw what happened."

"Yes, but how did it go from the camera to another object at the last second?" I begin to tuck myself back to sleep when he says, "Look. The camera is beginning to fade but something happens. That is when the request shifts to the other object. What made it do that?"

I sit back up and look at the video again. Cliffster puts it in slow motion. He is right. Something did happen. I take the camera from him and watch the video several more times to include in slow motion. I have my suspicions but that is all they are. I keep them to myself and say to Cliffster, "I cannot tell what it was that caused this. Probably the same thing that is causing these requests in the first place." I hand him back the camera and tuck myself into a ball. But I cannot sleep. I keep thinking about the video again.

About half an hour later, we reach a house that is somewhat away from the city. We get out of the truck and I stretch my body to the sky. It feels so good to walk about but I do have to pee, and I am hungry. The other three get out and do the same. We take a short pause to relax our bodies. The house is on a cliff. The front door faces east. It is a small one-story house in decent shape. There is a great view of the other neighborhoods and a large mountain to the east. I can only guess what the view is to the west. Koonzo does his secret knock on the front door which by now I find awkward. No one answers. He knocks a few more times. Still nothing. The look he gives telepathically tells us not to say a word. He decides to ignore the secret knock and bang on the door.

I roll my eyes as I tell myself, "I know we did not drive down here just so we can stand outside waiting for another nerd to not open the door. I walk up to the door, "Hey! If you do not open this door, I am going to kick it down! And then I will look for you and I will beat the nerd out of you!"

"Maybe Shaboomba is not in," Sung-Suu states.

Koonzo comes back, "No, we made our hack time. Shaboomba knows we would be here."

These nerd names are driving me crazy, "Shaboomba?! Are you serious? How does someone come up with…?"

"Shhh! Grab your gear and follow me." Koonzo orders. With our bags on our backs and in our hands, we head to the back of the house. We pass through the gate. Once we reach the back, I can see the San Diego cityscape. It is a beautiful sight. A 180-degree panoramic view. Wow. The boys have seen this view before, so they keep their stride. I actually slow my pace to soak it in. The back deck stretches the entire backside of the house. There is some patio furniture under an awning. In the love seat is someone covered up in a cozy blanket. Looks like he slept out here through the night. Two empty bags of chips and a tablet accompany him in the seat.

"Shaboomba!" Yells Koonzo. It does not work. He pokes at the motionless body under the blanket. It does not work.

He jumps on top of him. I hear, "Ouww! What is your problem, pal?! I was having a glorious dream!"

I hear a Polynesian accent. The blanket is pulled back and it is a girl! No way. She must be the sister to the nerd. She gets up and does her own stretching ritual. After a lengthy yawn she acknowledges her friends, "Hey cronies, it is good to see you guys again. You all ready to crank through another Comic-Con?" The three nerds embrace their friend like one of the guys.

Even for just waking up, she is very pretty. I would say she is possibly from a tropical island like Hawaii judging from her tanned skin, facial features, and long straight dark hair. She looks me over and sticks out her hand. I shake it and ask, "How did you get a name like Shaboomba?"

As I wait for an answer, I look her over some more. She is a little taller than me and seems to be in shape. With an irritated look on her face she replies, "Well Powa, let me fill you in on a short story." She walks up to me and tilts her face down to meet mine and says, "Princess, Lady Bird, and Fluffy Muffs were already taken."

The audience behind me keep their laughter to a minimum. I cannot tell if I deserved that or not. She probably gets that all the time. I tell her, "I get it. You like to tell people that story. Well I like that story, too. You have a beautiful view." I had to change the subject quick. If she is the only girl in the group, I am going to want her on my side. Besides, I think she can take me. She can tell I am backing down.

Shaboomba softens her look. "You can call me basically anything but never call me Boo," as she looks over at Cliffster. I can tell he made that poor decision in life and paid the price.

Cliffster looks away and then checks his watch as to illustrate he is occupied by something more important. Koonzo and Sung-Suu laugh at her latest comment. I want to laugh but since I do not know what that story is I figure I would keep it shut. Shaboomba tells us, "Bring in your gear. We need to plan this out. Comic-Con is not going to wait on us. By the way, I do not understand why you guys could not get here last night."

Koonzo replies, "You know this is expensive for some teenagers that really have no money. Gas, food, and even getting our tickets take their toll."

Shaboomba comes back, "And I tell you every time, I can front you guys the tickets and chow. I got you."

"Look, you are not going to take away our machismo, Shabby. And I know what you are about to say. Just give it a rest."

"Ok, ok, I will not say anything else about it...today," replies Shaboomba. Koonzo shakes his head.

I jump at the chance, "So how did you join Koonzo's group, Shaboomba?" She looks over at Koonzo who scratches his head signaling he is uncomfortable with the topic. She walks back up to me with a solid stare. What did I say? I know I did not say anything insulting. Come on.

She has her original glare, "Honey, I created this group. My house is HQ. And I have all the connections down here. Girl power." She blows me a kiss and a wink. That was pretty cool. There was no objection from Koonzo. But why do I get the feeling she relinquishes that leadership role when Koonzo arrives. I continue my questions, "So how did you guys meet?"

"Online in a chat room. Koonzo, Sung-Suu, and Cliffster were asking about Comic-Con. I filled them in and eventually invited them to crash at my place. That was about two or three years ago. But back then they came down with their parents. Since last year, these guys are too badass to travel with mom and dad anymore." The three do not bother commenting but they do give her the middle finger as they drop their gear on the deck.

Before we go inside, I hear another set of voices from the path we just came in from. From what I notice, it sounds like nerd language. Just what I need, two extra shots of geek wisdom to add to this rogue group. And here they are, two teenagers who are about my height with a slim build. Their Caucasian tanned skin does not convince me they are of European descent. I am done trying to figure out people's ethnicity. One has dirty blonde hair while the other has red and black hair. They are dressed very rockabilly-like which makes them look appealing and un-nerd like. They see us, and all nerds collide. Hugs and hi-5s all around. The dirty blonde one yells out, "Sung-Suu!" He prolongs the last syllable as it cues everyone else to join in. Everyone is doing some seizure of a dance as the red haired one does his beatbox. It does look comical.

They both walk up to me. The blonde one says, "Powa hello, my name is Noni."

"And my name is Goji. We have examined your video countless times and have taken notes. When can we speak with you?" They have thick Russian accents. It does keep my interest.

Koonzo steps in, "Easy, you two. She just got here, and she is slowly and sometimes painfully getting to know each of us."

Noni says, "We are twins but not identical as you can tell. But in case you are wondering, I am the smarter one."

Goji steps in front of Noni and says, "If you have to announce it then it is probably not true. Do not let us distract you from your objective. We are here to help even though Noni is not the smarter twin. But I do agree with his statement. We are fascinated by your video. But I get it, we firehose you with questions."

Then I hear Noni beatbox the opening segment of The Game's rap song "Westside Story." I know my rap music but that was really odd. I ask, "Umm, what was that?"

Goji answers, "Oh snap, sorry. That is just something we have been doing since we were itty bitty. At times when someone finishes a sentence, one of us will sound off with a conclusion beat. We do it every now and then."

Koonzo adds, "It gets annoying but after a while you will not even notice them doing it."

"Or you can be like me and slap them in the back of the head," Shaboomba added.

Goji replies to Shaboomba's comment, "This is abuse." Goji proceeds to display with his right-hand what abuse looks like as he air slaps his brother Noni. He does an excellent job acting out as the victim falling to the deck. Then he states, "And this is correction." To showcase correction, Goji air backhands his brother. Noni, in acting mode innocently says, "I am so sorry, sir." He sounds off with the conclusion beat. Everyone laughs at the comical demonstration.

Folks with street humor get it. I have to admit the conclusion beat does accent Goji's statement very well.

Noni and Goji give everyone hi-5s. Once the laughing dissipates, I ask them, "So are you guys joining us on our quest to Comic-Con?" That seems to strike a chord as everyone flails their hands in the air, grumbles and snickers all at once. I want to ask.

Koonzo explains, "These two are in the Comic-Con history books." Koonzo looks over at them, "Tell her. You knew this would come up."

Goji starts off, "Listen, we are teenage boys. We are going to do teenage things even if it is not a smart idea."

Noni takes over, "So we decided to sneak in to Comic-Con. It was pretty easy. The problem took place when we did our cosplay. It was me and Goji going at it. Then these two other characters that are not even in our character universe jump in. So we go with it."

Goji steps in, "So Noni is getting hit by this swordsman. And I can tell he is getting hurt. He tells the swordsman to tone it down. Well that did not work because he kept hitting him hard. Noni decides to hit him just as hard. Then another character with a mace decides to jump in and help out his friend. So, I jumped in. At this point, we are striking each other with a good amount of force. It got personal. Next thing we know, we are in cosplay war with every costume character. I have no idea how it escalated that fast. Security took us away. We find out the swordsman was a young adult with a disability. Oh man, that made it even worse. And they found out we snuck in. The entire Comic-Con organization was giving us the Riot Act as we sat in front of them during their interrogation. But we played it cool. The only thing we told them was our age. After that, we just stayed quiet. But the end result was that we are permanently banned from Comic-Con."

Noni says, "But we made the news!" Goji rolls his eyes. I can tell these two are crazy characters but not loose cannons. I understand the situation they were in, sometimes when you do something right it still ends up wrong.

Koonzo concludes, "So, they will not be joining us. But they will be here while we are away." And why would they not head back home? They cannot stay here for the entire weekend. Well that is none of my business, so I will keep my mouth shut.

Then something weird happens. Sung-Suu begins to do this weird dance as he stomps on the deck and chants something in a language I have never heard before. Then Koonzo jumps in with the same dance. Then Shaboomba stomps her way between them both and pretty much leads the choreography. Noni and Goji fill in behind them and partake. The dance is intense like they are angry or about to go into battle. Their screams are loud and vicious as their bodies are rigid and strict. Every move looks like a strike or kick. It looks similar to those old Kung-Fu scenes where they show off their martial art talent prior to engaging in battle.

After a couple of minutes, they finish as they are breathing heavy and start to sweat. A little skittish by what I just saw I quietly ask, "Is that your routine thing?"

Koonzo answers as he catches his breath, "That is from the Maori people."

"What country is that?" I ask.

Sung-Suu tags himself into the conversation, "They are the native people from New Zealand. From Shaboomba's stories, we can tell she misses home sometimes. So, one way we help her is by doing the Haka war dance when we can. We also do it whenever one of us needs that extra motivation."

Wow! I have never met a New Zealander before. Now the accent makes sense. She is powerfully impressive. Shaboomba smiles with pride for her friends.

They give each other strong hugs as we walk through the backsliding door and into the dining room. A dining table of four is all the chairs I see. She walks us through the kitchen, which is a bit small but functional. Then we see the living room that is also shared by the same space as the dining room. A sliding door and several large window panes face the city. I mean the entire city can be viewed from here. This house is already awesome. We make a left and into Shaboomba's room. It is fairly large for what I am used to. There is a loft bed, a couple of comic book posters, and an organized closet. My dad always told me you can judge someone's organizational skills by the way their hidden compartments are arranged. He also taught me to always make sure all my drawers, backpack, school, gym locker, and closet were presentable. Even my folders in my computer are organized. It drives me crazy to see things out of order. There I go again thinking about my dad. I wonder what he is thinking right now and if he found my note?

I always wanted one of these beds with a little desk area underneath it. She has made some space in her closet for us to put our bags in. As we drop our gear, we head back out to the dining room. The television is on but muted. It is the news, I think. Cliffster unmutes it and calls for our attention. Shaboomba comes over, "Yea, that is right. You guys have been dark the entire way down. Check it out. There is a company in Moravia that is taking anyone who can and is willing to request a camera which includes footage of children making their requests. Everyone wants to copycat you, Powa." I am not impressed. She points to the television again, "Right here is a third world country. One of its companies got busted in. The police raided this building and discovered some craziness. The new thing is that companies are pretty much snatching up homeless folks and taking them to a place like that one there to brainwash them into requesting anything in particular. People still do not know what this brainwashing process is. But from what they discovered, it is with illegal drugs and pharmaceuticals."

As the cameraman pans around, it looks like they are in a server room. But this room looks different. Someone put a flamethrower to the server racks. They are all melted. I see the newscaster and realize he is wearing a gas mask. The newscaster begins to speak. I do not recognize the language. I decide to read the subtitles out loud, "There must have been a gas leak as all the folks in these hospital rooms are dead. From what I can see, these people look like vagrants from the downtown district judging by their appearance. In world news, several organizations are close to instituting the new time schedule. They say there are multiple benefits to this major adjustment since..." "Alright Powa, we do not need to hear the entire segment. We do have a commitment to get dressed for." Cliffster adds as he mutes the television.

I get carried away when it comes to reading. It is one of my hobbies. But right now I am recalling the image of the facility. It is difficult to tell if the gas cloud lingering in the room is from the gas leak or the burned servers. That is absolutely absurd to kidnap these people and do that to them.

Shaboomba cracks open her tablet, "It gets even more twisted. Look here, an informant has come out to tell us what is going on in our country." She plays the video. It is a silhouette of a man with possibly a fake beard. I can tell the person's voice has been altered. He or she really does not want to be discovered. The video starts in the middle of his discussion. The person speaks with this deep altered voice, "Other companies have picked up this idea and have taken it a bit further. They are targeting suicide cases, folks that have mental disabilities, folks that take depression medication, and folks that are seeing the wizard. These companies are taking them to these large complexes disguised as your standard aerospace or high-tech company with its own personal security."

Sung-Suu attempts to slow down Shaboomba, "Whoa, whoa, whoa! Pause, Shaboomba. There is no way they can do that. They would have to kidnap each person and interrogate them on their medical issues. And even then, those people are not going to answer truthfully because they are scared for their lives."

Koonzo chimes in, "They hire hackers. These hackers hit the hospital servers and get the info that way."

Shaboomba jumps back in, "That is not all. They are checking out social media. Everybody runs their mouth on there."

Cliffster asks, "Wait. What is this other news story about? Are they talking about a hospital getting involved in this stuff?"

Noni clicks on the video as we shift our attention. The newscaster states, "At least seven staff members are being charged. One for selling medical information to the black market. Two for overcharging families for request surveillance packages. Two more for advancing the death cycle in cancer patients. Eight nurses and doctors are detained for selling patients to these underground companies. And two high ranking hospital officials are charged with masterminding all of it."

Sung-Suu says, "What is the human race turning into?"

Koonzo replies to that comment, "Hey Noni, mute that thing, will you? We need to stay on point and make sure we got everything set. Get our minds off this and back in the game." Goji provides the conclusion beat. I smile at the awkwardness it creates.

Shaboomba signals for her turn to talk. She leads off, "We already have a plan for Comic-Con. But what about her? We need to get her taken care of as well. When do we do that?"

Koonzo looks at me and then back at Shaboomba, "Well since she does not have a ticket, she can wait here."

I laugh it up, "If you think you all got me down here so that I can sit here while you all nerd out over your Comic-Con experience, then you have another thing coming!" I want to do my own conclusion beat but that would be weird. Koonzo knew what my reaction would be.

He grins and says, "Well, we can always sneak you in. Noni and Goji gave us the insight. But keep in mind, there will be a lot of picture taking as well as video recording. And did I forget to mention, those photos and videos will be uploaded? So, the risk of you being seen is about ten out of ten. And if you want to draw that attention back on you then that is on you. Or you can stay here and lay low until we get back. Once we are back, we will be ready to execute our plan."

This is crap, "The plan is, there is no plan until you are done with your nerd escapade and then will come up with some last-minute idea."

Sung-Suu chimes in, "You know we can get her in without being detected. Come on, fellas, this is Comic-Con by the way."

Cliffster joins in, "It is pretty crummy that we drag her out here and she has to wait here for us in hiding while we go and have our fun. I mean she cannot even go to the store or walk around the neighborhood. It is like house arrest."

Shaboomba even speaks up, "She can use one of my outfits. She has the body for it."

I look at all of them, "If you think I am going to get dressed up to frolic in your cult movement then will someone please wake me from this nerd nightmare?"

Koonzo repeats, "Or you can stay here and wait for us to complete our nerd escapade. Besides, we will be out there putting all the pieces together. We got this. There is no need to complicate things. Oh, and keep in mind, this is a four-day experience."

Sung-Suu looks at me, "Three and a half. Today is the first day and it starts in about four hours. Listen, I think Powa should come with us so that she can get cultured. She can see what we are all about. We will discuss our plan accordingly as she fills us in on any other details. She loses nothing and nothing big gets complicated."

Koonzo throws his hands in the air as he walks towards the dining room. He is making a lot of sense. Besides, as beautiful as this view is, being stuck here will only drive me crazy thinking of what is to come. I provide a nod.

Noni chimes in, "Hey, if she goes, we go too. The only reason we were going to stay was just to get to know the new girl." He looks over at Goji of which they both look at me with this cheesy grin. I do not give them the satisfaction of a reply, but I do manage to hold a stern look at them until their grinning transforms into an uncomfortable session of scratching and stretching.

Koonzo, "That is on you two. It is 1400. We leave at 1700. You know how dense it is going to be. Before we get there, remember the rules. This is for you, Powa. Never call us by our names. Call us by our character names. Spectators appreciate our dedication to staying in character. Besides, Powa is not a common name. People will pick up on that pretty fast. I will tell you the other rules when we get there."

Everyone heads back to the room and here comes my first close encounter with a nerd enriched experience. Cliffster and Sung-Suu stay behind for a quick chat. I stay behind as well for the sake of being nosy. Cliffster tells Sung-Suu, "You know those companies can start reaching out to other folks as well. I mean I reach out to yo momma whenever I want her to make me some chicken soup."

Goji laughs at the last remark and takes his seat again as he joins in, "Like who?"

Cliffster replies, "Well anyone in a crappy situation looking to get their families paid or at least make themselves a part of something bigger."

Sung-Suu asks, "Who else besides those folks dying in the hospitals, the bums on the street, the kidnapped, and Cliffster's momma is there?"

Cliffster answers, "Addicts of the worst kind, for one. And even the elderly in hospices. Those guys would get hemmed up easy. All you need to find those folks is a birthday."

Goji states, "That has to be weird. An entire generation of old folks turns into a commodity. Crazy."

I jump in with, "Oh I know, death row prisoners. They have nothing but time."

Sung-Suu replies, "That is a good one, Powa. I did not think of that. Except for Cliffster's momma. She is allowed conjugal visits. However, unless the warden is on their payroll, I do not see that happening. Nonetheless, it is an appealing thought. It does not stop there. I guarantee you there are those religious leaders that would sacrifice themselves for something like this. Not so much that they would kill themselves for this but quite possibly try and convince one of their fellow ailing members to request a camera. I mean, think about how that will change the world?"

Goji looks confused. I am confused.

Cliffster looks at the confused ones, "I follow you, Sung-Suu. Imagine if a certain religion succeeds in requesting a live feed camera or a tracker. What will that do for that religion?"

Sung-Suu answers without knowing the punchline, "It will be free advertisement that their religion is able to request such a device or even request what they want."

Cliffster points his finger at Goji, "Do you see? Religion gets a mad boost in recruitment which leads to a crazy boost in attendance. That religious leader is immediately idolized. His place of worship becomes saturated with all types of people to include people of money. And who knows, a possible religious war could start or at least a competition between religions if any other religion can do the same." Goji sits back, "Wow, that is some real deep stuff. I never thought of that." Ok, I am a religious person as I do pray for every meal as well as before I go to sleep. We never did go to church a lot. Not even on special holidays would we attend. But Cliffster is right. I can see how this could manifest itself into something hypersensitive among every believer of their higher power."

Shaboomba pops her head out, "Eyes on the prize, guys. Gear up."

Sung-Suu looks back at me, "Looks like you are getting hailed to put on your Halloween costume." Noni adds the conclusion beat. This time it makes me feel like I am about to experience something pretty awful. Please, do not let it be something nerdy. Who am I fooling?

Shaboomba presented a nice makeshift salon seat for me which happens to be one of the dining room chairs. Noni is in the room working on his costume and Goji went to the bathroom to start on his make up or whatever they call it. As Shaboomba is working on my hair, I ask, "Hey Noni, have you seen the latest Russian request video?" Noni keeps looking over his costume, "The one with the little old lady in the car crash? Yea, that was pretty crazy."

"No, the one with the teens in some abandoned building?"

Noni stops and looks at me, "What abandoned building? Umm, just to let you know Goji and I do not have cellphones much less a data plan. We are only connected when we are here or at our uncle's basement. And we are only allowed there once a week until we make more money to stay longer."

So where do these guys stay in the first place? Before I could ask, he hands me a tablet. I punch in the request description and there it is. Noni examines the initial frame, "No, we have not seen this one." He presses play. The video reaches the part where red shirt grabs the request." Noni's reaction is priceless. He covers his mouth, "I did not think we could do that!" Red shirt makes his first comment. Noni pauses the video, "Goji, come here man!"

Goji walks in with the top half of his face covered in black and gold make up. It makes him look evil. He looks at the tablet, "This better be good because you know how long it takes for me to put this stuff on my face."

Shaboomba strikes back with, "It beats having to look at your real face." Noni rewards her with a conclusion beat.

Goji heads back to the bathroom when Noni grabs his shirt as he laughs, "No, for reals. This is not Russian. This is Kazakh. You learned Kazakh better than me." He looks over at me, "We came from a city called Bishkek which is a city in Kyrgyzstan. We learned multiple languages in school until we were forced to leave."

Goji interrupts, "Before he rambles with that sob story…" He presses play. Red shirt makes his statement. Goji pauses and translates, "It is not as painful as I thought it would be. It is very hot." He continues the video. Red shirt attempts to pull the request toward himself, but it does not move. He attempts to pull with both hands and is not successful. The light from the request is still zigzagging inside his hands. The light gets brighter. Red shirt expresses his increase in pain or discomfort. Then the request disappears. A teenage boy then asks his question.

Goji pauses the video, "He asked how hard were you pulling?" He listens for the answer. Goji laughs as he pauses again, "This guy in the red shirt is funny. He said he pulled about as hard as he pulled on his momma's hair last night."

Red shirt cups his hands around his mouth and then starts to rub them together. The other teenager asks his question and Goji presses pause. Goji says, "This guy asks why are you rubbing your hands? You just said they were burning up." He listens to the answer and translates, "Red said it was very hot when the request was in his hands. He could feel the zigzag of the lights in his hands. When the request vanished, the heat vanished, and his hands went straight to freezing."

Goji plays the video and then laughs at the same time the people on the video do. He explains, "Then this other kid said that is how Ruslin is when he is trying to find…" He tries to wrap up his laughing seizure. We do not get the punchline and he is laughing much longer than our enthusiasm for the joke.

Shaboomba smacks Goji in the back of the head, "Hey, at least finish the video, pendejo!" She looks at us proudly as she expresses her ability to speak some Spanish. It only makes me feel further away from my culture. That catches Goji's attention as he continues the video. Then red shirt shows the camera his hands.

Noni, Goji, and Shaboomba's jaws drop. Noni speaks, "Are those the patterns of the…?"

Shaboomba replies, "Absolutely. This is crazy." Another teenager speaks as Goji laughs along with the video. He places his hands over his face and finally gains control of himself. He translates, "He said now he is always going to be accused of playing with hims…"

Noni and Shaboomba laugh at the joke before Goji could finish. As I finish the last word in my head, I do admit that is a little funny but not that funny.

Goji continues the video and translates what the cop says, "Hey punks, what are you doing here?! Wait, get back here! This girl is dead! What did you do to her?!"

We stay silent for a bit. I know what they are thinking. Those teens killed that girl. That is some selfish cold-hearted stuff right there. Goji leaves without adding any comment. I think he is disappointed that he was liking those guys until the last part. Noni resumes his attention to his costume. Shaboomba does not start on my hair. She stares at my hair for a minute until I cough for her attention. I recall the video now that there are no other distractions. We have a couple of hours to get ready for this so-called special event. I hope this turns out to be fun.

Chapter 9

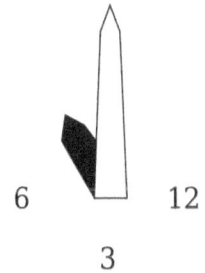

6   12

3

Saturday morning

Nope. I do not want to talk about it. I will never do Comic-Con again. Those two days were absolutely heinous! The media talks about Comic-Con as if it is the greatest event on earth. I do not see how they can say that. Sure, you get to see a lot of creative costumes. The nerds call it something else. The exhibits and panels for big movies coming out were a good experience. I got to see some of the celebrities I never would have seen in person. They even played some of the trailers for the new movies that will be coming out soon. A lot of people approached me about my costume. I did not know how to respond. I felt like an imposter in a land that I was welcomed. But what they do not tell you is what they should tell you. Never did anyone tell me about having to wait in line for over four plus hours to get inside. I surely was not told we would be sleeping outside while waiting in line to get inside that same stupid building the following day and the day after. Oh, and since we stayed there for the following three nights, guess what did not happen...showers. No showers equal body funk. And it is not just us, but it is everyone else that never went home to get a decent meal, a nice hot shower, or brushed their teeth. Oh, and keep in mind, it is July. 80 degrees feels nice and fresh outside. Was Comic-Con 80 degrees? Only if you like being hot, muggy, and a having a constant film of sweat on you to wear; every time you extend your arm you can feel your bicep skin unwrapping itself from your forearm skin. Now picture that feeling all around your body. Yeah, somebody hand me a wet nap kind of atmosphere.

I felt disgusting the entire time I was there. People's body odor was wreaking through their costumes. Even people that did not wear a costume were funky. We ate the same chow we ate on the ride down from Klamath Falls. I tried to be accepting of this experience but what I had to go through to see those celebrities, of which were far away because our seats were near the back, was a large price to pay. Very early Saturday morning before dawn, I woke up itching. That is when I realized something either bit me or I was having some skin rash from all the dinginess. I threw out the white flag right at all their faces. I made demands to get me back to the house or I would have been relentless in my pursuit to make them all equally as uncomfortable as I was. As upset as they all were, they decided to take me back. But they did not just drop me off, they all stayed with me. I am thinking they wanted a break as well. At least that is what I tell myself. I have a lot of respect for the hardcore Comic-Con fans that do this. They are devoted to this cause. They sacrifice their time, and money for those costumes, for something that really takes a lot out of them. If the Comic-Con organizers found a way to make this more customer and costume friendly, then sure I would give it another try. But until then, I am sticking to not doing this again. Thank goodness. We just arrived at Shaboomba's house. "Excuse me folks, I am going to sterilize myself for about three hours." As I exit, I tell myself, "And to think I made the decision to go to this thing rather than stay here."

Now I feel better. I cleansed myself of all things Comic-Con and took a healthy nap. Koonzo comes over and nudges me awake. I cannot judge his facial expression as he has already walked away. I do not get upset since I am happy to be back in civilization. I take in a long stretch with a yawn and follow him. As I came around the corner, I see they do not look happy to see me. I can tell I did not make it a pleasant experience. At least the feeling is mutual. Honestly, I do feel bad that I am the sole reason for the bad experience. A lot went into planning for this and I ruined their annual ritual. So, I speak first, "Before you all say something, hear me out. I know this Comic-Con sucked for all of us. I am sorry for that. It was something I was not expecting to endure. You all are used to this, but I have never done anything like this before. But what troubles me is that all this time none of you talked once about my plan. And not only that, if you put me through this without ever telling me what I was going to go through, how am I supposed to trust you will have my best interest when it is time to execute this plan? So, what I am going to do is head back to Klamath Falls and deal with this situation on my own. I appreciate your attempted effort to help me, but I think I am better off just going back." My audience remains quiet. I thought at least there would have been some grumbling.

I take their silence as a sign for me to start grabbing my stuff. As I walk back to the bedroom, Koonzo stops me, "Powa, there is something we need to tell you. We found out about it while you were taking your nap." Yup, that caught my attention. I was expecting an apology from them or some form of empathy. But instead, they are going to fill me in on some news. I guess I am right. They really could care less about my situation. I stopped in my tracks but do not turn to face them. Koonzo continues, "It is about your family. Actually, it is about one of your parents." My heart skips a beat. No, this cannot be happening. My dad's secret has been exposed. Or could it be something worse. Koonzo says, "The media has leaked out information that is very private."

Ok, I need to keep it together. I take in a deep breath with my mouth and slowly blow it out my nose. "I am sorry, Powa." I close my eyes and yell within myself, "Shut up, Koonzo, just shut up!" I squeeze my eyes tight hoping they can keep my ears from listening.

"We are sorry to hear about your mother's condition." My eyes slowly grow wide. My mom?! What about my mom? There is nothing wrong with my mom. This must be the media trying to get a rise out of me. I turn and face him still in disbelief.

Koonzo informs me, "Your mother has A-TAC. All they know is that it is a new strain."

No, this cannot be. A-TAC? The media is calling it the AIDS of our generation. An airborne virus or bacteria. I do not know which. First case was reported just after the new year. All we know is that it camouflages itself as intermittent blurred vision, fatigue, and minor headaches. Then the brain starts to deteriorate after four months. No one knows much about it other than all 57-cases have resulted in death. Some folks are claiming there is a connection with the requests but nothing substantial has been uncovered. Why my mom? She has always been the quiet bond in the home. I cannot contain it and tears begin to flow. It feels like someone has pierced my stomach with a hot blade. My teeth grind against each other to the point I wish they would crush under the intense pressure. My entire body goes tense. I feel the fibers of each muscle tearing alongside my chest. My face wrinkles in pain. The one person I allowed to be overshadowed. The one I speak of the least is the one that has guided our entire family to be peaceful and charming despite her quiet personality. Not my mom, please, not her.

After several moments go by, they show me the news. I go a bit numb. I want to call her. I want to see her! I yelled while grabbing two fists full of his shirt, "Get me on a flight back home now, Koonzo!"

"Listen Powa, I know you are in pain, but I need you to be logical right now."

Oh, I let him have it, "Logical?! You expect me to be logical? My mom is about to die, and I am here not doing anything about it. You know what? I do not expect you to understand. Forget it. I will find my own way home."

Cliffster jumps in front of me with his hands up, "Powa, we know what the love of a dying parent can do to a teenager. I went through it. My life has never been the same. And I went down a pretty bad road. Koonzo helped me get through that nightmare. I have him to thank for finding something for me to believe in. He turned me to comics, real-time strategy games, and a bunch of teens that feel the same as me. I cherish it. What we want to do is get the spotlight off you. We have someone that has a dying sibling. We just need you to recreate the conditions of Nhim's video."

Koonzo provides more information, "We will position ourselves so that you are never in the video. A second cameraman, Noni, will also record from his viewpoint. Once we get it on video, we will upload it which will take the spotlight off you. But if you go up to Klamath Falls now, the least that will happen is that the government will take you into custody and hold you there. They will use your mother's condition to force you to talk or coerce you to do what they want you to do. Then more interrogations will take place. And by that time who knows what condition your..." Cliffster did not finish the thought.

"I understand all that but what if it does not work? Or if I am unexpectedly discovered on the video from a reflection on a mirror? Or someone says my name? Then all that does is re-enforce to the government guys that I am the key to all this. No deal. There is too much at risk." I said almost shouting.

Goji instinctively makes his conclusion beat. Shaboomba smacks him on the back of the head, "Shut up, Goji bean!" Goji rubs the affected area and says, "that is a new nick name for me. I kind of like it."

Shaboomba now steps in, "Powa, we will not stop you from leaving. But we will still offer our services. Koonzo is good at organizing things. He is as obsessed about details as he is obsessed about Xenomorphs. Koonzo has someone lined up right now. We talked about this opportunity at great lengths before your discovery on the web. I would not have agreed to this had they not done a lot to convince me. My feminine intuition tells me this is the logical approach to take."

Oh Shaboomba, that is pretty slick adding that last part. "Let me have a moment to myself. I have to think this through," I tell them as I walk onto the deck.

What a beautiful view this is. How my mom would love to see this. Did my dad know? How much time does she have left? Did my brother know? Or did he find out like me, like this? Is the poor kid freaking out? I should stop with these questions before I drive myself half crazy. I miss them all, a lot, even my little brother. So now what? What should I do? Go home and see my family or stay here and let the gang work out their plan for me? The last thing I want is to see my mom and have the Goon Squad come in and take me away minutes later. That will only stress my mom out. I would not want her last vision of me being taken away by government agents. I am staying. It is the most unselfish of decisions. Before I tell them, I decide to take in more of the vista. I enjoy the simple peace it offers me. It reminds me of my room. My safe place to be when the world does not understand me. I close my eyes and take in the breeze and head back inside. Here we go.

There they are still seated in the living room. They become silent once they hear me enter. I decide to open up with, "I have to think of my family first. Having said that, how are we going to get the spotlight off me?" The expression on their faces tells me they were not expecting that answer.

Noni yells at Goji, "That was the time to do your conclusion beat, dummy! I told you I am the smarter one." We all laugh. I give them a smile to camouflage my troubled heart. If there is a group out there that can pull this off it better be this one.

Koonzo stands up and says, "We have another friend who could not join us."

I cut him off, "Let me guess. This friend is a nerd and he knows what we should do, right?"

Koonzo looks around before looking at me, "Why yes, yes he is and yes he does."

I reply, "You guys are too easy to read."

Koonzo, "Since you can read us so well, then you probably read the reason he did not join us is because his little brother is dying."

Oh crap, I did it again; I put my foul-tasting foot in my mouth. I really need to shut up sometimes, "I am sorry guys. I meant no disrespect."

Shaboomba says, "We know. You try to outsmart us. We get that all the time. You are not the first, Powa."

Yea, I do jump the gun sometimes. Man, am I like this at home, too? "But I still do not know what we are going to do. None of you have spoken of a plan since I have been here. And that is what has me concerned. You cannot go against these Bigs or the government without some type of plan. I mean you guys are nerds! You think of stuff like this. But here I am asking for a plan of which no dialogue has taken place!" I feel the blood rushing to my ears. I need to calm down.

Koonzo pats a space next to him for me to sit, "We understand how you feel. I would be too. We believe our plan is as close to completion as it will ever be."

I strike back, "Oh really? When was it completed? When we were waiting in line for that zip line ride for three hours or was it while we were waiting for Hall H, inside Comic-Con to open. Because that felt like an eternity. Now I know how cows feel like in the field. We were cattled for about four and a half hours?"

Koonzo looks over to his friends keeping me only in his peripheral view, "It was when we were sleeping under the stars Friday night. You remember? Everyone pitched tents to wait in line. It was a great night to talk."

I stand up and stop him right there, "I call BS. Besides the lame fact that we pulled a Black Friday stunt, you guys did not talk about a plan. You guys were talking about a video game. I remember it. I could not sleep because you would not shut up about it."

Sung-Suu joins in, "Powa, remember when we were talking about the pipeline to Venador?" I nod. "We were really talking about how we were going to get the video on the web without too much attention to you. Masking our web signal is important in order to ensure the attention is placed strictly on us and away from you. That requires more than just uploading a video."

I do not understand what he said or how that can help. I just nod to keep the explanation going.

Noni adds, "And do not forget about us. Goji and I deal with audio and video. You may have heard of our site called Scratch Cat. We go about interviewing people who share a horrible experience. Then we add animation to re-dramatize the experience. We try to make it funny but some of them are pretty jacked up. When ratings get low we tend to do some abstract projects."

"Nope. But I will check it out. It sounds like a great idea."

"Oh it is. We have been picked up by several internet stations and guest starred on a few podcasts." Noni says almost too enthusiastically. Goji happily provides his conclusion beat.

Looks like this team has a couple of hidden prospects here. I never would have guessed these two teenage boys would be impressive enough to create their own web show. Good for them. I just hope they are able to capture what is required to help me out.

Sung-Suu continues, "And I know you heard us talking about Operation: Open Passage many times. This is one of our favorite online games. Here we discussed our part when we begin filming. We all will have certain responsibilities to ensure we maximize the effort for the request. Once we are set up, you will see what is going on."

I reply, "Okay. I was wrong. I underestimated your talents. And it makes sense why you did it this way. I appreciate your encrypted dialogue. You guys need to find a different way to make me feel like crap. This one is getting old." They all break out laughing. And I continue with my curiosity, "But why 'Open Passage?' Is that supposed to be something significant? And what is Venador?"

Cliffster's eyes brighten, "I got this, guys." Everyone takes a second to get comfortable as if they know they are going to hear a story they have heard several times over.

Sung-Suu yells out, "Nerd alert!"

We all laugh as Cliffster comes back with a lame response, "Takes one to know one."

Cliffster scoots his chair closer to me as he waves at me to sit down. He begins his explanation with a storyteller's tone deep and spooky, "You see Operation: Open Passage is a game that has an evil character named Mark 4. He created a mysterious passageway that leads through a waterfall. Everyone thought it was someplace wonderful even though no one knows anything about it. Well a group of scouts went through it. The first several hundred meters of the path were very exciting. An entirely different world was on the other side. From the trees, the grass, and even the animals there were all different. The scout leader sent a message of what they were observing. Another party walked through the waterfall. The path came to an end which was a cul-de-sac of extremely large trees. But these trees had these butterfly type of insects and some odd chirping birds. The first two groups decided to set up camp there as the trees would provide cover for their fire. Once everyone got comfortable…"

"Dude, she gets it. Short stories, Cliffster. I told you about your storytelling technique," explains Shaboomba.

I play it off like I was losing interest but to be honest, that story held my attention. I will have to ping him later about that.

Koonzo informs us, "We will leave in ten minutes. Everyone, grab all your gear." And sure enough, we leave on time.

Chapter 10

Saturday late morning

We reach a neighborhood that is very poor. It took only a couple of short minutes to get there. This Saturday morning is going to be a little hot, I can tell as the clouds have retreated from the sun. Shaboomba rode her dirt bike. Her dad must have raised her to be a tomboy. I like dads that make their little girls competitive in activities typically dominated by men. The front yard of the house is cluttered with junk. We go around back which I am beginning to understand is a nerdy thing to do. More junk has taken over what used to be a well-manicured backyard. The secret knock is answered. A teenage boy opens the door. He is a white kid about Koonzo's height. I make the mistake of thinking this house belongs to immigrants. The only reason I say this is because my little neighborhood looks a bit cleaner than this one and a close-knit group of us are Hispanic. But there is something different about this guy. His right hand is missing. I lean over to Koonzo and whisper, "What happened to his hand?"

"A few months ago, his older brother drank a gallon of acid. He was not high or anything. His brother wanted to commit suicide." I give Koonzo the 'Oh my goodness' face. He continues, "Crazy, huh? He saw him drink this stuff right in front of him. Then my boy saw the label on the bottle and naturally responded by jamming his finger down his brother's throat to make him puke it out. In the process, the acid began to dissolve his hand. To make things worse, his brother still died. And to add to that, our homie was right-handed. Poor guy." How does someone recover from something like that? Talk about a tragedy.

He greets his friends. Cliffster gives him a hug, "Hey there Captain Hook, where is your hook? Did you let Sung-Suu's momma borrow it?"

He responds with, "Argh, Matey, I must have left it in your sister's room." They both laugh at his comment. Sung-Suu shakes his head. The others make light of the situation with similar jokes.

I smile at their humor. Then he walks up to me with a welcoming tone, "Powa, it is good to meet you at last. We have gone through great lengths to keep your arrival top secret. I am Mort."

Well at least Mort is not a nerd-sounding name like his friend's. Mort continues, "But please call me Munch."

Dang it. I cannot win. I notice something familiar. Partially hidden by his shirt at the base of his neck are these burn marks like that from the Kazakhs video. My smile turns to a scowl as my disappointment settles in.

Munch realizes I have noticed what he is trying to conceal. He says, "In case you are wondering it is not what you think. Yes, they are the marks from a request. My brother gave me his necklace when we first saw a request video. I told him I was afraid of them especially after viewing the Moldova and Russian video or wherever they are from. He gave me his necklace to protect me. But when he died I placed his necklace around his neck to protect him in the afterlife. I should have known his necklace was his request. For some reason, once I saw his request I became guilty that he gifted me this necklace for my protection. The only thing I could do was place my neck in the path of the request to forever mark my brother's gift for me. I was focused more on the pain from my neck than on the request. I got a lot of those same looks you are giving me. That is why I try to cover them up."

I change my expression. This was not his doing. Munch was trying to save a life. Not take it away. He grabs my hand and guides me across the other side of the backyard. From the clutter I can see a small shack the size of two garden sheds put together. It is camouflaged with all the junk surrounding it. We walk inside. It is a studio style layout like Sung-Suu's flat. A lot of cardboard boxes and plastic crates with clothes inside. This must be Munch's place. A bed sheet hangs from the ceiling separating the common space to the far corner of the room. As Munch pulls the bedsheet back, I see an entire family of eight huddled around a boy on a cot. They are all Hispanic, but Munch is a white kid. One of those European genes must have squeezed through. As for his little brother, he looks seriously ill. Munch tells us, "We got a hold of a Gevity device for him and he already got his first alert."

I ask Sung-Suu, "How does it work?"

He replies, "Well you first have to place the two strips…" I do not let him finish.

"I know about that part. My dad hooked up the whole family. I just do not know how it works." Sung-Suu changes his tone to be oddly more enthusiastic, "You know that euphoric sensation you get when those two strips dissolve in your mouth? Those are the Nano-machines coming alive. We call them Nanites for short. Well those things go all over your body. The Nanites are so smart, they not only report everything about your body. They analyze it, provide medical recommendations, and dump all that info into your medical records. By the way, this company so happened to have developed the first nationwide medical database. Talk about deeply connected. The infant version of this was created to detect cancer. But with all that has changed in the world, they have managed to introduce this technology at the opportune time."

Sung-Suu keeps talking as I get distracted by the coughing from Munch's brother.

I ask Munch, "Is there any way we can get your brother into your parents' house? I know it may be hard because of the situation but it would help to have more space."

Munch looks at me, "We all live in here. This is our home. We are undocumented. This is the main reason we cannot go to a hospital. We have no papers and we have no money. We are lucky the Gevity alert is not connected to the immigration organization. But I am sure the government will be tapping into that resource in the future.

I quickly feel a sense of obligation. I always read about these situations and even questioned how destitute are these families? I will never ask that question again. But wait, "There are laws that allow treatment for anyone regardless if you are undocumented. You can still get him help."

Munch replies, "He gets taken in and then what? There will be forms to fill out. We cannot give our address. We will be jeopardizing the family that took us in. And if my little brother does get accepted to the hospital, we all will not be able to stay there. We will not be allowed in. And we are a very close family. We went through all of this with my uncle. It was a horrible and desperate experience. And when we are home and the Gevity device sends an alarm, how are we to get there? We have no car or enough money to pay for public transportation. Most of our money goes toward the rent and food. We are stuck here."

Munch's statement overwhelms me. Their situation is dire, and they cannot do anything but to watch their relative die in pain. An overwhelming sadness knocks me down to the seat behind me. I want to help this family out of this bad situation. There must be something I can do.

Koonzo steps up to me, "Powa, Munch knows about our plan. We should talk."

We all head outside and gather around Munch. He opens up with, "Thank you all for the love. It means a lot to us. Times are tough right now. I am definitely on board with getting Powa to do her thing. Unlike those other request videos, my family is going to stay inside with him throughout the entire session. No way around it, sorry. You guys do what you guys do. And yes, I am still good with being a cameraman. Now I have been priming my brother to request this camera which will be on a live feed on the new account Shaboomba created just for… this." Munch begins to get a little emotional. Noni and Sung-Suu come over and hug the guy.

Koonzo takes over, "Just like Nhim's video, we will only upload the beginning portion. What we are hoping for is the Bigs will look for us. Since we anticipate they would be extremely interested in the footage they would actually pay for the entire video. Noni will make sure Munch's face is seen clearly on the video but not make it obvious. This way these guys can take the bait. Whatever is offered is what we will split. The money will help his family find a better life here in the States."

And there it is. This is the way I can help this family. I will not tell them no. That was never an option in the first place. I feel I am doing this more for them than for me. And I feel good about that. This family deserves a life worth living. They deserve a lifestyle like mine if not better. After all, these are my people. I tell Munch, "I want you to give my portion of the money to your family."

I can see the reluctant tears piling up on Munch's eyes. That is all the thanks I need. He puts his head down and throws out a few coughs. I want to give him a hug but decide against it. For some reason I think he would take it as a form of sympathy. I would rather not challenge his machismo even if I am wrong about him. I walk to the other side of Cliffster.

Koonzo orders, "Alright everyone, looks like it is time to review Nhim's video before going live." I breakout Nhim's tablet. Koonzo yells at me, "Hey, what's the deal?! We have been Daedalus all this time! That tablet is going to get us caught!"

I yell back, "For your information, this tablet's web connection has been disabled! Look at the web icon. It has a red 'X' on it. So, ease up on the drama and stop being a drama queen!"

Noni sends me a conclusion beat which makes me feel good. Koonzo wants to say something but the silence from his friends keeps him quiet. The nerds huddle behind me. I feel like I am about to unveil the biggest secret of my failure. It is not guilt that I feel, I really do not know how else to describe it other than I cannot take back the promise I made to my dying friend. Still, in order to make ALL this go away I must do it. Someone nudges me from behind. This time I decide to prop the tablet on a chair and press play. I stand up and walk behind the chair. It is important to me to see their facial expressions. I need to see what everyone else in the world is going to look like. My spectators look on examining every detail that leads up to the request disappearing. Then comes the special part. Each expression is different. Some of their eyes grow wide in surprise while others squint trying to understand what they are seeing. And this is the response I wanted to see. This is what

Nhim deserves. My own alligator tears begin to form but I suck them back in. This is not the time. But I do present a smile that they do not see even though I am right in front of them. They are utterly amazed. I keep hearing, "What is that? Where did that snow come from? Where does that lead to? Are those what I think they are? The color of the sky looks weird. What is that way back there?" Some of those questions make me want to look at that video again. I do not remember any detail about the sky.

The video ends and these guys quickly start to nerd out. I put the tablet back in my backpack. They are asking more questions and coming up with these crazy theories.

Goji breaks out with, "Oh my goodness, heaven is an ice planet. Snowboarding for everyone!"

Cliffster jumps in, "Shut up, Goji. For real, I think that is some place we do not know about. And did you see that part at the end? Was that a city or what? We are going to have to rewind that part."

Shaboomba breaks into the conversation, "That cannot be heaven. It is nothing like what we were taught. There are no pearly gates. I did not see any fluffy clouds, birds chirping, angels flying around, and I definitely did not see God."

Cliffster replies, "No one really knows what heaven looks like. All the movies, the books, the sermons do not know what heaven looks like."

Shaboomba fires back, "And what about those folks that actually have died and claim to have seen heaven? They all describe the same thing."

Before Cliffster could reply Sung-Suu takes his turn, "Maybe it is another world. Maybe death is the real wormhole."

Noni smacks the back of Sung-Suu's head, "Did you just say that? You better not ever talk about me and Goji not being in our right minds. That is clearly the afterlife. And the afterlife is all about shredding that snow! Give me some!" Goji sounds off with the conclusion beat accompanied by a hi-five and a bro hug.

Shaboomba smacks Noni and Goji in the back of the head, "You are too young to smack anyone in the back of the head. And you, shut up." Sung-Suu looks at Noni with the intention to break him in half. The glare and the message are well received by Noni as he looks away.

Koonzo calms them down, "Whoa, whoa, whoa, keep it down guys, will you? I appreciate how excited you are about this mission but, we got a job to do. Everyone take your places. We need to mock our positions for the video before we go inside. Some adjustments have to be made since this room is significantly smaller than Nhim's." I have my place to shoot while the other two find their spots. As Koonzo plays director, we reenact Nhim's video. Without wasting time, we review our responsibilities. As we watch the video, Munch's father comes out and tells us they have received the second alert.

Munch looks over at us and said, "Time is up. The reaper must celebrate Christmas."

We all give each other the gas face. Koonzo asks, "What do you mean by that, Munch?"

Munch takes a few moments to gather his thoughts and then says softly, "I know we are in the middle of July but since my little brother will not make it to Christmas and he is the most precious gift we have, the reaper is coming to collect him." It looked like Munch was about to say more but could not find the words.

That one got me for sure. One tear falls without my permission. I wipe away its existence. No one notices as they immediately scramble to rush inside.

I get inside, and notice Munch's little brother does not look good. I grab the camera and begin recording. Munch is trying to push his family away from the bed, "No, let them be with their son. I can work around them." The rest of the team stands behind me except for the other two cameramen. All we can hear are the prayers from his family. My mind goes blank. I cannot remember if I talked to Nhim or just kept quiet during this part of the video.

Koonzo begins to talk to the little boy. It is not part of the script but he can tell I am not feeling at ease with all this. He kindly tells the boy, "Hey there little one. I was told this is your favorite toy right here in my right hand. I do not know how this became your favorite toy, but it is an amazing stuffed animal." Hearing Koonzo talk to the boy like that makes me feel like a fraud. I know this is not what I told Nhim in his final moments. But I am here to help this family, so this is the way it has to be.

Koonzo continues on, "Better yet, what if you requested this camera instead?"

What is he saying? This kid is not going to fall for that! The poor boy raises his hand wanting to touch it. Koonzo walks closer to him. Once he gets within arms distance, we hear his hand thud back down to the bed. Koonzo lowers the camera all the way to his side to get a better look at what happened. His family already knows. The crying starts off slow and low. They lean in almost on top of him. We move out of their way. His mom is kissing his little limp hand. She wipes her tears away with it. The loss of a child must be the worst moment a parent can ever experience. I am about to close my own eyes when I begin to see lights on the wall in front of me. This must be it.

Koonzo puts the camera back up to his face and focuses on the lights. But these lights look familiar. They are not like the lights of a request. They look like everyday lights, like from a lamp or a... but I never get to finish that thought because a big crash rambles the entire shack!

A gaping hole replaces the door as smoke enters the little house. Everyone is startled. A lot of yelling and screaming takes place. We all turn to the commotion. Yelling ensued along with a pouring of people with bright lights on their weapons. Weapons?! Who is bringing weapons here? Is this the immigration service? Oh no, they are going to think we helped Munch's family cross the border illegally. Or maybe they will think we are the ones that supplied them with illegal documentation. Everyone tries to escape. As I run away, I see a light flash. I look over and see the boy's request vanish. But I am unable to look long enough to decipher what it was. I must grab my stuff. They cannot discover Nhim's video. I take the tablet out and open the digital folder. I am hesitant to delete the video. I tell myself, "I am so sorry, Nhim." The intruders are getting closer. Then I shove the tablet in the microwave and turn it on. Shaboomba's bike screeches over the yelling. I take off running with the hope of reaching beyond the front yard.

Buzz... Now that is a sensation I never want to feel again. That taser shot feels like it lasted for a long 60-seconds. I try to get up and am reminded of another shot of electricity. My muscles tense up again. I can feel my teeth clinch and my head rattle. Once the taser feeling stops, I learn quickly and stay down. I hear a male voice say, "Load this one up, too. Ensure you keep them all separated. Grab all of their gear. Toss the place and load up the family as well. I want everything." A bag is placed over my head. It smells like someone spilled a strong liquid on it. I pass out.

Chapter 11

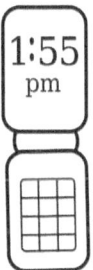

Saturday afternoon

Man, this is a pretty bad headache. The bag is off, but my vision is blurry still. The light above is extremely bright. I rub and rub my eyes several times. My sight returns as I realize I am in a jail cell, I think. I am laying on the floor. It smells sanitized and not one speck of dust to be found. As I look around, all I see are four walls. I walk along the walls and place my right hand on it feeling its smooth texture like glass. I begin to feel some anxiety.

These walls seem to be getting a little closer together, but I am not claustrophobic. Then I come across a wall that feels exactly the same but looks different. My eyes must not be completely recovered. It looks like there is a hallway inside the walls. I rub my eyes hoping they will fix themselves. I look closer. Oh, I get it. The cell door is made of clear glass and the wall on the other side of this door is the same type that is in here. Serious optical illusion. The hinges were either invisible, I would not put it pass this fancy-futuristic looking place, or built into the wall and there is no door handle.

I can see its thickness by pressing my face against the glass door and looking at its sides. While my face absorbs the cool surface of the glass door, I look down the hallway. There is nothing there to see. It just disappears into infinity. More than likely the door is either bulletproof or some other type of high-tech glass that is not easily broken.

I will not insult my own intelligence by trying to break it. But I do try screaming while banging on the door in hopes that someone will hear me. I yell for several minutes until my voice gets hoarse. All the screaming did not help my headache either. No one answers.

This is not the normal immigration jail cell or the standard county jail. Not that I would know what one looks like. But I have enough street smarts to know this is not one. Besides, this cell is exquisitely clean. There is a sink and toilet combo and a cot that is connected to the wall. I have seen my share of prison documentaries. And it is all painted white. Not a smudge of grease or blood anywhere. It looks like I am its first tenant. There is no way this is a standard jail cell. Ruling that out, I would venture to say this is either one of those secret prison facilities the government uses to house really bad guys or the Bigs have created their own facility. Either is not good because they both have unlimited resources to do what they want without anyone ever finding out.

Then I hear a door open. Footsteps from possibly a high-end designer shoe comes closer. I am just guessing at that because of how loud the wooden soles tap against the floor. Nothing for me to do. Nothing to use as a weapon. I am as helpless as I am useless. Finally, a tall figure appears in front of the glass door. An African American man; his hair is short and well groomed. The hair matches his goat tee and sunglasses; that for some odd reason he is wearing indoors. The light directly above him accentuates his features.

His jawline is solid. His suit is well tailored to his body. Maybe a little too well. His suit jacket looks a little too tight around the waistline. It is difficult to tell if he is now getting into shape or if he has stopped eating his usual healthy diet. For someone so arrogant looking you would think he would have checked himself out in the mirror before starting his 'normal' duties of kidnapping and terrorizing teenagers. Oh, the useless chatter that runs through my head while my life is in danger. "Typical Powa," I tell myself. But I still cannot tell if he is a government agent or one of the Bigs.

He speaks with an accent that is either from a western or North African country. I can tell by the dialect. So put a pause on my assumption about him being African American. He informs me, "You have something we want. We would appreciate your cooperation. It will be entirely up to you on how long that takes. And for you, time is of the essence." His voice is not as stern as his jawline.

It is soft with a tone of caution rather than threat. He makes a gesture with his left hand and the door opens. He stands aside as if telling me to exit the cell. I feel apprehensive about moving much less following this person, but I know better than not doing what he wants. The last thing I need is for this guy to lose that 'soft' tone. And so that is what I do as he leads me down the hallway. As I walk, I notice there are more cells. The cells are identical to the one I was in. They are on one side leaving the prisoner to face four blank walls rather than three. I can see how that would mess with someone's mind. At least when a prisoner sees a door, there is a sense of hope knowing it will open. Somehow, I know this place is not meant to treat people but to hurt them. And all these cells are empty. I do not know if that should be a good thing or a bad thing for me. We enter another corridor and I see my friends! Yes, I am not alone! At this point, they are definitely my friends. I am grateful to see them. Knowing I am not here alone makes me feel more at ease. As I walk by, they rush to the front. I see Sung-Suu, Cliffster, Noni, Goji, and Koonzo banging on their assigned glass door barely making a sound. I stop and run back and forth trying to talk to each one of them at the same time.

The walls and door are soundproof. I can barely make out what they are saying. As I bang on the cold glass, I tell them with tears running down my face, "I am going to get you guys out!" I feel like such a girl right now but the emotional relief of having them here is worth the stereotype. My escort behind me points to the other side of the hallway cueing me to keep walking. Unintentionally, I gaff him off and continue to communicate with my friends.

I feel a heavy hand grab a hold of my left shoulder. His grip is strong. I look away as I wince at the pain. He squishes the muscle between my shoulder and neck. I grab for his hand by mere instinct, I definitely did not mean to. My small grip does not wrap around his hand, so instead, quickly I reach for his wrist. What I find is an inopportune sturdy metal bracelet around it which made it impossible for me to do the maneuver my dad taught me for situations just like this one. Sorry Dad, I did not make you proud this time. Nothing I do will break this grip. The pain causes me to lean against the wall across from Koonzo's cell. I notice something minutely particular. But I will get to that later.

As I think of how weak I am, my thoughts turn to Shaboomba. I recall she was not with the others. I hope she got away. At least she will get some help to break us out. Do not ask me how she will do that, but I con myself into thinking she is capable. As I continue my forward march, my friends follow my steps with their eyes. All the banging they are trying to make makes no difference to my kidnapper, he marches on.

I wonder what his name is. It is not like his fancy suit has a name tag on it or anything. He looks like a Clive to me, but I do not think it matters, does it?

Once I am out of their eyesight, my escort releases his grip. I feel the blood returning to that muscle. We continue walking when I look up and identify several cameras on the ceiling and possibly one in front of each cell. They must be embedded into the wall. I noticed it when I was leaning on the wall across from Koonzo's cell. It is the size of a pinhole. I do not see a guard anywhere in the entire facility. 'Clive', I might as well call him something, pushes me out of the corridor and into a room.

We walk through to another hallway that has one door to the right. Now I am scared. This room is mostly dark except for a single light shining on a metal chair. It is a scene straight out of a detective movie where an interrogation is about to take place. My escort guides me towards the chair. As I take my seat, he has a seat somewhere in the darkness. With the light blinding over me, the mystery man disappears but I can hear him breathing. Will I be restrained to this chair? I decide not to ask that question out loud. This is frightening enough but bringing that up is only going to make me freak out even more. Then there is the comfort level. I mean I do not know much about being kidnapped or being a prisoner but times like this is when my dad pops in my head. He always told me if I am ever in a difficult situation to find a way to get comfortable whether it be physically or mentally. "Never hype up a problem," is what I hear in my head. So, I focus on my chair. There is no padding on the seat and armrests would help. And a table would give me an option to lean forward.

My mind plays this game for what feels like five-minutes. Knowing that I have an audience, my mental critique manages to keep me from talking and expressing any emotion. It is his move. But my mind game can only last for so long. The fear of what may come overpowers my dad's advice. I become dreadfully scared again. There is probably some type of torture in my near future. I try another mind game as I place my anger on the invisible man in front of me, the one preventing me from getting to my mom. That does not distract me for long as I hear the mystery man's suit fabric ruffle about. He must have made a signal since all the lights come on in the room. It takes a few seconds for my eyes to adjust.

I realize my surroundings. This is a hospital room. Behind Clive, there is a glass partition with another room on the other side. This glass partition is another soundproof barrier. I can see through the glass that there is a hospital bed with several hi-tech medical devices I have never seen before. From my vantage point, I can tell someone is laying on it as the impression of a pair of feet are left on the sheet that covers them. Wait a second! Do not tell me that is my mom! I jump out of my seat and open the glass door heading straight for the bed. Clive does not bother to stop me. As I approach, I see another window beyond the medical devices. It is an observation room that has several people crowded around it. They look as distinguished as my gentleman escort.

My heart rate accelerates, and my anxiety gets worse and worse with every step I take. Finally, I reach the bed and I am relieved. It is not my mom. It is an old man. But should I be relieved? This is someone's son and quite possibly someone's brother, or father. To hell with the request this is too much even for me. The potential for my mom in a hospital bed overpowers me. A dark image of how helpless she must look in this very moment just like this old man paints a scary picture. The old man is very thin and frail. The top of his head is mostly bald, but he still has wild strands of white hair that act like a crown on his tanned head. The wrinkled skin does not end on his face. His arms are pretty wrinkly too as they lay on top of the bedsheets which are neatly tucked in. He has a tattoo on his upper left arm, but his hospital gown is concealing most of it. There are IVs in his arms as well as an oxygen tube up his nostrils. It is difficult to determine what his ailment is but at this point I would rather not know. He is awake and staring at me. It is not a frightful stare but more of a look of satisfaction. He extends his right hand.

I can tell it takes a bit of effort for him as his hand shakes while suspended in the sterile air. I quickly extend my hand to prevent it from falling back onto the bed. I am fine as long as he does not shake anymore. For some reason, people shaking uncontrollably makes me feel helpless. His hand is surprisingly soft like a baby's cute little butt. He smiles. His eyes accent the smile. I do not feel as scared as I was a few minutes ago. He draws his left hand towards his chest signaling me to come closer. As I move in, he says, "You are a pretty young lady. Thank you for being here. I appreciate you giving me this moment." A lot of questions are floating in my head right now. Why is this man thanking me? Does he know we have been abducted? Was it him that ordered my kidnapping? Naw, it cannot be that. If this man did arrange to raid an entire house full of people, then he has a lot of money that is connected to even more people's money. And if that is the case then he does not need to make money. Which means he does not need to make a special request or sell a request video to the Bigs. Not much of a motive there. No, he is part of the experiment just like me.

The well chiseled man enters the room and speaks, "All you have to do is get him to request the camera. How you make that happen is entirely up to you. The sooner this happens, the less we are involved." I think to myself what does that last sentence mean? Will they start hurting me? Or hurting my friends? I do not know. It is better if I just focus on this old man.

He squeezes my hand. I take that as a sign for me to look at him. He whispers, "I have a lot to be grateful for, but this moment is my greatest."

I ask, "Why is this your greatest moment, sir? You have much more life in you." A familiar noise sounds off.

The old man points with his eyes at the Gevity device, "That contraption should have never been invented. Knowing when you will die is the worst thing to know in life. Some say the moment you find out is the moment you actually die. Others might contend that the opposite of that argument is equally relevant. The chime this device sends out is death regardless of how cheerful and playful it may sound. If you really think about it. It almost turns any pleasant melody into the sound of death. Now tell me, who wants to be frightened before they die? Who wants their final moments, the culmination of their life's efforts to be rewarded with such fear?"

This old man is wise. I can tell he spent a lot of time thinking about this. He is right, especially if you are an older person. There is a lot to look back on. You would think there is a reward for making the best out of your life or even that there would be a ceremony for a long and permanent departure. So, I tell him, "Maybe the way you view death should not be so grim. Maybe the Gevity Alarm should not be a chime but more of a pulsing light." I pause and think of what I am saying. I sound ridiculous. I adjust my response, "Oh what is the use. No matter what it is, people are going to automatically associate that noise or whatever they choose as the sign of death. There is no way around it besides not getting the alert." The old man sinks back into his deathbed with a long deep chuckle. I do not know if he thinks my idea was dumb or if he agrees. I keep hold of his hand.

The Gevity Alarm goes off again. Its pleasant sound startles me. The old man chuckles again and says, "The first alert has arrived. The sound of angels coming?" With a confused look on my face I said, "I thought the other chime was the first alert." The old man keeps his focus on the device, "No, my dear, what you heard was the chime of a diagnostic check. The new generation of Gevity Alarms will automatically conduct a thorough body scan after a traumatic event such as surgery or a severe injury. But do not fret. This is the only one of its kind out there. The next chime you hear will be death entering the room."

The old man's statement paints a picture of the grim reaper standing behind me. Maybe this whole thing is not supposed to be warm and inviting. Fear pulls me away from the old man. I cannot help it. I think of my mother possibly being in this same situation. Is she scared? Is she worried about me? Is her being worried about me making her condition even worse? I do not know but I would not want her final moments to be like this. Then the sensation that I may not get to see my mother's final moments begins to add to my growing anxiety. I may be stuck here for a long time. The anticipation is overpowering, and an overwhelming sadness brings involuntary tears to my eyes. I have to control myself before I start whimpering because once I hear myself make those little crying noises it only gets worse from there. So, I grab the camera that was on the table and begin recording. I decide to treat the video like an interview, "Well, sir, I am sure you would like to say something to all your viewers in the World Wide Web. Here is your big moment."

The old man opens his eyes wide as if a movie director just shouted 'action!' on a film he is starring in. He adjusts his posture and fixes his hair. Then he begins to speak, "Let me tell you a story about two lovers. Both were married to other people. This is a sad story but one worth telling." As I keep recording, I get the feeling this story is more than just a personal experience and it is more like a secret/confession type.

Several short moments later, "And that is how I left." This old man tells me this sad yet inspiring love story. The pain they both felt. I especially liked the part where he was trapped and how he broke free. As I lower the camera, the tears I have been shedding over the last several minutes are uncovered. I really want to ask if this is his story. I can tell his eyes are replaying the story again. I imagine the film projector in his head rewinding to the day he met her and how much he misses that moment. I do not ask. Let him have this moment. He deserves to have at least that.

Chapter 12

Saturday dusk

A teeth-rattling explosion shakes the walls and everything inside the hospital room. The commotion knocks me to the floor. It sounds like this building has its own alarm system as it sounds off. Gunshots! I hear gunshots in the direction of the door to this room. I quickly assumed but even quicker eliminate the possibility of a science experiment gone wrong. The trading of gunfire tells me the security here is prepared for such an assault.

More explosions rock the room and the air within it. I have never felt anything remotely close to this sensation. Now I hear shouting. I cannot make out what it is over the gunfire, but they are close by. Is this the government attacking the Bigs or vice versa? I get up and head for the old man. With the alarms and beeping going on, if I was in this bed I would be freaking out. So, I caress his hand as I crouch on the side of his bed to protect myself from the destruction that is taking place outside. I do not know what else to do. As I look around the room I ask, "Sir, how did you feel when you finished telling me your story?" There is no reply. I shake his hand to get his mind to focus on me. The gunfire, which echoes inside the hallway, makes me duck my head for some unknown reason. The old man still has not answered me. I face him and notice he has this blank stare but is looking at me if that makes sense. He does not blink, sheds a tear, or smiles. It is just a blank stare.

A large explosion replaces the door I entered. The concussion shatters the glass partition. I fall to the floor again as the sound of combat boots rush in. I get back up and wave off the smoke-filled room which has me coughing. There are lights that follow the sound of the boots. My ears are ringing. The shouting I hear is muffled. I stumble back to the old man. He is covered with the broken glass from the partition. I can hear the men clearly now. They are sweeping the room. The old man is still. His eyes remain with the blank stare he gave before. The ringing in my ears is from the flatline tone of the machines. The old man has died. I think the explosion is what accelerated his death.

Coming from the smoke, I hear a voice say, "He is here. Looks like he is dead." Then I hear silence, it takes me a few moments to realize what is going on. I decide not to look at him in order to prevent any unwarranted threats. "Will do. We also have a girl here. A teenage girl." The person stops talking again. He is talking to his boss over a radio. Probably the evil person behind the explosion. Then I hear the guy say, "Very well." He ends the radio conversation and barks out orders, "You and you, grab the old man! She is also coming with us."

They begin to wheel the old man out as they grab me. That is when I notice they are wearing these black masks. I do not know if I should be worried or grateful. Then the thought goes from my mind to my mouth, "Do you guys know Shaboomba? Did she send you guys here?" No answer. I want to ask again but I can tell there is a sense of urgency here as we are speed walking through the destroyed building. I go with it. We leave the room. Sporadic gunfire ensues. We are heading through the large gaping hole that used to be an exterior wall. The sun has already set. What remains of its light is tinted in an orange and purple sky.

I can smell the crisp night breeze along with the scent of burnt gunpowder. There are these really bright lights that soak up the dusk of night somewhere high above the complex. What day is it? How long have I been in there? I gain a cowering sense of freedom from all the activity. I look around and see the assault team is still engaged with the security of this place. Several folks receive medical attention at one of the vans, but it is not your standard ambulance. It looks like the other black vans that are a part of the attack but with medical equipment on the inside. Once I realized I was sort of okay, I do not know why but I think of my nerd friends. I cannot leave without them. I pull in the gentleman who has a hold of me, "Sir, we have to go back! My friends are in there!" He tells me, "We are not going back in there! The security is gaining the advantage! We do not have much time!" He keeps pushing me forward. I lose sight of the old man.

Several other black cars, diesel trucks, and vans are parked in front. I am heading towards one of the vans. That is when I dig my shoes into the ground to stop the momentum. It does not work. I fail to remember that I am only a teenage girl and these men are trained to fight back. He lifts me into the van and that is when I reach out to grab his gun that is tactically holstered on his chest and point it at him, "We need to go back in there! There are several others still inside! I cannot leave knowing they are in there! Please, help me!" The man holds up his hands as a sign of nonaggression and tells me, "Please wait inside, Miss. We will figure out who else is left." The man gets on his radio and informs the people on the other end the situation. I am surprised he let me keep his gun. It has been a long time since I held one. Thoughts of my dad's training enter my mind, but it is a perishable skill. This one is heavier than I would have guessed. He steps away and disappears around the corner. I cannot hear what is being said because of all the gunfire. He comes back and says, "Wait in the van. Someone will be here to see you."

What is that supposed to mean?! We are in a gunfight! We need to get my friends and get out of here. There is no time for chatting. But I keep quiet. None of the vans have left. This gives me some comfort in believing they will entertain my request. I take the chance and go inside the van.

This is not your normal looking van. It has several flat screen televisions with captain seats all around made of peanut butter leather. It looks very high end. I take a seat near the back staring at a blank screen thinking of the nerds I call friends. Another van pulls up. Since there are no windows at the rear of the van, I am unable to see anyone approaching. But I do hear people exiting the van and heading towards this one. It does not sound like combat boots. I see two faces appear from the open sliding door. One is that of a Caucasian man in his thirties and the other is an elderly woman. It is difficult to determine her ethnicity but if you were to tell me she is the daughter of the old man, I would believe you.

The woman introduces herself, "Hello darling, I deeply apologize for the chaos. I am Mrs. Bellows." Her voice sounds dignified and high class. It almost has a hint of an English accent. And she sounds like she has a smoker's voice. It is very raspy and rough like she has been yelling at people all night. Her upper lip makes those wrinkles when she speaks with words that start with the letters O, U, J, Q, W and Y. I know plenty of adult smokers and I would stare at their lips every time they spoke and soon realized words that started with those letters are what makes the lips form the unpleasant wrinkles. You are wondering how come I know so many smoking adults? Cause my dad loves to host parties at different venues. One of the things people like to do is smoke and drink amongst each other. I would mingle with the adults just to see how the life of an adult compares to the life of a teenager. To me, I believe being a teenager is more exciting than being an adult. Everything is fresh and new. Exposure to different things is a constant. All the emotions are raw and sometimes unwarranted. But I digress. There is a war going on here!

"I am Powa," I say. Even with all that is going on I did not forget my manners. My parents would be proud.

Mrs. Bellows responds, "It is a pleasure to meet you, Powa. Such an unusual name. With the gunfire going about, may we enter the car?"

I do not miss a beat and say, "Please come in. It is dangerous out there. Do you know what is going on?"

Mrs. Bellows jumps inside as an explosion takes place about 50 yards away. The gentleman jumps in as well. He turns to me and says, "If it gets to the point where we need you to use one of those, I will give you a quick 30-second class. Until then, let me be the hero." His voice is strong and confident. If his tone had been more uplifting it would have been a smart attempt to break the ice. But this man is not that type of person. Without hesitation, I relinquish the gun. I cannot tell if Mrs. Bellows and the suit have guards assigned to them, but I would bet they do. Their clothes look expensive. They look like they are about to have dinner at a fancy restaurant or something. Her jewelry as well as the clothes look top of the line. They shut the door as the debris from the explosion peppers the roof of the van. Mrs. Bellows looks to the gentleman and says, "Carter, she cannot be associated with them. She does not fit their profile."

Carter replies, "Mrs. Bellows, I believe you are correct. I think there may be another one inside."

I have to say something, so I do, "The best you can do is talk to each other as if I could not hear you. That pisses me off. So, before I enter a new level of irate, can someone tell me what is going on here?" I close my eyes and take a deep breath and continue on, "I am sorry. Everything has me freaked out right now."

I no longer hear the gunfire outside. Even the vans are soundproof? My mind feels like a horse racing without a finish line. Mrs. Bellows looks at me and says; "I apologize, darling. That is rude of me. I must be more compassionate. We discovered a group of teenagers. The problem is they look nothing like you. At least you seem to have enough social skills to get along with the rest of civilization. The other group is a big mess."

She barely finished speaking when I screamed, "Those teenagers are my friends! Where are they? Are they almost here?"

I get interrupted by the radio. A loud voice says, "We cannot stay any longer. There are six cars in high pursuit heading this way. We have three minutes left if we want to make it out of here. We are leaving, Mrs. Bellows."

She waves her hand to the driver. The driver replies to the messenger, "We acknowledge. See you all at the rendezvous."

I get a little worried. "So, where are they?"

Mrs. Bellows can tell I am getting more anxious, "Darling, they are in one of the other vehicles. They are all fine. We are heading back, and we will figure out what is going on." Her tone calms me like a grandmother soothes a wounded child. It lowers my stress level. I want to ask where are we headed?

But I keep that question to myself. If they told me I would not know where it is anyway. I will feel better once I see my friends again. I take a seat behind the driver and lay my head against the window wondering where in San Diego are we going now.

Chapter 13

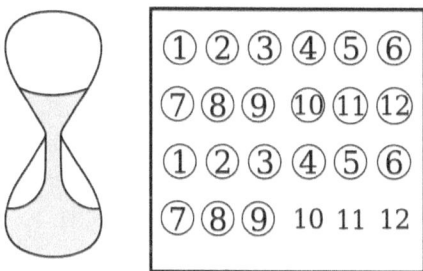

Saturday evening around 21:04

I wake up slightly disorientated. I must have passed out. It feels like I have been asleep for five or six hours since I feel kind of rejuvenated. I look around and notice I am in someone's living room. I see an antique grandfather clock. It reads 9:04 pm. From the expensive furniture, I would bet this is Mrs. Bellows' place. I sit up to see if there is anyone else around but see no one. However, I do hear whimpering. It is coming from the room next door. It is probably Cliffster. I picture him being the softer type. The whimpering guides me around a corner. I quietly take a peak. It is a well-dressed man hunched over with his face in his hands resting on top of this small dining room table. This wooden table looks nice but does not match the high-end contemporary décor of this home. Just imagine one of those houses featured in a lifestyle magazine. Exactly. Ultra rich. I focus back on the gentleman at the table. Oh, it is Mr. Carter. I present myself, "Hello, Mr. Carter. Are you ok?" The man looks up. The first thing I see are handcuffs around his wrists. I notice this man has been crying for a lengthy amount of time due to the bloodshot eyes and dry snot around his hands and mouth. But it is not Mr. Carter. The man turns his whimpers into a low cry. Maybe I remind him of his kid.

It receives the attention of someone. The footsteps on the nice hardwood floor grow at a slow steady pace.

They are also soft and light unlike the combat boots from before. From around another corner, "I see you have met my younger brother, Gerald, darling. Oh, what magnificent stories has he told us, huh Jerry?"

The low volume crying increases as he speaks, "Please, I was doing right by him. You have to see that."

I ask, "And what does your younger brother have to do with any of this, Mrs. Bellows? Why has he been handcuffed? And where are his shoes?" Gerald's feet are exposed and have taken some serious punishment. My dad told me the feet are the hardest parts of the body to bruise. Gerald has been through some tough times recently.

She walks around her crying brother still seated at the table, "Let me tell you a short story."

Mrs. Bellows decides to take a seat next to Gerald which is directly across from me. She starts, "I do not know if you saw an elderly gentleman inside. That man was our older brother, Pendleton. He died while inside that makeshift prison. He was taken from us by our younger brother here. We are a total of six siblings."

I would have guessed Mrs. Bellows as the wife of Pendleton instead of his sister. I guess my theory that this lady was the same person Pendleton was referring to in his video confession was wrong. The mystery continues, I guess. She goes on, "Have you heard of HyphenDash, Incorporated?"

I reply, "Yes, they have been making a killing off people's requests."

Mrs. Bellows chuckles, "Very odd choice of words, darling."

I realize what I said but saw no need to stall the conversation with explanations. I add, "I think they also made the Gevity Alert."

Mrs. Bellows smiles, "No darling, that is made by the grossly powerful Betahouse, Incorporated. They are HyphenDash's fierce competitor. That is another interesting story that is indirectly intertwined with ours." My mind tries to picture the battle between these two mega companies, but Jerry's cries are distracting. Mrs. Bellows puts her arm on Jerry, "Now Jerry, please keep calm and quiet. If not, then we will have to find other means to communicate that to you." Jerry quickly chokes back his whimpering. She must be talking about the technique that was applied to Jerry's feet. Mrs. Bellows continues, "Ok so HyphenDash approached my older brother to create a concoction to make it easier for a request to be accepted. In other words, the person would arbitrarily pick an object instead of letting their soul do the picking for them."

I interrupt, "Mrs. Bellows, not to be disrespectful but picking a request is not that easy. This company can ask anyone to make a special request but from what I gathered, zero special requests have been accepted. Making these cocktails are nothing new and each one of them will fail. The Bigs as well as opportunistic manufacturers have tried every drug from illegal, prescription to a hybrid of both and none of them seem to be effective."

Mrs. Bellows smiles, "That is what the internet wants you to believe, my dear. But here is something you may not know. Prior to working for HyphenDash, my brother Pendleton was a scientist for a company that makes the three drugs the government uses for lethal injections. He was able to modify the sodium thiopental which is used to induce unconsciousness.

You see, during this part of the lethal injection, the mind should be shut off from all the senses to include that of pain. It was later discovered this was not the case." I raise my brow displaying my confusion. She responds by saying, "You, just like everyone else, believed otherwise. Knowing this information, my brother modified this drug in order to relax the subconscious."

I knew I should have paid more attention in chemistry class. She continues, "The second drug is Pancuronium bromide prescribed for respiratory arrest and muscle paralysis. Students at a university discovered the drug provides a semi-hallucinogenic effect. The only reason we found out about it was because they got busted selling the stuff at their college parties. Mixing this with sodium thiopental allows the subconscious to be 'hypnotized'."

Without even meaning to, I again interrupted Mrs. Bellows, "Which makes it easier to get someone to make a special request."

She tells me, "Yes, among many other opportunities it presents. There was one problem though. After several trials, my brother, for some reason, wanted to get out of this industry. We are guessing his dementia was getting the best of him. HyphenDash reached out to my little brother and convinced him to get a phony medical power of attorney much sooner than necessary. So, when an opportunity came to take control of my older brother, little brother Jerry jumped at the chance."

I think I am following, "So HyphenDash takes your older brother and tries to get him to make a camera request."

Mrs. Bellows grins, "That is what I originally thought; however, the main objective was not to get him to make a special request upon his death. They wanted him to provide the formula for the cocktail which he called 1X. He had hidden the formula and all the 1X serum." I cannot believe there is a way to make any special request happen. If the government knew about this, they would get off my case for good!

Carter appears out of nowhere and turns on the nearby television. A video is being played. It looks like your typical request video. A man is strapped to a gurney while two other people dressed in hospital scrubs tend to him. He looks dingy like he has not showered in a long time. By the look of his bed sheet the poor guy has been there for days or maybe even weeks. A book is only inches away from his face. A drug is injected as he attempts to resist. Almost immediately the man dies judging from the flatlines on the monitoring equipment. Suddenly the camera pans to the book. Unfortunately, there is no audio to this surveillance video, but by the looks of it the two staff members exchange words. We can tell by their hand gestures that they are writing down the time of death and then suddenly they get distracted by the wave pattern in one of the monitors.

The book flashes with lights. Those lights pop out from the book like purple firecrackers. The flashing tempo goes from fast to slow and back up to fast again. And then the book just vanishes. The book was not a photo album or a book he had written. It was an ordinary dictionary that no self-respecting soul would request. After that video ends, we watch several other videos with the same sequence. The requested items were so random and mundane, like shed tools, a car seat, and even a blank piece of paper. Those poor people were stripped of the one opportunity to take with them something meaningful to the other side. Imagine how disappointed they will be when they reach the other side and realize a blank piece of paper is what crossed over with them. That is a horrible way to start off a new beginning.

Out of nowhere (or so I thought) three burly men enter the room and grab the cuffed, sniveling Jerry. He begins to yell, "No, please, I did not mean to harm anyone! It is not my fault! They made me!" They lift him up and I immediately realize

Mrs. Bellows is no small fish in this pond. Jerry's knees are bleeding through his pants. The left pant leg is torn, and I can see bone sticking out. My dad told me one of the most painful places to strike is the knee cap. There are many nerve endings that will bring any size man to the ground. And Mrs. Bellows' team knows this. Who are these guys?

Jerry is dragged away still pleading his case. Once he is taken away, the silence in the room almost becomes deafening. But I have a question, "Did Jerry tip off HyphenDash about Pendleton's medical situation? How else would they know about his dementia unless that fact was already disclosed by your older brother to HyphenDash?"

Mrs. Bellows, "I like how you pick things up, darling. Not a lot of girls your age care to do that. And no, Pendleton never told anyone of his dementia.

What Pendleton did was what the rest of the world is feverishly doing. He got himself a Gevity Alarm. Keep in mind he got his before getting hired by HyphenDash. And they knew he was registered but the ingenious thing about the Gevity Alarm is that once you are in, there is no 'CONTROL ALT DELETE.' The Gevity Alarm has been around for about a year. So, the device requires all access into your medical records. No one really pays attention to the popup window that states 'You agree to the terms of this application.' Folks just want the app or the device. They could care less about the details. This is especially true for those who are gravely ill or their family member without thinking much about the potential consequences. What we recently discovered from Jerry's latest Q&A session is that individuals with dementia are the optimal patients for 1X. Under these circumstances, a last-minute change of plans in terms of coercing a random request does not require much convincing from a bedside fellow. This is how confidently we have transferred our most private possession, our medical history. We are giving HyphenDash every piece of our medical information for them to manipulate for their own gain."

"Mrs. Bellows, you told me the Gevity Alarm belongs to Betahouse. How is patient information going from them to their rival HyphenDash? I doubt they would want to provide any of that private information to their competitor. Besides, is that not illegal?"

"Bravo, darling, that is the big question. How is HyphenDash getting this information? We do not know, and Jerry keeps claiming he does not know either.

But we are doing our best to find out, in fact, right now my men are having another 'chat' with him. We are going to ask him several more times to make sure. Maybe HyphenDash has a mole inside Betahouse. Or maybe HyphenDash and Betahouse are in bed with each other and there really is no competition. What we do know is our medical history is being used for their personal gain. Both of those companies are making billions off it. Everyone with a Betahouse Gevity Alarm has given up their medical records as well as their loved ones' personal contact information. That is the genius of the app's design. In order for someone to register they must also provide an emergency point of contact or anyone else they would like to be notified.

And guess what? Betahouse uses that contact information to also promote the Gevity Alarm. You see? It was never about the Gevity Alarm or the service. They could care less about charging people for it or if the patient makes it or not. It is about getting them to be impulsive about registering for the Gevity Alarm. All that newly registered information is what gives them the money and the power they have now. They sell that information as fear. HyphenDash's special request project only needs patient information for trial purposes. Once 1X is proven valid, they will lose interest in patient information. That serum will amplify their power and possibly diminish Betahouse's position of influence. People will buy the serum and carry it with them everywhere they go like a cellphone. In the end, people that buy the Gevity Alarm will ultimately buy 1X. Why? Because instead of not knowing what their last request would be, by taking the 1X drug they will be able to choose the EXACT item (which of course they are carrying with them) they want to take with them to the after-life. And all those backpacks, travel cases, little wagons, and pockets stuffed with photos and jewelry will finally come to an end. Who knows what these big corporations will come up with next?"

Mrs. Bellows stops talking and stares off into the air. She then starts again, "Poor Pendleton. My brother was married once, you know? Happily married to be accurate, at least at the beginning. Then someone got in the way and when that ended, he was never the same. He never gave himself the opportunity to have children, but looking back, I think that was for the best. He would not have made a good father. He dedicated too much of his time to science. Besides, with him and HyphenDash, the concept of death and the type of work he was doing for them would have been a lonely road (with no space for a loving spouse and needy children). HyphenDash is working on making it as automated as possible."

"You lost me on that last part, Mrs. Bellows. Automated? Like having robots inject 1X?"

Mrs. Bellows snaps out of her flashback tone, "No darling, I mean having the dying person in a room by themselves and using subliminal messages from some electronic device to influence the requested item."

Wow. Just when I thought the ceremony of death was getting worse, in comes HyphenDash to make it even more miserable before a person dies. I look back at Mrs. Bellows giving her encouragement to continue with the details, "From my other sources, I heard the company discovered the dementia connection from Pendleton himself by accident. Listen, they were about to perform their experiments on a subject that happen to have dementia. In the beginning, they did not check for disabilities like mental illness. One day when Pendleton was conducting an experiment on a subject, he injected the 1X drug.

Pendleton presented the subject with a playing card. He only showed it to him one time since the drug was expected to work almost immediately. No sooner than 30-seconds had gone by and the subject died. My brother wrote down several notes. Six-minutes later, when his mind stopped working, the playing card vanished. Pendleton did not witness the disappearance of the playing card, but he did look for it. Every staff member involved with the experiment examined the video. All experiments were to be recorded and later studied in order to perfect their technique. Sure enough, the card had been requested. Judging from the footage from the building we found you in, the room was well illuminated to the point that the light source from the request was not bright enough to catch Pendleton's attention. If you ask me he should have been watching in the first place. Well, a later performed autopsy revealed the subject had dementia. So, what did discovering this fact do? You guessed it. HyphenDash put out an all-points bulletin to their data miners to generate a program that will consolidate a list of every Gevity Alarm registered patient with dementia. And the big discovery was that their top scientist also had dementia. Once he learned HyphenDash was gathering a hit list of dementia patients, he knew for certain what that list would contain: his name in black and white. And he believed that at the cost of this discovery even he was expendable. When my brother Pendleton no longer wanted to cooperate, all it took was finding the most vulnerable and ambitious sibling to take custody of his medical power of attorney. From there, HyphenDash convinced Jerry they would provide medical care for his brother. HyphenDash already did their homework. They knew what type of person Jerry is. He was their perfect fall guy. HyphenDash convinced Jerry they would provide the medical facility which happens to be the same building they conducted their tests.

It was easy for them to convince him they would take care of my brother. I do not know if Jerry knew they would be caring for him at the same facility they conducted their experiments." Right then Mrs. Bellows gestures to Carter to come over. She whispers in his ear. He immediately takes off. I really want to ask but instead I decide to keep my mouth closed. Then I hear a horrifying scream. It frightens me to the point of standing up. It sounds like it is coming from a house next door, but the screaming is so intense the person could have been right outside the room we are in. Then I look at Mrs. Bellows. She is as calm as can be staring directly at me. That expression tells me what is happening; Jerry is getting another beat down. It is likely a reaction from Mrs. Bellows recalling what he put Pendleton through.

I do not blame her. However, I do ask, "Will the screaming alert your neighbors, Mrs. Bellows?"

She stands and takes in a deep breath and says, "Darling, my neighbors know better than to meddle into my affairs."

The screaming is no longer heard. No way did she just have her little brother killed. That is too cold blooded even for her. She gestures for me to follow her. We head down the hallway and into a conference room. Along the way, I see no pictures or portraits on the walls. If this is her home, she keeps no record of her family. And did I mention? It is exquisitely clean like a model home.

She looks at me and says, "Wait here." Her raspy voice echoes in the room. I take a seat at the head of the table. The walls are bland. There are two large televisions with cameras on top. A contraption is in the middle of the conference table which has a standard key pad as well as phone features. I hear footsteps, a lot of footsteps. This must be it. Either Mrs. Bellows sold me out and I am done for or she has assembled her team and we must be leaving soon. The door opens, and I see them all. It is my nerd friends! I run to hug them, "Cliffster, Sung-Suu, Noni and Goji, I missed you guys!"

Sung-Suu does not skip a bit and says, "Mrs. Bellows, I do not think this is our friend Powa. She usually does not act like this." We all break out laughing.

Cliffster decides not to be outdone and adds, "We thought our wishes had been granted when we did not see you when we arrived here. Ha ha! I am just kidding, Powa. I actually thought we were going to see Sung-Suu's momma bring him a fresh set of underwear." It feels good to see them. It feels even better to know they are also glad to see me.

I see Koonzo in the back of the group. I run up to hug him and whisper in his ear, "I missed you, but do not tell anyone that."

We smile at each other for a little longer than normal. Then he leans in. His eyes close like a sunset. His mouth becomes partially opened.

His lips look fresh and appealing. He is closer now. I can see a mint in his mouth. It smells inviting. I realize my surroundings. Everyone is quiet and staring at us. And then I tell him, "What?! Are you serious? Maybe if you would have rescued me and in the heat of the moment...maybe, but oh no you are not going to try that on me."

Goji makes his conclusion beat with perfect timing. All the guys crack up laughing. The Ooohs and the Aaaahs go on for a while as the guys cannot believe Koonzo FINALLY went for it. Never mind that he did not pass go and did not collect $200. Koonzo's eyes pop open startled by everyone's input. Hearing his friends make those remarks makes him react with a half-hearted smile muscled by shear rejection. Koonzo's now reddened face cannot hide his embarrassment.

Even I know my reaction was a dick move, I could have played it down some. Dang it. I need to change the subject, so I ask them, "What happened to Munch? I did not see him at that crazy building."

Koonzo tilts his head down and everyone gets quiet, then he says, "They probably took him somewhere. He is messed up, his nub busted open when they tackled him; it was pouring out blood. Hope the dude is ok." From behind us, we hear a tap.

In the doorway is Mrs. Bellows and Carter. Mrs. Bellows inserts herself into the group, "It is good to see you all together. Please have a seat. We have some refreshments coming." As we sit, I try to anticipate when will we be released. Possibly after we eat. I am starving. She continues, "While we wait, we should discuss a few things." Another mystery looms. I knew this was too good to be true.

Mrs. Bellows starts again, "With HyphenDash possibly in disarray due to the threat of someone attacking their secret facility and the potential of that information getting out, we are in position to make a potential deadly strike."

I ask the question all my nerd friends' faces are asking, "Who are 'we' exactly, Mrs. Bellows?" She gives me the look that tells me I am wearing down on her hospitality. It makes me a little uncomfortable as I break eye contact from her.

Mrs. Bellows answers my question contrary to her facial expression towards me, "Darling, your attention to detail is a skill I appreciate. I guess I should tell you a little more about myself. 'We are an unknown conglomerate of developers, discoverers, inventors, and providers. I will not bother with what we are actually called or the name of any of our affiliates. But I will tell you we have a concerted interest in 1X. Jerry is not a connected man. So, he does not have a security detail or a high-end vault to hide the 1X injections and formula." She is interrupted by a text. As she reads it, I look to my friends. They have the same confused look as me. Then she says, "Hmm. Interesting. Ok, so let us not waste any more time and get down to business. Jerry has 'volunteered' some life-saving information. You see, Jerry is a well-known introvert and paranoid individual. If he cannot do it himself then he does not do it at all. We know he has hidden the formula and injections. And now we know its general location. Here is where you all come in. It is located in the same convention center Comic-Con is taken place. Jerry has attended every Comic-Con for the past 17-years. We do not know whether he has been able to befriend the staff at the convention center or the Comic-Con organization staff. What we know is 1X will be at Comic-Con. We turn to your expertise in this department to determine its location."

Goji inquires, "Hey, how do you know we have anything to do with Comic-Con? We are just a bunch of teenagers. None of this has to do with us!"

Mrs. Bellows smirks as she walks over to the large wall mounted television. She turns it on and an image of Noni and Goji getting hauled out by security is in freeze frame with the Comic-Con banner behind them. Mrs. Bellows informs him, "Jerry pointed you and your brother out. He said you two should never have been kicked out of the conference."

Goji looks at the rest of us and says, "And you know what? He is absolutely right! Can you guys get me a copy of that video? It is the highlight of our Comic-Con experience." Noni comes up with the conclusion beat. The rest of the group shakes their head.

Noni adds, "Can I get one copy as well? After all, I was the main reason we got kicked out."

Sung-Suu interrupts, "What happens if we find it? Is there a reward for us?" We all look at him as if he were crazy for asking.

To our astonishment Mrs. Bellows replies, "Yes, dear. Of course, we will offer compensation." She looks at all of us and then says, "I am prepared to offer each of you $10,000 cash and five-year's worth of Comic-Con tickets upon delivery of the 1X drug. No strings attached, and no further obligation."

I feel the need to add to Sung-Su's question, "How will we know you will not pursue us after we deliver the drug to you? How do we know you will not come back after us later?"

Koonzo jumps in and answers for her, "We will never know that. They can tell us anything we want to hear. They can offer us each one-million dollars, and we would have no way of knowing if their offer is on the up and up. Look, these guys infiltrated a fortress. What do you think they will do with us once we have the formula?"

Then Koonzo leans in and stares straight at Mrs. Bellows as to offer a dare, "Just to let you know, you are not in tuned to the teenage world much less Comic-Con. A real incentive would involve in-person interviews with all the topnotch stars, party passes, on-set studio visits, movie stand-ins, and private screenings for the next five years. That is the premium package that is on every Comic-Con's real fan bucket list."

A stand-off presents itself between the two. All is quiet. I am excited for Koonzo and his courage. I did not think he had it in him. The others are frozen. No confirmation is offered, not even a conclusion beat is heard. Mrs. Bellows sighs, "Koonzi dear..."

Almost immediately he interrupts her and says, "It is Koonzo with an O at the end, Mrs. Bellows." I gotta hand it to him, the boy has some big ones.

"My apologies, Koonzo. I know I am not up to speed with today's lingo. I can only offer what it is I know. What I will do is my best to accommodate you all. The easiest course to take would be money. It requires less personal interaction, less logistics, and funds can be made available quickly. And you are correct, a large amount of trust is required. I wish I can get you to trust me. The problem with trust is that if it is not already there then asking for it will only make it more difficult to reach."

Koonzo replies, "Then I ask you to compensate us well above your thought of generosity. One more thing. And what of Powa? She should be able to go free. She has done more than enough."

I feel a sense of loyalty growing within me towards Koonzo for this request. I got so caught up in the mystery of the 1X drug that I forgot all about my own situation. Mrs. Bellows' pleasant aura changes to a concerning and uncomfortable expression. She has difficulty starting, "Koonzo, you are correct. Powa does not have any further connection with any of us." I exhale. For a second, I thought I was going to be mixed in with this Comic-Con search mission. "Except she does have a connection with you all," concludes Mrs. Bellows.

All eyes focus on me. I try to make sense of it; however, the shock that something bad is going to be said is making me feel anxious. So, I ask, "Someone tell me what is going on? Because I have nothing to contribute. But what I do have is a dying mother that needs her daughter by her side." My voice cracks. I have to keep it together. I cannot stand crying in front of people I do not know. It makes me feel weak and vulnerable. And I am neither of those things.

Mrs. Bellows looks at Koonzo and says, "I need you and your friends to find that formula. We will protect Powa until you arrive. Then I will provide the required funds and we all will go our separate ways. Easy as that." She concludes.

"Wait, so you go from rescuing me to holding me hostage? This is kidnapping!" I exclaim almost out of breath.

Cliffster chimes in also, "Man, that is a buster move. We will get you the formula, but you do not need to put her through all that. Just messed up." As soon as he is done talking the rest of the gang voice their opinions of the situation at once. I feel a genuine appreciation for them as they rise up to defend me.

Koonzo adds, "Here is a better deal for you. Powa comes with us. We both know you need the formula more than we need Powa, so it is this way or there is no deal." Now that catches my attention. Did he just say what I thought he said? Even his friends give him the gas face. Koonzo continues, "If you really want it that bad then you are going to allow it."

Mrs. Bellows sits back in her chair. She lights up a cigarette. As she inhales the tobacco, we all can hear the burning of the tar and paper. She blows out the smoke accentuating the lines on her lips. Mrs. Bellows makes her move, "Then she must wear a tracker. Certainly, a degree of trust can be attained from this. I have compromised. This is my counteroffer."

The room goes quiet until Noni blasts out the conclusion beat. Everyone looks over at him. Sung-Suu says, "Pff. And he said he is the smarter one."

I almost laughed at this quick little break in seriousness. Mrs. Bellows and Carter (who up to this point has been staring at his tablet) sit quietly. My mind contemplates the worst-case scenario, but Mrs. Bellows beats me to the punch with this, "Think about this before you answer. If you decline my offer what do you think will happen next?" She makes no other gesture other than to take another puff from her cigarette. The question makes me think of many different things. But one thing that does not cross my mind is them letting us go no questions asked. She wants to fill our minds with the endless evils people will do to protect themselves. It is a harrowing thought. I look at my friends' faces. They all are thinking the same thing. If I refuse to cooperate, she can make my life miserable as well as my mother's. And my mother does not deserve that. My turn to compromise, "So what is the play?"

Mrs. Bellows grins at my question, knowing she has gotten her way.

"You all will be taken to Jerry's house. There, you will assist my people in search of any piece of evidence that may lead us to the formula. If you have to return to ask Jerry more questions, then that is what will be arranged. He is supposed to return to Comic-Con tomorrow to pick up the 1X formula. From my understanding, tomorrow is the final day of Comic-Con. The order is if he does not retrieve it before the conclusion of Comic-Con then the formula is to be destroyed. So obviously time is of the essence." Mrs. Bellows tells us this with a sense of apprehension.

Cliffster takes over, "Jerry knows someone." We look at him like he is the stranger in the group. "Think about it. If he gave it to someone then he has to know that person. He may not trust the person. Maybe that person does not even know what the formula is or what it is for. He may have slipped this stranger a couple of bills and gave him simple instructions. It is better than getting a friend involved. Is any of this making sense or is that way too over the top for you guys?" It makes sense to me. But Comic-Con is not a small place and I guarantee you it will be packed once again.

Packed with funky bodies and sleepless zombie-like nerds. Carter interjects my train of thought, "We are leaving for Jerry's place now. I have mapped out our route." He breaks out a small black piece of plastic, "This is a tracker. We will know your location at all times." He places it inside a gel cap, "Now swallow it."

Oh no he did not just tell me that, "I do not think so. I am not putting that thing inside my body. To hell with your formula."

Mrs. Bellows picks the right time to speak, "Then to hell with your mother." I quickly turn to face her. She is looking directly at me as if she is daring me to reply to her comment. It is a cold, hard stare. The comment stings my ears. I never would have thought Mrs. Bellows could be this heartless. However, regardless of my shock I understand why she said that. The same tears that have been threatening to spill over before begin to flow, making it hard for me to see clearly. I become embarrassed; exposing myself like this but at least it is not the whimpering type of crying.

I hear her come closer to me, "Darling, I am sorry. That was out of line. Listen, once we get that formula I will do my best to provide your mother with the best medical care money can buy." I stop listening to her. I bite down on my cheeks as the tears continue to roll down my face. I can taste their saltiness. "No whimpering. Not right now, Powa." I say to myself.

"Mrs. Bellows, we do not need Powa with us. She will not even know what to look for. Let her go and just deal with us," pleads Koonzo trying to take the attention off me.

I admire his futile attempts. Mrs. Bellows does not entertain his recommendation. She waits for me. I grab the pill and swallow it, and say, "Once we have the information on the formula's location, we either come back here or head straight to Comic-Con. Once we find it, we give it to you guys and we are free. Nothing more, nothing else."

Noni brings up what the rest of the gang was thinking about, "And do not forget about the money." We all look at him. He shrugs his shoulders, "What? I am just reminding them."

Mrs. Bellows replies, "Yes, darling. This is what will happen. My people will be with you throughout this process. You and your friends may have the knowledge to crack Jerry's hiding spot but remember who is holding all the cards."

Carter radios someone, "Does he have anything else? We are about to punch out." Almost immediately the person on the other side begins to talk to Jerry while keeping the mic open, "Hey, you wanted to say something so say it!" We can hear the grunting of pain over the crackled radio static. A short pause ensued and then we all hear Jerry say, "You never bothered to ask why he did it, Mona. You never bothered to ask him." Then it sounds like the man holding the radio used it to punch Jerry in the face. The radio is still transmitting, "How about giving us something we can actually use, you pathetic excuse for a man?" The transmission stops.

That name reminds me of old man Pendleton. On his video he mentioned her name. Mona is Mrs. Bellows? And Mrs. Bellows is... No way! Did Pendleton... Regardless, Mrs. Bellows is the star of Pendleton's story. Now I really have mixed feeling about her. She was such an inspiration to him. A sense of sadness settles within me as I look at her. I walk up to Mrs. Bellows. She takes a step back with the anticipation that I might lunge or strike her.

Those eyes of hers do lie but this time they tell me she is slightly afraid. I pull out from the inside of my thin red jacket the camera I swiped before I was taken out of the building, "He did not make the video because he wanted to relay a message to someone. He just told a story. A happy story with a sad ending."

I place it in her hand. Mrs. Bellows' face is unreadable. She puts her arms around me and whispers in my ear, "Go, darling. Find that formula. I want to get you back to your family." Her kind words make my eyes welt with tears again. I hug her a little harder as if she were my mom. I say nothing in return. We let go of each other and discretely wipe our faces. After all, we both have reputations to maintain. I wish I could be mad at her, but I see her soft side. Everyone remains quiet as they stare. I can tell they are thinking we just had a female moment. If they only knew her little secret. We all head out and follow Carter to the garage.

Chapter 14

Sunday before dawn

We reach Jerry's house. It appears to be in a secluded area. I cannot really tell. It is still dark out. The rolling hills on this small road make it even more isolated. There are no street lights. Anyone could easily pass by this place. From the little illumination the moon provides, I can tell the landscape is very well manicured. The three-van convoy finally parks at an expensive looking one-story house. There are no fences here. Behind the house are more hills. The air is still crisp, and the area is rich with little critters making their nocturnal noises. I love the sound of the night; it reminds me of when my dad would take us camping which we always did last minute, but never as often as I would have liked. We enter the house. Carter enters the alarm code (probably beat it out of Jerry too), disarms the security system and turns on the interior lights. This place is nothing like I expected. It is absolutely horrendous. The house is a total mess. I am not talking about just the messiness; the place is filthy too.

Things are stacked on top of other things. There is a foul odor that makes me want to vomit through my nose. I mean it smells like someone threw up in a full bag of trash and forgot to toss it out. I can hear everyone else grumbling as the same smell assaulted their senses.

Carter informs us, "Sorry kids, Jerry is a hoarder. Mrs. Bellows made countless attempts to get him help but he is addicted to not living well. Let me tell you what little I know about Jerry, it might help with our little mission. I can tell you he likes his Japanese cartoons. He really likes his exotic animation. The guy is a total loser."

Koonzo rolls his eyes, hoping Carter knows something about Jerry they can actually use, "Besides that, what does Jerry like to do?"

"We really do not know. He stays to himself. We only know about the exotic cartoons because we traced his credit card to several of those websites." Says Carter.

Koonzo takes charge, "Alright, Noni and Goji, check out all his anime files in that room right over there. I can see a laptop in front of that couch. Be quick. I am sure there is a lot to go through. Sung-Suu and Cliffster, start in the garage looking for anything Comic-Con related. I will head to his bedroom and dig in his computer and search there."

Carter asks, "How do you know there is a computer in his room?"

Koonzo answers, "All introverts are very private and insecure about a lot of things. The bedroom is the most secure place." Everyone looks at Koonzo knowing he just exposed a private piece of himself unintentionally. Carter looks agitated by the remark.

I ask, "and what about me?"

And almost immediately Koonzo replies, "You can help me out."

Koonzo barely got the words out when Carter screams, "Whoa. Look kid, you may be King Kong on the web but here I make the calls."

Koonzo is not caught off guard, after all, he set Carter up. Men and their big power egos.

"Alright, if you have a better way of finding something you have no idea what it looks like, then please, tell us. And when we do not find it, we can all tell Mrs. Bellows you were the one who wanted to lead the search instead of letting me do what I do best."

Carter stays quiet for a while. Everyone stares at him waiting to see what his reply will be. We can see him picturing the conversation between him and Mrs. Bellows not going well. He rubs his eyes hard before speaking again. He does not want to say it but, "For now we will stick to your plan. If we do not come up with any results, then we will go with my plan instead."

No one says anything. After a few seconds Cliffster starts laughing.

It starts a chain reaction. Even Carter's guys snicker. This really upsets Carter, "Hey, cut that out before I have you all start in the bathroom! I am sure it is one of the 'cleanest places' in this pigsty."

It is a lame comeback. Everyone's laughter eventually dies off as we all begin our assigned duties.

We find Jerry's bedroom. Koonzo spots the computer. He looks at me with a grin that tells me he was right. We take our seats in front of Jerry's computer which happens to be a top end computer brand. I only know that because my dad got me one to do my virtual reality artwork. But this piece of expensive technology is given no respect. The touchscreen monitor has smudges and flicks of boogers? Gross! The keyboard has crumbs between the keys. The space bar and enter key are loose enough to pull off. I completely forgot to examine the seat. I just want to bath in hand sanitizer right now. Koonzo grimaces at the same sight as he begins his search.

As he taps away, I ask, "So what are we looking for?"

He looks around. No one is nearby. With a low tone, he tells me, "What we are doing is checking the Comic-Con schedule. Looking for something we could tie Jerry to. So we find what Jerry was into and we will find where the 1X drug is hidden."

"So why are we almost whispering?"

"The best way to play chess against an opponent is to not broadcast what you are doing," he tells me.

I quietly reply, "What? Now you are talking in riddles."

Koonzo chuckles, "It sounds better than a boring explanation and I thought you would appreciate that." He is right. I would rather hear a creative answer. That was pretty cute.

Koonzo finds the Comic-Con website and heads straight for the events page. He tells me, "Ok, as I figured, the big movie companies will not be there. The big television series will not be there, either. However, there are some decent line ups that day and that will be our best shot. There are two anime events, five comic books events, and a panel for a television show I never heard of. Powa, I am going to need you to deliver this information to our team." He hands me the list.

I have to ask, "Just to be clear, you are talking about us, not including Carter's people, right?"

He gives me a look that says, "Wow what a stupid question." I knew I should not have asked that question. Then he says, "Make sure Carter and his goofy goons do not catch what we are doing. If not, then we are screwed." I nod and make my way to go find them.

As I am walking through this maze of a house, I am greeted back by the foul odor. I use my shirt to cover my nose. It really does not help but in my mind, at least I like to pretend my shirt is filtering whatever high levels of toxicity are in the air.

I find Sung-Suu and Cliffster. They are in the garage, and their task looks overwhelming. Boxes and trash bags are stacked up all the way to the ceiling. The small pile they sifted through made no impact or dent to the rest of the garbage/stuff.

They are in a deep discussion. Sung-Suu tells Cliffster, "Breathing through your nose is better because whatever is causing this stench will be trapped by your nose hairs."

Cliffster stops him, "First off, if that is the case then my nose hairs are failing miserably because I can still smell this funk that closely resembles yo momma's armpit funk. And if my nose hairs are reacting like this then yours must be reacting the same way. Second, breathing from your mouth will prevent you from gagging which is what I am trying not to do."

Sung-Suu comes back with, "Ok mouth breather, so you would rather breathe in the toxins of this place than protect your body from it?"

"Would you rather puke in this box or that one with the dusty dishes in it? Because you are going to puke, dookie-doo driver," Cliffster finishes with.

Sung-Suu stops what he is doing and looks at Cliffster telepathically telling him that was a low blow. This is the opportune time to step in, "Hey fellas, looks like you got it just as funky as we do." I signal for them to bring it in and make the hush signal with my index finger against my lips, "Keep a look out for anything related to these Comic-Con events." I show them the list.

Sung-Suu whispers back, "Well at least this list will narrow down the stuff we actually have to rummage through. I found a flattened rat; it has been here so long it no longer stinks. I am requesting a bio suit. This stuff is disgusting. Tell Carter I need one and a lot of disinfectant."

"Yeah, this detail is the worst out of all of them. I think Jerry used the garage as a dumpster. I actually want to take a dump in here and wipe my butt across the floor like a Chihuahua. Or even better, I can use Sung-Suu's Gallon Man costume to get rid of the dingleberries. Hey, Sung-Suu, yo momma kind of wore it last night when I had her make me a quesadilla. She got some cheese on it," Cliffster adds while laughing.

I simulate the vomiting motion as the image of that description enters my mind. I leave them to their pain and head off to find the twins. As I walk away, I hear Sung-Suu, "Yo man, call Gallon Man a costume one more time and I am gonna…"

Cliffster cuts him off, "Or what? You going to cosplay fight me? Or you going to stop calling me Daddy every time I come over to your house? Besides, that costume does not rate to be called cosplay worthy."

Poor Sung-Suu, Cliffster never lets up. As I walk to my next destination, I hear squealing and other unusual noises from a room. Sure enough, it is the twins paying stern attention to their duties. They are mesmerized by the video as they share a ragged love seat. I am not going to tell you what that video is. Let me just say the squealing is not what you think it is. It is much worse. I kick a box near the entrance to interrupt their 'work'. They spring out of their seats and cover their groin area with some nearby magazines. I laugh at their expression. Goji speaks first, "Powa, hey girl! We are knee deep in videos. There is a lot to go through."

Noni backs him up as they both sit back down, "This guy has thousands of videos. We are going to be here all night."

I tell them, "Have you any idea what Jerry may have been doing in that seat you both are sitting in?" Their reaction to my comment is priceless. They have the look of someone who just stepped on a hot pile of dog crap with their Sunday shoes. As they creep away from the love seat, I whisper, "Once you both are done sterilizing your behinds, Koonzo wants you to focus on these events to get the ball moving."

They take a look at the list. I offer to let them keep it but Goji whispers back, "We got it. The Sunday schedule is the least active. Easy to figure out."

I turn to walk back out when I hear someone sit back on the love seat. As I stop in the hallway, I hear Noni exclaim, "Hey G, how are you going to sit on that nasty thing again?!"

Goji presses play on the monitor, "Well I am not going to stand watching all these videos. Besides, I farted on it so now my butt is protected by my own germs."

Noni replies, "Dude, that makes total sense!" I shake my head as I walk away.

Then I hear another body sit on the love seat accompanied by laughter. I hear Noni, "I just did not want to look like the biggest pig in front of Powa. I may have a shot."

Goji fires back, "You are not getting a conclusion beat for that." Then I hear someone fire off a clapping fart and hear Goji break out the conclusion beat. They both laugh aloud. If he did have a chance, which never was the case, he does not anymore.

I head back and see Carter talking with Koonzo. I wait behind some stacked boxes as either have not seen me. I hear Koonzo tell Carter, "We have to look into the oddest of all things and maybe there will be a chance we catch a clue. There is a lot to scroll through."

"Alright, I will get my guys to look for those strange things in the house which is practically anything." I start to walk into the room before Carter sees me. We cross paths and he gives me a quick frown. I know he does not like me, but this particular time I did not do anything to deserve it, so I shrug it off. I ask Koonzo, "You hanging out with your new friend now?"

He gives me a huge smile, "Well since you were not around, I decided to find a friend that will respect me in the morning." We both chuckle. I am sure Carter heard us.

I take a computer break and head out to find a restroom. I locate the kitchen and it is utterly foul. There are dishes in the sink with mold growing from them. Mold is even growing from the drain! I cannot understand how someone can live like this. This is the worst moment to have to go to the bathroom, but it cannot be helped. There has to be a restroom somewhere around here. I might end up peeing myself while puking. Yes, that is how bad it smells in here. I see a door and get excited, but as much as I need to use the bathroom my father's training comes in handy. He always told me to never just pull on a door. To look around for any foreign devices or things out of place. Sure enough upon closer examination I see the hinges are off. My dad would be so proud of his little warrior. I get sad for a quick second just thinking about my dad, but I do not have time for sentimental reminiscing. I got a job to do.

Several plastic storage bins are in front of the door to keep it from falling over. I push those out the way. I carefully move the door from the frame without making any noise which would attract the attention of Carter and his squad.

Once I push the door to the side, I walk in. Oh, my goodness, I cannot make heads or tails of this place. What is going on? The bathroom is more like a storage room. By now I understand every room in a hoarder's house is for storage; however, this is different. This bathroom is a bit larger than the typical washrooms I have seen inside kitchen areas. But the peculiar part of all this is that it is spectacularly clean. Sure, the crates inside make the room a little cluttered but overall this room is very clean. Even the crates were not covered with cobwebs or dust.

Of course, the big question is why is this room so different from all the others? Why the room next to the kitchen? Why not a secret room in the attic? Who knows at this point. I begin to look around. I check under the sink cabinet and the normal household goods are there. It is quite organized. I thought it would be packed with garbage. Behind me and to the left is a shower stall with glass sliding doors. No soap scum on the windows or the shower walls either. I imagine taking a shower right now in this thing because I cannot remember the last time I had one. I am starting to smell like those Comic-Con extremists. How is this my life now?

There is body wash and shampoo. As I pick them up, I can tell they have been used. The medicine cabinet is my next venture. I bet there are pills and toiletries. Sure enough, all that is in there. It is nicely organized. The only odd thing is there are about ten pill bottles of ibuprofen. At least, that is what the labels say. Nothing left to examine but these crates. They are not the normal milkman crates. They have lids on them and are more like storage bins than crates, I guess I stand corrected.

I open the first one. Inside, I see cartoon magazines. There are many of these magazines and they are all in Japanese lettering, but that is just a wild guess. I push that box to the side and open the next one. Action figures still inside the packaging, several old movie posters, and several other trinkets like keychains and bottle openers lay inside the second bin. The final bin contains photos of Jerry posing with some dressed up characters like the ones on the magazine. Some of them look like the cartoon characters and others look like staff members of that company wearing their yellow shirts.

I pull out several old lanyards with Comic-Con access passes that have Jerry's name on all of them. One has this year's date on it. There are two other passes going back to last year and the year before. Oh, this is starting to get juicy. I have to tell Koonzo about this. I grab this year's lanyard, several photos, and a cartoon magazine and shove them somewhere on my body. I do not want Carter to find out about this. I head back out ensuring I pushed the door and the boxes back to their original placement. The foul smell hits me again. It is seriously stronger now. I sneak past one of the goons in the living room. I make it to Koonzo and find him deep in concentration on something on the computer screen. I ask him, "What did you find?"

Koonzo keeps his eyes on the monitor, "Jerry is all about this NDW. That is what they are terming the new nine-day week stuff. On this website, there is a debate about the nine days and how that affects God and how he rested on the seventh day. Some people joke that God went and traded places with the devil those next two days. Then it gets serious as people start to chat how the devil will allow all types of sin for those two days. Stuff like that." Koonzo keeps reading.

Even he is getting hooked on this NDW news. I break his concentration by dangling the lanyard in front of his face. The trick works as it catches his attention. He looks at me with a question mark. I whisper to him, "I found a washroom in the kitchen area, and all this stuff was in there."

I pull out everything I brought. Koonzo looks at all the items and says, "No way. This is the 9Lock magazine series. These are the cleanest things in the house! Did you wipe them down or something?"

"No, the entire washroom is spotless. I wanted to go pee in there. I got so excited about my discovery that I forgot to pee. So, what do you make of all this?" I ask.

Koonzo turns to the computer and begins typing away as he replies, "The restroom is squeaky clean, huh? Well I am going to have to check that out once I am done here. Naturally, Carter will discover it. It looks like even though Jerry was a hoarder he was still able to preserve these things. They must have meant a lot to him. Like one of those dedicated super fans that..." He stops mid-sentence and begins to type away. Then he finds it, "So predictable. A super fan that writes his opinions on forums and even has his own blog under a surname. You see, this series has been around since the beginning of anime. These magazines are not as valuable as other more popular magazines, but the fact that they are kept in such pristine condition indicates that they are a big piece of the puzzle." He clicks back to another window, "Look, they are on the schedule for this afternoon. And that is where we need to be. The problem is if Carter and his guys find the washroom, they will easily pick up on this clue as well."

"So, what do we do?" I begin to get nervous. We have everything we need but no means to escape and no means to destroy the evidence in the washroom. We hear someone coming. Koonzo hands me the lanyard and signals for me to hide it. I tuck it inside my sports bra.

It is Carter. He walks around the room and then stands behind us. Neither of us turn to look at him. We keep staring at the monitor. Carter pushes our chairs in opposite directions splitting us apart. He scrolls through the open windows reviewing our work. I can tell by the look on Koonzo's face there is something wrong. He uses his eyes to signal to me to look at the computer. I squint to focus on the small font. There it is. The 9Lock event is scheduled for Sunday. And Carter is one window away from clicking on the event page.

I try and think of something to possibly distract him. But all I can do is focus on the mouse swaying from left to right hoping it does not make its way to the next window. If I do something I am afraid it may make Carter curious as to the diversion we are attempting. Screw it! I look up and whisper to myself, "Forgive me, this must be done."

I muster up some tears and begin to whimper. Koonzo picks up on my intention and puts his arm around me, "Hey, everything is going to be ok. Relax. Do not get yourself worked up." My whimpers grow into a low cry. Koonzo wipes my tears, "Powa, what is wrong?" The low cry escalates into an out loud cry. The mouse pointer stops.

Carter turns and faces us, "What is her problem?"

Now that was pretty insensitive, even for Carter. So, I let him have it, "I will tell you what is wrong, Carter! I am here wasting time on your boss' mission; my mother is dying, and I am not there! The thought of me not being there for my mother's final moments, that my mother will not get to see me before she dies is what my problem is! That my mother will die with the sadness of never saying good-bye to me is my problem! And that I will carry that against you and Mrs. Bellows until my very last breath is going to be your problem!"

In the beginning, I was only trying to get Carter's attention. But as my impromptu speech went on, I genuinely became angry at him. I pick up a nearby desk lamp. With all my heart and might, I cocked my arm back and threw that thing as hard as I could at Carter's face. He is experienced enough to duck smartly. The lamp misses him and crashes through the window behind him. Koonzo leaps out of his seat from the shattering glass.

The crisp, dark morning air rushes in. I have forgotten how disgusting the air in this house has treated my nose. Then something strange happens. I hear the shattered glass on the grass outside crack several more times. Carter hears the same thing. He draws his coyote colored pistol. He cautiously creeps towards the broken window. With his side arm at the ready position, he peeks into the night. He looks left and then to the right. Carter looks directly below him when the rest of his team enters the room. Their guns are drawn at the window carefully pointed around their boss. Carter says, "It is alright. The girl here had a dramatic moment." He is really pissing me off. I want to throw something else at him. I pick up a plate with petrified food on it.

The next window breaks just as surprisingly as the first one. All weapons point at the curtains blowing in the breeze from the second window. Koonzo turns to me, "Powa, stop it already!" I look down at my hand. I still have the dirty plate. Carter looks at the floor, "Get down!" Right then I see something spring up from the floor. Next thing I know there is this loud explosion. The concussion is much stronger than the one at the make shift detention hospital. It takes my breath away as we all fall to the floor. I feel myself losing control as my lungs flex all the air out of my body. I try to inhale but the air keeps escaping me. All the while, I hear furniture tumbling over. I can smell things on fire and can see the bright light of the explosion in my peripherals. The explosion thrusts the computer desk along with me to a corner. The impact and the lack of oxygen makes me pass out.

Chapter 15

Sunday still before dawn

I wake up groggy and with a real bad headache. I feel like I am tumbling. Koonzo is carrying me. I can tell he is either running or speed walking. He tells me something, but I cannot hear him. I look around and see gunfire in the darkness. We are still at Jerry's house. From all the chaos, I am able to see other bursts of light. Are these smaller explosions or the muzzle flash from the weapons' fire? My eyes have not been able to focus still. I squeeze them tightly hoping this will help regain my vision. I can hear Koonzo now, "It is going to be ok! We are almost there!" As he is looking at me, I can tell he is scared. These types of things do not happen to nerds except in the gaming world.

My voice is weak, "What are those flashes?" I ask Koonzo. He looks at me and says, "It is a spectacular yet unpleasant sight."

At that moment, my eyes begin to work properly again. I focus on the flashing again, "Koonzo, those are the requests from the dead!" I tell him with excitement and surprise.

"I know. I have never seen a request at night outside before. There are so many of them. They look like a new generation of mini fireworks. Alright, Powa, I am lowering you down." He places me inside one of the vans, "Wait here. I am going to look for the others."

My body is not responding the way I want it to. I hear someone else tell Koonzo, "Do not go back in there! It is swarming with bad guys! We have to go!"

Oh no, Koonzo may get left behind. I am not going to let that happen. Mustering all my energy, I roll back out of the van. The unknown voice grunts profanities as he heads over to pick me up. That is when I tell him in a vulnerable and weakened state, "Please wait for my friends, mister."

The man radios in, "A teenage boy just went back into the house for his friends."

Another replies, "We have all of them in my van! We need to get out of here, now!" This is not good.

Koonzo went back into the house looking for his friends. And that is going to take a long time, especially since Jerry's house is packed with junk. The man screams, "Pop smoke! We are leaving! Move out!" I can hear the screaming from the other van. They must be right next to us. Several pops go off and then a large plume of smoke covers the vans. The engines rev high and the tires screech along the driveway slowly gaining traction. This cannot be happening. Koonzo will die if they find him. I make a jump towards the driver. But the man next to me must have anticipated me doing this. He grabs me by the back of my shirt. It chokes me and whips my head into my chest. I retract back into my seat.

A familiar voice transmits on the radio, "Meet me at the rally point before the enemy gets here." It is Carter. I totally forgot about him. It appears his team thought he was dead.

We pull up to a spot on the road next to a rock formation surrounded by brush. I look back at the house. I can see the headlights of their vehicle's turnabout facing the road we are still on as the cloud of smoke dissipates. From the dark brush appears a tall man with a bloodied face. He is breathing heavy as if he had been running for a long time. The team inside the van point their weapons at him. The bleeding man opens the door. "Carter, I cannot believe you are still alive, man," says the driver in disbelief. Carter walks up to him and punches him square in the nose. Blood erupts from the center of his face as the man falls back into the driver's seat. Carter, still breathing heavy, looks back into the brush and yells, "Clear." From the dark brush appears a short and frail silhouette.

"Koonzo! I thought you were captured or dead. How did you get out of there?"

I open the van's sliding door and rush to help him into the van. Carter grabs us both and puts us in the vehicle, "He will tell you all about it on the way." Carter shuts the van's sliding door, sits in the passenger seat behind the driver and we take off. Behind us are the same headlights that attacked us at the house. I look at the road and realize one set of headlights is closing in on us. Carter tells the guy he punched earlier, "Turn the lights off and pull over. Place an explosive in the middle of the road with a pressure switch. You have less than five-seconds to do it."

The bloodied man gets out and heads to the rear of the van. He does what Carter told him and jumps in the van again. Probably took him about ten seconds to do it instead of the five Carter gave him. But who knows, it just felt like it took a long time to me, maybe because we were being chased by some bad people. The driver takes off so fast that the momentum pulls us back into our seats. We all look back at the road. Any moment now. I stare deep into the headlights. They catch up to our dust trail. The headlights swerve left and right. We are going so fast that I can see the rear brake lights reflecting off the road and dust. They brake so much they appear to be strobing. Then boom! I feel the explosion. I guess Mr. Bloody Nose did his job after all. The headlights disappear. Even through the night, I can see the column of smoke and debris. No other headlights break through the smoke in tow. A sense of relief envelopes me. That was a close call. We all finally take our seats. Carter takes in a deep breath, "Now go on and tell them what happened."

Koonzo clears his throat like he is nervous to speak, "Well after I dropped you off, Powa, I went back into the house. The place is in shambles. All the windows are blown out. Whatever was standing or hanging before the explosion was scattered on the floor. Smoke filled every room. I was trying to look for any of the guys. I come across a hand in the rubble. At first, I thought it was one of my friend's hand. But when I lifted the hand as the rubble fell away, I noticed it was Carter. I wanted to keep looking around, but I could not leave him there. So, I lifted him up; he was partially in shock as we stumbled towards the front door. Another explosion blew us through the front door and onto the driveway. I think that really woke Carter up because he began looking around. He found a rifle and we headed towards the vans.

When we notice the vans leaving, he got his balance back and told me to follow him. We took off running towards an old dirt road. Carter told me that if we did not sprint, those people back at the house would find us and torture us before they kill us. I did not need to be told twice. I ran so fast I passed up Carter and kept running. Then I got popped in the back of the head with a rock; it almost knocked me out. I looked back and saw Carter signaling me to come back. Apparently, I ran so far ahead that I had passed up our stopping point. And that is how we got here."

Koonzo rubs the back of his head as he is still recovering from the impact of the rock. I can tell he ran for his life. Carter picks up the radio and transmits, "Let us put aside the short amount of time I have had to mesh with you all. We all know how I ratted out half my old squad when I discovered they were up to no good and that did not buy me any sympathy points with you guys. And let me share that I know none of you want me to lead this team. However, that does not excuse what you guys did. Seriously? Not one of you felt the need or the desire to go back and look for us? Putting all that baggage aside, you left us to die."

It is at this moment that his voice went from relatively loud to uncomfortably loud and angry, "And I got this kid who is not even old enough to join the military come in and rescue me! How pissed off do you think that makes me?!"

Carter is gripping the transmitter so tight that for a moment I thought it would break in his hand. The bloody nose man says nothing. He keeps his eyes on the road making the appearance to be concentrating on his task. No one says a word. I have to say I do agree with Carter. Those guys left him to die. They never talked about going back. We got out of there pretty quickly. Then again, I did blackout from the initial blast.

Still fuming, Carter lunges forward and snatches Mr. Bloody Nose from his front seat and into the back with the rest of us. Carter is so fast, the man looked like he was made of cotton when he snatched him up. The man in the front passenger seat realizes what happened and jumps in the driver's seat. Mr. Bloody Nose is pinned up against the van wall. Carter's face is so close to the man's face, I bet they can smell each other's breath. The crinkled cloth from the man's shirt is bunched up and gets stained by Carter's bloodied fists. Carter wants to hurt him bad. His breathing tells me so. The man's face says only one thing, "I really done it this time." Then Carter looks to his left and focuses on me. His angry face then goes back to his preferred no expression appearance. He lets the man go and points to the open front passenger seat. The man jumps to the front just as fast as he was jolted to the back a minute ago. Carter adjusts his tie with blood around his white collared shirt and says, "Drive faster before something else goes wrong." I hear the engine rev into a higher gear and the van begins to move faster.

The driver seems to know where we are going, even though Carter did not name a location or address. I am almost afraid to ask where we are heading, but looking at Carter's face, asking him would not be a good idea. Almost immediately another thought popped in my head, were those guys attacking us enemies of Mrs. Bellows or the government? Maybe they are people affiliated with Jerry. In some way, I really do not wish to find out. They appear to be the type to attack first and then ask questions later. Along the way, Carter mentions something about going back to the main house and finding out what is going on. Well, we have about 30-minutes before we reach Mrs. Bellows' house. I am going to digest what just happened and hope to crap it out before we get there. Wow, I have been hanging out with these guys for far too long. I am beginning to sound just like them. I can only hope I go back to my normalish self when this is over.

Chapter 16

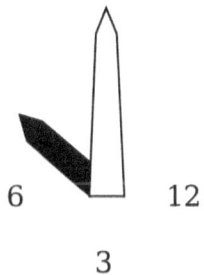

6   12

3

Sunday early daylight

I am thrusted into the back of the bench seat in front of me. The tires are skidding on the pavement. Carter's voice sounds concerning. In a low tone he points as he tells the driver, "Pull over behind those trees." I look back and see the other vans are still with us. Carter gets out and fiddles with his cellphone. He leaves the sliding door open. I decide to get out to have a look. As I exit the van, I reward myself with a well-deserved stretch. It is early enough and cool enough that I can actually see my breath. Something is different about this morning air though. It does not smell quite as crisp and fresh as I remember. It smells polluted with something I cannot quite put my finger on.

Did Carter take us to an oil refinery or a processing plant? I turn to Carter. With his phone up to his ear, I can tell he looks distraught. He is speaking with someone so quietly that I cannot decipher what it is. I trace his line of sight to the object he is focused on. Through the trees, I begin to see where the toxic smell is coming from. The morning air is dragging along its blue orange sky a trail of smoke that looks like hair whipping in the breeze. I follow the smoke trail to the point of origin and I see something I could barely believe. Mrs. Bellows' house is completely destroyed! I am not talking like what happened to Jerry's house. I mean a full-on assault took place here. Debris is scattered all over the place from what looks like several large explosions.

Carter returns to the van and says, "Hey, we are leaving. Get in."

I naturally ask, "What happened? Is Mrs. Bellows alright?"

As I closed the door, Carter tells me, "I do not know what happened. My guess is whoever hit us at Jerry's house are the same ones that have done this. From what I gather, they came here first. The guys probably tortured Mrs. Bellows and the rest of the staff and that is how they found out we were at Jerry's house. They must be big time if they are able to prevent emergency services from responding. I mean in both instances no cops or fire trucks came to the rescue." Carter flings the sliding door open and jumps out. He points at me, "You, get out!"

Is he pointing at me?! I look around and sure enough, he is. I question the request, "What for?" I can sense something has Carter spooked or upset. He grabs me by the jacket and yanks me out. This guy is strong! I begin to yell when he puts his hand over my mouth, "The last thing we need is someone getting a lock on us. You are close to jeopardizing us all. Calm down and let us get through what I must do next." He does not realize his hand is covering both my mouth and my nose. I panic a little as I begin to suffocate. I give him a quick nod in order to get permission to breathe. Must be some black ops technique he learned to control his subjects. He removes his hand and I gasp for air. As I recover, he tells me, "You need to vomit. The tracker Mrs. Bellows made you swallow a few hours ago is still inside of you. That has to be how they made us at Jerry's."

I give him the stink eye, "First of all, you trying to suffocate me is BS. I am not one of those bad guys trying to kill you.

Better watch who you get angry at..." Next thing I know, I am hunched over with a finger jabbing the back of my tongue! I bite down. Carter grunts knowing that finger of his is coming off if he does not stop. He lets me go. I am catching my breath when he grabs me by the back of my neck and jams his finger in my throat again. How did he manage to get his finger in my mouth that fast? I bite down again but something is different. This time he has pinched my nose and is wearing a glove; I can tell because the leather is pressing past my taste buds. How did he put on a glove that fast? This time my biting is not successful. His finger eventually makes its way to my gag reflex and I begin to vomit. I hear everything I have eaten hit the gravel. My eyes are shut tight; yet, tears manage to escape.

I hear the other van doors open and footsteps running in my directions. I hear Koonzo's voice, "Hey man, get off her!" There is a slight struggle as I am jostled around a bit. Koonzo falls to the ground. Other footsteps stop around us but do not get involved. Carter removes his hand from the back of my neck to give me a chance to recover.

He then explains to the rest of the gang, "The tracker she swallowed is still inside her; that is how they found us. We cannot move on until she pukes it out."

Sung-Suu asks, "Well then they know where we are at right now, so, what is the point in getting it out?" The driver of our van says, "Because all of our vans are equipped with jammers. If we are bugged, the jammers will prevent..."

Cliffster cuts him off, "We get it James Bond. We have seen the movies." Goji provides the conclusion beat. The driver gives him a dirty look that makes Goji break eye contact with him as he hides behind Cliffster.

Sung-Suu still fires back, "But she is outside the van now which means they now know where we are."

The driver answers again, "If you know your James Bond movies then you would know a jammer's radius extends approximately five yards beyond the van." He smirks at Cliffster knowing he gained one victory out of that discussion.

Carter comes back, "She needs to puke it out before it enters her large intestine. If the tracker gets there, then we will have to leave her here and keep moving."

And if that happens then I will get picked up by these bad guys. Something tells me these guys will not be as inviting as Mrs. Bellows (and she was no picnic either). Knowing I had no other choice, I put my finger in my mouth and vomit some more. I can see the other folks are not entertained by this. As I puke, Carter is sifting through the gravel infused vomit. Then he puts his hands directly under my mouth to catch the vomit as it comes out. Gross! Seeing that makes me throw up even more. I hear other people begin to vomit as well. The chain reaction is unstoppable. Nerds or guards, it does not matter. We all vomit off each other's cue. Someone is puking so bad it is making him fart. Laughing ensues. More puking and farting takes place. This has to be the most disgusting activity I have ever been a part of and I am pretty sure I will never forget it.

Carter shouts, "There it is! I got it. You all can stop this unimpressive act of solidarity. Rilo, get the RC out and bring the portable jammer." Rilo happens to be the driver. The driver after Mr. Bloody Nose. It is amazing how long it can take before you learn someone's name. Anyway, Rilo returns from the rear of the van and comes back with a remote-control truck. It looks pretty techie and expensive, too. It has a camera on it. The controller has a video screen and all types of cool buttons. At this point everyone else has recovered from the short vomiting epidemic.

Rilo reports to Carter, "Here it is, boss." Carter looks at Rilo as if it was the first time anyone called him that. He does not show it, but I can tell he likes it. Carter hands the transmitter I swallowed to Rilo. He is a professional. The man did not care that the device was still covered in vomit. He places it in a certain spot on the expensive looking little truck.

Rilo then tapes a device with three little antennas on the truck. He makes a few other modifications on it and tests the controller out. He looks at Carter and gives him the thumbs up.

Carter instructs Rilo, "Make sure the jammer is on or else all this is for nothing." Rilo checks the three-antenna device and gives him another thumbs up. Carter adds, "Drop the pill at a nearby house." Rilo lowers the truck like he is about to release a puppy at a park. He grabs the controller and flicks a few switches. And just like that, the little truck whizzes into the woods. We all crowd behind him. At this point, Rilo is fascinating us with his reality show. Carter asks him, "You sure you got range on that thing?"

Rilo replies, "I do not know how far the next house is, boss, but we will surely find out." It is funny how all of the sudden Rilo is all boss this, and boss that. That is what happens when you see someone getting beat up for leaving the boss behind. Well done Carter, well done.

Several minutes go by. The grey monitor on the controller highlights the brush and trees as the little machine zooms past the terrain. Finally, the little truck reaches a nicely manicured house. It heads around back to an impressive yard. I could not help noticing again something I have not seen back home; it is unusual for me to see a house without a fence. I guess I am that far away from home and everything familiar to me.

The little truck catapults the pill behind a garden shed. Carter instructs, "Park it somewhere hidden but keep it pointed at the pill." Rilo nods and he parks the little truck under a set of bushes. The monitor turns from the grey screen to a regular color screen like a T.V. With the daylight approaching, the night vision feature must have automatically disengaged.

I turn to Carter, "So what are we going to do now?" I am still recovering from a sore throat and exhausted tear ducts.

Carter responds, "We are going to Comic-Con to finish what we started."

That does not seem right to me, so I said, "Wait! We should at least go back to the house and see if there are any survivors."

"We cannot risk it. Those guys more than likely left a few eyeballs behind." Said Carter almost unapologetically.

That makes no sense to me. And here is where I get him back for all the things he has done to me; I almost yell my words at him, "You are a hypocrite! A yellow belly hypocrite!"

Carter leans in very close and gives me the same glare he gave Mr. Bloody Nose.

I answer the question his eyes are asking, "You nearly broke the man's chest for not going back for you. And now look at you. I bet if Mrs. Bellows was out there and later found out you did not go back to look for her, she will be more inclined to properly handle that 'sign' of loyalty."

Within those vein popping eyes, I see him thinking of what I just said. He holds his pose for a short while. From my peripheral, I can see everyone focusing on Carter, including Mr. Bloody Nose. Carter is in a no-win situation. However, if he is a tyrant then he could care less about hypocrisy. I realize I am holding my breath and say to myself, "Please do not hit me; and if you do hit me, do not hit me in the face. I bleed pretty easily."

He moves his face away and says, "Everyone, get inside your vans. Rilo, cautiously make your way back to Mrs. Bellows' house, or what is left of it." We all jump in the vans. This time my fellow nerds pack in my van; it feels good having them around. I intentionally take a little longer to get inside just to express to Carter that I got the best of him. Carter does not bother looking back at me but I can sense he knows I am gloating right now. He jumps in the van behind us. He must be tired of me. The driver puts the van in gear and we slowly begin to move. Mr. Bloody Nose occupies the front passenger seat as he gives a wink as payment for my killer comeback to Carter.

Chapter 17

Sunday Early Morning

We pull up cautiously to the demolished house. Carter comes over the radio, "Listen, we move fast but quietly."

Goji quickly states, "Silent but deadly like a quiet yet pungent fart." Noni gives the conclusion beat.

Carter continues with the plan, "If there are eyeballs here then prepare to defend yourself. Jump in the vans and head to our rendezvous point like always. We will know within the first 30-seconds what is going to happen. Look around and see if you can find any survivors. Remember, our fellow warriors were inside this house. Time is critical. The pill is exposed so whoever is monitoring that tracker is on the move. Rilo, keep checking on that shed for activity."

Now I get it. That is why he wanted the little truck to stay behind. That is pretty smart. Carter is definitely a professional. We get out of our vans. The smoke has dissipated a little, which helps keep the coughing down. Carter's guards make their way swiftly through the debris starting from the van and fanning out. My nerds and I take our time walking towards the house, so we do not stumble over a body. The house is completely destroyed. There are bullet holes everywhere. Several walls still stand but for the most part everything has collapsed or has been blown out into the yard. I mean there is no roof. That is how bad it is. It is a blessing the sun is coming out because it helps us to better see where we are going. I see pieces of furniture and even pictures scattered about. Whoever destroyed this house was viciously prepared. I mean who destroys an entire house? From a short distance, we notice a request is taking place. We head over there. I do not understand why we have this impulse to view the request. Maybe it is to show the dead our respect. Or maybe it is curiosity. It is one of Mrs. Bellows' guards which means it is Carter's guy. The request disappears as soon as we arrive. I look over at Carter. He is in no rush. He is probably a realist and understands there is nothing he can do.

"I found one," is heard from one of the guards. We all sprint over to help. This time Carter gets there first. I really do believe he wants to be there if any of his teammates are alive. After all, most leaders have some type of connection to their subordinates. My dad is like that because when he gets a special phone call he takes off immediately to help one of his teams. But I do not want to think about my dad too much, tears would probably follow.

The guard who found someone is removing the rubble off him. The victim is face down covered in debris dust. I cannot see much damage on him, so my guess would be he either suffocated or died from smoke inhalation a while ago. Carter puts his hand on his neck hoping to feel a pulse, "I do not feel anything." He goes to flip him over. His team gasps. It is one of their own.

I hear Rilo say, "Gustafson, oh man, I am sorry this happened to you my friend." Rilo is not crying or hinting that he is broken up about it. It is a half-hearted emotional statement. Maybe he said it like that to keep his edge and tough guy reputation around the other guys. Or maybe he really did not know the guy too well. But then I see Carter bow his head next to Gustafson's left ear and say a few words. I could not figure out what he said as his tone was low enough for just him and his deceased comrade to hear. I do not risk asking what was said or why he did not do this with his other teammate. It is none of my business.

A few more people say they found survivors. Two members of the house staff are found. There are no requests taking place. They obviously are either alive or have been dead for some time now. It does not matter to us, we rush over to them anyway. It is confirmed, both are dead. One of them is missing his legs and his left arm. The second is missing his entire face. I can actually see parts of the skull. It does not scare me, but it does burn the image in my mind. I stare at the man with the missing face for quite a while. To think we all look like that underneath. Six more bodies are found. All of them dead. As I look around, I notice the guards are becoming a bit demoralized. I empathize with them, after all they used to know these guys. They probably know each other's families. It is a horrible way to die.

I head to the dining room area where I last spoke with Mrs. Bellows. It took some time to orientate myself around the rubble. There I see the table where we sat while Mrs. Bellows explained to me about HyphenDash. I wonder if she meant it. If she really meant to help my mother out or if she was just saying that to get me to help her. What a pleasant surprise that would have been, if she had meant it.

I pick up one of the fallen chairs when I see a hand underneath a crushed cabinet. Is that what I think it is? I yell for the others, "I got a hand over here!" I sprint to the cabinet. I hear them pass the word. I go to touch the hand. I brush off some of the debris dust away. As I am doing this, the hand moves. It acts as if it were suffocating as each finger sprawls for something. I yell out, "This one is alive! Hurry!" I hear their steps move even faster. I yell at the hand, "Help is coming! Hold on!" The hand is trying to lift the cabinet. I assist in its action. Everyone soon arrives, and they work on moving the cabinet. I can hear their heavy breathing from their recent sprint.

The cabinet is not moving fast enough for us. The expensive wood is heavy. Instead we decide to lift it up enough to drag the wounded from underneath. It is another friendly face. This is a much younger man. He looks like he just graduated college. His face has dry blood mixed in with the drywall dust. His uniform reflects the same. His poor hands are shaking. His stomach has a large piece of lodged wood from the cabinet. The piece of wood along with the surrounding portions of cloth from his shirt seem to be containing the bleeding. It makes no sense, but he is not bleeding out. However, the placement of the stake being in the exact center of his stomach would lead me to believe this is a terminal wound.

His friends take a knee around him. I hear them console and put him at ease, "Hey Trent, looks like you will do anything to get out of work." They all chuckle as some have tears down their faces while others maintain their composure. Trent's chuckles turn to weeping quite fast. They try to make him feel comfortable.

Trent says, "Inside my left breast pocket is a letter to my ex-wife. It is my confession to her. I never treated her the way she should have been treated because I never stayed…" He pauses as he flexes through the pain. I can tell his pain is agonizing as well as emotionally difficult. Someone reaches in his left breast pocket and pulls out the letter and hands it to him. He grunts through it all, "I did not fight enough for our love." That even touched me. Then he says, "Make sure she gets it. In my other pocket I have a toy car." The same hands reach in and hand it to him. Trent explains, "My son put this in my bag before I left for work three years ago. I took it as his first sacrifice towards unselfishness."

That was pretty cool. I tell him, "That is a sweet gesture, Trent. He loves you very much."

Another voice says, "Geez Trent, no wonder why you are always a slow runner. You keep carrying around everything including this complimentary wooden stake." That comment made me and everyone else laugh aloud.

Trent laughs with us which reaches his pain level. This time he begins to cough blood. There is not much time. I can tell his friends are able to comfort him better than I can. Trent speaks while spitting out blood, "Someone record me. I would like the world to know I died with my brothers around me."

Rilo breaks out a small camera, "I gotcha, buddy. Say whatever you want. I got plenty of storage space here. I already deleted those videos with me and your momma." As they laugh, I begin to appreciate their camaraderie and the ability to erase any sensitivity during the most traumatic events. That is probably how they keep their edge.

This must be difficult for them as well. As I well know from experience watching someone you care for die in front of you is an event that messes with your mind and emotions. "Yeah, well my momma said she felt sorry for your lack of depth if you know what I mean." They keep laughing it up. It is a happy moment which has been different from the other deaths I have observed in the last couple of days.

Rilo continues his comedic attack, "Well your momma definitely does not have a lack of depth in her part. I mean you do know she was everyone's girlfriend at one time. And by that one time I mean at the same time." They all bust out laughing so hard even my nerd friends had to chuckle that one out of their system. Sung-Suu and Cliffster even raise their eyebrows taking mental notes. Carter is in the back almost invisible.

Something is up with him. I thought he would be up close and personal with Trent. What gives?

The second alert chimes somewhere in Trent's back pocket. We all know what that means. Trent's laughing turns to coughing. More blood starts coming from his mouth. His body starts convulsing. The area around the stake now has a large spot of blood that is growing. His body is calm now. The team starts to tear apart the shirt. Carter speaks up, "Do not add pressure to the wound. Adding pressure to a wound with an object still inside will only make the injury worse. Let him enjoy his final vision of us the way he would want it. We should send him on his way as a happy soul."

Everyone gathers around and starts telling stories about him. But they tell their story including him in their conversation. They all laugh while some of them try to conceal their tears behind their sunglasses. Others conceal their whimpering with stubborn coughs and clearing of their throats. I thought it would be odd, but I appreciate watching it. If my mom dies in front of me, this is how I will honor her final moments. For as much as I really do not like Carter, I have to respect the type of guy he is with his team even though he may be a bit cold at times. Then I notice several rings of light. That can only mean one thing. Did Trent pass away already? Has six minutes passed? The request is taking place now. I want to see it. Naturally, it is his son's toy car. It is a lime green Formula One little toy car.

The lights are somehow orbiting through the little car. There are rings all around it. The rings of light are like that of a comet. There is the head and the tail of the comet. Now connect the head to the tail. It is like a snake chasing its tail. This is what those rings look like but in different colors. I have never seen anything like this! The heads of these rings are orbiting extremely fast now. This must be the time when the toy car is about to transfer from this world to the next. The intensity of the light grows fiercely bright. We all squint to keep our eyes on the toy car. The light overpowers all of our vision and the toy car disappears.

Everyone else gets up and continues the search. Rilo grabs the letter from Trent and stuffs it in his left breast pocket where I see another letter already in there. Could this be his final letter? Who could he be addressing it to? I stop with the questions and just focus on Trent. He is still, quiet, and at peace. A voice breaks our silence, "Is it me or does anyone else feel a sense of calmness right now? Like all the stress and anxiety has been lifted from you?" The voice is right. I do have a sense of peace. I am not sad he has passed away. And I do not mean that in a heartless way. I mean I am pleased he has moved on from his suffering. Wherever his soul is right now is in a better place and in better condition than when he left here.

Something just as odd happens. "Help me!" Is heard from a weak voice attempting to scream through its whisper. Everyone gets up to find this voice. Underneath more rubble in what used to be one of Mrs. Bellows' grand living room, we find the source of the voice. Everyone begins to move the debris out of the way. We move quickly hoping we are able to save this comrade's life. Finally, the body is uncovered. It is not one of the guards. It is a woman. She seems to have passed out. Carter moves in closer and says, "She is not one of ours. This is interesting."

Koonzo surprises me with his voice when he says, "But she is not wearing one of those tactical uniforms. She seems to be wearing business attire underneath the bulletproof vest."

"You are right, kid. Which means she is even more important than a worker bee," Carter adds. He checks her over to see if there are any wounds. Miraculously, she only has a bad bump on her head.

At that very moment we hear Rilo coming from the radio, "Hey boss! Got a team at the shed. Whatever we are going to do, we better do it fast!" Carter instructs, "Everyone get in the vans. Bring her along. Move it!" We all scramble. At this point, I have declared Carter and company friendlies. I have to convince myself of this to prevent the yo-yo emotions of who to trust. I sure do hope this does not backfire on me.

Chapter 18

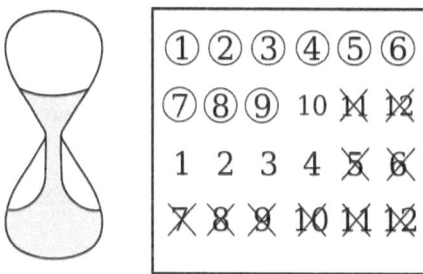

Sunday early morning still

We jump into the vans. Our recent discovery heads into the second van with Carter. "Hey Darryl, take over the radio and the wheel. I am busy monitoring the shed," informs Rilo. So, Mr. Bloody Nose's name is Darryl. At least I can stop calling him that now.

Darryl takes the driver seat and replies, "I gotcha." He pushes a button, "Hey boss, I am driving. Rilo is working on the little truck situation. Where are we headed?"

Carter's radio voice answers, "Convention Center."

"Copy that," Darryl acknowledges. Our driver steps on the accelerator and we chirp out of there. The other vans follow suit.

Rilo keeps us informed on the activity at the shed, "They are trying to locate the tracker. Another group busted in the house. I feel bad for those folks. I am going to reposition the truck to see if I can make out who these clowns are."

My mind is on the lady that is with Carter. What things may he be doing to her to get the information he needs? As I am thinking that Carter's voice comes over the radio, "Stop the convoy now. Tell Powa to get into my van."

I have no idea why he wants me in there with him. I do not know anything about interrogations. I open the sliding door and hop out. I see Carter pulling out some of the captain chairs from the van. He gestures for me to come over. "Please do not have me torture this lady," I say to myself.

Carter states, "I did not call for you."

I reply, "Oh, yes you did. I heard it on the radio. But I am good with going back."

Before I could turn around, Carter replies as he is still taking out more seats, "Not you, him."

I look behind me and am pleasantly surprised he would come to see what was going on. Koonzo acknowledges his presence, "If Powa is going to be in there then she is going to need someone to keep her calm unless you want two uncooperative women in your van."

Carter finishes offloading the seats, "I do not have time to argue. There is no place for you to be comfortable but that is your problem now." Koonzo gives me a look that says he got himself into something he probably should not have. Too late, buddy.

Before I jump inside, I see the lady chained up and anchored to the van floor. She is unconscious with blood still on her face. I look at Carter as he offers, "She is ok. But we have to act fast before she wakes up." We all find a spot in the van. Carter slams the door shut and the driver takes off on cue.

Carter opens up a black case. Some metallic devices inside that I imagine are used for torture. This is not for me. I cannot do this. Carter tells Koonzo, "Hey, since you wanted to join your friend so bad, chain her left leg. I will do her other hand."

Koonzo argues, "I am not going to chain up a lady. This is not my thing. This is on you. Plus, you can get one of your goons to help you."

In a matter of seconds Carter snatches Koonzo by the throat and grits his teeth ferociously while talking, "My goons are trying to make sure we stay alive especially if we are ambushed right now! I need them to do what they have been trained to do. I need an extra set of hands to help me out with this as I was not expecting to take on any prisoners this morning. But if you feel inclined to deny my request then sit there and watch your friend's mom die before she ever reaches home. This lady is a part of our problem now. We need to get some serious information in a short amount of time which we do not have much of. Is that not right, Powa?!"

I sit still as I am shocked the conversation would pivot towards me and my mother again. That is a dirty trick, even for Carter, but I guess the employee does not fall far from the employer's tree.

Carter continues, "I will torture her if that is what it takes. And for your information neither of you will physically touch this woman when I begin. But I need her chained up in order for me to do my part. So, move it!" He releases Koonzo's throat which allows him to regain the blood to his face. Carter's hand marks are left on his neck.

I can see by the face Koonzo is making that he does not want to do this task but knows he has no choice but to do it. He grabs the leg cuff that is anchored to a post in the van's floor. Carter has already finished with her hands. He props open her mouth with one of those devices used by dentists. He uses special tongs to grab her tongue. What is he doing? Please do not tell me he is going to cut off her tongue. He pulls out an odd-looking spike. Now I cannot help myself; I have to ask, "Carter, what are you trying to do?!" With the spike, he expertly pierces the lady's tongue.

Koonzo tells him with a sour face, "You wanted to pierce her tongue? What kind of a sick individual are you?" Carter looks like a mad scientist as his eyes are thinking five steps ahead of his hands that are moving quite swiftly. It appears he is enthusiastic about this procedure. The odd spike part is screwed on with a cap on the bottom of the tongue. The top of the tongue has a loop. Carter put a short cable through that loop. He adds a few other rods that attach to a base which is on the neck of the lady. Picture someone with a halo neck brace; the kind that rests on the shoulders and cages the head with metal rods that are drilled into someone's skull. That is pretty much what he is putting on her head, with the exception of the drilling even though I would not put that past him. There is a lever on one of the bars. He connects the cable to it and ratchets it once and her tongue extends slightly.

I am in shock, "Is this some whacko torture device? I cannot do this. I will not watch you do this to this lady." At that time, the lady awakens from her newly inflicted pain. Her eyes go from groggy to panic. She tries screaming but it does not seem to help. Carter removes the mouth piece that keeps her lips apart. She attempts to scream some more. It helps a little but not much. She looks around and sees me and Koonzo. Her speech is impaired from her tongue being suspended by the ratchet. The pain she must be feeling must be unimaginable.

Carter pulls out a purple glass bottle. He swirls the dark liquid contents inside it in front of her. The lady has a confused look on her face. I have a confused look on my face, too. What is inside that bottle? Carter has that Doctor Jekyll look on his face again. It bothers me. To be honest, it scares me. He leans in close to the lady and says, "I will give you multiple opportunities to answer my questions. But this first opportunity will be your easiest." I do not know what that means but I am frightened for this woman. Koonzo looks paralyzed with fear and actually passes out.

Carter continues, "First, what is your name? A simple enough question worthy of a proper answer."

The lady wastes no time answering. Her pronunciation is horrible, "Everest is my name." It sounds like her tongue is frozen on a flagpole. If the conditions were different, I would be laughing right now.

Carter smiles, "Everest, that is almost as unusual as Powa. Thank you! That was not so bad, was it?" Carter continues to swirl his magic purple potion. His smile has turned even more devious. He asks another question, "Who do you work for?"

Everest must have known this question was going to be asked. She takes a little bit longer to answer. I can tell she is swallowing her own blood from the puncture. She painfully replies, "I am with the government."

Carter yells at her, "That is a lie! The government is not interested in killing people over these requests."

That statement might be untrue but right now I am not going to argue with Mr. Torture. His adrenaline is making him breathe heavy. Everest's hands and lips are shaking with horror. Koonzo is still unconscious. I must be in some paralyzed state as I cannot stop this from happening. Carter continues, "Last chance."

Everest replies desperately, "I am with the government! That is the truth!" Her cuffed hands make that metallic sound when being yanked quickly. Her hands are in a white-knuckle fist and shaking with fear. Still, I can tell that if she could she would blood choke Carter regardless if he tapped out.

That devious smile finally unveils his plan. He hits the lever one time. The ratchet lifts her tongue from her mouth just a little more. It is enough for us to hear her scream and know more pressure is being applied to her tongue. Carter unscrews the cap to the purple bottle. He swirls the contents one more time and says, "Bottoms up." He pours it into her mouth. It is a thick grey, almost metallic type of liquid. It takes a little while before the contents are emptied due to the viscosity. Whatever this stuff is, I can tell it is much thicker than oil.

Everest tries to move away from it, but her head is braced in place, and she has no choice but to swallow the foreign liquid. With her tongue still suspended, she is unable to prevent the liquid from entering her throat.

I break free from my paralysis, "Carter, what are you doing?! If you wanted her to drink that stuff you could have used tongs. Why are you using all of these medieval contraptions on her?" Carter's demented face looks at me. Those eyes threaten me to shut up. He does not answer as he turns his fervent attention back towards Everest. All I can imagine is that whatever he did in his previous job had to be sick and twisted.

While I am focused on the pain on Everest's face, Carter manages to insert an IV in her left arm. A clear plastic bag hangs above her swinging with the moving van. I have no idea what cocktail he created but none of this is good. Then I see him pull out a large grey rectangular block of stone. Maybe it is one of those knife sharpening stones. I am done with playing the guessing game with Carter. He has too many wicked surprises for me to be stunned anymore. Whatever he injected is beginning to show its effects on Everest. Her eyes wander from left to right in a drowsy state. Carter gets close to her left ear and whispers, "So we are going to play a little truth game. Lucky for you I am not playing this time. Powa and you are. You keep playing the game as I showed and nothing bad will happen to you, but if you resist, then…well you will find out soon enough."

Everest attempts to lift her head and fails from either the weight of the contraption or the drug in her veins. In a groggy voice Everest says, "I do not want to play your stupid game."

Carter looks over at me, "You will ask her the questions I provide to you on this doodle board. The game is that simple."

I do not bother looking at him as I strongly reply, "I am not going to do that! That is YOUR job! Do not get me involved in your torture sessions!"

Carter naturally knew I would react this way. He tells me, "I know you do not want to do this but the serum I injected in her works better when a soothing voice asks the questions. In this case, her hearing your voice will produce better results than if I were the one asking the questions. We are running short on time, are we not?"

That is another reference about my mom. I am getting sick of these people using my mother's illness as a form of coercion. If my mother were dead, I would not be at their mercy now. No, no, no. I take that back, I am not going to talk about my mom like that. She will be just fine.

Carter begins to write on the doodle board. It reads, 'Introduce yourself. Give her some information on who you are. We need to establish a peaceful tone. It is part of the serum process.'

I look at her. I can tell my voice will be shaky when I speak. I clear it several times. Carter moves out of Everest's peripheral view. I clear my throat one more time and say, "Everest, my name is Powa. I am from Klamath Falls and am a sophomore in high school. I am really scared right now, and I am in no way in control of what is going on." Everest looks at me and nods. She replies with a soft voice, "I know who you are. I met you at your school. You bailed on me. I was trying to help you."

When did I meet this lady? She does not look familiar. I dampen a nearby rag Carter left out. I wipe some of the blood away from her face. After several wipes, I begin to see who she is. I speak out loud without meaning to, "Special Agent Cross? You look so different. What are you doing way down here?"

She gives a little chuckle, "Please call me Everest. And this is what I look like without make-up on."

I show her my appreciation for her humor with a few chuckles of my own. I hear a tap that catches my attention. Carter has written a new message. Before I read it, I order Carter, "Reduce the tension on the cable. I need to understand her clearly." Carter firmly presses his lips together in disagreement, but I release the tension. Everest moves her tongue around as I watch the cable between her closed lips wiggle from side to side.

She mouths to me, "Thank you."

I smile knowing she is not in pain. I read Carter's message aloud, 'Who do you work for?' Everest shakes her head and rolls her eyes, "I just answered that question. I am with the government. How many times do I have to say it? Idiot. That last part was for him, not you, Powa."

Carter is not satisfied with that answer. He grabs the block of stone and holds it about four inches above her stomach. Everest begins to scream in pain. I look from her face to her stomach. Then I see a large bubble grow from underneath her skin.

I yell at Carter, "What are you doing to her, Carter?! Stop it!" I make a go at grabbing the stone. Carter's defensive training blocks my attempt and within a few seconds. He has my attacking arm in custody. I can feel his excitement through his strong grip around my wrist. My hand is shaking from fear.

Now the blood being trapped in my hand makes it swell. I do my best to hide the pain, but it is getting pretty tough to keep it concealed. I grit my teeth and hold my breath to not show any weakness. But it does not work.

I cry out, "Okay, okay, let me go!" He releases his grip and the blood that has been blocked for those lengthy 30-seconds begins to circulate again. As if nothing has happened, he writes on the doodle board, 'I gave her metal shavings mixed with a syrup that does well with magnets. Where I place the magnet is where the syrup will move inside her. Move the block over an area several times and the shavings begin to cut through the inside like glass. I thought of this idea all on my own.'

I can see the pride on his face as his grin telepathically lectures me that coming up with medieval torture schemes is something to be prideful for. Carter must be pretty sick to think of this type of stuff. I wonder if Mrs. Bellows ever knew how sick Carter is or if she hired him because of these very skills?

I tell Everest, "Please tell me the truth. I do not want to see you go through this again." Everest, with the metal syrup bulging from her stomach grunts, "I am with the government! Make him stop!" Carter finally gets it. He moves the block away from the pain riddled agent.

Carter writes another message, 'What were you doing at Mrs. Bellows' house?'

Everest still catching her breath from the punishment replies, "We were trying to find more information on Jerry. We knew he had the formula and several syringes loaded with the serum."

Carter's written reply, 'Why would you believe Jerry had the formula? He knows nothing about the serum.'

Everest continues even though she sounds like she is about to pass out, "Because Jerry sold out his brother for money. HyphenDash offered Jerry such a generous amount of money he could not refuse. Per the medical power of attorney, all Jerry had to do was periodically check up on his brother and report anything unusual to his siblings. No other family members would have been easily convinced to cooperate as they were deeply consumed with their own affairs. This is how Jerry became involved in Pendleton's affairs. He is the only unestablished sibling. When Pendleton learned he had dementia, he made one request of his little brother. He wanted Jerry to administer the formula to him when his time to die arrived. This is also reflective in the power of attorney. The underlying intent was to have the Gevity Alert updated voluntarily by Pendleton to strictly provide Jerry with Pendleton's first and second alerts. This will prevent anyone else from receiving notifications as well as his current location. Prior to that update, Mrs. Bellows was the only one on that contact list. Pendleton wanted himself to be a test subject for the formula. Naturally, HyphenDash had no qualms with this decision, after all, other subjects have been used before with success. Pendleton figured his lifelong legacy as a dedicated scientist would live on with a recording of a short commentary and his request."

Carter's next message, 'So what does Jerry wind up doing with the formula? Why does he steal the formula anyway?'

Everest looks extremely pale. She is either going to vomit or pass out. But the truth serum keeps her awake as she answers. Her voice is gritty now, "Unknown. Maybe for greed, the attention, or maybe he is working for one of HyphenDash's competitors. Establishing a motive was not our primary focus. We were going to find that out after we had conducted our interrogations. But he knew HyphenDash would notice their precious serum missing as well as the only handwritten copy of the formula. Pendleton worked off paper and chalkboard. The guy never used a computer. This was a plus for HyphenDash as they did not have to worry about cyber threats. Funny how that countered against them. So, Jerry anticipated there would be conflict, and he reached out to someone to hold the formula for him. We did hear unconfirmed reports that as a failsafe, Jerry instructed his contact that if he is unable to pick up the formula then that person is to destroy it."

Carter points to his next message, 'Who has the formula?'

That must have sparked Everest's consciousness because she begins to shake her head, "I cannot tell you that because I do not know."

Carter holds the stone above her stomach. We watch the bulge pop up from her torso. It looks very gross and painful. I can now picture what a hernia looks like. I feel nauseous just looking at the image of what her insides must be going through. Everest yells out a gut-wrenching holler. It is not a high pitch tone. It sounds like what I imagine a death metal woman growling while giving birth may sound. Things like this I know I will never be able to forget.

Carter removes the stone and the yelling stops. Everest attempts to catch her breath. She is panting from the pain. Carter points to the same message as he finishes injecting more of the truth serum. Everest calms her breathing again. The serum must be affecting her. She answers, "I do not know! I just know that it must be someone he has identified with from the stash of comics in the bathroom outside the kitchen or the online chat rooms he often visited. We matched some of them up with a tent at Comic-Con. The plan to intercept will be in a few hours. We may take the entire tent staff depending on how big the group is."

Carter has another message. I try to ignore it, but he keeps tapping at the board. His message reads, 'What does the government want with the formula?' I have to admit. It is a legit question and one I never would have thought to ask. I relay the question to Everest.

She looks over at me with her eyes half awake and her face pale green again, "My division is responsible for understanding anomalies such as these requests. A common trait among the recent human genome is that of greed.

When man sees an opportunity to benefit himself, he will go to great lengths to acquire it. The request anomaly is one of these opportunities. Currently, humans view this anomaly as a symbol of hope and faith. There is money to be made now that people are observing this natural phenomenon when a someone dies. Now imagine if this anomaly is morbid and horrifying, the context changes to fear. People will fear death more than how they feared it prior to the requests. Corporations will capitalize on the opportunities to prolong the human life by utilizing elixirs and invasive surgeries. Businesses will also attempt to deny potential requests as the dying would not want a photo of their loved ones or a sentimental item taken to a place of fear. People will believe everyone will go to hell. Religious practitioners will utilize this information to promote their religion for recruitment. One religion battling over the others defending theirs is the one that will deliver them from evil and the vehicle for them to be accepted by their supreme being in the afterlife. A potential religious war may come from this issue. All this stemming from the reception or the perception of what is actually seen by the live feed on the other side of a request.

My division is entrusted with preventing this potentially worldwide, sociological catastrophe. The meaning of death has changed. And if that live feed is something we should fear then the meaning of death has a gruesome and hopeless meaning entirely different from what people are experiencing and feeling now."

Everest finally passes out. We all pause to digest her latest confession. It sounds logical if this change of events takes place.

But would the human species really make the other side of death a money-making machine? Well they already did it with the requests, so anything is possible. Carter removes the cable from Everest's mouth. He disassembles the contraption around her neck, head and places it all back in the black case. He leaves her in restraints and tapes her mouth shut. It does not matter. She is not waking up anytime soon. I am still upset about what just happened; I feel the last bit of innocence left in me has been stripped away, but I have to get my mind right. Comic-Con awaits.

Chapter 19

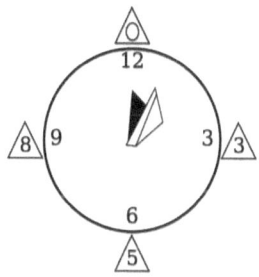

Sunday Late Morning

Here, again. I am not excited about this, but it beats being in that van with evil Carter and Everest. En route, Koonzo finally comes to and I do my best to recap what happened while he took 'his nap'. He then assured me the Comic-Con crowd would not be as thick as it normally is during the first three days of the convention. I am still apprehensive about the whole thing, but I have no choice. My goal is the same as Mrs. Bellows' and Carter's. We have to get that formula. My intentions remain the same; I only want to get it for the purpose of fulfilling my forced obligation to Mrs. Bellows so that I may go home.

What she really wants with the formula could be anyone's guess. But then again, Mrs. Bellows is not here to answer any of those questions. We do not even know if she is alive, but that does not seem to stop Carter's loyalty. And I figure Carter will ensure Mrs. Bellows' request will be upheld. That is why I have not made any attempt to escape. Now that I have seen Carter's dark side, I dare not ask their interest in the formula. I definitely do not want to give him the impression I might run. He already demonstrated not even the opposite sex will discourage him from taking brutal action.

We park on the street next to a bar in the Gaslamp district, at least that is what the arched sign reads. The convention center is across the street and trolly tracks. And here we are on a warm Sunday morning in sunny San Diego. Koonzo is right. The crowd is not as thick as before. We all get out of the van and stretch our bodies. It is quiet, and I appreciate how peaceful it feels. As I am closing my eyes and begin to take in the sun, Carter interrupts my peaceful thoughts and says, "So here is the play. We already have access into the convention center. But I am unable to get you and your friends inside. The Comic-Con staff is giving me a hard time about letting minors inside to assist with my investigation. Now that I hear myself say it, it does sound pretty ridiculous to recruit teens for such a mission. So, you guys have two options, you can either stay here or you can find your own way in. But remember, you all have to get back here before we leave. If not, then you run the risk of becoming our enemies and that would not be good for you guys." Carter gives us each a hard stare. I just want to find this formula and be done with these folks. I need to get home and see how my mom is doing, I just hope I get back in time...

I return Carter's stare and ask, "May I make a phone call to my mother before we begin?" I keep my tone simple and emotionless hoping he cannot see how badly I really want to talk to my mom. Carter is doing his best to interpret my request. He replies, "You get your phone call when I get the formula." His tone is unequally heartless. I do not reply but I do grit my teeth to the rejection. Carter continues, "Keep in mind, the government is or will be here. They know about the comic character and its tent. So, we will have to blend in with the crowd."

Cliffster and Sung-Suu break out laughing. Rilo asks, "You guys got a better idea?"

Koonzo chimes in, "You all look like stiffs. The tent staff will be on to you right away and the government spooks will identify you quite easily. However, they do not know who we are or what we look like. It would not be hard at all for us to walk up to that tent and see what is going on there. But if you have a better idea please go ahead and enlighten us."

Goji perfectly sounds off the conclusion beat. The nerds give each other high fives. It has been a while since I heard the conclusion beat. I actually have missed them. I am sure the goons are questioning themselves on what that was. As they look to each other for a counterpoint, I give Koonzo a wink. That was pretty clever and quick.

I can see Carter is desperately attempting to find a comeback as he turns his focus at Koonzo's face. But he has nothing, so he said, "Very well, you made this even easier for us and more consequential for you and your friends. The burden is now on you guys to get the formula. We will hang back and provide support in case the government folks get frisky. Plus, it will give us a better chance to see who is who inside the convention center."

Noni provides us with an unwelcomed conclusion beat. The nerds give him the stink eye. Anyway, I think Carter just flipped the script on us. I am telling you, Carter is no dull knife. This guy is good. Koonzo smirks at him and begins to walk off. We all follow suit. Carter and his guys begin to change so they can blend in a little more while concealing their weapons. These guys are ready for every scenario. They even have a container filled with additional clothing and accessories. The team picks out what they want. We do not bother waiting for them to finish so we ahead towards the convention center. And that is how I found myself at Comic-Con, again.

Luckily for my nerd friends, they still have their passes. I pull out Jerry's pass and lanyard and hang it around my neck like the rest of the guys do. Before we enter, Koonzo huddles us up, "Ok everyone, we all need to find the 9Lock tent and scrub each person there. Noni and Goji look around the convention center for potential cosplay characters milling about the place and see if they know what is up. And remember, the government agents will be here too. Act natural."

I have to laugh at that one, "I am sorry guys. But you have to admit that piece of instruction is funny." As I look around, none of them are laughing. I clarify, "Act natural? Here, at Comic-Con where nothing is really natural?!" They only give me blank stares, so I tell them, "Oh forget it. I thought it was funny."

Koonzo hands me some phony glasses and a hat he got from Carter's container, "Put these on. There is still the risk of you being identified." He is right. I totally forgot about the public eye.

Cliffster looks at Noni and Goji and says, "You guys better fix your faces, too." They do something weird with their hair and some weird paint for their eyes and their lips. They look like two freaks.

Koonzo puts his hand in the middle of our huddle. Sung-Suu asks, "What is that?"

Koonzo replies hesitantly, "This is where we break from our huddle."

Sung-Suu laughs, "Pfffff. We never have done that before and you know it, Koonzo! Stop showing off to Powa. You increase my odds of being her man every time you do that. Let us just bro hug it out like we always do. How about that?"

Sung-Suu winks at me knowing he is just teasing Koonzo. I wink back at him which Koonzo catches me doing. His face gets a little red. I can tell he misinterpreted my wink. Before I can say anything, Koonzo gestures with his arms wide open to bring it in. We all get close and hand out bear hugs and bro hugs. It almost feels like we are leaving on a trip and not coming back. In the beginning of our hugs, the feeling is euphoric. But it quickly turns melancholic as these embracements become longer and stronger. I do not understand why they are acting like that, but I do not let my not knowing disrupt this unusual emotion of theirs. A second round of hugs comes over us but this time each embrace lasts a little bit longer. The bro hugs went away and just bear hugs are all that is left

Even though we just gave each other meaningful and heartfelt embraces, we all walk side by side with confidence, after all, this is their turf. They feel at home here. Thankfully, no one is inspecting our passes. Koonzo informs me, "Since it is Sunday, the security becomes a little more lax."

I ask, "So what do we do now that we are inside?"

Koonzo tells me, "Once we find the tent, we will immerse ourselves with the tent staff. Find out what we can and then head back. Easy as that. Powa, you just hold back and see if you can spot the government peeps." We all give him the thumbs up. I have no issue with the plan, for once all I have to do is just chill.

After walking through the convention center, I realize the folks here on Sunday are just as weird (to me anyway) as all the other days. We reach an area that has strictly comic books. I ask, "I did not see this here the last time."

Goji replies, "A few years ago, the Comic-Con committee was confronted by the two big comic book giants. Their fans were upset about how the spirit of comic books has withered. These guys stood up and told Comic-Con that they have gone so mainstream that they forgot about their roots.

So the committee was convinced to add an entire section dedicated to nothing but comic books. But logistically they could only squeeze them in on Sunday. The other three days are booked with superstars."

I give him an 'Oh' face when Koonzo draws our attention to our objective. There it is. The tent with their staff members wearing yellow shirts. It matches the shirt Jerry was posing with in one of his pictures. The nerds keep walking as I head over to another booth to perch. I see them all engaging with the yellow shirts. A lot of nerd interaction. Nerds seem to give each other good vibes; I have not seen much bitterness around. I have to admit; these people are not a violent bunch.

We 'regular people' could take a page from their playbook. Oh, my goodness, I must be dead tired, here I am thinking about nerd behavior. I refocus on the group of nerds in front of me. So far, it does not look good. I see many of the yellow shirts shaking their heads as they answer questions from Koonzo and company. A man not too far off does not seem to fit in. Possibly an off-duty cop, if I could envision what an off duty cop looks like. He looks uptight and uncomfortable. His face gives it away as it looks stern and partially angry especially with those sunglasses. Now that I have something to go off, I can start looking for others. And sure enough, as I pan my eyes around, I see three more of them. None of them have focused on me, yet. So, I turn around and act like I am interested in what the booth next to me has to offer.

It is an unusual booth. The staff seems to be talking with spectators about the request. I find it a bit odd this type of tent would be here at Comic-Con but there are people here showing interest. One of the audience members asks, "What does the request have to do with Comic-Con? It seems out of place."

A staff member replies, "That depends on what topic of the request we are talking about. We are here to discuss these requests in relation to comic-books. Our company is developing the storyline for the comic. You see, in our comic series the request is just the beginning. A team of investigators will look into the history of the request and what elements may have led to the development or the initiation of the request. After all, everything has a beginning."

Another audience member asks another question, "The premise is very promising. If you are doing a storyline then what is the point of being here? I mean why not make the comic and then publish it?"

The staff replies with a lot of enthusiasm, "That is the beauty of it. We are soliciting writers and illustrators for an opportunity to work with us. A new hero and a villain will be developed by an undiscovered talent pool rather than using the conventional standards. And this scouting effort has never been done at Comic-Con before. Our investors find it very appealing."

The audience member replies, "It sounds like a long shot, but I think it might work. I hope the comic will be out in time for next year's Comic-Con."

I become distracted by another conversation. Two men are dressed up as a vampire and werewolf. The vampire has some white make up, slick back blond hair, and fake vampire teeth along with a red shirt that has 'Suicide Matters' in bold black letters and black pants. The werewolf has the mask and a long sleeve shirt with werewolf hair popping from the sleeves and neck and khaki shorts. Neither of them put much effort into their costumes but I am intrigued by the shirt.

Werewolf informs vampire, "I agree, suicide does matter. People should take it more seriously. I lost a friend to suicide a few weeks ago."

Vampire replies, "Oh no, that is not what this means. Suicide Matters means committing suicide is a life choice kind of like the abortion issue. Pro-life or pro-choice."

"What type of talk is this," I ask myself. Werewolf, just like me, keeps quiet as vampire dude keeps on, "You see these requests have made death a beautiful thing. You die, and you are granted permission to take something from this world into a new world as possibly a reminder of the world you left or just as a keepsake or who really knows."

Werewolf is visually upset as he crosses his arms and asks, "So are you promoting suicide?"

"I am promoting a beautiful death. The act of death, any type of death, should no longer have a negative connotation. All death is beautiful, and suicide should not be discriminated against anymore." Vampire dude had the audacity to say this with conviction.

Werewolf steps closer to vampire. He speaks in a stern voice like a father scolding a child, "Look pal, have you lost your freaking mind?! You must think this Suicide Matters movement is going to take off, but that is the dumbest thing I have ever seen and heard!"

Vampire guy remains quiet, but after a few seconds he replies, "Suicide is on the rise around the world, not just here. You want to know what else? Over 70% of their suicide letters talked about how happy they are for this moment. Not because their lives were pathetic and dismal. But rather how they looked forward to their new world. How they will be equally welcomed there as they were here on earth. And how their request will be used to spark new dialogue with other people on the other side. Suicide is no longer meant to be a bad thing. And those request marks on people's skin, that adds to this cause. When those suicidalists leave this world, they grant everyone a final opportunity to be marked... to be remembered."

Werewolf is breathing heavy as his chest rises and falls as he stares at him. Vampire must know that the classic showdown between these two may happen right here, right now. Werewolf finally speaks, "You are an idiot, a completely blind fool! You are twisting this phenomenon in a way that does not help anyone. Do you think when someone commits suicide it only affects that person?! No, it does not. Families are not celebrating when they hear one of their own committed suicide. That person's family is destroyed. Images of that suicidalist's future is taken away from them. Visions of a successful career and a beautiful family are obliterated. You think suicide is on the same level as the other types of death in this world, but it is not. There is a reason it is discriminated against. Because everyone associated with that suicidalists has failed. Which makes suicide a result of a combined lack of effort and concerted failures.

No vampire, you do not get to glorify suicide; for there is no glory in it at all. I will tell you what is left for the family and relatives: regret, remorse, anger, pain, mental torment, depression, a further fractured family, blame, broken dreams and lost hope. That suicidalist leaves nothing for the family to celebrate.

The world did not get better because he or she committed suicide. He or she was probably one of the few things keeping the fractured family together. So, do not tell me how you believe suicide is to be viewed as an act of beauty. Because I have plenty of stories to contradict that statement."

At this point, Werewolf is standing nose to nose with vampire. Werewolf is about six inches taller than his nemesis and his body looks like it is built for these types of confrontations.

It looks like he wants to start a fight, but at the last minute he changes his mind as he remains quiet. Vampire takes the silence as an opportunity to silently move away. But before Vampire is out of earshot Werewolf makes a final statement, "Just to let you know those request marks are not just from the requests of suicidalists. They are from everyday people who left someone behind."

As Werewolf walks away, I notice the back of his left calf has those request marks. Werewolf wins that battle. Good because I was rooting for him.

But I have a job to do. As I focus back away from this tent, I recall this odd conversation. How are people like Vampire thinking of this stuff? It is a selfish attempt to justify a desperate cry for help. But these folks want to politicize it as if it requires a campaign to be viewed as a legitimate viewpoint. I cannot stand behind that logic.

Chapter 20

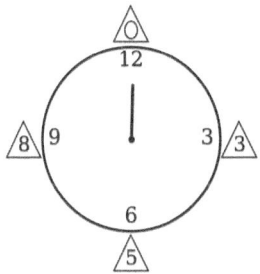

Sunday High Noon

Koonzo surprises me with a tug and grabs my hand, "We have to go."

As we start walking, I inquire, "What is going on? Did you find the guy?"

"No, we have not found him, but we know who he is. Do you want the good news or the bad news?" Koonzo asks.

I reply with, "Stop stalling and tell me what is going on."

We keep walking away from the yellow shirts when he tells me, "The good news is that the guy is here in the convention center and we have a description. The bad news is the convention center's security guards are looking for Noni and Goji. Those two got caught up in a conversation when one of them did their stupid conclusion beat. One of the security guards happened to hear it and recognized who they were. We need to find this yellow shirt guy quick. I told Noni and Goji to beat it, but they wanted to stay. They told me they want to maximize this opportunity for their web show Scratch Cat.

Plus, if they get caught they will draw all the attention and we can continue our search of our mystery guy.

As we speak, they are playing hide and seek with the guards. Now our guy is also wearing a yellow shirt. He is a little shorter than me, of middle eastern descent and has the matching accent. That is all we have to go on."

We are power stepping through the convention center looking around to find this character. I would rather run to help release the anxiety I am feeling but Koonzo's grip tells me he is dictating the pace. I hope the guards do not catch the twins. I like those guys.

Koonzo whispers in my ear, "Every couple of steps I want you to look back and see if we are being followed." I squeeze his hand in acknowledgement. How I miss my cellphone.

I whisper to Koonzo, "How do we let our guys know we found this person?"

Koonzo still scanning as we are walking says, "Whenever the two hours are up, we head back."

I look at him in disbelief and say, "If we get the formula in our hands within two hours, really? That is the plan?!"

Koonzo stops power walking and looks at me at eye level. He asks, "Do you have a better idea?"

I waste no time to reply, "Actually, I am hoping you have an alternative plan." His eyes ask the question, so I keep going, "I mean all this time we have been at someone else's mercy. They tell us where to go or what to do and we end up doing it. They dangle my mom's illness every time they are crunching for something. I say it is time we dangle a few carrots ourselves."

Koonzo's eyes shift from my face to the ground; I can tell his mind is on thinking mode. Several seconds later he says, "If we all meet up before reaching Carter and we have the formula, we will tell the rest of the group to not head for the vans. Once outside, we will negotiate our terms. Preferably in the presence of security cameras. What those terms are we can think of as we find this guy. One of them for sure is that you be released with a paid ticket home. I do not like the fact Mrs. Bellows dragged you into this."

I look at him and say nothing. His hero speech does give him bravado I did not think he possessed. But I do not tell him; I am hoping though that he can read it in my eyes. And from what I see, he is reading it exactly the way I want him to, I hope. But then I see his eyes shift slightly left, and I notice the look of surprise on his face. He tells me, "There he is. It has to be him." I look in the same direction and notice a middle eastern-looking guy wearing a yellow shirt guiding a young teenage girl to another room. And just like that we are on the prowl. Too bad. If there ever was a chance for him and me, it is once again gone.

We reach the door the yellow shirt went through. Koonzo slowly turns the knob. It is still unlocked. We walk through and notice a stack of chairs and folded tables. We continue our walk quietly. Is that kissing I hear? At a dead-end maze of chairs, we find our guy locking lips with a very pretty girl.

This guy looks pretty dang good; way better than any of Koonzo's friends. No offense to those guys but this guy is not a nerd at all. At least he does not look like one. From the hair to the suede shoes, he does look impressive. His eyes open midway through his French-kissing session and is startled he has been caught in the act. At first, he pushes the girl away, but once he realizes he did not get caught by security his shock turns to anger. He yells, "Hey, go find your own spot! This one is taken."

Koonzo somehow grows taller. He does his best to look bulky and says, "You there. I recommend you leave before things get really ugly. My girl here is an MMA coach and loves a fight. Plus, she has taught me a few tricks." I dare not look back at Koonzo. Instead, I roll up my sleeves and give a smirk as I fake my toughness. I better give my best acting performance because I have never been in a fight before. What would I do? What if she punches me in the face? She looks back at her kissing friend and then starts to walk towards me. Oh no, this is going to get ugly... for me. Koonzo, what did you get me into?!

The girl is a little taller than me. She asks, "An MMA coach, huh? You look a little young to be teaching anything and you do not seem to have the build for that type of aggressiveness." She is going to punch me right on the nose. I just know it. A broken nose on this face will be devastating. What do I do?!

Then I hear a faint yelp. We both look and see the yellow shirt guy in a rear naked choke. He is grasping at Koonzo's forearm that has a firm lock around his neck. Then Koonzo says, "Is this right coach?" Without hesitation I play along, "Push his head down some more." To my delight Koonzo does just that. Then for effect I point to the yellow shirt dude and say, "And if you want him to stop just tap your hand on his forearm so he knows you have given up." The poor guy just kept looking at me. Why stop the charade now, right? I go for the kill by telling Koonzo, "But if he tries to attack you then next time he taps just keep the pressure until he no longer taps. He will more than likely pass out or have a broken neck. But that is his problem." I can barely believe how convincing I sounded.

Koonzo pushes the yellow shirt guy's head down even more. The yellow shirt grunts even harder and quickly taps his forearm many times. Koonzo holds his grip and looks at the female spectator and says, "Coach, whatever you do, do not aim for her mouth. You are still paying for the dentist bill of the two boys you messed up last time. I still think the court should not have sent you to juvie." The girl looks back at me with an incredulous look of awe. She covers her mouth and runs off.

The quick taps are much slower on Koonzo's forearm. He realizes this and immediately releases the choke. The yellow shirt gasps for air while dropping to his knees. I give Koonzo a wink for his Oscar winning performance.

Koonzo picks up yellow shirt guy and gets straight to the point, "Where is the package Jerry gave you? We do not have much time." It takes a short while before he gets back to his senses. Once he comprehends the question, yellow shirt's expression is of denial as he looks away crossing his arms.

Koonzo becomes impatient, "I will wrap my arms around that scrawny neck of yours and ensure you are conscious for every ounce of pain. And then when you are passed out I will scalp the back of your head so that you have a permanent bald spot. Now tell me, where is it?"

I wave my hand in front of Koonzo to slow things down. I step in front of yellow shirt and ask, "What is your name? Mine is Agnes."

Yellow shirt guy is staring at Koonzo but replies, "Dedrick but I go by DeadRick." I smile and say, "DeadRick, I like it. It sounds hot. Hey, we need Jerry's package. He told us you are holding it for him."

DeadRick still massaging the pain on his neck says, "Well Agnes, I think you should give me a little credit. If you want something, then you have to give me something. Right now, I am going to take something. Is that fine with you, Agnes? But you look more like a Rachel, Karen or maybe a... Powa."

The jig is up. Dang it. I thought I was going to pull this off. DeadRick smiles and says, "Your face is all over the web.

Besides, I can look past your cheap disguise. Your request is the biggest talk of the town. You are lucky your boyfriend had me in a chokehold or I would have called out the BS MMA coach stuff. Too bad that girl is not up to date with what is happening all over the net or she would have made you out regardless of the bogus glasses and the hat. But I have to admit, that skit you two pulled was pretty quick and pretty clever."

Koonzo extends his hand. DeadRick reaches out and shakes his hand. Koonzo says, "Sorry about the neck, DeadRick."

He waves it off, "I get it. You guys want Jerry's package. Well here is the short story about that. I do not have it."

"What?! Did Jerry already pick it up? Tell me!" I shout at DeadRick.

Koonzo leans in closer to DeadRick, "Hey, we are on the same side! Same side." Koonzo grits his teeth and asks, "Tell us what happened."

DeadRick takes in a deep breath, "Look, every year during Comic-Con we meet up at a certain spot during the evening. Since there are diehard fans out there, we decide to get together and talk about the future of 9Lock. We know not everyone can pay for a trip to San Diego, so we set up a forum and chat rooms for our extended fans. A few Comic-Cons ago, a vrana introduces himself to our group."

I do not want to, but I have to stop him, so I ask, "Vrana?"

"Yea, in the comic series these are created creatures from…"

I stop him again, "It is a nerd definition. I got it. Move along please." I say in a prissy manner.

Koonzo interrupts, "May you get to the punchline? We have to move quickly, and we do not have time to get acquainted with the story of how you and Jerry became BFFs."

DeadRick looks over at Koonzo and says, "If that is the case then my story is done, and I am walking out. You can go ahead and choke me out again. This time I plan on not tapping. At least if I am passed out you cannot continue to badger me."

Good thing I am here, this situation requires the finesse of a lady. I put my hands gently on DeadRick's left arm, "We understand. You want to tell us the story. Please go on."

I give Koonzo the look to keep quiet and go with it. DeadRick continues, "Thank you, Powa. So, Jerry enters one of our meetings which is normally at a speakeasy but for teenagers. For our newcomers, we ask them to introduce themselves. I remember Jerry being the last one to speak. For a gentleman older than our average age of attendees, he seemed very timid. I took a personal liking to him only because I felt he was a very sheltered individual. In the end, no matter how much I tried to get him to come out with us he always flaked. But anyway, Thursday night he shows up again. He tells me he wants me to hold onto something for him. He has this blue and red plastic case. Jerry tells me to never open it because it is dangerous. Before I could ask anything else, he slips me a grand in cold cash. He looks at me and tells me not to ask any more questions. Before he leaves, he said he would pick it up on Sunday, today; and would give me $5000 when he gets his package back from me. So, of course I shut my mouth and took the money. As he is walking away, he tells me he will reach out Saturday night on a private chat to tell me what time Sunday he will arrive for his package."

Koonzo is getting anxious, this is some long story. He heads over to the door to see if anyone is coming. DeadRick keeps going with his long story, "So last night I am back at our speakeasy hanging with my crowd. I have my laptop open on our page monitoring the chat rooms. One of our regulars sits next to me and asks what I was up to. I tell her about Jerry and show her the blue and red case. She gets interested and convinces me to show it to her."

I have to understand, so I cannot help the interruption "Hold up, DeadRick. You said 'she.' Who is this girl?"

DeadRick says, "I never got her name. I have seen her at our meetings in past Comic-Cons. Our get-togethers get to be a little large at times, so I never had the chance to actually get to know her. Next thing I know, she tells me she needs to take the case with her. I tell her about the money, but she convinced me to let her hold onto it."

This is getting ridiculous, but I have to ask more questions, "How did she convince you to forego $5000?"

DeadRick smiles, "She told me there are more important and sensual things in life than money and leans over and kisses me right on the lips. I love peppermint lipstick. Oh man, she could have asked for all my passwords and even my ATM PIN number at that point. And that is how she romanced me into giving up the case." DeadRick still cheesing as his eyes stare beyond the ceiling replaying that entire scene again.

My next question, "What did she look like?"

DeadRick wastes no time to respond, "She has blonde hair, just like you, and a slightly thicker body than yours." I think he just called me skinny. I take the compliment and smile.

From the door Koonzo rushes over to us, "We have to go, now! The convention center guards just snatched up Noni and Goji. Time is up." He grabs my hand and pulls me with him.

DeadRick calls me out, "Powa?" I tug back against Koonzo's force and ask, "What DeadRick?!" He yells back, "She has a dragonfly above her collarbone. I can never forget that tattoo."

Koonzo does not waste time, "Stay close. We need to get back to the vans before these guys catch us. Right now, Carter looks like a good friend to have." We leave the room and head toward the escalators. I can hear Noni and Goji screaming. It is a good thing because they are creating that distraction for us as planned. Security rushes over along with several of the stiffs to assist with Noni and Goji. As we go down the escalators, we can see more government agents observing the commotion. There are at least seven of them. We head down the second set of escalators.

I say out loud, "Blonde hair." Koonzo has no idea what I am talking about, so he gives me an inquisitive look. I reply, "DeadRick said the girl has blonde hair like mine. Do you know any girls that have blonde hair?"

Koonzo responds, "No. Shaboomba is a brunette and our other friend is in Oregon. No way she would be here for this. She cannot afford to come out here."

Now I get curious, "Oh so you have another girl in your group? When were you going to bring her up?" He looks at me as if saying that is something I should not worry about. And you know what? He does not answer my question. Then I tell him, "She has a dragonfly tattoo on her collarbone. Those things are ugly. Who would get that on their body?"

Koonzo looks back at me and says, "Dragonfly?! Oh no, we have to find a way out of here and find Shaboomba." We start walking down the last escalators. Finally, we reach an underground parking garage. He is still tugging on my hand when he says, "We need to ditch Carter and get to a phone as soon as possible."

I am surprised to hear this, "What do you mean ditch Carter? Right now, he is the only one that will save us from getting caught. We need to get to the vans before they take off."

He keeps tugging away. I am trying to slow down his pace, but my body keeps getting yanked forward. I finally rip my hand away from his and stop in my tracks. "Come on! They will have the garage blocked off soon!" Exclaims a desperate Koonzo as his voice echoes throughout the concrete, shaded structure.

I am angry and concerned, "Carter is here to help me. I cannot walk away from that." I say the last part as my voice is beginning to break.

Koonzo walks up to me in a slower than expected speed, "Listen Powa, I know where we need to go. But I cannot tell you until we are clear from this place. Because if they catch us they will probably torture us until we tell them what they want. Just trust me, please."

My heart is beating so fast right now. I want to cry from frustration but that is not going to help the situation. Instead, I extend my hand. He grabs it and kisses it. It looks uncomfortable for him. This is probably due to a lack of experience. But the notion is very adorable. I raise my eyebrows in a pleasant surprise, "I was not expecting that."

Koonzo raises his head and says, "I actually thought that is why you put your hand out like that. Well I hope you liked the friendly gesture." I feel a little sad he did not do it out of his own free will, but my look of surprise seems to be masking that emotion.

We near the exit of the garage. It is bright outside. I can feel the heat. We get close to the edge of light and two men appear from the darkness. Our eyes must have been affected by the intense contrast of light and dark. I cannot tell if those men were standing there all this time and we walked right into them or if they came down the stairs and coincidentally saw us.

Either way, they are heading toward us. Ours eyes adjust. They are dressed like the stiffs we saw in the convention center. These government guys need to learn how to adapt to their surroundings. Koonzo pulls me in a little closer. We veer to the right of them. I would guess the opportunity to get away is higher in this direction. The stiffs match our course of action. Koonzo pulls hard and we sprint to the open light. I look to the left and see them sprinting towards us. One of them leaps and lands on me. I lose contact with Koonzo and fall on the cold garage floor. I can feel his gun on my back. He is heavy. I scrounge to get up, but he is able to wrap up my legs. The second stiff manages to pull me up by my armpits.

Koonzo yells, "Powa!" I watch him disappear into the light. One of the stiff radios in, "We got her. The boy confirmed who she is. Requesting pick up." I do not put up a struggle. These men have overpowered me physically and psychologically. I hear the sound of handcuffs clanging in the echo of the garage. Then I hear light footsteps. As one of them puts one cuff around my wrist, I hear a dense thud. Then the sound of a body falling makes me look over at its origin. It is one of the stiffs. The other one looks around to see who the culprit is. But he is too slow, another whack hits him. His body falls to the floor.

"Powa, get up. We need to get out of here!" He came back for me! I knew Koonzo would never leave me behind. He picks me up and we restart our trek to the outside of this garage. A car skids to a stop directly in front of us. We jump out of its way. Did that driver purposely try to hit us? We move to the left this time and the car door opens. Two men jump out and tackle Koonzo. We lose contact once again, but we all fall to the ground. Koonzo and I are the first ones to pop back on our feet. He looks back at me when I hear a loud bang. Koonzo falls immediately to the floor.

I run to him. His eyes are closed. I put my ear to his chest to hear his heartbeat. But I cannot concentrate. No, please, not Koonzo! My tears begin to flow almost immediately. I hear a female voice yell out, "My weapon is jammed!" She struggles with it.

Then he screams while his body automatically folds into the fetal position, "Arrh!

That is one hell of a slug!"

Thank you. He is still with me. Reality sets in quickly. I try to get him up, "Koonzo, we need to go! Get up!" Koonzo quickly grunts as he explains, "I cannot move. That shot got me in the wrong spot. Go find her and figure out what is going on. I will stall them. There is a piece of paper in my pocket that I was able to acquire. Put it in my hand and go." I grab the paper from his pocket and place it in his hand.

He tells me to go. I hesitate but the sound of the men getting up scares me into a sprint. As I start running while looking back, I see a woman dressed in what looks like a SWAT outfit step out of the car. She has a shotgun in her hands.

Koonzo yells, "Powa, comeback! Take the formula! Take the formula!" I stop for a second. Was that piece of paper the formula? I yell back, "Koonzo, why did you not give me the formula?! What have you done?" Koonzo remains still with a shocked look of regret. After about two seconds he yells back, "Get out of here! Get back home before it is too late!" The other two men have already jumped on Koonzo. I see him start to tear up the formula. The woman sees what he is doing and snatches the tattered paper. I run away. Every couple of steps I look back. Koonzo puts up a good struggle but all three of them restrain him and load him in the car. I see another car swerving to reach the point of commotion. Now I have to get moving before that car starts to hunt for me. After one last look at Koonzo, I pick up the pace and get lost in the city. What am I going to do now?

Chapter 21

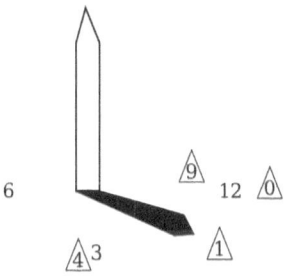

Sunday afternoon

Power stepping is what it is called. And that is exactly what I am nervously doing through the streets of downtown San Diego. I do not have to look back to know those government goons are after me.

The sweat dripping down my back is a reminder that I must remain evasive. However, the perspiration is starting to create armpit circles. The sweat glands on my face are working overtime, too. I got to do something about it. I talk to myself until I calm my rapid breathing, and by slowing my pace enough to let the San Diego breeze cool me down; I compose myself while remaining on the move. I dip into an open mall. I have never been to one of these malls before, but I have always heard of them. This particular one looks like a high-end mall. It has several floors of some ritzy shops. I do not bother going in any of them. Right now, stopping is not an option. As I step onto an escalator, I wonder, what am I to do next?

Finally, the emotions of what just happened catch up with me. Why would Koonzo hold on to the formula? Why did he not try to negotiate for our release? Maybe he just received the formula and did not have enough time tell me. My mind weaves in and out of multiple scenarios. I have to think of something else. How about home? I am done with San Diego. Not to take anything away from my nerd friends but I think this is a sign for me to just head back. I miss home. I want to leave but I do not have the cash to get there. If I get a plane ticket, I will surely get pinged. Same goes for the train. Best thing would be to hitchhike back home. And that goes against everything I was taught. But at this point what options do I have?

As I am thinking of what to do, I exit the fancy mall. These goons could be anywhere by now. Here is where I hear my dad's voice in my head. I remember him telling me that when there are no longer any options or decisions to be made, another piece of my destiny would be revealed. I really do not understand what he meant by that but right now I feel like all my options are gone. My mind switches to Koonzo's last words to me. He told me to find Shaboomba. Without a cellphone, my chances of connecting or finding her are extremely limited. The only place I could start is her home. But I do not know her address. What I do remember is a water tower and a tall tree. I also remember that I can see the cityscape from her deck. So, if I could see the city from there then that means I could probably see her house from here. Hmm. The first thing I must do is get to the top of an extremely tall building and then, well then what?

I am really hitting a lot of dead ends. As I look up to the partially clouded sky, I tell myself, "Come on, Nhim, hook a sister up." There is no sparkling light or supernatural anything leading me towards the right place to go. As I begin to feel a little more than desperate, I decide to get to the top of one of the skyscrapers and find out if I can see anything from there.

I keep on walking for at least three blocks. At this point, I am not sure of anything. Finally, I choose to head inside one of the tall structures. There is a security guard watching folks entering the building. From the middle of the lobby, I hear a woman screaming, "You better not keep all of that to yourself, Lincoln! We are all family! We all deserve it! Not just you!"

Another female voice joins in, "You are wealthy enough! We should not have to beg!"

The gentleman named Lincoln remains calm and replies, "Listen, first I will take care of father the way he would want it. Then I will settle any of his debts. After that, I will look into possibly distributing some of the funds. But if you continue to act this way, I will not entertain your request."

The poor guy was barely done with his passionate discourse when the two women leap on top of him with flying fists. They all fall to the floor. The funny thing is no one is pulling the scuffle apart.

One of the women yells out as she hammer-fists the bloodied man, "I am a good mother, a good sister, and a damn good woman! No way do I deserve to be treated this way, you dirt bag!"

Finally, the security guard decides to do something, and heads over to the middle of the lobby. It was now or never, "Thanks, Nhim." I say looking up. I manage to sneak into the elevator with a small group of teenagers that appear to be taking a tour. There is also a strapping young man already inside. He is a tall white gentleman who is definitely not young enough to be in high school still. He does not pay me any mind which, in this case, is good. This sure is a fancy elevator, there is a television playing a reality show.

The reality show was providing much needed distraction when all of the sudden the show was interrupted by some breaking news. The newscaster begins, "Law enforcement officials have busted a cult in the outskirts of the San Diego city limits who were providing illicit drugs to an array of people.

Interestingly enough the people found there were homeless, runaway kids, addicts, and many with mental disabilities. During the raid, officials found over 35-dead bodies. But the eerie part of all this is that the items found there have been modified. The items range from toys, photo albums, and random appliances like microwaves. All of the items were retrofitted with some type of explosive. What we may possibly be seeing are failed attempts to request these improvised explosive devices. From what we know, this is the first of such an attempt. We will have more details as the story unfolds." And with that the update ends and the reality show begins to play again.

My goodness this is madness. First the suicide conversation and now this? People are losing their minds.

The elevator reaches the seventh floor and the tour exits. This is when the gentleman looks over and realizes it is just the both of us in the elevator now. He says, "Looks like your floor request did not register, which floor are you?" I keep quiet as I did not expect to be asked anything. But I choose to ignore my anxiety and then reply, "The top floor, please."

He looks at me oddly, "Do you visit the building often?"

This question is just as odd as the one prior. What is he getting at? Did I mess something up? At this point, it can be anything, so I answer, "Of course, I work on the top floor."

The guy smirks at me and then says, "Well this elevator does not reach the top floor because the top floor is a maintenance floor. There are no office spaces up there. The maintenance elevator serves that purpose."

You know, being caught in a lie is the worst. But much worse than that is being caught while in an elevator. Nowhere to run. I take in a deep breath and slowly let it out. I decide to try the truth, "Look sir, I am not from around here. I am trying to get to my friend's house. I figured if I could get to the top floor I would be able to get a general sense of what direction I need to go."

The guy takes his finger away from the elevator control panel since it was hanging there waiting on a floor number from me.

After a few seconds he adjusts his glasses and says, "Unless your friend's house is downtown, you are not going to figure out where it is at. Here is my cellphone. Type in the address and you will know where to go." I take his phone but pause. I tell him, "I do not know the address." I say sheepishly.

"So how did you get to your friend's house the first time?"

Now I remember the conversation between Sung-Suu and Cliffster. They were talking about using landmarks. I begin to talk out loud, "Something about Cholas and Water." The guy interrupts, "Chollas Creek? I know where that is at. It is about a five-minute drive south from here." He types the name on his phone and shows it to me.

Then I remember the nerds talking about tracing a line eastward. I take the phone and do the same. I talk out loud once again, "I keep moving east until I find a landmark. I finally reach the green patch of grass that they were talking about. He leans over me and pushes a button, "Here is satellite mode. This might help you recognize the house.

And sure enough, I scroll around that area and see Shaboomba's house. I am certain because I could never forget such an impressively large deck. I am so happy I could cry, but that would not be helpful or appropriate right now. Instead I choose to say, "This is the place I need to reach."

He takes his phone back and says, "I got it."

At that point, the elevator bell rings. I did not realize we had gone back down to the first floor. He steps out and I follow. The commotion from earlier is nowhere to be seen. The guy says, "It appears the Jerry Springer like fight is over now. I can only imagine there are going to be many like that one from now on."

I ask him, "Do you know what that fight was about?"

He replies, "It is over someone's estate. They were about to have a meeting concerning their father's will." He told me.

"Oh, I hear those things can get quite ugly."

The guy replies, "Definitely. Those were his daughters and the son is a small-time business owner. Those poor ladies are stuck in the ghetto. But what makes this situation concerning is what the will dictated." This is where the guy decides to tell me the rest of the story.

A little bit of mystery, huh? I can use the distraction, "Please go on."

He looks at me first and then continues, "The father recently changed his will. Oddly enough, his will stated that if a photo of one of his children was requested then that person would get his estate."

I am in shock and almost immediately say, "No, he did not do that? Oh wow, it looks like his son is the winner then. What would happen if none of those photos were picked?" I have to ask as this is like nothing I have heard before.

"Then the estate gets split evenly. A lot more of these cases are going to start popping up as the dead continue to let their requests dictate to whom their inheritance is to be distributed to."

I add to his comment, "It is like they are using the request to announce which one of their family members they loved the most. I can see how people might get disappointed and angry with their loved ones if they feel these requests are signs of who is to be awarded the estate." I hear myself say those words and still cannot believe this is the world we are starting to live in.

"Yeah, let us hope this does not happen within our society. But then again, I doubt it."

The gentleman states.

"Because I am the son's attorney. I have two other cases just like this." He answers cautiously.

No way, this is nuts! The world is about to crush its own little heart. I walk out of the building not expecting him to escort me out. He did not give off the impression of being upset with my trespassing attempt.

I will forever be grateful for his assistance and that is when I hear, "Hello, Miss. Over here."

It is not the gentleman's voice. It sounds more authoritative. I am stunned. This guy did not just hail the cops, their security guard, or even those government folks because I went on their stupid elevator. I am really about to go off on this dirt bag if that is the case. I turn around thinking my run is over or should I just start running as if my life depended on it. Rather, I see the guy with a taxi behind him, "I will have the fare taken care of." He tells me.

I run over and give him a big hug, "Thank you, sir, for helping me." He smiles.

As he heads back into the building he tells me, "I hope you find your way back." My mind takes his statement an intellectual step deeper. I blurt out one last request, "Sir, may I borrow your cellphone one more time?"

Chapter 22

$$16:22 = 6.432$$

Sunday late afternoon

As I head to Shaboomba's house, I compose myself. After all, the ride there was not as bad as I thought it would be. But maybe that is because there is so much going on. I am sure it will hit me once I reach her house. After a twenty-minute ride, I arrive at my destination. I am hesitant to knock on the door. What are the odds that she will be home anyways? What will I do if she is not home? My goodness, if she is not home then I am going to knock door to door and will ask for a free ride to Klamath Falls.

I ring the doorbell hoping Shaboomba answers or for anyone to answer. Nothing. I knock a few more times. The same. I knock a little harder thinking she may be wearing her headphones. I am getting nothing. This is it! Game over. I am tapping out. She is not here. Her parents are not here. No one is here. What now? And I really do not want to knock on every single door asking or begging for a ride. I do not think I can even beg for a ride. But asking would be just the beginning. The worst would be when I tell them I have no money to offer for gas or accommodations. Screw this! I am heading around back to clear my head.

As I reach the large deck, I see those inviting lawn chairs I remember from before. I sit on one of them; the weather is perfectly cool, and the sun is fighting against the cool breeze. Somehow my body finds the most comfortable position as I close my eyes. I am close to dozing off when I hear a voice say, "How did you get here?"

The voice sounds familiar, but it still startles me. I pop out of the chair and concentrate on the voice. My eyes squint to focus and I realize it is Shaboomba! I rush to embrace her, "Shaboomba! It is so good to see a friendly face! You have pink short hair now. I like it."

She reciprocates my hug but not as enthusiastically. I can tell she is a little standoffish. We pull away and she asks me, "Where are the rest of them? No way you are the only one to make it out of Munch's house! What happened, Powa?"

I scale back my temporary jubilation and proceed to tell her, "They are fine, I think. Noni and Goji were caught by the Comic-Con security. Koonzo is in the custody of the government or the Bigs, I do not know which. Sung-Suu and Cliffster are the only ones I do not know about."

Shaboomba flails her hands in the air, "And you call that fine?!"

She is right, of course. If I heard a similar report, I would probably have the same reaction. I get closer to her and try to explain, "I am sorry. Things are not well. Koonzo sacrificed himself in order for me to get away. He even kept the formula with him, so they would not chase me, but that has thrown me off."

"What did he do? Take a bullet for you?" Before answering her questions, I look at her and notice she has a satchel over her shoulder and then say, "As a matter of fact, he pretty much did. It was one of those rubber bullets. It knocked the wind out of him. We discovered someone reached out to one of the 9Lock people before we did. When we confronted the person, he confessed he had handed over the case to a girl with a dragonfly tattoo. Koonzo said to find you after hearing that, so I made my way here. And now I am stuck at a crossroad. If Koonzo did have the formula, then the government now has it. So, what is the point of me trying to get the case? I feel as though I should just walk away." After saying that I head towards the rails that lead to the San Diego cityscape.

Shaboomba walks up next to me and says, "Listen, if Koonzo had the formula, I am sure he had a reason for holding on to it. But maybe that was just a decoy to draw their attention away from you."

I ask, "Why would you think that?" A tug on my shoulder makes me look in her direction. She pulls down her shirt to expose her left collarbone. There I see a pretty little dragonfly. It is the cutest thing ever. Then she opens her satchel to reveal the blue and red case. I do not know why but my anticipation gets caught in my throat and the words fail to leave my mouth. When I am finally able to speak I ask her, "That is it, huh?! Oh my goodness, my entire world revolves around this case. We have to ask for help. There is no way we can do this on our own." I can see Shaboomba has a question written all over her face.

I answer her question, "We need to ask someone that you may not agree with but is worth the risk." I grab her hand and begin to walk towards the house.

She withdraws, "Powa, DeadRick told me this guy of his has requested to meet up at the drop off place. He said he is willing to double the payment amount for the case. I can care less about this thing. Powa, I just want to wash my hands of it. Do you know I had to change my appearance several times since Munch's house? These guys have to know where I live if you were able to find me. I am scared they are going to come to my home or that they may hack into my life or my parent's life and steal all our money and then we become homeless. No, no, I cannot let that happen! I am going to give back the case."

I empathize with her reaction. All the things she said are realistic fears, but I have to slow things down, "Shaboomba, I know you are scared. But we cannot fall apart now. We are sharp enough to keep up with the smartest brains out there when we work together. Please believe, we have to work together if you want to return to your old life. We need to get some help. And DeadRick is not the help we need. If you give this case back to DeadRick then you are putting a life sentence on Koonzo. Noni and Goji will eventually be released since they are young minors. But Koonzo, who knows what those government goons will do to him. With the formula, I can negotiate his release."

Shaboomba replies cautiously, "What about your mother? Will you not negotiate to be freed from all this to go see her?"

I face the blue sky and bite my tongue to prevent me from crying and say instead, "I will deal with that issue when the time comes. Right now, the priority is to get Koonzo out of wherever they have him." Shaboomba closes up the satchel. This is not a good sign. I may have to fight her for it. This is not going to be fun or easy.

Shaboomba walks up to me with a stern look on her face. Here we go. Bam! I strike her in the face with a quick left cross! The punch lands on the right side of her chin. I hit her so hard her face turns from left to right. She does not fall but does stumble a few times. I cannot tell what is going to happen next. She slowly turns her face back towards me. I can see a line of blood coming out the right corner of her lips, but she does not bother wiping it off. I know I have awoken the dragon. This chick is pissed. She slowly walks towards me. What am I to do?

My eyes grow large with fear. She does not say anything. Is she mad? She has to be mad, but does she understand where I was coming from? I can tell this is going to hurt. I still have my guard up. She is almost directly in front of me when she grabs me quickly by the shoulders and forces my body to take a bow.

All I can do is grit my teeth and squish my eyes shut. Thud! I feel immense pain in my stomach as her knee impacts viciously into it. It feels much worse than a punch. I collapse to the floor, coughing uncontrollably. My eyes fill with pain and drenched tears. I fall over in the fetal position to protect myself from further attack.

In front of me, I see the satchel being lowered to the deck. Well I guess she is making herself comfortable now. I can anticipate the kicks to the ribs when Shaboomba squats down and says instead, "Idiot, I was going to hand you the satchel when you punched me! And here I thought I was high strung. No hard feelings, Powa. Just make sure next time when you punch someone, throw a flurry of punches. Not just one."

I feel completely embarrassed because I jumped the gun like that. I camouflage my embarrassment by exaggerating the pain still coming from my gut. She helps me up and immediately I hunch back over. Shaboomba grabs me by the shoulders and places the satchel around my neck. We walk inside. After a couple of minutes, I tell her, "I have no way to reach them, but I know where they might find us. We just need some wheels." Shaboomba gives me a smirk as if telling me wait till you see our wheels.

Chapter 23

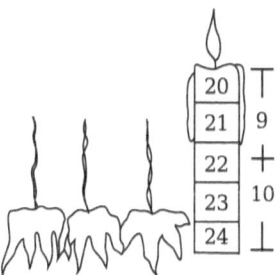

Sunday dusk

I do not know if I was more afraid or thrilled by what just happened. What I do know is that we are back at Mrs. Bellows' house of shambles. The ride took a lot longer than I thought. Luckily, I remembered the landmarks that led me to this place. However, I could tell Shaboomba was losing her patience with me as I kept having to change directions. But hey, the ride was not easy for me either. Having to yell over her loud dirt bike did not help.

The withering smoke coming from the house is still present as evidence of the battle this house experienced. But what I cannot understand is how not even a single emergency vehicle has responded to this place yet. How is that possible? Are the Bigs this powerful? Or is the government able to intervene even in such fancy and luxurious neighborhoods?

We take off our helmets. I look at Shaboomba's expression. It is the same as mine when I first saw the destruction. She looks around and asks, "Why are we here? Are we going to start rummaging through that rubble?"

My hope was that Carter would be here for some unknown reason. Now that I am thinking about it, there really is no reason for Carter to come back. If there is a time to feel hopeless again the time is definitely now. The wind has left my sails. I am at a complete loss. What can I do? There is nothing here. I mean if anything, the government probably still have their goons around here. Well maybe not here but probably back at the nearby shed where...

"Put on your helmet, Shaboomba. We have someplace to go." She looks over at me and I can tell she is hoping I do not take her on another blind road trip. I ignore her likely thoughts, so I can keep my mind clear and find the little shed. We mount up and go on a short ride. I tell her to keep the engine noise as low as possible. I do not think she heard me. We park the bike in a hidden spot behind some brush. After a five-minute walk to the house with the shed, we look around to see if there are any people around. The area is clear. No cars, either. I search for the hidden little truck. After several minutes, I find the little green RC truck underneath a bush. I pick it up to examine if it still has power. Shaboomba comes over to see what I am doing, and I tell her my objective. She takes the truck from my hands and removes the undercarriage. We see a nice bright red light glowing off our faces. I know exactly what that means as I smile.

Shaboomba recognizes that she found what I was searching for and replaces the panel. She asks me, "Now what, Powa?"

"Well, all I can think of is to stare into this camera and hope they can see us. It is all I have left in my magic hat."

Shaboomba does not look impressed by the thought, "You must understand this radio control truck may only have a short transmission range. They may never receive our feed. But we can take this to my friend's place to see if he can pinpoint the reception point. Something about matching frequencies. Of course, that possibility is only a viable chance if your friends still have their controller on and that my friend is able to search for this type of frequency. We got a lot of uncertainty here, but it is a much better option than just sitting here staring into a lens that may lead us nowhere."

I think about that for a second and come up with, "Hey if anything, we can take the truck with us while I am making faces at it trying to get someone's attention. Ok, time to boogie." Shaboomba rolls her eyes for whatever reason. I do not bother asking. We ride off into the early night. I hope this is the last time we see this place. This entire area gives me the creeps no matter how rich these people are.

Chapter 24

Sunday twilight

We finally reach our destination after about a 30-minute ride. It is dark out, but the night is still vibrant as the summer season keeps people on the streets. Oh, and my brilliant idea about making faces to this little truck did not work. Nope it sure did not, considering I am wearing a full face helmet. The way Shaboomba rides, I have to use both my hands to hold on. So, I had no choice but to sandwich the little truck between the both of us. I take off my helmet and look around. It does not look shanty, but it is nothing like Mrs. Bellows' neighborhood either, that is for sure. Then again, it is dark so maybe some of the beauty is concealed in the darkness.

I hear her voice both whisper yell at me, "Hey, move it!" Shaboomba is at an open gate that seems to lead to a backyard. I leave my helmet on the rear-view mirror of the bike and speed walk while ducking my head making myself even more suspicious in the dark. I do not know why I just did that. Once I went through the gate, I can see that the back of the house looks more appealing than the front. The yard is manicured and the bench swing as well as the love seats add a swanky touch to the place. The flowerbeds also add to the peaceful vibes.

Shaboomba gets to the door and performs a familiar knock. These nerds are engrained in their secret society lifestyle. I have to ask, "Why do you all have to have a secret knock? It is not like visitors make a habit of knocking on your back door, or do they?"

Before she could answer me, the back door opens. It is a little pudgy white kid who is probably about six-years old wearing pajamas. I look at Shaboomba with the 'How is this little kid supposed to help us' face. The kid turns around and waves us to follow him. We walk in and see a home that matches the swankiness in the backyard. It is well kept and clean.

The little kid leads us into a bedroom and there I see a taller version of the little kid. He has a few more freckles and is skinnier. His room looks like the front yard; cluttered but not messy. If that makes any sense. He has his action figures on a dresser re-enacting a battle scene and Japanese anime posters everywhere. Some of them are quite exquisite while others were borderline inappropriate.

He stands up and approaches Shaboomba and says, "Hey there girl! You cannot get enough of me, huh?"

She looks over at me with a guilty smile and makes the introductions, "Powa, this is Mack. He is a close friend."

Mack comes over and hugs me as if I were royalty, "Oh my goodness, it is you. Ms. Powa, we talk about you every single day, all day long. You are the reason so many of us want to learn more."

It is an odd introduction but still I reply, "Thank you but I really did nothing special. I also make for a sorry ambassador of education."

Mack releases me from the short-lived bear hug and stands at the edge of my personal bubble, "The video you shot of your friend's request is making people go nuts about the potential mysteries beyond this realm. You have the news reporting about it. Talk shows and radio shows keep bringing it up. The web will not shut up about it. Professionals and amateurs alike have picked apart your video and are still confused and lost." Finally, he finishes his passionate discourse.

"I am sick and tired of everyone making a big deal about the request, Mack! When will people understand, I lost my little friend!" I notice my right index finger is close to jabbing his eye out. My other hand is clenched awaiting any form of retaliation.

Mack puts up his hands as if saying he did not intend to offend me, "I am simply stating what the rest of the world, not just California or this nation, but the entire globe is saying. This is better than them doubting your video and just calling you nasty names." My eyes focus away from Mack and onto something else as I envision the entire world looking at my video at the same time. That is a powerful image.

Shaboomba steps in the middle of the both of us and says, "We need your help, Mack. We need you to trace the freq of this little truck."

I pull the truck out on cue and hand it to him. He says, "Sure. But keep in mind if the main console for this thing is offline then there is nothing I can do."

Shaboomba replies, "I have confidence in you. Do your voodoo." Mack gives her a wink, takes a seat at his desk and goes to work.

He powers up a device and hooks up some electrodes to the truck. Mack starts to take it apart. I kind of wish he did not do that because this little truck has some sentimental value for me. At this point, sentimental value needs to take a backseat. Plus, Mack is able to take the top layer away rather quickly. He punches a few keys on his keyboard and grumbles as he keeps digging into the unrecognizable little machine. Mack uncovers the plastic panel Shaboomba discovered back at the shed. The red light is still on.

Mack looks at another one of his devices, "Well ladies, we are in luck. There is a device receiving these images. I am going to use one of my homemade tricks to see if I can pinpoint the reception point." He delves back into the truck and comes back with another remark, "Now this little thing is interesting. It is also emitting a frequency. Do you guys have any idea what this may be?" He turns around and holds up this dark pill. Wait a second. That looks like the pill Mrs. Bellows made me swallow. Carter had that thing ditched at the shed. I saw them dump it off before the little truck went into its cubby hole. So how did it manage to get back into the little truck? I do not understand. I hear tires screeching to a halt out front. The rays of the headlights from outside indicate something is going to happen. I go to the front to peek at these visitors.

Shaboomba tells Mack, "Find the signals for both. Hurry, Mack!" He replies with a statement that sounds confusing even to himself, "I already found them. Both reception points are here."

Wait, what? I get a little nervous from hearing that and ask, "Was it here all along?"

"No, the signals cleared as soon as the headlights showed up," states Mack as he begins to register what may be happening. I peak through the edge of the living room blinds. The headlights prevent me from seeing who they are. All of a sudden there is a knock on the door. Right now, I wish it was one of those nerd knocks. The silence makes everyone even more nervous, and then we hear more knocking. We dare not move.

"Powa, we know you are in there. We saw your ugly mug on the controller."

I run to the door and open it, "Sung-Suu?!" Shaboomba jumps in front of me and jumps on him with a powerful hug and a kiss on his cheek, "Sung-Suu, you had all of us scared to death! I freaking missed you!"

Sung-Suu's eyes grow wide with surprise, "Oh dang! What about Cliffster? Will he get mad?"

Shaboomba smacks him on the face, "Shut up!" As I laugh, I turn to hug this nerd with such force I feel I could break his neck.

Sung-Suu finally replies with a little whisper of a voice, "Ok, Powa, ok. You can stop with the brutal greetings."

I hug him a little more and ask, "What are you doing knocking on the front door? I thought you would come around back. And why would you not use one of your nerd knocks?"

Sung-Suu looks around the house, "I told Carter you would be more receptive to opening the door if you saw a good-looking and friendly face."

Three silhouettes cover the light shining on Sung-Suu's back. They come closer, "We need to go before we are made." I recognized his voice immediately.

"Carter, you guys came back for us," as I walk up and hug him for making such an effort to come get us. I am even glad to see his two guards behind him.

He replies, "Grab all your things. We need to get moving."

His abrupt response interrupted my warm welcome, but I understand the urgency. We all start to collect our things. I did not have anything but the little truck and the satchel.

I look back at Carter and ask, "Why did you put the pill back in the truck? What was the point in that?"

Carter's face tilts like a dog trying to understand its command, "What pill?" Mack comes up and shows him, "This pill right here. We found it inside the truck. Carter grabs the pill and examines it. His face went from stone cold to surprised.

Mack further explains, "Yea, I was able to register both your frequencies to our location."

Almost immediately Carter pulls out his weapon and tells me, "You better get all your friends out of here now!"

"What is going on, Carter?" My intuition screams for attention.

He looks at me and says, "We dropped this tracker towards the shed, remember? If you found this on the truck, then that can only mean the folks at the shed placed the tracker on the truck. Not us."

Mack replies, "Yea but if both signals are pointing back to here then that means…"

Boom!

A large explosion takes down the entire rear facing wall of Mack's house. How that happened I could not tell you. Then a flood of flashlights begin to enter the house. The odd thing is there is no shouting coming from those flashlights. Normally a string of barking orders proceeds a large invasion. But the flashlights are only accompanied by the scuffing of boots. Do not get it twisted, it is still frightening. We all rush to the front of the house where friendlier lights await us. The dining room seems to be the area left to take refuge in.

Two of Carter's guards inside the house point their machine guns to the flashlights. Those flashlights do not proceed any closer. Carter looks at his vans. His men are at the ready but there is a problem; he recalls what Mack told him a short while ago, "Both frequencies are tracked back here and showed up the same time we did." So that must mean someone on my team is a traitor.

Carter calls out to his team behind the headlights, "Rilo?" A voice from the other side says, "Yea, boss."

Carter barks, "Who is the newest person on the team?"

"Augustus got to us two years ago. He is the newest bum on the block. Why?" Responded Rilo.

Carter tells himself, "Augustus has been with us too long to flip."

"You need us to come in there, boss?" Then from behind Rilo, another set of headlights turn on. They are much brighter and many more of them.

Carter's guards quickly face about. None of us can see these people because their headlights just make us squint.

A voice from behind them calls out, "Mr. Carter, am I correct?" The voice sounds foreign like the person could be from Europe or something.

Carter speaks up, "Who wants to know?"

The voice replies, "We have a common enemy. The government is trying to stop both of our advancements. I would like to offer you a truce."

Carter looks back at me. I show him the blue and red case and mouth the word '1X.'

He registers to me, "Good. We hold the lottery ticket."

I squeeze the strap a little tighter. Carter exits the house and walks towards the voice and shouts back, "Which government are you referring to? And what truce are we talking about?"

"You know the answers to your questions, Mr. Carter. We should talk more about the details."

Carter steps towards his van as I keep cloaked behind him. As he reaches his van he whispers to Rilo, "Smoke check them all if these guys turn me into a redhead."

Rilo replies while still locked in on the headlights, "But I like redheads, boss."

Carter holsters his weapon. I figure if they want him or all of us dead then they can pretty much do it at any time. I wait next to Rilo. I fear for Carter's safety; I know he has not been the best role model, but he has a great way of showing up as a dark hero at just the right time.

Carter reaches the headlights and asks, "What can I do for you, sir?"

The voice calmly replies, "We would like the girl, Powa, for obvious reasons."

Carter stops the voice, "No deal but you already knew I would say that. How about we start with two basic things, your face and your name?"

The voice softly yet surprisingly replies, "My apologies. That is rude of me. My name is Rutherford. I am a representative of HyphenDash." Rutherford steps into a beam of light. He has a dark complexion. I would say African American but that would be incorrect going by his accent. African European or possibly African, maybe. Either way, he looks young, possibly in his early thirties. He is a little hefty in the mid section, but I can tell he is strong by his neck muscles. I am sure he also knows self-defense and other tactical skills like Carter. Oddly enough, he is wearing a suit with what looks like expensive dress shoes. But I am distracted by his request.

Carter says, "HyphenDash has you chasing little girls, huh?"

Rutherford comes back with, "Well actually she was already in our custody when you rudely interrupted our little experiment with Pendleton, remember? I am proposing a compromise. If you hand us the girl we will release everyone we have captured. Oh and Ms. Powa, that includes Noni and Goji."

"So you were the guy behind that sinister looking hospital. I was wondering when we were going to see you again." Carter said, wondering how come Powa did not recognize the guy or the name from before.

Now I remember, I knew his voice and face looked familiar to me. I must be more traumatized than I thought if I am able to block evil people from my memory. In my defense though, I can barely keep up with all these Bigs.

And another thing, how could they take custody of two minors from the convention center security? This is not good.

Rutherford addresses me, "I see by the expression on your face you comprehend how serious HyphenDash is about getting what it wants. But I also want to express how compassionate we are with you. If you come with us willingly, we will get you in touch with your family. I know your mother is in dire straits right now."

There I go again getting pissed off about these jokers using my mother to control me. This guy is no different and wants to use my mother as bait. I am beginning to not like him.

Carter sounds off before I get my chance at him, "If we do this, we need to see if they are alive. We are not going to make a sucker's trade."

Rutherford replies, "Naturally. Because HyphenDash likes to keep a low profile of its facilities, you may either ride with us or we hitch your vans to ours."

Carter replies, "We keep our weapons and ammo."

Rutherford's response surprises me, "If that will move things along then yes."

Carter walks back to the van and says, "What do you think?"

Rilo replies, "Well it is…"

"I was asking Powa. She is the one they want."

Beyond Rilo, I can see Cliffster sitting in the front passenger seat. He sends me a comforting smile with a cute little wave trying to disguise his fear of the people behind the headlights.

Carter leans in and redirects my focus, "Hey you, over here. What are you thinking? If you go with them then you sacrifice yourself for those prisoners. But if you stay, then you sacrifice us to include yourself because it is going to get really bloody. Besides, who lets the enemy walk in their facility with their weapons? These guys must have some serious firepower and bulletproof walls not to worry about a potential fire fight."

Well thank you for no sugar coating it, Carter. I tell him, "I do not want to do it. But I also do not want to see more people die just so I can protect myself. I just do not want to be alone in there."

"You bring up a good point. Remind me to tell Rutherford that. I think we will work out that detail."

I ask, "Why not ask them to provide a live feed of the prisoners?"

Rilo answers before Carter can even respond, "You cannot trust it. If these guys are as good as they sound they would have already prerecorded them and then slap a 'Live Fee' logo on it. Meanwhile, the guys could have been dead for over a day." I must admit, it is a scenario I would not have entertained. Carter's guys are very good indeed.

Chapter 25

1	2	3	4	5	6	7	8	9	10	11	12	13	14	15	16	17	18
1 2	4 3 1 3	8 8 1 5	6 5 1 5	7 2 1 2	4 1 1 1	8 1 1 1	0 8 1 8	4 4 1 4	0 0 1 0	4 1 1 1	8 5 1 5	0 2 1 2	7 3 1 3	7 5 1 5	6 6 1 6	5 9 1 9	5 9 1 9 0 0 1 0

19	20	21	22	23	24	25	26	27	28	29	30	31	32	33	34	35	36	37

Still twilight

C arter tells Rutherford, "Time to get hitched."

He looks at his vans and says, "Hey team, Bravo Foxtrot. Do it right. Guide their trucks for link up and then jump in. Kids get in that van over there."

Carter points to a different van than the one I have been riding in. I do not think about it too much, but it does not seem like Carter has a plan cooked up, but one thing is for sure; we are heading into unchartered waters. Carter knows how difficult it was to extract Mrs. Bellows' brother out of the makeshift hospital. And Rutherford, more than likely wants to go another round and finish up what they started when we got away. They will be more than prepared for whatever we may bring them. But there is nothing we can do right now.

We all head inside the same van when Rutherford stops us, "Hey, that little one is not going with you. He will go in one of our vehicles and we will reunite him with his parents."

The pudgy little boy hides behind his brother. Mack replies, "He is not going anywhere."

Rutherford, "Then no deal."

Carter comes over to Mack, "Give them the kid so we can get this over with."

Mack gives him the gas face, "I will not do such a thing. My little brother going alone with those guys?! I do no think so."

Carter yells over to Rutherford, "The little kid and his older brother will go."

Rutherford, "Done. Can we speed this up, please?" Mack glares at Carter for making the call without his consent. Carter looks back confident Mack will not do anything. The little boy grabs Mack's hand and they step into one of Rutherford's vehicles.

I grab Shaboomba's hand and tell her, "It is better than having them with us, especially that little kid. We are old enough to take care of ourselves, Shaboomba. The last thing we need is to have that little kid screaming for his mom. Let it go."

Shaboomba stares hard at me while taking her seat, "I doubt they will bring them back home." She crosses her arms and looks at the vehicle Mack and his little brother entered.

Rilo shuts the sliding door to our van and hops in the driver seat. The inside of the van is quiet because no one knows what to make of the situation. Finally, Cliffster asks, "And what happens after they let us go?"

The question gets me thinking, too. Shaboomba beats me to the punch with convincing sarcasm, "We go home, stupid. They will just open the door and leave us alone. What do you mean 'What happens afterwards?"

Cliffster clarifies, "Not us, but the rest of the world? If this company figures out how the dying can hone in on a particular request, then they get a first-hand look at what the other side really is. With that information they could influence how people feel about death. Let me ask you this. Do you want to think of death as a fearful place that you will enter after serving your time as a good person on earth?"

Sung-Suu interrupts, "Cliffster, no one wants death to be a transition to hell. People are going to want to live a worthy life. I get what you are saying. If we find out that after death is hell, then this world will be crushed by the false hopes given by every religion. That will not happen. She will not let that happen." Sung-Suu looks straight at me.

As if my current stress meter was not high enough, I look away and think about what those two just said. It is a frightening thought if my mother was dying and all she thought about was her soul going to hell no matter how good of a human she was here on earth. Oh man, this is really going to mess with my head.

I can hear the metal grind against each other as the ball and hitch find the perfect path to finally mate. I can tell these guys have done this before, how many vehicles have they hitched together under the same circumstances? What happened to the other hostages, did they make it back home? I do not even want to think about that right now.

Rilo and Carter enter our van. Carter shoves Cliffster out of the front passenger seat. Cliffster takes a seat next to Shaboomba in the second row. She gives him a hard look like their past is still an open wound. Poor Cliffster quickly looks to the front acting like there is something more interesting to pay attention to. I am in the third row and scan the van. This one seems to be more spacious than the other ones even with the flat screens mounted on the walls.

The surveillance cameras are on. One of them catches my eye. It is focused on the house. I can see several of Rutherford's guards doing something inside. Then out of nowhere, the screen goes black. I look at the other screens and they all go black too. I can hear what it is. The noise makes its way to the front. A black tarp covers the windshield from the world.

An overwhelming sensation of fear gravitates me closer to Sung-Suu sitting next to me. He asks, "Does anyone else feel this was a bad idea?" No one answers, not even Carter. But I would guess this feeling is shared among everyone as the tarp anchors to the undercarriage. Then I hear an ultra-high-pitched noise like that of an old disposable camera flash recharging itself. And just like that all the lights turn off. It is pitch black in here. I mean I see nothing. No reflections of light nor a glimpse of it from the outside.

Cliffster chuckles, "So this is what sleeping in Sung-Suu's mom's room feels like." It is a funny comment, but we are too scared to laugh. Rilo goes to start the engine but the van remains silent. Not even the dashboard lights respond.

Carter breaks the silence, "These guys are good. They used an EMP (electromagnetic pulse) to knock out all our electronics. This transaction is going to be a chess match for sure."

We hear a knock on the window and a voice on the other side of the tarp, "Make sure the emergency brake is disengaged and put the van in neutral."

We hear their engines turn on. After several minutes, our modified convoy begins to move. I hear the glove compartment open along with several snaps like someone is breaking a twig off a branch. Some shaking takes place and I turn my blinded eyes toward the noise. From the dark I begin to see colors of green, orange, and white. Glow sticks! Always good to have those things around.

Yea, Carter is one well-prepared professional. Then he breaks out a doodle board and writes something on it.

Shaboomba begins to ask, "What are you writing, Carter?"

He looks over at us, "How about you and all your lame duck friends shut your trap. I am making out my will. So shut up already!"

We all raise our eyebrows to that demand. Has Carter gone cold on us? Is he admitting defeat? He looks at us and puts his index finger in front of his lips and gives us the signal to remain quiet. He finishes writing on the doodle board. It reads, 'If I were these guys, I would have placed a bug on the outside of the van just to hear what we are saying. If you want to talk then talk about anything else other than the formula or how we are going to get out of here. Talk about being afraid, needing to use the restroom, feeling sick, etc. But do not start talking right now. I do not want to hear your voices just yet.'

I switch seats with Cliffster and make the gesture to use the doodle board. I write the question, "What happened to Everest?"

Carter frowns as he scribbles, 'I left her back at Mrs. Bellows' place. We got pulled over once we left the convention center. She somehow got one of her legs loose and banged on the van wall. Would not have been an issue had there not been a squad car right next to us at a traffic light.'

I finish reading it and stick my hand out to take back the doodle board. But Carter flips it back around and erases it. He begins to write some more. I guess there is more to this story. He writes, 'So we are pulled over. As the cop is walking up to the driver's window, I went to the back to do something about Everest. I could not kill her with the cop right outside. She signals me to remove the tape from her mouth. As I replaced my hand with the tape, she informed me to let her make one phone call in order to call off the cop. In exchange, she demanded to be released. I was hesitant, so I refused. She banged on the van wall again. The cop gets freaked out and requests Rilo to get out of the van. At this point, I have no other choice. Either the gig is up, or I take a chance and let her make the phone call.'

Carter erases the doodle to make more room. He continues, 'I pull out my phone as she gives me the number. I put the phone up to her ear. She tells the other end to have the police officer that has pulled over a van in downtown San Diego near the convention center to disregard that van, immediately. She provides some special numerical code. The cop stopped talking almost immediately. I can hear him trying to plead his case on the other side of the radio and then goes quiet again. He tells Rilo to get back in the van as the police officer returns to his squad car. Once Rilo began to drive off, she told me to remove the battery on my cellphone and to ditch the phone. I was going to do that anyway but her telling me so proved she was doing her best to stay on my good side.'

Carter erases the board and starts to write again, 'She requested to be dropped off at Mrs. Bellows' house and told me her people would pick her up from there. I am sure she just said that so she could be released.'

Can it be? No way, Carter looks like he feels bad for making that decision. He finally hands me the doodle board.

I write, 'So why do you look like that? Like you made a mistake?'

His reply, 'Because it was a mistake. I went from having just one adversary to having two. And this one is going to have a bad chip on her shoulder. I know this will come back to me and bite me you know where.'

I write, 'I get it, Carter. You are getting soft in your old age.' I crack a smile hoping it would lighten his mood. It backfires. He snatches the doodle board from my hand and throws it on the dashboard. Yup, I pissed him off. He moves past me to the rear of the van and starts dismantling the rear right panel. My nerd friends' eyes are blazing into me as if telling me to not piss Carter off anymore. Behind the panel is a little compartment. He takes out a screw driver and a can of paint. I do not know how this will help but I do not dare ask any questions.

Carter begins to remove the carpet from his little area. He seems to be searching for something. The creepy silence in the van keeps us from asking Carter more questions. We dare not allow ourselves to interrupt his plan. He finds what he is looking for at the corner of the van. It is another panel. Carter unscrews it and exposes the undercarriage. I can hear the roaring of the tires on the pavement along with the thrashing of the tarp.

The outside air is making its way to us. It is still night time. I can tell by the crispness of the air even though it is mixed with the smog from the vehicle towing us. I cannot see all the way through because of where I am sitting but I would imagine Carter's view is limited to only the road. The open space is too small for any of us to crawl through. And even if one of us did, we could not just jump off. The cars behind us would run us over. Carter uses the screwdriver to pop off the lid on the can. The van shakes due to the road conditions which allows for some of the purple liquid inside the can to spill over. I want to ask so badly right now. He pours a small portion of it down the open space. He waits a few seconds and pours a little more. He repeats this.

After several minutes, I think I figure out what he is doing. I go in and take the can away from him. He gets it. He moves out of the way and I take his spot. He motions with his index and thumb to use a little bit. I look inside the can. It is still mostly full. Who knows how long this drive will take; I have to make it last. Carter goes back to the front and just like that I become the owner of this little mission.

It feels like two hours have gone by. All four of us have been taking turns pouring this stuff through the little hole Carter found. I feel a little tired; maybe it is from the complete darkness we have been cocooned in. It is my turn again and I realize we are almost out of this paint.

I get Shaboomba's attention who is asleep and signal for her to get Carter. He comes over and sees my dilemma. Carter's face tells me that he is about out of tricks. He puts up one hand signaling me to stop.

He grabs the doodle board and writes, 'Only dribble a small amount of paint when we turn. If we run out, then we run out. It is all we can do for now.'

The message gives me the impression Carter is being outsmarted. He tries not to show any emotion about it, but I can feel it. Even Rilo appears nervous seeing Carter this way. Cliffster decides to take over. I show him the doodle message and I take a seat to relax myself. What have we gotten ourselves into with these folks? The fear I was feeling before comes back. Bad idea, I should have stayed pouring the paint.

I look back at Cliffster and see he is zoning out. I guess it is taking his mind off everything we are going through. I do not attempt to take back my paint dumping job. Shaboomba is awake and now sits quietly. Her mind is on her friend, lover, or whatever you want to call him. Sung-Suu has fallen asleep. We all poke him every time we hear him snore. I think about the formula and my family. I tilt my head back and thankfully my brain decides to go blank.

Chapter 26

Monday early morning

Iwake up to the sound of an electric gate opening; I can only tell from the humming of the motor because I do not hear any squeaking or squealing of any moving parts. This place must be high end because even the electric gates are topnotch. The convoy stops briefly and then we are back to forward motion. The gate we passed through must also have one of those concrete barriers that are staggered to prevent anyone from driving straight through without proper clearance. I can tell because our bodies swayed gently side to side as we passed it. My nap was quick and uncomfortable. I look back and notice Shaboomba had taken over the paint task. I can tell by her purple fingers. She has fallen asleep but not before using up all the remaining paint. Carter is still awake. He has the same stone-face he had before.

Sung-Suu and Cliffster are leaning on each other as they sleep. The orange glow of the glow stick makes them look cute in a funny kind of way.

About half a minute later, the van stops again, and the engines turn off. It signals everyone else to wake up. Before the grogginess could wear off, I hear the wrestling of the tarp on the side of the van. The sliding door opens as the tarp still covers our view. The same voice from before calls out, "Exit the van one by one slowly through the sliding door only." It is morning time. I can see the light from under the tarp. It is going to be another hot day. The light beats out the glow sticks as it causes us to squint.

Rilo is the first to move towards the sliding door. As he exits the van, I catch a glimpse of what is beyond. All I see is Rutherford's vehicles. We wait to see who moves next.

Carter tells us, "If they wanted us dead they would have found a much clever way of doing it." He exits the van as we all look at each other with a sense of panic. Did he say that to make us feel frightened or is it his dark humor under the circumstances? Does not seem like there is anything bad happening outside. I go out next. My heart is beating restlessly but there is no time to be bothered by that small detail.

As I pass through the tarp, the newfound light causes me to place my hands over my eyes. I look through the cracks of my fingers and notice Carter and Rilo facing the HyphenDash guards. We are inside a loading bay. It is a very wide-open space the size of a warehouse. This place must get a lot of action for them to have such a large size bay. The guards still have their weapons holstered so Carter and Rilo do the same. This is another compound that appears to be quite massive. It looks new or very well kept. I hear the tarp wrestle behind me as the others exit the van. They all adjust to the light. Carter's other guards come out as well. They have their guns drawn at the HyphenDash guards. This causes Rutherford's guards to put their weapons at the ready. Carter whistles to his team to get their attention. He signals them to lower their weapons as he wags the barrel of his rifle to the floor. His team adheres to the order. From the inside of the bay, the sliding garage door lowers shutting out the bright morning light.

Rutherford walks out from the door across from us, "Welcome everyone. We have water and food. That door is the restroom. It has a shower and toiletries. We currently do not have clothes for each of you."

None of us make a jump for the food although we are all hungry. I just want to use the restroom.

Rutherford signals for his guards to eat and drink from the lineup. His guards obey and eat willingly for just a few seconds and then they step back to their original positions. He knew we would be wondering if the food was okay to eat (we did not doubt for a moment that this guy was capable of poisoning us). He is sharp. Carter is taking all this in and it must not make him comfortable. We do not wait for a signal from Carter. The nerds dive in as well as Carter's team. Shaboomba and I head to the restroom. We notice there is only one toilet. Who cares. We shut the door and lock it. I go for the toilet as she turns on the shower. I feel a little more human right now. Rutherford sure knows how to play psychological games.

After about ten minutes in, I hear a knock on the door. I guess the guys want to use the facilities as well. I finish up my shower. It feels real good to be clean again and it relaxes me too. We open the door and as we are getting out Cliffster enters.

Then Carter calls out, "Hey, if we all are not done in ten minutes then we are all done in ten minutes."

Sung-Suu rushes to the restroom. Cliffster yells out, "Hey man, what are you doing?"

Sung-Suu continues to push to enter the restroom and says, "Listen, if the rest of us do not get a chance to shower and we have to stay funky for however long, I will break into your Narcata Cloud account and post all your embarrassing videos."

"What?! Oh yeah, well I will take all your videos from the Pino Pin Server and make them global. And you know which ones I am talking about. Yup, all access videos of me and Yo momma on your peepee stained bed."

Carter walks up and pushes the door wide open. Sung-Suu smirks while Cliffster's arms ask what is going on. Carter looks back and gives an eye twitch in my direction. I feel a little uncomfortable by it. Then Carter's team maneuvers between me and Shaboomba. They keep walking right on through into the restroom. Sung-Suu's smirk morphed into shock. Cliffster mimics the shock.

Carter looks at his watch, "Nine minutes and thirty-seven seconds remaining. Get to stepping." He closes the door behind him showing us a big smile as he knows he got the last laugh.

Shaboomba and I laugh out loud as we watch Sung-Suu and Cliffster's petrified look. The men behind them begin to undress. It is a memory worth saving.

I look around and notice our vans have been unhitched but left in the middle of the bay. The tarp has been removed for whatever reason. Their cars have been moved to the far-right side of the bay closest to the garage door.

As we finish lacing our shoes and fixing our hair, Shaboomba asks me, "Do you think death sees life the same way life views death?"

Now that is a question I would not believe came from this particular girl unless I had heard it myself.

I answer with a question, "Are you asking if death were an entity, would it look at life as part of the process that leads to death? Wait, let us get our definitions straight. Are you defining 'Death' as the transition to the other side or as the 'After life?'"

Shaboomba thinks about it for a few seconds, "Hmm, I would have to say 'Death' as the after-life."

"That makes more sense. First, I believe life would look at death as the reward for living a good life or as good as one could make it. It is inherent that humans do good in the world because it gives us a sense of satisfaction. That satisfaction is fueled by a sense of belonging or completion. To succeed at something is what makes us seek happiness. During our lifetime, we do not think, 'when I die this is one of those moments that should count towards me getting into heaven.' But when we are on our deathbed, we are hoping we have done enough to get into heaven. That is when life walks us down memory lane as death spectates from afar. Death as the transition is judgment. Death as the after-life is the reward we seek or the punishment we deserve."

Shaboomba sits back in her chair and says, "Life is the servant of death."

I look at her surprised by her response and say, "Dang, girl. I thought I was deep. You are really dropping some intellectual knowledge right now."

She smiles, "You make it seem like I am not an intellectual type of girl. This brain does a lot more than just compliment this face." We both laugh out. Honestly, I did not picture her as a thought-provoking person. I give her credit for not being one dimensional.

Chapter 27

Monday mid-morning

The restroom door opens, and steam escapes the small room. Sung-Suu and Cliffster are the first ones to run out.

Sung-Suu exclaims, "That is almost as bad as my shower experience after football practice! This is why I do not go to the gym."

Cliffster laughs, "Man, you have not played football since you were 13-years old."

"Shut up, Cliffster! Still, that does not mean I was not traumatized by the experience."

Cliffster fires back, "No, traumatized is having to shave yo momma's back every other day!"

Carter and his team emerge from the restroom. They look refreshed. Carter still has that look of concern on his face. I can tell all of this bothers him. His team help themselves again to the food and drinks.

Carter comes up to me and says, "You good? You better be. We will have to figure this out. I cannot relax here." He is right. I have to remember why we are here. I hope Koonzo and the rest of them got this same treatment.

Rutherford reappears from around the corner. His armed entourage accompanies him. He looks at us and says, "I hope the hasty accommodations made you all a little more comfortable. As much as I would like to keep the atmosphere uplifted, we must proceed with our original intentions. Mr. Carter, shall we?"

Rutherford waves his hand like a magician presenting us a new trick. In this case, Rutherford presents us with a door. This is not the same door he came out from which implies this other door leads to a more secured area.

Carter looks at me and then at his team, "Bring it in." His team huddles around him. This must be the big pep talk. Carter pops his head from within his huddle, "Hey, that means all of you. Get in here." My nerd friends and I jump right in. Carter gives his quick speech, "Listen, everyone, keep your weapons lowered. That also goes for everyone's mouth. No one get froggy out there. Remember, we are on their turf walking through their security system blind to anything that may come at us. We do not have the advantage. The only time you are cleared hot is when shots are fired, or you are being targeted. No other exception. We cannot afford to mess this up.

Powa, keep your head on straight. Do not let them con you into anything. Think of what you are in search of before telling them anything. Better yet, I will tell you when to speak up. It is safer for all of us that way."

Rutherford interrupts with a half-hearted cough. Still in the huddle, Carter gives us a last piece of advice, "Bring it in tighter. I do not want them to see this. Powa, this is me keeping my promise to keep you safe."

Promise? What is he talking about?

Carter unholsters his gun and goes on, "Rack the weapon. Switch the lever to red. Put your booger finger on the trigger only when you are ready to squeeze. If one of the steps does not work, go to the next step. Repeat the entire process if needed."

What? Is he actually giving me a class on how to use a gun right now? And he wants to do this now?! I tell him, "No way am I going to remember that."

"Rack, red, booger, squeeze." Before I can reply, Carter orders me to say it.

So I do, "Rack, red, booger, squeeze. There, happy?"

Rutherford speaks up this time since his other attempt to get our attention did not work, "Mr. Carter, let us carry on, please."

Carter looks to the rest of the bunch and says, "Chew slowly."

I am a little upset at that heinous cutting remark. Who does he think we are? We know how to control our emotions; for the most part. Okay, Carter knows exactly who we are and telling us to keep our cool was not out of line. All this tension has my hormones raging wild.

"Rack, red, booger, squeeze," there I said it. Now I have to remember it when the right time comes.

Carter's 'Chew slowly' directive is not all that inspiring. I would have said something more motivating than that but, this is just how Carter works.

Rutherford heads towards the door. We all mob our way towards him. He looks back and stops. Everyone stops. He tells Carter, "You can bring the teens but none of your other teammates may come along. To keep it peaceful, I am the only one walking with you all. Fair?" We all look at Carter. His mind speeds for an alternative disposition. Technically, if this is the case, we would be outnumbering him.

Carter replies, "Make it two more so we can keep it moving." Rutherford holds up two fingers. Two of his guards run to their new position which is behind our group. Carter keeps a lock on Rutherford as he calls out, "Rilo, Darryl on me. Everyone else hang back. Stay frosty til we get back." Rilo and Darryl take their spot on both sides of Carter while the rest of his team walks back toward the buffet table. Our group went from 17 to seven. For some reason I think Carter should have negotiated for more of our team to come with us.

As we resume walking, Sung-Suu has his eyes closed repeating the ditty over and over, "Rack, red, booger, squeeze."

Shaboomba nudges him, "Hey, make sure you piss your pants while you are at it."

Cliffster and I giggle loud enough to get his attention.

Sung-Suu opens his eyes, "Hey, my mind needs to hear it seven times in order for it to stick. I am not taking any chances."

Cliffster asks, "How many times have you said it already?"

"Eighteen times. Trying to get to one hundred though."

We all roll our eyes as Cliffster replies, "I remember when you did the same thing for your calculus test. What did you end up getting anyway?"

"That is beside the point, Cliffster. This is life and death. I got a 42 on that test."

Cliffster and I giggle quietly as Shaboomba rolls her eyes again.

Carter turns his head slightly towards us and utters his command, "Shut up." And that is the end of that.

Three of Rutherford's guards keep the rear of the mob company. Carter takes me by the arm and escorts me to the front of the pack. The door is already open before we even get to it. We continue to walk through. The walls are grey, and the lights mounted near the ceiling create an eerie mood as the ceiling is abnormally high. It makes the hallway appear narrower than it actually is. There is nothing here but a long hallway and the bright lights. I wonder what is on the other side of these walls. The rooms must be large. I bet that is where they are holding Noni and Goji. The door in front of us also opens up before Rutherford walks up to it.

One thing strikes me as odd. I did not notice any cameras in the hallway and unfortunately, I did not pay attention while we were at the loading bay. One thing is certain, we are being watched. Here comes another door.

As we approach, I can tell the room is completely dark. Once Rutherford walks in, the lights automatically turn on. I walk in and notice to my left a row of doors. But the doors are prison-like cell doors made of glass. Well that answers my question; these guys are the same ones that kidnapped me. But I do not ponder long on that as I must stay focused. There are at least twenty of these doors. I wonder what happens if they have more than twenty prisoners? I better not ask. I do not want to be a part of their count.

I rush to the first cell in hopes of seeing a familiar face. It is empty, but the layout is familiar. There is a toilet sink combination in the back of the cell along with a piece of metal highly polished, their weird version of a mirror I guess.

On the left is a small bed attached to the wall. The cell is slightly wider than the door but not by much. Overall, it is much smaller than the one I was in before, but the accommodations are obviously better.

The cell walls are the exact same color and texture as the hallway. For me, the optical illusion of only seeing four walls is what played tricks with my mind. Not really seeing a door made me think there was no option of getting out. This is a very strong psychological trap.

At this point, I notice the rest of the crowd has stopped while Rutherford is on the other end watching me. My nerd friends look on with the expression that they want to help me search these cells. However, it looks like Carter is the one that is stopping them from doing so. I do not understand why he would want me to do this alone. Rutherford's guards make no attempt to have them keep moving. But it does not occupy my attention for too long. I hop over to the next cell. Inside I see somebody! I knock on the door to get this gentleman's attention. He looks up at me, but it is not a face I recognize. The guy is wearing an orange jumpsuit. Whoever put this place together went all out to make it feel and look like a prison. The man does not look like he has been beaten but he does not look pleased to see me. He looks either depressed or detached from what is going on.

Carter and the rest of the group come from behind me. Carter looks and says, "He is not one of mine." I move onto the next one. Another man is in there, but his reaction is equally depressing. He looks to have lost all hope, as if he is waiting to die.

Carter repeats what he said about the first man. I stop at each window and I do not know any of the people inside the cells. Rutherford remains quiet as the rest of us keep walking to the other end.

Carter reaches the last cell, "If you are trying to find a way to piss me off then this is a good way to do it, Rutherford."

Rutherford holds up his hands, "Mr. Carter, I was not the one that assumed that some of these folks were your people. What I will tell you is that I hope you took note at how motivated these men are to see a fresh face. I want you to think about that when we start our conversation. If you like, you may proceed through the next door." Rutherford walks past us to the rear of our group to link up with his two guards. We split the hallway while our eyes follow him as he walks down the center.

Carter keeps his eyes locked on Rutherford. He talks quietly from the left side of his lips, "Rilo, open the door slowly. Darryl, be prepared to shut it or shoot through it."

"Got it, boss." Rilo whispers almost automatically. Darryl provides a thumbs up with a nod.

I turn around to see what is awaiting us. Is it a trap? Is this the reason Rutherford went to the other end of the room? So that he may force us into this room which may be another cell? This is a bad idea. The door opens.

Chapter 28

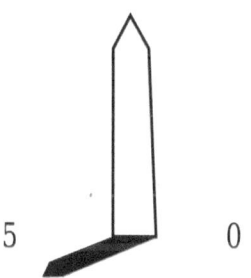

5   0

Late morning

The lights are already on inside. Rilo opens the door a little wider. Another row of cells. On the other end is another door. Without realizing it, I am the first one to step through the doorway. I walk up to the first cell. It is empty. The second cell also has a man I do not recognize.

Carter walks through as he taps his booger finger on the side of his rifle. He turns to face Rutherford who happens to be at the entrance of this hallway. I can see what is going to happen. They are going to shut that door and lock us in. We walked ourselves into this trap voluntarily. This guy is really good. Rutherford speaks before Carter can say anything, "There are more cells."

I am not optimistic about this as I look into the next cell, "Koonzo? Koonzo, it is me! Come here!" Koonzo looks at me and rushes to the window. Shaboomba, Sung-Suu, and Cliffster almost push me out of the way to see him. We can barely hear him. The cells are soundproof.

He places his hands on the window. All four of us reach out for his hands. It looks like a prison visitation scene. I can faintly hear him, "Hey guys! They catch you, too? No. You guys are supposed to be the rescue team. Hell yea! Hook it up!"

Shaboomba replies with, "No, we heard this is where you found love. When can we meet him?" Everyone laughs at that one. I even here Rilo snickers at that.

Sung-Suu speaks while laughing, "What do you mean by him? It is more like 'When can we meet them?' Because we all know Koonzo's flat butt must be shared by more than one guy." The laughing gets a little louder.

Cliffster adds, "Let me guess. He wears the pants in the family. You always did look good in a dress." Koonzo laughs so hard he has tears rolling down his face.

Carter looks inside the cell and reveals no excitement; I can tell he is hoping to see one of his guys. I rush over to the next cell as Shaboomba, Sung-Suu, and Cliffster stay behind with Koonzo. It is not one of my friends but looks like one of Carter's guards.

Carter comes over, "Vendervich, you hold tight, brother!"

I hear a muffled, "I am not going anywhere, man."

In the next window there was another one of Carter's guards. The next few cells also had Carter's men.

Then I see him, "Goji! Are you ok?!" Shaboomba and the others leave Koonzo and sprint towards me.

Goji runs up to the window, "Oh man, Shaboomba you look hot!" A quick silence overcomes us all as we look at Shaboomba to see what she will say. But then Goji tells us, "I am starting to lose more of my marbles in here. Cliffster, sorry you messed it up with her, man. Would you be mad if I...?"

Goji stops as he can tell Cliffster wants to break through the cell door and his intentions are not heroic.

Shaboomba giggles which makes me and Sung-Suu laugh. Goji keeps talking, "Hey man, it is either her or your momma. Sorry, Cliff. I cannot help it. You know how I get when I am in my freak out mode!"

Cliffster walks away as he looks into the next cell, "Noni?! It is good to see you!"

Noni runs up to the cell door and yells, "You are a sight for sore eyes! What are you doing here?"

Cliffster's expression turns to frustration, "Your brother is going to lose more than just his mind if he keeps talking his crap."

"Is he talking about Shaboomba again? Yea, he gets like that when he is trying to cope with a bad situation. Speaking of which. Yo, get me out of here. These walls are starting to curse me out."

The rest of us come over to see him. Carter shoves us along to keep the tour going. Noni keeps shouting, "Hurry because these walls are starting to talk to me and they are not saying anything good!" Noni does not seem like he is doing well in there at all.

I head to the last cell before the next door. I look inside and find, "Mrs. Bellows?! Is that you?!"

Carter shoves me out the way, "Mrs. Bellows?! We are going to get you out of there, ma'am." Carter is keeping his composure under these circumstances.

I can hear Mrs. Bellows, "Carter, my boy, I trust you will do what you can for me."

Carter looks over at Rutherford with a glare that could cut steel, "I will find a way to hurt you, Rutherford; treating a lady like Mrs. Bellows this way."

Rutherford smiles and walks towards us, "Now, Mr. Carter, if I had better accommodations for Mrs. Bellows, I may have used them if she would have cooperated a little more with me."

I look at Carter and he is not happy at all. I grab his hand and whisper, "Chew slowly."

He looks at me, "Gotcha, kid."

Another smile forms on Rutherford's face. He knows how to push Carter's buttons. After he soaks in Carter's silent rage, "So, do we have a fair trade, Mr. Carter?"

Carter is still looking at me. I can tell he is thinking of something as his eyes go from squinting to worrisome. I give him a little smile, but Rutherford's question has me scared too. Be strong, Powa. Just be a little brave.

Carter finally turns to face his adversary, "No deal." We all focus directly at Carter. Even his guards are surprised by what he said.

I tug on Carter's shirt and whisper yell at him, "Are you crazy?! These guys will shoot us all. That is stupid!"

Carter keeps his eyes locked on Rutherford and whispers from the side of his mouth, "Think about it. He has anticipated my every move from the beginning. The guy is a pro. If I hand you over, more than likely we are dead. Either our vans are tripped with explosives or we get ambushed while being escorted out of this building. Face it, the guy can shoot us right now and we would have no control over that. But I do know he needs you more than he wants you dead. So, if anything, you are our meal ticket out of here. But I have one small problem."

I realize everyone has huddled around the both of us. I ask, "What is it?"

I never expected to hear Carter say the following words, "I do not know what to do next."

Oh crap! I suddenly feel nauseous. Oh no, oh no! What can I do? I have to do something. I look at everyone's faces. They are as terrified as I am. Then I see Shaboomba. Her outfit matches her hippie satchel. Why am I thinking of her outfit?! Wait a second, I have her satchel!

I break away from the huddle, "Rutherford!" I can feel the eyes from the group stare at the back of my head.

Rutherford, previously scrolling through his gauntlet on his left wrist, looks up at me. I have no other name for it; it appears to be a tablet/smart watch hybrid of some sort. Very impressive looking. I bet he can control this entire building with it. I continue, "I have the formula with me. It is right here. I also have all three serums. Two syringes, one which is already loaded."

Rutherford looks at his three guards and begins to laugh. Carter whisper yells, "Hey, do not use our freaking lottery ticket now!" I whisper back without losing eye contact with Rutherford, "I am about to cash in this lottery ticket to get everyone out of here. I got this, Carter. Chew slowly."

"What?! Chew slowly?! You are going to choke out there!" Carter cannot believe I am doing this.

I hear a friendly voice, "Carter, you just said it. Every move you have made so far has been countered. This guy is your reflection. What we need is for you to figure out Rutherford's next move. Let her do her thing. She is equally invested in this as we are if not more." I look back at the voice of reason. It is Sung-Suu of all people to speak up. I knew he liked to shy away from any confrontation with strangers, but I am glad he stepped up to the plate.

I keep quiet waiting to see how Carter takes the advice. More importantly, I wait to see if any of Carter's teammates speak up against Sung-Suu. The only thing I hear is Rutherford laughing.

"You almost had me, Ms. Powa. I almost believed it. But once again, you teenagers talk too much, and you put yourself back out of control again. You see, there are only two serums to mix for 1X, not three. You have your information mixed up. The cocktail for lethal injection, on the other hand, is three serums. But hey, I applaud your bravery and creative spirit. It is a better performance than anything I have seen from Mr. Carter." Rutherford states.

Oh, I can tell Carter is not happy about that comment. He must be biting his tongue right now. I keep my bearing, "You are good Rutherford. I have to hand it to you." I begin to pull out the case and open it as I talk, "You have had us pegged since you caught us. And you have managed to outwit Carter every step of the way. You even have been able to stump me. You know your stuff, sir."

I open the case and pull out one of the pages, "Let me see. Step four, place 18-milliliters in a vile. Step five, hmm, a certain amount in the same vile and mix for approximately 20-seconds. Well it does not matter because it is all fake anyway, right Rutherford? I am sure your video surveillance cameras captured what BS I just read off and the contents within this case which means I am full of crap. Therefore, this is what I am going to do."

I pick up the loaded syringe and hand it to Carter. He has a shocked look on his face and takes the syringe. I know from here he can make his own negotiations, but I am hoping he follows my lead. I continue, "Carter is going to insert this needle into my arm and enter the fake contents into my body. Rutherford, you are an extremely smart man. What do you think I am doing with all these fake chemicals?" I feel the skin prick. My eyes look down in surprise. I was not expecting Carter to inject my right now. But I refrain from showing Rutherford my surprise. The needle prick is a bit painful but not enough to wince. The cocktail is cold which contrasts with the warmth of my blood.

It is a thick substance as I can feel my arteries expand a little more. It dissipates as it befriends my red blood cells along their travels. I begin to feel a bit anxious, but it is hard for me to tell if this is from the cocktail or because of the current situation. Only time will tell which one.

I see Rutherford squint his left eye as he attempts to predict what happens next.

The squint goes away and he nods his head, "Very smart, Ms. Powa. If the contents are real, then we will not want to shoot you. If we do, then we run the risk of killing you. And if that happens then your request will more than likely be that piece of paper that has the formula. Very smart, indeed. But that just means we have to aim carefully. And my men can do that."

Okay, this guy is calling my bluff, so I hold out my hand. Almost immediately, I feel a heavy piece of steel placed in the same hand as the serum was injected. The weight of this object makes me drop my hand to my side.

As I look down, I go along with it, "You may be able to shoot them but in the middle of all that I may use this on myself. Plus, Carter, Rilo, and Darry know to shoot me first anyway."

I reference the pistol in my hand along with the three behind me. The wheels inside Rutherford's head are spinning again. He is in mannequin mode (not moving, barely breathing and probably going through 10,000 thoughts a second). To throw him off a little more, I say "We talked a lot about this in our little huddle to include our secondary options."

Sung-Suu whispers to Carter covering his mouth with his hand, "Did we actually talk about these things in the huddle because I was busy with Rack, red, booger, squeeze?"

Carter does not reply. I can tell he is fiercely locked onto Rutherford's face. I add more pressure, "Well Rutherford, are you going to just stand there, or do you plan on making a move?" This bothers him even more. He looks agitated as he searches the clean, cool floor for an answer.

Then I hear a metallic double click followed by the pressure of an object to my head. From what I would gather from the movies, I immediately understand this is a pistol. I do not bother looking to see who it is. My guess, Carter is pointing his weapon at me. I get scared. I know this is for show, but it only takes one fidget and I am done.

Rutherford finally replies back, "Smart play again, Ms. Powa and Mr. Carter. What are your terms in exchange for all the contents inside the case?"

I waste no time thinking, "Everyone here is released. We are allowed to exit the facility with our vans. And $10,000 cash in five-dollar denominations for each of us to include those that are imprisoned here. While we wait for the cash and several cash counters, we will wait in the loading dock with all the prisoners. Ensure food and water is there. Your timeline is…" I look back at Carter. He peeps out, "One hour."

I repeat, "One hour. As big of a company HyphenDash is, this is a very small request." Rutherford is in deep thought. The weapon on my head is pulled away and I hear Carter's voice, "He is thinking of how to gain the upper hand again. What else you got?"

"Nothing. I pretty much showed my hand."

Carter expels a long exhale, "Well, then it is his serve."

Rutherford snaps out of his personal think tank, "No deal. Even HyphenDash is unable to pull that much cash with those requirements in that short amount of time. I may possibly put together that much money in two hours, but we need to be reasonable here. Even two hours is pushing it. We can either all get down right now or we can compromise which is a logical choice, no?"

A counter-offer is what I was trying to avoid. Now we have to get into the haggling game and I suck at that. I tell Carter, "I knew this was not going to be easy. I mean when I go to the swap meet I pay full price. I just suck at making deals."

Carter sounds cool, "No need to overthink it." He raises his voice towards Rutherford, "Two hours, done."

Rutherford quickly adds, "Depending on how difficult it is to get the cash it may…"

"Two hours, done!" Exclaims Carter.

Rutherford stops his disclaimer. He is back to his thinking mode.

A minute goes by and Rutherford finally breaks his silence, "Fine. But I have a demand. Your terms will be met as long as we also get the case that has the formula, the three serums, and the second syringe. And I even have an incentive for you, Ms. Powa. If you are willing to partake in our experiment, we will provide the formula to anyone you choose free of charge when their time comes. This service will get extremely expensive once we mass produce it. But it is a task that will require your life. I am an opportunist, and since you already have 1X in your veins you will make for an excellent candidate."

Did I hear him correctly? Does he want me to kill myself for the sake of a science experiment? This guy has another thing coming. Rutherford stands there with a cheesy smirk like he just made me an offer I should not refuse. For all his collective demeanor, he just lost all his cool points with me. At least Carter does not have the heart to tell me to do something like this for the benefit of science or in order to save anyone. Then again, I remember what he did to Everest. Yea, scratch that.

I am getting worked up here. I remind myself to chew slowly, "One deal at a time. Your two hours start now. Release all these prisoners. Make good on your part." I hear someone fidgeting with their watch.

The big question is what do we do if the money does not show up in time? I do not bother thinking about it. What is Rutherford up to?

Rutherford walks up to Mrs. Bellows' cell. He reaches out and pulls it open. I wonder if his powerful hand is the universal key to all the cells or is someone watching us pushing buttons? The door silently open and I see Mrs. Bellows struggle to stand up. She begins to walk towards the door and then Rutherford slams it shut. I can hear the tinker of Mrs. Bellows' strong attempt to bang on that heavy door. Carter almost lunged at him as his body jolted against my back. Rutherford takes two steps towards me which now puts him about a foot away from my face. I look up at Rutherford and realize he is much taller than I originally thought. As he looks down on me, I can tell he is fit. No double chin, his cheek bones are pronounced, and I cannot hear him breathing.

By the way, I have learned loud breathing is a big pet peeve of mine. Anyway, he stares at me as he shares his thoughts, "Change of plans. We will not be releasing the prisoners. Your friends may wait in the loading dock while we wait for your money. But for you Ms. Powa, I want you to come with me. I have something to show you."

Carter says it before I could get it out, "She is not going anywhere. We made a deal. Now stick to it!"

Rutherford replies, "Mr. Carter, I will not have the prisoners released. They can wait here. There is no harm in that. I have not exhibited any form of violence on my part. But for me to be tactically sound, I will feel safer if your friends stay where they are at and keep the atmosphere neutral. You are a chess player, Mr. Carter. If these roles were reversed, you would do the same thing if not better?"

I do not play chess, but I agree with the move.

"I come with her and none of your guards follow us." Carter demands.

Rutherford, "Agreed but only if you leave your weapons behind. Ms. Powa may keep her pistol to give her a sense of control."

Interesting Rutherford would say this. He would rather I have control yet put Carter in a vulnerable position. If anything goes down, Carter will have to get my weapon before someone is able to shoot him. Tough call.

"Done," Carter states. He looks to everyone else, "Rest up and keep thinking. Rilo, you get to be the star. Here is my rifle and here is my pistol. Look for chinks in the armor. See you all when we are done."

I hand Carter the case. His eyes ask the question, "Why are you giving this to me?" But he quickly realizes it is safer in his hands. He one ups my gesture and hands it to Rilo and says, "Hold onto this. It is the only thing keeping us in the game. They can take me out pretty easy at this stage. And with Powa walking around with that stuff in her veins who knows what she is going to do with it."

I add, "Besides, if they kill me the formula does not have to be close by for me to make it the object of my request."

Rilo takes the case and puts it in his tactical backpack. Carter and I look at each other both wondering if breaking away from the group is a good idea. Without an answer, we walk as Rutherford leads the way.

Chapter 29

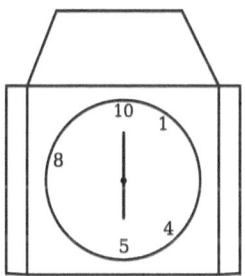

Monday High Noon

We make our way through several different hallways. I think Rutherford is trying to get us lost by taking this intricate route. I do not bother trying to map it. I am too nervous wondering what he could possibly want with me. After about a brisk two-minute walk, we finally reach our destination. Rutherford goes through a retina scan as well as some device that scans his forehead. The door opens, and I see a room filled with photos, sketches, and maps on the wall across from us.

The lighting is dimmed which accents all the little lights on the computers, monitors, and other little gadgets. Several of the same devices are found on the wall to the left.

To the right is a brightly lit hospital room separated by a glass wall. The hospital room has a large surgical light that looms above a gurney along with several other contraptions I have never seen before. More medical equipment is lined up along the walls. I keep looking and I realize there is an observation area with seats and tables on the other side of this hospital room. There is only one other individual here but from the amount of computer desks I would say the other folks were told to leave. The person is working on a computer. I can tell it is a male with glasses but that is all the illumination will provide for details.

Rutherford welcomes us inside, "Please come in. This is our glorious hovel. It is not the main brain of this project, but it does play a large part in it. Those maps indicate an occurrence we are tracking. We also have some potential candidates we plan on acquiring."

I cut him off, "What do you mean by occurrence? And what are you acquiring? What is this place?" The way he talks is different from the way I talk, and I want to make sure I understand. I have to clear this up before I get lost and frustrated. It is all about definitions.

Rutherford holds his hands up as a sign to let me know he can sense my irritability, "I am sorry. I get carried away sometimes. The occurrence is when we identified someone requesting what we wanted them to request. As for acquisition, I am talking about people that meet our requirements. We already have a hospital here, but this new industry is in constant demand."

Carter decides to speak up, "So you are telling us this huge facility is filled with people that are about to die? What do you do with them afterwards, cremate them or just dissolve them in a bucket of acid?" It sounds like Carter has done some of those things before.

Rutherford has a cooler head and replies, "Oh dear no! We properly send the bodies back to the families. We pay for all the funeral costs as well as a handsome payment for allowing us to make our observations without their interference. There are many families who are taking advantage of this opportunity."

"Basically, you bribe them," Carter states.

Rutherford sighs, "Call it what you will, Mr. Carter. These families benefit from us more than if they denied us. Go out there and see how each of those families are living. We accommodate them as best as we possibly can. We are not monsters. But if we were to be, we would like to be known as kindhearted monsters."

I change the subject, "How do you track an occurrence? Once it is gone, it is gone, right?"

Rutherford escorts us over to a monitor mounted on the wall, "That is a big misconception, Ms. Powa. Look here." I have a seat as Rutherford taps on the keyboard to my left. Carter remains standing attempting to take in his surroundings.

Rutherford's voice becomes eager, almost like he could not contain the excitement regarding what he is about to explain. I must give him credit though, he does his best to compose himself while doing so. Rutherford rolls his computer chair over to mine, "We saw this by accident. But eventually we would have come across it. The dark circle is the earth. This image is from one of our satellites. Currently, we are looking at the dark side of our planet."

I cut him off, "Let me guess. You see the requested object in space, right? No way am I buying that. NASA or someone else would have discovered that by now."

"Well smart little girl, if you let me finish you will understand." I just keep looking at the monitor. Rutherford starts tapping on the keyboard again, "Initially, we thought we were seeing lightning strikes. You know, the ones that strike into space. But then something tragic happened. Remember the Apatou event which people are calling the Apatou nightmare?"

I nod my head to indicate I remember the event, "It was horrible what happened down there. What made that catastrophe worse is that it happened in the middle of the night."

"Exactly! About 4,000 people died. At the time, our satellites were equipped with an experimental spectrum filter. One of them happened to be over that area at that time. This is what we saw."

After Rutherford taps on more keys, the same image of the dark earth is focused on the Southern Hemisphere. A dime sized white spot is directly over the town of Apatou. "And look here." One more tap on the keyboard and the white spot is replaced by multiple specks. Another tap and the white specks lessen. Rutherford taps the key several more times until there are only a few specks left.

He explains, "You see? Each of these frames are a millisecond in between. These specks of light do not linger at all. There is no way a concentration of lightning strikes took place at that exact same time in the exact same place. I zoomed in because I wanted to see exactly what these spots of lights really are."

He taps a few more keys, "And here we have a ray of light. These are those specks of light you were just looking at. When we magnify the image, we see this. These rays of light do not point to the infinite. They are angled. We have generalized the path to several different areas in space simply due to the trajectory we are able to calculate."

"Wait a second, are you saying these rays of light are the requests? How do you know that?" I have to ask.

Rutherford dips his head and taps on the keys again. Another image pops up of the same dark earth but from the silhouette the area is in the Mediterranean, "Here is one of our sites. We had the time of dissolution, when the request disappears, correlate to this ray of light."

He magnifies the ray of light. It becomes pixelated when he finally stops magnification.

I ask myself, "Is this what the soul looks like?"

"If I had to guess, I would say yes." I look over at Rutherford and realize I spoke out loud.

I continue, "This is something people will probably freak out about."

Rutherford calms his excitement, "I know. Since we currently have the only means to detect these rays of light, we maintain control of potential scientific advancements and any other favorable spin we may choose to give this. That is why it is imperative we get a complete understanding of what this is before people jump to frightening conclusions."

I do not know how to react. Rutherford adds, "We all know when the request reaches dissolution it disappears on earth. Get ready for this. We found it reappears on the outer side of the troposphere. We kept our lenses focused to the night sky when the dissolution took place, but we did not see the ray of light from our point of view."

I look at Rutherford, "You are not just a representative for HyphenDash, are you?"

"I hope I am not that obvious. No. I am the chief scientist for several of these stations. I volunteered to pursue you as I believe I am more approachable than their initial selection. I am very honored to have you here with us, Ms. Powa. You have taken this entire project to a new dimension."

I am a little perplexed, "I did nothing special or different. All I did was record my friend's death. I have no skill or special talent. I am not super smart nor am I very athletic. I am not popular in school nor have many friends. I am simple or at least I try to be."

Rutherford gets creepy and attempts to touch my hair, but I pull away, "Oh Ms. Powa, you have no idea what you have done. One thing for sure, you are very popular. You look on the web and your name is at the top of the list."

He switches to another computer and jumps on the web. He pulls up a chatter board, "You see? Your name is plastered all over this site along with many other sites."

I grab the keyboard to punch up a site I regularly visit. He is right. My name is more popular than the superstars of the world. But how would I have known that? With all the chasing, running and hiding, I have not had time to catch up on my web news. I have to ask, "But I do not understand why. I did nothing special. All I did was hold up a camera. That does not make me an inventor or even a discoverer. It was all accidental. If anything, Nhim is due all the credit. That camera was his creation."

Rutherford tells me, "You fail to see the observance. When Neil Armstrong first step foot on the moon, all he did was just take one small step. That was it. He did nothing fantastic. But the world recognizes him as being the first man on the moon. The same goes for you. The world saw you in the middle of this new type of request. Sure, it is coincidental or even accidental but to all of us we see it differently. We see you as the only one to have the ability to see beyond our world. You are the face of the request movement, Ms. Powa. Your life will never be the same. Regardless of how much you would like to ignore it. After all of this is done, you still have to contend with the real world. Grow up fast, Ms. Powa. If not, the real world will turn on you."

I do not know what he is talking about. If he has not noticed, I am not exactly living a peaceful life right now. And here I am thinking my life is only a plane trip away. How naive I am to have thought this. I stare into the dark world in front of me recycling what has been said.

Rutherford dips into my thoughts, "And this is where you will be." He is looking at the hospital bed in the other room. He adds, "We will track every movement your mind and body will make. We have our satellites honed in on the anticipated spot the ray of light will present itself. Every resource is being maximized as we speak, Ms. Powa." A beep saves me from having to hear his morbid plan.

Rutherford answers to it by punching several more keys. All this talk is starting to make me feel nauseous. My head feels light. This feeling is all too familiar. To think the entire world or at least the entire World Wide Web knows who I am. I should feel thankful, but I do not. I feel like a cheat. Like someone who is passing herself off as a talented person but has no proof when the time presents itself. This is overwhelming. My head is starting to bead with sweat. Now I am starting to feel anxious. 'Do not freak out, Powa. Hold it together.'

Rutherford holds my hand and escorts me inside the hospital room. This does not seem right. How did I allow myself to get in here? I look over at Carter for a vote of confidence. He is sitting down and asleep. Why is Carter sleeping right now?! My mind is not working correctly. Is that a rope around his chest? I should be worried now but something keeps me calm and floating.

Rutherford sits me down and asks, "How are you feeling, Ms. Powa? You look a little pail. Can I get you something?" Everything is starting to feel unfamiliar and it suddenly scares me. I do not know how to explain it. But I do know I cannot speak. I am mumbling right now.

Rutherford has a camera up to his face, "How about one of these? This will make you feel much better, Ms. Powa. Here, hold it. It is your most prized possession." I feel the weight of the camera. It is heavy for me. Rutherford holds it up, so I can get a closer look at it. He explains how precious this camera is to me. I do not understand why it is so special, but I am believing it.

Something is wrong. I feel my heart race exponentially. I can hear the heart monitor beeping faster. It freaks me out and the beeping on that machine pulses even faster now. I can actually feel my heart pounding through my chest. My sternum feels like it is going to crack. I attempt to squeeze my chest with my arms to subdue the pain. They are restrained just like my legs are. When did that happen? When did Rutherford take the camera back? My eyes are slow to locate it, the camera happens to be directly in front of me at eye level. I must not be paying attention.

Then I hear a different type of noise. It is a familiar ping. Rutherford, "This is good, Ms. Powa. Your first alert has sounded off. One more and we will be on our way. You are doing great. Keep it up. That camera is your key to feeling much better. Focus on the camera." I look at it once more. Thoughts about this camera begin to run through my mind. I look to my left and can see a monitor with an image of me. I raise my eyebrows to see if it is a live stream and it is. I look horrible.

Rutherford answers a call, "Hey, if that is what it takes. Not like we have any other choice at this point."

He leans over to me, "As promised, the money you demanded has been collected and is en route. We will hold onto Mr. Carter's portion. Your cut will be sent to your family along with an added bonus. And I want you to know your body will be sent directly to the nearest funeral home, immediately. We will pay for all the accommodations. I want to thank you once again for doing this. You are an honorable lady. Thank you, Ms. Powa."

He squeezes my hand and I, for some unknown reason, return the same squeeze. It reminds me of when my brother was messing with me when I was going through the Gevity euphoria from the two strips dissolving. Man, that really upset me. But that feeling is kind of like this one but this one is much trippier.

Wait one second, is this... Rutherford interrupts my thinking as he pulls down a monitor from the ceiling. He turns it on. It is a video surveillance system. I can see multiple camera angles. There are about nine of them on the screen at once, but I am sure there are more. Rutherford tells me, "This is so you can have peace of mind knowing I will keep my word on paying your friends. And you will see your friends and Mr. Carter's team drive away unharmed."

I attempt to point to one of the cameras. Rutherford puts his finger on the touch screen. I shake my head. He pushes another camera pane. I shake my head again. He turns back and hands me a mouse, "Here Ms. Powa, you can choose any camera you like. There are over 70 cameras, I think. Your friends can be found in cameras eight through 15." I move the mouse and double click on camera eight. There they are. My vision is not as clear. I think I see Koonzo. Wait. Koonzo is still in his cell. Is the little camera recording this? Why am I thinking of this camera at a time like this? Looks like some activity is going on.

A car and a semi-truck pull up to a guard shack. This is not the same guard shack as there are no barriers like the ones we went through. I am sure that semi-truck would have a fun time with that. Four guards come out to greet them. They all know each other. I can see them smiling and giving each other their bro shakes. They still search the vehicles. One of them breaks out a mirror on a stick and checks underneath them. The semi-truck's rear doors are opened. I click to find a better camera angle. Two guards enter with their flashlights and other gadgets while the fourth guard sets himself just outside those doors with his rifle in his hands. I cannot see clearly what is inside, but I would guess it is the money. After a minute or two, they exit the rig.

Rutherford comes over and sees the action on my monitor, "Looks like it is payday!" A beep goes off and Rutherford says, "If you say they are green then I am green."

The barrier poles slide back into the ground. They wave to each other. I switch to one of the cameras in the bay. The vehicles take about 30-seconds before they show up on screen. They pull inside and park. The car pulls off to one side as the semi-truck parks in the center of the bay. The entire left side of the metal cargo container drops down slowly like a tailgate on hydraulics. I have never seen something like that. And there it is. Two of the largest piles of money I have ever seen. And I mean these two pallets are extremely large and the stack is high. A larger than normal forklift comes over and extracts one of the pallets. The pile of money appears gigantic once it is placed on the floor next to one of our vans. It must be about ten feet high and in a perfect cube.

The second pallet is unloaded next to the first. It is gargantuously symmetrical to the first. The two pallets tower over the guard standing next to them. It catches everyone's attention. There is no audio, but I can tell one of the guards directs Rilo's folks and my friends to keep away from the money.

I scroll through the other cameras to see what other action is going on. Rutherford tells me, "Camera 22." I double click on camera 22 and see the cell doors open. One by one the imprisoned walk out of their cells. There must be a speaker in the ceiling as the prisoners exit their cells looking up at the lights. There I see Koonzo, Noni, and Goji. I even see Mrs. Bellows walking out. Camera 23 has the unknown prisoners creeping out of their cells. HyphenDash managed to snatch up everyone, huh?

Some hugs and handshakes are exchanged. That group enters the group of unknown prisoners and they greet each other with handshakes and hugs. From their reaction, the voice in the ceiling commands them to continue exiting. I scroll through more cameras following their short journey back to the bay. The reunion is a beautiful one. A lot of hugs are exchanged. I can see their love for each other. Noni jumps on top of Koonzo. It is the funniest thing. Goji heads straight for Cliffster and tries to mimic his brother.

Cliffster keeps his arms crossed when Goji makes his leap. This causes Goji to lose his grip on Cliffster as he falls off him. Shaboomba is laughing as she points at Cliffster. It makes me want to laugh but that emotion seems to be disabled. Oh man, they even have DeadRick and Munch. Munch does not look too thrilled to be free. DeadRick is happy but also frightened by the entire ordeal. They both walk towards the group and are received with bro hugs and words of encouragement. Mrs. Bellows walks gingerly towards her guardian staff.

I completely forgot about them. They huddle around her. I can tell she is asking for Carter. Her guards use their hands to explain a story I cannot hear. Someone even gets her a chair from the table of food. Her employees are demonstrating strong loyalty towards that woman. I would love to hear her story. More bro hugs for everyone again. What I would give to be there with them.

Chapter 30

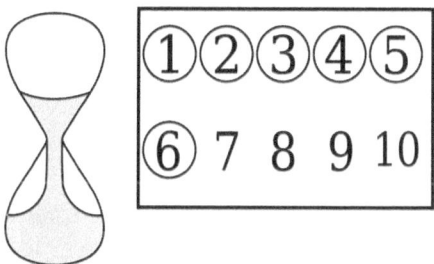

Monday early afternoon

The guards gather around the pallets as the money counters are set up. One of them even goes so far as to caress the cash. As I zoom in, I can see them smiling as they mill about waiting on an order to distribute the funds. I zoom back out to see the recently released group huddled in the far-left corner.

Rutherford seems to have wondered off to his desk. The lights are bright inside this hospital room, but I still manage to locate Rutherford. He is deep in concentration and looking at whatever is on his monitor. I refocus back on my assigned television. One of the guards pulls out his cellphone. Interesting as I realize none of the guards have reached for their cellphones. They are highly disciplined, except for this one. He looks at it and then puts it away. Dang it. I thought he was going to be the one that goes against the grain. So far, I have not found the chink in this place's armor.

The cellphone guard gathers some of the other guards. After a short speech, they all disperse and head to the pallets. They cut the steel ties that hold the money in place. I can see the block of money swell slightly. My eyesight must be getting better. Details such as this were difficult for me several minutes ago. However, I still am unable to talk. One of the guards takes a brick of money from the pallet and flips through it. From my point of view, it looks like he is letting the scent of those dollar bills waft into his face as he takes in a deep breath and a smile. Some of the other guards wind up doing the same thing. From their reaction, I would say this type of delivery does not happen very often. This makes sense as HyphenDash is not a laundry mat. A few more guards take a brick of cash and conduct an informal inspection. One of them notices something within the pallet of money. I can see him taking a closer look as the other guards keep their attention on the money in their hands. The curious guard removes several more bricks from the pile. This causes the bricks above to topple on top of him. Everyone turns to the commotion. The guards already have their weapons drawn. Once they realize there is no threat, they lower them as they laugh at their guardsman who is pushing the cash off him. But he does not lose focus on his curiosity. The pile of money remains tall. Only a corner of it has collapsed. He removes several more bricks. I can see an object protruding from the stack. I magnify the picture and notice is it a dark cloth like protrusion. The guard obstructs my camera angle as he tugs at the object. I switch cameras and can see he has two hands on it. The other guards take note.

Their curiosity grows as they begin to remove the bricks of cash from both pallets. One of them looks at the brick in his hand and realizes a portion of it has been cleanly shaven. Imagine a secret compartment inside a book with the pages cut through and this is what the guard is seeing. The other guards find the same thing as they continue to remove those bricks. One of the guards tilts his head sideways. He must be hearing something. Another guard comes over to listen in.

By this time, the guards at the second pallet have also reach the same type of protrusion. Then both cloth protrusions extend themselves about a foot straight up at the same time.

This freaks the guards out as they fall back and grab for their weapons and aim. The cellphone guard waves the others to step back. He walks cautiously towards the pallets as he calls for someone else to come and assist him. The assistant continues to remove the bricks from the second pallet. Several more bricks fall to the floor when he stops. He hears a noise as his head is tilted once again. Cellphone guard orders his assistant to move back. I zoom in and can tell he is yelling. It is difficult to determine if he is yelling at the assistant or at the object within the money. Then the assistant starts yelling at the pile. An alarm sounds off within the bay as emergency lights go off as well as a flash on my monitor.

Rutherford moves to another computer and pulls up the same image as I have on my screen. I can see he is calling someone. I look back at the screen and notice cellphone guard reaching for his phone. From the second pile of cash, an object explodes outward. This object flies from the stack of cash like a banshee as the dark cloak covers it. Several bricks of money impact the assistant guard as he is knocked backwards. The banshee object ends up striking somewhere out of my camera's scope. I pan the camera and see a cable is tethered to a dark cylindrical object that currently attached itself to the concrete wall near the ceiling.

The dark cloak must have fallen on its way to the wall. Whatever it is tethered to is still hidden within the pile of cash. Cellphone guard drops his phone from the commotion and fires off a shotgun round at the pile. The other guards quickly take this as a sign to open fire. The released prisoners along with Rilo's group squat down and make themselves small from the gunfire. I switch to a different camera angle and see more guards pouring into the bay. The first pile of cash introduces itself by thrashing six of these tethered objects onto the walls near the ceiling as well. One of them also looks like the banshee from before but its cloak is now wedged between the tethered cylinder and the wall.

I can see what they are tethered to now. It looks like a mechanical scorpion with six legs but without the stinger tail. The dark metallic color makes it difficult for me to make out the details. With the cables extended, it looks like a halted carnival ride that rotates and swings round and round but in an evil way. The automatic machine gun fire from the guards continues while these machines remain still.

Then the second pile of cash wakes up and strikes one of Carter's vans directly behind it like a donkey kicking with its hind legs. The impact is powerful enough to knock it towards the entrance of where more guards are filing in from. The crushed van seems to have wedged itself into the doorway and the wall next to it. No other guards can come from that area now.

The second pile of money reveals the second scorpion infiltrator. It looks the same as the other with the exception that it has a larger underbelly. More guards begin to drum through another entrance, that is not worthy of my attention right now, amidst the barrage of weapons fire. I change camera angles again and realize these scorpions are starting to take some serious damage. Why are they not attacking? A better question is 'Are they here to save us?' If the HyphenDash guards keep this up, these scorpions will be an expensive waste of time.

The fresh group of guards bring in some heavier fire power. This livens up the scorpions as the second one extends its antennae. I am going to call the scorpion with the underbelly Momma and the one with the six tethered cylinders as Poppa. Poppa is hit in what I would believe to be one of its optics. I pan around through several camera angles. Through a sliver where the ceiling and the walls make contact is a compartment where a sniper is firing from. More snipers are seen as I trace this wedge along the ceiling.

What is taking Momma and Poppa so long to do anything? I click to a camera at the exact moment an RPG explodes on contact with Momma. It knocks everyone to the floor. Shrapnel scatters all around. Smoke accompanies the debris. I cannot see what happened to Momma. I still cannot scream but I can feel tears running down the side of my face. I do not know why I am crying. I do not feel sad or frightened. If anything, I feel calm and slightly entertained.

Rutherford looks on waiting to see the final damage. The bay finally clears itself of the debris. I can see Poppa. It looks fine. But Momma looks bad. Its left forward leg is partially destroyed at the knee area. Momma finally takes action and moves around to locate its first target. The front leg is proving to be an obstacle as its other five legs compensate. I can imagine how Momma's gears and hydraulic lines must be straining to keep up with its commands.

Rutherford laughs, "This must be someone's foolish idea of training my guards. If anything, my men are getting a kick out of this except for that door that is destroyed. That is a triple steel reinforced door with titanium braces." An alarm goes off, "Oh man, I almost forgot I have to start up this sequence." He heads back to his desk and starts punching on his keyboard.

More ammunition is expended on the two scorpions. The RPGs sidewind uncontrollably as they whistle through the smoke-filled air. They add to the mostly destroyed vehicle bay. The snipers are picking apart pieces of Momma and Poppa. There is a large crash. What was that?! The concussion reaches me.

Rutherford says as he refocuses his attention back on the monitor, "Those guys better tone it down on the fireworks before they blow up the building."

I pan around to see if they used a larger explosive device on the scorpions. But they remain intact, for the most part. I keep panning around. I notice the guards are looking up. I search for a higher camera angle. There it is. One of the tethered devices launched an explosive attack on the compartment one of the snipers was firing from. Then I see something chaotically wonderful. All the tethered objects begin shooting at the guards on the ground. Beams of light begin emitting from them as it scrolls throughout the bay picking their targets. Massive firepower is being unleashed towards the guards. The scorpions awaken with their own hellfire. Momma engages in machine gun fire along with some whacky strobe lighting. Poppa shoots off its two canons that are protruding from its front. They are loud and nasty like artillery sounding off. I can faintly hear them from my hospital bed. The oversized casings eject from Poppa and clang against the battle torn floor. From the chaos, there are bright lights; it is not the target lights from the scorpions.

It is different, yet familiar. I know what that is. They are requests! As the smoke from the expended gunpowder and debris billows the bay, more requests are seen. They glow like little angels hovering above those bodies. The scorpions' stumble as they move about. The damage they are sustaining is impeding their forward progress.

I hear Rutherford, "There it is! Do you see? The satellite is recording the requests. They are beautiful, are they not?" I focus back on the screen and take note to some activity within the destruction.

The other recently released prisoners seize the opportunity by picking up the weapons from the fallen HyphenDash guards. This is a risky move. The two scorpions may track them as hostiles. "Be careful guys," I say to myself. Rilo and his team along with their new additions begin to shoot the HyphenDash guards.

Mrs. Bellows is still there being protected by two of her loyal subjects. Rilo's men are more precise in their marksmanship than the scorpions. I see someone tug on Rilo's shirt. A short exchange of words takes place. Rilo makes a hand gesture and the entire group moves toward the van that is wedged in the wall. Explosions knock some of them to the floor. I pan over to the explosion. Poppa is hit. The right side of Poppa has been blown off. Its mechanical parts are exposed. The enemy shoots at its new target. Poppa keeps firing but is moving much slower than before. Momma realizes Poppa is damaged and maneuvers to Poppa's exposed side. She is slow but manages to reach Poppa. Momma's heroic actions rescue Poppa from imminent destruction; however, this now makes it easier for the guards to shoot in one general direction regardless of the thickness of the smoke inside the bay. Poppa's tethered cylinders receive different orders. Each cylinder fires at a designated target. I can tell as there is not a barrage of gunfire expended from them. There are pauses between each shot. These cylinders are now acting as snipers. It makes sense. By design, there probably is not a lot of room for all those bullets in those cylinders.

I scan over to find my friends huddled behind two of the vehicles that are closest to the doorway I went through before. Then I see DeadRick speaking to Sung-Suu with his hand up to his mouth acting as an amplifier as a result of the battle taking place. But what happens next is what really shocks me.

Sung-Suu's face turns red and angry. He darts over to Munch and lands on top of him. Sung-Suu begins to punch him in the face repeatedly. And to make it even more appalling Munch does not make any attempt to defend himself. My body tenses at the vicious attack of one friend to the other. It does not take long until the rest of the group realizes what is happening.

They split them apart. Koonzo restores order quickly. Sung-Suu is yelling at Munch as he wipes away the blood from his face. Koonzo raises his hands towards Munch as he mouths off a statement. Then a large explosion goes off sending a piece of shrapnel directly at the vehicle where Koonzo and Sung-Suu are behind. This quickly makes everyone refocus on taking cover. Shaboomba holds Munch behind their vehicle as it appears, he is crying. This is something I am going to have to ask them about when I get out of here.

Chapter 31

Monday Mid-Afternoon

R ilo's guards are searching for a way to enter through the wedged van. Rilo pushes Koonzo's body inside the van probably to find a way through to the other side. Koonzo pops back out shaking his head. This does not look good. A cluster of guards have shifted their fire towards them. With the guards shooting and throwing grenades at the rescue squad, the situation looks very bleak. Several of them are wounded. Mrs. Bellows has her ears covered. Someone has to get them out of there! From another camera angle, I see a guard with an RPG on his shoulder.

"Get out of there, Mrs. Bellows!" I mumble at the screen. They do not see him. "You guys have to turn around!" Why are they not looking at this guy? The rescue squad needs to be rescued and they know it. Any moment now that guard is going to pull the trigger. Seconds after I had that thought a bullet strikes the RPG. It explodes, disintegrating the guard. I switch cameras and notice one of Poppa's tethered cylinders is pointing its barrel in that direction. That is amazing, Poppa is able to recognize their threat is our threat. How would it know that? There must be an operator inside them. But if that is the case, why the delay in the beginning?

Poppa breaks away from Momma's cover and heads towards the rescue squad. I think it is going to provide them cover from the fire while they figure a way inside. Momma moves towards the main cluster of attackers. At this point, there is one main cluster and two smaller clusters all of which are in different locations at the farthest wall from the wedged van wall. The main cluster is at the left corner. There is a slow turnabout from Poppa as it tries to aim its weapons to the rear where the enemy continues to attack.

The cables are twisting as Poppa does its turnabout. Several explosions take place above Poppa's top area. How did I miss that? I am staring right at Poppa. Then I see the cables dangle from the hanging cylinders. This is good and bad. Poppa is able to turn all the way around now. The bad part is Poppa's sharpshooter cylinders are no longer active. Momma open fires on all three clusters. As it moves toward the main cluster, her single tethered cylinder seems to have reached its maximum length as the tension on the cable is rigid. An explosion detaches the tethered cylinder. There was no activity coming from that cylinder to begin with. Poppa completes its maneuver and begins to engage its targets with canon fire. The rescue squad has no other option but to shoot its way out of that bay.

What is going on down there? I see Poppa raise both its rear legs. This clues the rescue squad to move away from that area. Just as fast as it cocks its legs, bang! It donkey kicks through the wall with the van wedged in it. A large gaping hole enough to fit Poppa reveals what is on the other side. That is amazing! That operator knows what is going on. Now I get it. Poppa, to include the operator inside, would not expend its explosives on the wall since the rescue squad would not know to move out of harm's way. I guess a donkey kick works just as good. These machines are incredible. The squad realizes the gift presented and bolts inside.

Could they be coming for me? Or are they looking for a vantage point to help out the scorpions? Either way, we both need them. Poor Mrs. Bellows. Her body must be taking a beating from the concussion of those explosions. She is not going to last much longer. More requests are seen against the walls where the HyphenDash guards are defending their position. Several armor-plated shields are propped up to aid the guards from further casualties. I could not tell you how they got there. As for the guards, how much firepower does this place have? This battle has been going strong for quite some time. What is a place like this doing with this much ammunition? This is a small army attacking us.

I scan over more cameras and find the rescue squad. They are in a firefight with the guards in a hallway. I do not know where they are at, but it is not close by. I do not here any gunshots from my end.

Rutherford comes in and tells me, "You know, no matter how hard they want to come in, you will keep them away." My mouth only murmurs what I want to say. But he already knows what I am going to ask.

He fills in the blanks, "Keep away from what? Oh no, Ms. Powa, I have seen enough movies to learn not to give away the secret. But you are obliged to watch your friends fail." As he walks away, Rutherford laughs with the sense of confidence that his plan is foolproof. What is it that makes him believe they will not reach me? But the real question I want to ask is how will I manage to keep them away from saving me? I already feel sick to my stomach and this is not going to make it any better. I wish I could do something other than stare at a television screen.

But since I cannot, I continue to watch my reality show. I scan through other cameras looking to see if there is any other action taking place other than the battle in the bay. There is more. There are other cells here. The layout is the same as the ones I have seen before. Was this a prison at one time? This is probably where DeadRick and Munch were locked up. Some of the cell doors are opened while some others remain closed. I cannot tell if there is anyone in them. I am going to have to remember camera number 34. I scroll through and find a hospital room with someone occupying it. He looks gravely ill. Wait. No, he has passed away. The machines in the background all show flatlines. There is someone else inside. Looks like medical staff. I cannot tell what the gender is as he or she is covered up with the standard surgical apparel.

In this case, I am going to call this medical staff member a her to make it easier for me to explain. There is a small wooden block like that of a toy about a foot away from the dead man's face. It looks like she was trying to get him to request it. These people here are disgusting. She could not pick a photo of his family to be a request? They have to pick an insignificant object to be the one thing he takes to heaven?

Unbelievable.

The medical person looks at her watch and shakes her head. She looks over and does something. The camera is unable to pan about. It looks like she is unwrapping something while talking to someone. I can see her facial visor moving up and down. She injects something into the dead man. Seconds later, the man comes back to life. They give him another injection. Just like that, the man dies again. What kind of torture chamber is this? How cruel can a human being be towards another human?! Several minutes go by and the box begins to light up.

HyphenDash is getting what they want. The wooden block begins to elevate and slowly spin on its y-axis. More lights spring from the block. And then poof. A blast of bright light and then nothing. The block falls to the tray and the lights disappear. The lady scrambles to give another injection. The machines bleep back to life after she injects another cocktail.

How is that possible? The request has failed. What are they up to here?

Rutherford thankfully breaks my concentration, "He is already dead. What I mean to say is he initially died an hour ago. We have been trying to get him to request that block. We realized something. When the heart stops, it takes the brain around six minutes to stop functioning completely. The challenge is actually knowing when exactly the brain stops functioning for each individual. When we discovered this, we realized we can reanimate the brain and the body. And when we do that our patients get another chance to make a request. So far, we have not been successful. But from what you can see we are getting close. Pretty impressive, huh?"

My mouth still feels restrictive, but I manage to mutter this off, "You people are dirt bags. If you can bring his mind back, then why not use that to keep him alive? Why not share this serum with hospitals so they can save lives? Why torture him?"

"Ms. Powa, you do not see anything beyond your little world. Once we perfect this process, we will surely provide this medicine to the masses. No use in keeping it to ourselves. We will also reveal our discovery of request manipulation. As you can tell, this is about getting a loved one to carry a message or something even more meaningful to the other side. The possibilities are endless. The research is endless. Who knows, maybe we might be able to enter this other place and then come back to our world. Hmmm, let me write that down."

As Rutherford picks up a pencil to annotate his brand-new idea, I get confused so I have to ask, "If you have a process to manipulate a request, then what is the purpose of the 1X formula? Why go through all of this if you already have an alternative? Does HyphenDash have anything to do with the new week and calendar changes?" That last question just popped out while going through my mental filtering process.

But I figured since they are knee deep in this type of activity maybe they are involved with the big calendar shift too.

Rutherford finishes writing his latest idea as he replies, "For your last question, we are involved in a lot of major programs but that one is not one of ours. Betahouse gets the honors in that department which explains a lot of their recent activities. The 1X formula has a severe side effect. It accelerates the process of death. Pretty much, taking the formula means killing the person. The FDA would never approve this if they ever found out. HyphenDash was going to put a team together to lobby to get this pushed through. Fortunately, that is when another one of our sites found an alternative way to the request process. Surely, we want to keep the formula to ourselves to prevent our competitors from perfecting 1X."

I could not believe my ears and state, "So, I just injected myself with a lethal serum?" Rutherford lowers his head and nods slowly. Stupid. How stupid can I be? What if he is lying? He has to be making that up. But then again, I did receive my first alert.

Rutherford adds, "Hey, listen, your situation does not change. You are still set to make an honorable sacrifice for all mankind." Now I understand why I feel so drowsy and why it has been difficult to speak and breathe.

I hear another crash much larger than the one Poppa generated when he kicked in the wall earlier. I focus back on the monitor and pan back to the area where the sound came from. Poppa and Momma have switched places. Momma seems to have burrowed herself inside the busted wall while Poppa provides cover. He is taking a beating right now and the rescue squad realizes this. Momma lowers her underbelly. Now we get to see her precious cargo. The rescue squad gathers around. I zoom in and see there is some hardware in her carriage. Rilo hands out the gear. It does not look like there are any weapons or extra ammo. A monitor pops down from Momma. There is a man speaking on the screen. I cannot tell if it is a recording or a live feed. I can tell you it has the rescue squad's attention. Another large explosion takes place followed by a second. The squad looks over as do I. Poppa is down. Its exposed body and a portion of its face are blown out. Hydraulic fluid and other liquids pour from its main body as it bleeds out.

Poor Poppa.

Momma launches one of her tethered cylinders. It manages to strike a guard as it throws him against the wall it is now attached to. Rilo has the squad in a huddle while Momma provides the gunfire. They quickly break and now form two groups. After a final word from Rilo, the two newly formed groups venture off.

Some of them are heading downstairs. I would not have pegged this place as having a basement, but I guess I was wrong. I follow them down several flights of stairs until they finally reach the only visible door. But the stairwell still continues downward. I want to know what it is down there but there is no use in following it down to its final destination. I have to keep up with these guys. They are fast. I hear gunshots. I pan around to see where they are being ambushed. Hold on. If I am hearing gunshots and there is no audio on these cameras, then there is a firefight nearby. I switch cameras and locate them. The other team is down several corridors from me pushing through. The HyphenDash guard count seems to be dwindling; there are not as many now. As I follow along, I cannot help thinking about the dead man the mad scientists were working on. Is this how zombies come into existence? I think it is a legit question. That man's brain can only take so many shots of whatever they have been injecting him with until something even worse happens. I abandon that crazy science fiction thought and focus back on the monitors. The gunshots are much louder now. Rutherford is looking at the door. He seems a little nervous as he returns to his chair and punches in some more keys. I see the rescue squad right outside the door. Yes! They are putting something on it. It looks like clay which could only mean explosives.

Chapter 32

Same mid-afternoon

Rutherford rushes over to me with a device in his hand, "Tell them to stop! Tell them quickly before you lose your chance!" My face went from 'Whatever' to 'What do you mean' in a matter of seconds. His face looks serious. There is a gloss of sweat forming on it. I cannot tell if this is a life and death situation for him or if this is fear of losing his job with HyphenDash. But why should I care? He has not done me any favors. He gathers himself while he squares away his hair and wipes the sweat from his face. His breathing is calm now. Pretty impressive recovery time considering ten seconds ago he was in panic mode.

A loud explosion sets off and for some reason Rutherford flinches, we both look at the monitor. The explosion caused some damage to the door but not enough to open it. A slightly concerning look is on his face again.

Rutherford moves in closer to my bedside and asks me in such a forgiving voice, "Ms. Powa, would you like to see your mother one last time?" Oh man, is this guy that desperate? If this is his way of trying to convince me to do what he wants, then I take back every compliment I have said about this guy before.

Still straining to speak, "Do you think bringing my mother up is going to make your situation any better? Are you that stupid or did someone train you to be that way? I have nothing more to say to you. You can stop asking me now."

And there it is, that sneaky grin he likes to share. Did I just fall into his trap? I probably did. But I also have an ace in my hand. I look back at the monitor and see the squad placing more explosives on the door.

Rutherford looks at me and says, "My dear Ms. Powa, your mother would applaud your fire and grit. Young ladies your age do not develop such a trait until after high school. But that trait also blinds you from different realities. One such reality is the power of this company and what we are capable of doing."

"No point in using my mom as a crutch. I already beat you in that brain game. What are you getting at?" I ask as I stare at the monitor.

He goes on, "Okay, okay. It is a touchy subject for you. How about your father? You idolized him while you placed your mother in his shadow."

I can hear my breathing getting louder. The beeping machines are increasing in their tempo. Yes, I am surely pissed off, "What are you going to tell me now, Rutherford, that you are holding my father hostage?! Leave my family out of this conversation!"

Rutherford fires back, "No, Ms. Powa, I would not do that. There are too many eyes on your family. But I have to ask, why do you continue to neglect your mother?"

I lift up my arms as the restraints thud them back to the bed and yell, "To hell with you, Rutherford! My mother is dead and all you can do is talk crap about her! But you cannot use her name anymore. She is gone. She cannot be your lab rat. I called her while in a cab. She died as I was talking to her. So, you see, Rutherford? You lose! You hear me? You lose!"

I feel exhausted as I give up my only ace. Hopefully that shuts him up. As tears run down my face as I whimper, I believe what he said is true. I left my mother behind every time as I kept my father with me. I messed up. I am sorry, mom. I am so sorry. This is the real reason for the tears. Remorse is such a painful lesson.

I hear his voice, "I am sorry for your loss, Ms. Powa. Losing a parent is not easy especially when they are a large part of your life."

That is another stab at my lack of attention to my mother. I do not reply to his comment. My whimpering has temporarily locked down all other emotions and motor functions. He says, "But you already knew that." My face turns to lock eyes with his. He continues, "When your mother's first alert was relayed to HyphenDash, I immediately had our satellite move into position. Would you like to see her ray of light?"

I question his gesture, "That ray of light can be anyone's. All you would have to do is paste the time and date. I am not that naïve. Go find yourself another sucker, Rutherford."

He starts tapping on a tablet he now has in his hand, "This is true with how technology works these days. But something we discovered is that every request exhibits a light frequency, naturally."

"Like I said, Rutherford, you are telling me nothing," I tell him so he can shut up. But he does not catch my drift.

"Okay, then you must know that each request has its own unique light frequency. HyphenDash has been working on a device to measure such sensitive frequencies that can register to the peculum. The peculum is the overall measurement of each frequency.

I angrily interrupt yet continue to strain my point, "Now how would you know what frequency my mother's light was if you were not there?" Rutherford remains silent. Did I beat him at his own game?

After a brief pause he speaks up, "Like I said, you fail to understand how grand this company has grown. We were able to get in close as we planted a nurse assigned to aid your mother. She was there when your mother passed away. She also was able to record the request. So, I used our peculum device to register your mother's light frequency from her request. I compared it to the ray of light peculum and it is an exact match. Would you like to see your mother for a last time?"

It makes sense now. And HyphenDash seems to have their hands in everything. I would be a fool to think they are not capable of this. He can tell I am thinking about what he said. He holds up a device, "This is a video intercom. Once you push the red button, they will see you. But hurry. The deal is off once they break in."

I grab the device and waste no time pushing that red button, "Stop! Rilo, you have to stop! I am fine. But I need you to stop." I can see them on the intercom device. They all stop what they are doing and focus on the door monitor that somehow has not been destroyed by the explosions.

Koonzo pops up, "Powa, what is he trying to make you do? Do not trust him! He will lie and cheat you. We have to break in!"

"No, Koonzo, please stay out. I promise, I am fine, but I need to finish this with Rutherford. Afterwards, you can do whatever you want. Trust me, Koonzo." I begin to worry he will not heed my request.

Koonzo replies, "No, you are in danger! He has manipulated you into thinking nothing is wrong. There is a war going on out here! We have to leave before we all die!"

I look at Rutherford, "Tell your men to stop attacking." He heads over to his desk puts on a headset and transmits, "Mike 2 Actual, do you read, over."

He turns up the volume on his radio. Only static is heard in return. He transmits again, "Mike 2 Actual, do you read? Cease fire, cease fire!" Still only static is heard. I listen behind the walls. The firefight still continues. But then it calms itself down. I can only hear one type of gunfire. Who is the rampant warrior that does not understand we are no longer attacking?

I hear Rilo on the mic, "You two, go back and tell me what is going on over there." Two men take off.

Rutherford comes back to me, "Listen, who knows what else is going to happen. Everything is going to be in a free fall here soon. Tell them to stay out. Tell them to not do anything else!"

I begin to feel the anxiety rush back into my veins. I push the red button, "Rilo, Koonzo please stay out. I have to do this. It is about my mom. Please."

Mrs. Bellows enters the view screen. I did not know she went with the group. She must be hard as nails to want to go through this. She tells me, "Darling, we should go. This place is not suited for people like you and I." Interesting to know she does not look bothered by all the chaos.

I am about to reply when the two men return. One of them reports while trying to catch his breath, "It is not the security that is firing. It is the six-legged machine. We tried to communicate with the operator, but the antenna is destroyed. It is essentially acting under its last received orders."

Rilo looks back into the intercom, "Well you heard him. It is that machine out there. Nothing we can do."

Rutherford grabs the device, "Well my guys seem to have heard my transmission since they stopped firing. Maybe they will take out that thing."

Rilo attempts to say something but Koonzo stops him, "Ok, Powa. But all we will give you is five minutes regardless of what you say. We are not going to wait forever not knowing if he has killed you and found a way to escape."

I turn off the device and tell Rutherford, "You are up." He heads back to his desk and picks up his headset, "Mike 2 Actual, do not fire upon the visitors. They have ceased fire." Just static on the other end.

He removes the headset and begins tapping on more keys. My monitor changes to the dark earth. It zooms in. I hear Rutherford say, "There is a dimmer switch located on the right side of the mouse if you want to see the monitor more efficiently." I feel the dimmer lever. I use my ring finger to test it out. It works. The lights dim down to the point where the bulbs are a light brown. The dark earth is magnified some more. I recognize my home state. The image enhances continuously until it is focused on a building.

Rutherford explains, "This is the hospital she was staying at. Third floor in a room just for her. She received a lot of attention because of you. But it was good attention. We had staff on hand to ensure she was not harassed."

I do not know if I should be angry at him for spying on my mom or pleased he told me folks were kind to her. I look on as Rutherford tells me, "And there it is." I see a quick white bleep and just like that, it was gone. I hear, "Hold on, let me slow that down considerably." I can tell he is rewinding the footage as I see the bleep once again. The image is paused. Now I see it. It has a light green elongated hue like a falling star. Rutherford remains quiet. That is my mom. I reach up to touch the beautiful stream of light, but the restraints prevent such an act of love. I begin to cry not because of the restraints. Well maybe it is because of the restraints. I am quickly aware of an eerie metaphor; just like these restraints, I have been prevented from seeing my mother one last time. And yet here I am looking at her in a way no one on this earth has ever seen their loved one. I miss you, mom. "You look beautiful today." The image enhances some more. It begins to look a bit pixelated. As I stare at my mother, I see something.

Rutherford breaks my concentration, "Would you like to see her request?" Then the lights dim and flicker. The humming of the computer fans and other electrical devices slow for a second and return to normal operating speed. Rutherford scrambles to his other computer.

He tells me, "Your friends are…still at the front door? What?" He continues to scan through his monitors. He yells, "They are at the server room! Another group is attempting to break into the server room."

I reply, "So what?"

"If the servers go down then a trip protocol will commence. It is basically a failsafe that transfers all data here to another offsite location while destroying all the files. The servers will pretty much melt themselves. We will have about ten-minutes before the meltdown reaches these files. Thirty-seconds from then the second protocol would begin. This is when the compound is filled with poisonous gas for obvious reasons. Tell your friends to stop!"

I turn the intercom back on, "Rilo! Tell your team downstairs to stop trying to take the servers off line!"

He replies, "Why?" He looks back at Koonzo, "You better talk to your girl. She is tripping."

I reply, "Because there is a failsafe if the servers are taken offline. A poisonous gas will fill the entire complex in ten-minutes after they go down!"

Rilo's face gives me the chills. He says, "Just like the other complex. Hey, we cannot contact them because we do not have any communication assets."

Rutherford grabs the intercom, "Then you need to send a runner to tell them to stop."

Rilo, "Why should I send a runner?! This is your complex, get one of your guards to do it!"

Rutherford calmly replies, "If I sent one of my guards down there, do you think your people are going to think he is there for some tea?"

Rilo searches the floor for an answer and then looks back to his team, "You two are up again. Miracle yourselves down there and tell them the news before we are all dead." The two men take off again.

Rutherford turns off the intercom, "They may not stop them in time. We must be quick."

I try to remain calm as Rutherford rushes back to his desk. The monitor goes blank and switches to a video. As the video plays, Rutherford begins to rummage through his space. The video begins with a crowd around my mother's hospital room. It is dimly illuminated like mine. The camera pans around as I see my little brother who is crying and in the arms of my dad. I cannot tell if he is crying as well. I miss my family. My tears only continue to flow.

Then the camera finds my mother. How soft and serene she looks. That is my dead mother as the medical devices would reflect. I thought I would get to see her alive before this part. This is so overwhelming. I look away although this last image of her burns the inside of my eyelids. Then flashes of light are seen reflecting off the walls in the room. I look back at the monitor. What did she request? The camera pans over to focus on a little clay ashtray my little brother made her when he was five. I remember I busted that thing when we were fighting. I felt bad and glued it back together. I did a horrible job. We were fighting over who loved mom the most. "Mom, I am so sorry for everything. I should have treated you better."

The little ashtray continues to light up. The flashing lights pulse as they spin into a vortex upward like a reverse tornado. Then more flashing lights spin into a vortex but on the left, right, and bottom. So now there are four of the little light tornados. I can see my dad and brother's faces clearly now. My dad was crying because his eyes are red and puffy. And then it disappears. The room is dark again. It takes a few seconds before the camera adjusts to the lack of light. Before it finishes its adjustment, the video stops.

Finally, my crying ceases as I am trying to process everything. The urge to weep overtakes me again. Rutherford comes to my bedside and places something in my hand, "This is your mother. Everything you saw on that monitor is right here. I hope when my time comes, I am afforded the same opportunity."

What do I say to Rutherford's gesture? I did not ask him to do this, but I think I should be appreciative that my captor has done this good deed. He holds up a drawing of two angels on a piece of paper. He tells me in a somber tone, "My little girl made this for me the night of the Apatou event. My entire team from HyphenDash brought our families out there since they knew we would be in that region for at least two years. How was I supposed to know there was a gas pocket in that area? Why was the spectrum analyzer not picking that up? Why did I have to lose my little girl that night? We all lost everything in Apatou." His eyes are filled with tears, but he wipes them away.

I catch a good look at his right hand. The inside of it has request marks and continues down his forearm. The discovery stops my crying for now. I attempt to put that puzzle together. But then I remember, we should be rushing right now. We do not know if the first failsafe protocol issue is going to go off. How come Rutherford is not trying to get me out of these restraints? I hear his footsteps and then I feel this sudden thud on my chest. By chance, my finger brushes the dimmer lever to high illumination. The room is blasted with light as I squint to adjust.

I feel a burning feeling entering my chest. I look down at where this pain is originating. From my chest, I see an extremely large syringe sticking out of my chest. Betrayal! I scream from shock. My hands automatically attempt to remove the foreign object, but the reality of their restrained condition hits me again. My hands pay no mind to the restraints as they continue to make their perilous attempts to remove the syringe. As I watch my hands fight for centimeters, I feel a device being placed on my head. It forces the back of my head onto my pillow. It is metallic and heavy. Rutherford is clamping it down to the bed. I resist but the device has cinched itself firmly onto my head. I cannot move it at all. I ask him as I strain, "What are you doing, Rutherford?! Let me go!"

"Not just yet, Ms. Powa. There is something else that needs to be done," as I hear him fidgeting with something on a metal tray. As he does whatever he is doing, he tells me, "During our research, we realized after the first alert that we are able to manipulate the request within a strict process. What we found is that we can get the mind or soul to change its original request. The secret is that we have to provide an adrenal boost. Then we inject a special serum that strains the brain into a short term amnesiatic state. In order to make all this work, we bombard the senses with visuals of what we want to have as the request prior to administering the adrenal boost. Consider this 1Xa formula."

I can feel the adrenaline tense my every muscle. Through my struggle to speak I tell him, "If you already have a means to make custom requests, why the effort to retrieve the 1X formula?"

Rutherford leans in, "I already told you this, Ms. Powa, 1X was the first-generation serum. Keep up. Rule number one. Never put all your serums in one basket."

As I grit my teeth from the adrenaline, "In case you missed it, you forgot the first step, pal." Rutherford gives me that heinous grin I really want to watch turn sour.

He continues, "Like I said, we bombard the sense. The way we do it is with a monitor such as this one. We play the subliminal images throughout a prolonged exposure while the subject is watching something such as an attack on our compound."

I interrupt, "Or the video of a mother's request." I try and turn away not to face him but the contraption on my head prevents it. He beat me. I fell for all his tricks and traps. I cannot outsmart this guy. He brings the monitor a little closer. The only thing that is on the monitor is the door with Koonzo and the rescue squad waiting. I should have listened to him. My anxiety adds to the adrenaline. My heart is pounding so hard it physically hurts me.

I muster up the will to say, "You used my mother against me. For that? I hope when my time comes, your request is what I choose."

Then Rutherford jumps on top of me. I tell him to get off as the adrenaline has taken control of my body. But something is wrong. I look at his face and there is a look of terror I do not understand. Blood starts dripping from his open mouth. I hear another alarm go off. Rutherford strains as he speaks, "Ms. Powa, that is your second alert. I look forward to seeing your request. Or should I say, my request."

As Rutherford falls and my vision becomes hazy, I see Carter emerge. His eyes look bloodshot. He looks at me and says, "Powa, second protocol has been set. We got to get out of here." I pass out. It must have been a few minutes later when I wake up to the sound of a deep heaving breath. Looking around, I realize I am sitting up.

Carter says, "Powa! Can you breathe? Can you talk?"

I nod and ask, "What happened?"

Carter gives me a funny look and says, "I figured you would want to handle him."

On the floor is Rutherford with a piece of an armrest sticking from his back. Carter tells me, "He is going to bleed out. He does not have much time."

I stand up and struggle to gain my balance. A few seconds go by and I kneel to Rutherford's side. I place my hand on his face, "Thank you for this. None of this would have happened without you." He has that sick grin again. The grin of a person who thinks he did me a favor.

Then I hold up the drawing of the two angels that he had in his right hand. And my wish is granted. His smug grin melts into despair. I tell him, "You tried to kill me to deny me my request."

I hold up my left hand and Carter fills it. I then say in as calm a tone as possible despite the rage and enlightenment I am experiencing, "This request you have here as you lay dying will not go with you. Where is HyphenDash's power now?" In my hand is a lighter with a soft flame. I place it under the drawing. It slowly catches fire. I take a long look at Rutherford. I can see the horror on his face.

I can tell he has thought of his final moment before and this is not how he planned it. I win. His face has gone limp as his eyes fade away. Carter leans in to see if he can hear a heartbeat, "He is gone which is weird. No first alert or second alert went off. This guy never even signed up for the Gevity. I guess he had a problem with his company knowing too much about him. Probably did not want to have the same fate as Pendleton. We have to go now. We may still have a chance."

I ask, "A chance for what? It is over."

Carter tells me, "Not exactly, Powa. Rilo's guys were not able to reach the server team."

I have to ask, "How do you know about the server team?"

"When I woke up, I heard the conversation. I just kept my eyes closed. I broke off the armrest to cut off the wires wrapped around me. The technician that was in here, yeah, a nice blood choke took care of him. Then I went for your other boyfriend here."

"What happened to me?" I need to know.

He looks at me, "You died and then I miracled you back." Carter points to my chest. I see a second syringe sticking out from my chest. He tells me, "I gave you another adrenaline shot. Your breath stinks so CPR was out of the question."

I smile because I get his lame joke. Carter cannot fool me, he is a big softy. He would have given me CPR if necessary...I think. Oh my goodness. How many injections am I going to get before this day is over? Carter stands me up as he turns on the intercom, "Hey fellas, get us out of here, will you?"

Rilo jumps in front of the intercom, "Boss, you been sleeping on the job?"

Carter laughs and says, "Yea, with your mom." Everyone laughs but Carter brings it back, "Look, we have to hurry. The server team set off the complex's defensive measures. The servers are set to melt, and this place is going to get fumigated real quick."

Rilo tells his team, "You and you go down there and tell them this place is going to get gassed. We will meet you all at the loading dock. Be prepared to battle through the gas and any bad guys." The two men run off.

Mrs. Bellows speaks up, "Carter, my boy. Thank goodness you are still with us."

Carter feels the need to say, "I would not have you in the hands of Rilo, Mrs. Bellows. That guy creeps me out." Rilo cracks a smile.

Chapter 33

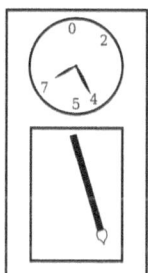

Monday late afternoon

From all the gunfire, I can hear the alarms go off. These alarms sound different than the previous sirens. I scroll through the cameras while Carter stands behind a filing cabinet waiting for them to blast through. The HyphenDash guards seem to have amassed only a few more men and weapons. They know what that alarm means as they load up their vehicles. Momma still is putting up a fight but is not able to reach them, which are around the corner. An explosion finally blasts the door off the hinges.

Carter yells, "Time to go, kid!" I exit the hospital room and reach out for Carter. On the floor is the technician that gave Carter the complimentary nap.

He makes it simple, "Lead the way, Rilo." Carter releases my hand and scoops up Mrs. Bellows.

Shaboomba extends her hand, "Come on, girlfriend. We need to boogie." I quickly accept. I still do not feel 100%.

Everyone heads out into a fast-paced run. We reach Momma. She is all battered up but still unloading on her adversaries anchored behind what used to be two trucks. Large chunks of her armor have been shot off or blown off. She has taken a considerable amount of punishment. I pass by her for the first and last time. She does not bother to look down at us. I can tell she knows we are here. I get the chance to place my hand on one of her legs. It is somewhat hot with ricochet marks on it. She increases her barrage. I hear the brass shell casings dance off the floor. For the first time, I see the bay we arrived in. It is scattered with twisted metal, concrete chunks from the interior walls, and five-dollar bills everywhere. And I do mean the floor is littered with these bills covering every open space here.

Carter peaks around and then tells us, "One of our vans is still out there but it is pretty shot up. Who knows if it will run. The other two are on the right destroyed from the battle. We will have to put ourselves in the line of fire in order to get there. Our second option is to bogart at least one of those vehicles from the HyphenDash guards. We will be under fire as well but this time it will be life or death for those guys. So, they will give us all they have in order to escape."

Noni from nowhere asks, "And our third option?" We all look at him like a stranger.

Carter looks out into the bay, "We stay and suck up the poisonous gas and have a real good time."

Goji provides the long awaited and inappropriate conclusion beat. Shaboomba smacks him so hard in the back of the head, Goji stumbles forward a few steps.

He immediately regrets his timing. Goji adds, "I cannot tell if he is trying to be funny or if he is really serious." No one bothers explaining it to him.

Sung-Suu gives his vote, "I say we go for the HyphenDash vehicles."

Cliffster seconds the vote, "At least we know they work unlike Sung-Suu's momma. No use going to our van knowing it has been in the middle of a war zone." Most of us shake our heads as Noni and Goji smile at the remark.

Rilo also agrees, "Boss, it is more of a risk but with time being a factor here, we need to reach for those vehicles and head out of here."

Carter comes back with, "I am thinking the same thing. Too bad this hunk of metal cannot help us out. Ok, Rilo, take two of your guys and head to the debris next to the van. If you can reach the van, then give it a shot. If not, then just lay cover fire while we take our spot. Most of my guys will follow me. You kids and two of my guards will stay with Mrs. Bellows. No need to bring her into all of this until we have secured a ride."

Everyone rogers up. Carter is about to give his team the go ahead when Koonzo yells out, "Stop!" Everyone stops in their place.

They look at Koonzo with questions on their faces. He answers them, "If we can get this machine to shoot off one of its cylinders then maybe it can use that to help with targeting the bad guys or it can use it as a wench to help pry itself loose."

Rilo has an important question, "Kid, how do you expect us to do that? It is not like we can jump up there and play charades with it."

"I figured you guys would know that," states a confused Koonzo.

Rilo looks at Carter, "Hey boss, why not just go for the gusto?"

Carter smiles, "Just like Fallujah when we were kids. We stick with the original plan." Koonzo looks a little disappointed his plan is rejected.

Rilo and Darryl rush; the enemy shoots at them as they return fire and reach their spot. This signals Carter to make his Medal of Honor run. He reaches his mark along with two other teammates which are slightly past Rilo's position. Carter's group spray their machine guns as Rilo attempts to reach the van. Rilo and Darryl are hit. The situation is bad. Darryl appears to be dead. Rilo looks like he is shot in the stomach.

He yells to Carter, "Boss, I am not going to reach it." The problem is the guards are firing accurate shots at him. From the chaos, another alarm catches everyone's attention. It sounds more urgent than the current alarm which is no longer sounding off. I look over at the HyphenDash guards. They put on their gas masks and finish loading their vehicles. The anchored down guards also do the same.

From the corner of my eye, I see Koonzo sprint towards Rilo. I react, "Koonzo, what are you doing?! Come back!" It is no use. He reaches the injured Rilo. Koonzo crouches under the debris with a fearful posture.

Carter fires at the guards while he yells at Koonzo, "Kid, pull him in!" Koonzo has a look of fright and regret that comes over his face as he tries to reach for Rilo. Carter yells at him again, "Kid, if you do not grab my guy I will go over there and shoot you myself!"

Koonzo looks over at me. I over exaggerate my words, so he can read my lips "You are too hardheaded for me." It is the only thing I can think of. The panic on his face changes to a smile. He grabs a large piece of shrapnel and covers up the side of his body facing the gunfire. Koonzo crawls out to Rilo who is about five feet in the open. Gunshots are pinging off the metal makeshift shield. He reaches Rilo and looks him over. Rilo grabs the shield, "Thanks, kid. This may put you in the running to get the girl." Fear prevents Koonzo from smiling at the remark.

Koonzo attempts to move Rilo, "A little help would get us over to the van much faster."

Rilo grunts as he replies, "Not going to happen, kid. For some reason I cannot feel my legs. But I got one free arm to get us somewhere." Koonzo is able to move Rilo but at a snail's pace. Carter realizes the situation. He tells his guard to his right, "I'm going to make a dash for it. Once I am there, I will…Hey kid, get back here!"

I look away from Koonzo and notice Munch sprinting towards Koonzo and Rilo's position. Has everyone lost their minds?! There he slides behind the makeshift shield. Munch yells, "I just pissed my pants!" Koonzo laughs as Munch asks, "What is so funny?!"

"I did the exact same thing!" Munch smiles and immediately helps Koonzo move Rilo towards the van. They reach the battered vehicle and take cover on the opposite side of the firefight. Rilo looks around and asks, "Where is my rifle?" Munch sees it at their former position. He sprints back out to get it as Rilo yells, "Get back here, kid! They got us dialed in!"

A shot strikes Munch to the left of his chest. His back is blown out exposing the bone structure of his upper rear torso. Munch falls backwards from the momentum of the impact. I want to look away, but I cannot. DeadRick breaks down in an uncontrollable sob which I would not have expected since he did not know Munch that well. Sung-Suu immediately looks away. I can tell by his body language that he is ignoring what just happened. I guess he did not want to think about their earlier fight or see more blown up bodies. Shaboomba, Noni, and Goji watch in disbelief as their eyes remain wide open while they are crouched behind a pile of rubble.

Munch's body lays limp near Darryl's whose request is a trinket I cannot identify.

Carter hand signals to Rilo letting him know the van objective is off the table. He focuses his attention on the HyphenDash guards in front. Carter signals to his three-man team the next bounding point. They lay cover fire as one of them reaches the new position. Through several military maneuvers, all three reach their new fighting position. I realize another three-man group has reached Carter's previous position. The HyphenDash guards begin to throw grenades along with their gunfire. Then the garage door behind the guards opens. They turn on their vehicles. The guards on the ground hop in while the ones in the turrets continue to lay suppressing fire. Once all their men are in, they chirp the tires. One of the vehicles circles around and heads towards the anchored group of guards. Carter and team shoot at it as that is one of the few vehicles left to acquire. Momma has a new target and unloads her arsenal. She must have hit a sensitive spot because that vehicle exploded and burst into flames.

The burning SUV careens to a stop once it hits the garage door wall. The other vehicles exit. One of the them stops just outside the bay as one of the guards jumps out. Koonzo uses the opportunity to run towards the battered van. He jumps in and turns the ignition. The first turn does not work. He resets the key and tries it one more time. It starts up! Koonzo jumps out of the van and yells at Carter, "It works!"

Shaboomba looks over at the garage entrance, "Carter!" She points to a guard who is in a turret. He has an RPG pointed right at Koonzo. Carter aims his weapon at the attacker. He fires off a round. It hits the guard but not before he launches off his ordinance. The little missile flies upward and hits the wall near the ceiling behind us where we are tucked in. Pieces of the wall fall over the opening we are huddled in. I get knocked on my butt.

Mrs. Bellows falls to the floor face down. Oh, she better not be dead. I shake her awake. Mrs. Bellows opens her eyes and says, "Darling, do not worry, I have been through much worse than this." I pick her up while I smile. The other guys are removing the debris. They are moving fast. We can smell the gas now as some of us start to cough.

As we gather ourselves, I hear a lot of yelling. What happened? I look back at Momma. She is done. A large chunk of the wall has crushed her head. Rilo is still hanging on. The gunfire has ceased now that there are no other HyphenDash guards in the bay.

Carter tells us, "We need to open that garage door."

Sung-Suu states, "That door was just open. Did those guys shut it on us after shooting a rocket in here?"

Cliffster replies, "That is how heinous these guys are. Where is Carter?" He is on the other side of the van. I run over to see what he is up to. Carter is kneeling next to Koonzo.

I think out loud and say, "What happened?"

Koonzo replies, "The explosion hit the wall over there. A piece of it broke off and hit this glorious specimen." I know Koonzo is trying to be funny, but his witty response does not put me at ease.

Carter informs me, "This piece of metal is from the ventilation."

Not understanding I say, "It looks pretty bad, but it looks like it hit him clean on the collarbone. He is not breathing shallow. That is good. His lungs are not punctured, right?"

Carter replies, "Yes, but the problem is those vents are spewing out poison. This poison is now in his bloodstream." A sudden rush of familiar panic strikes me again.

I yell at everyone, "Get in the van now! We have to go!"

Carter yells back, "Not yet! I still got to get this door open." Carter jumps in the driver's seat.

Everyone takes the opportunity to comfort Koonzo, but I stand back. It hurts too much to see him like that. I wipe my tears away to compose myself. I bite the inside of my check.

Carter puts the van in gear. He steps on the accelerator. The van's rear wheels screech towards the door. Upon impact, it creates a large indentation, but it does not break through. He puts it in reverse and gives it another go. The second time it breaks partially through. We can see the gas escape through the opening. Our coughing is getting chronic now. Some of the guys are coughing uncontrollably.

The van heads towards the garage door one more time. That jacked up van finally breaks through. Carter opens the door, "We need to move, now!" He goes back for Mrs. Bellows. We all exit the poisoned vehicle bay. The server team reaches us. I had forgotten about them. They are extremely winded but without question they help load up the wounded. It is extremely crowded in the van, but we all manage to fit in or hang off the sides. We even have a few of those other prisoners with us. Carter jumps in the driver seat and smashes the accelerator but due to the damage the van has endured we are not moving very fast.

Rilo speaks, "We have to offload everyone in case the authorities get to us, if that happens we will all get snatched and what is the sense in that?" Finally, the battered van exits the poisonous complex and past the guard shack that is also abandoned.

Carter heads behind a tree line not far from the bay. As he stops the van he tells everyone, "Hey everyone, get out, except for Mrs. Bellows, Rilo, and the kid. Move fast, people. You two, help me stabilize Rilo before we leave."

I speak up, "I am staying with Koonzo." I am expecting him to tell me no, but I am determined to stay in this van.

Carter and the other two guards are busy trying to stop the bleeding. Carter gives me a nod probably not understanding my request but at this point I am not going to argue. I see my friends outside. They are talking with Koonzo. I join them. The mood is laboriously jovial. They are trying to make him feel at ease.

I see DeadRick walking off as I call to him, "Hey, Comic-Con is over here!" DeadRick stops knowing the comment is directed at him. He walks back and notices me and my friends are watching him. His face looks bothered. Has all this shaken him to the point where he wants to run off on his own? It looks more like he is hiding what he wants to say. He stops in front of us and says, "I appreciate you guys getting me out of there, but this is not my group. I got my peeps just like you, Powa, got yours. It is time for me to head back."

DeadRick gives me an unexpected hug and walks off. I am slightly shocked that he would not want to form a bond with us.

That is when I hear Carter's voice yell out, "You, stop!" DeadRick stops and turns around. Carter hops out with his hands stained from Rilo's blood and points at DeadRick, "Do you think that walking down this road is not going to get you picked up? Do you think when you get picked up that you will not get tortured into saying something you should not be saying?"

DeadRick is about to answer when Carter answers for him, "No, you will not walk off and put all of us back in the very danger we just left. No, you will stand right next to my guys until we tell you what needs to happen." DeadRick takes his place next to Vendervich. The air is silent and the division between DeadRick and the rest of us becomes that much larger.

Then my friends turn to me. Sung-Suu tells me, "You make for a horrible nerd."

I give a half-hearted laugh with a hug, "Thank you for taking me in. And not knocking me out with your chin." I look down and see a wad of cash sitting in his left hand. Sung-Suu notices my eyebrows making their contorted yet silent question. He grabs my hand and fills it with that cash. I look up and he answers, "With all that money in the bay, we figured we would take some for our troubles. Then Koonzo told us to grab some for you since you decided to bail on us." He puts a smile at the end of it. That wonder chin makes his comment even more sincere.

I tell him, "No, Sung-Suu. That is for you. Keep it."

He leans in and says, "It is ok. My other pockets are filled as well." Then my hand gets heavier as someone else plops more money on top of Sung-Suu's cash. I use my other hand to catch the excess crumpled bills from falling. I look over and it is Cliffster.

Cliffster breaks us up, "Enough of all that. Hey, we are press for time. Here, I got five on it. On Sung-Suu's momma. And that is with tip. Make sure you do not blow it all in one place. But if you do, go to a quality hairstylist. Oh, and you are invited to come to Comic-Con anytime. But you still have to get dressed up. And you cannot go shadowboxing on people's privates. Just saying."

I tell him with a strong hug, "As long as it is a cosplay outfit with cornrows. And I learned that nut shots are not a good first impression." We laugh as he strokes his hair.

Shaboomba steps up. Oh wait. We are saying our good-byes now? The realization takes me by surprise. My heart squishes a little but it gets worse when Shaboomba puts her share of the cash in my hands. Then she puts her left arm around me, "You hit like a girl."

I smile with my comeback, "And you smell like a boy. You are the baddest nerd chick I ever met. They should do a show on you." She says nothing as we embrace.

Carter yells, "We leave in one minute!"

Goji sings, "The wheels on the bus go wait, wait, wait." Carter starts walking towards Goji as he runs behind Shaboomba. Mrs. Bellows puts her arm in front of Carter causing him to return to his place next to her. Goji sticks out his chest as he steps in front of Shaboomba.

She nudges him, "Stop it before the back of someone's head gets more knots in it." Goji quickly covers the back of his head anticipating a strike.

Then Noni and Goji hop in front of us. Shaboomba smacks them both in the back of the head probably for good measure as she walks away.

Noni places the money from my hands into a paper bag as he says, "You think someone would have thought of this. But then again that is why I am the smart one. Here is my donation to the Powa Hitchhiker Fund. Make sure when you come back down here that you find us. We will be trying to break into Comic-Con again."

Goji adds, "Yea, we decided we get more viewers just by trying to break in. And here is my donut donation. There is probably enough to get a car full of nerds to pick you up and harass you about Comic-Con."

I tell them, "You crazy twins! I am going to subscribe to your show. I am a forever fan."

Noni replies, "Look for our next episode. You might recognize some folks you know." Noni flutters his eyebrows with a cocky grin knowing the web is going to love it.

Goji jumps in, "Yeah, you might even be more famous than me!"

Shaboomba smacks Goji on the back of the head, "She already is, dummy. And you Noni, come here. I am going to smack you just because you are his brother." And that is when I give them the conclusion beat.

The twins say on cue, "Oh, that was smooth girl!" We all hug as I hear the doors on the van close.

Mrs. Bellows huddles everyone, "First off, Powa, your friends are very honorable in giving you some of that free money. But do not worry. We are not going to take it from you. And no need to give Powa the extra money. We will take care of her arrangements."

Noni immediately snatches the bag full cash ripping the handles off. Everyone looks over at him. Noni explains as his face has the look of guilt, "What? It was a reflex." Shaboomba begins to march over to him with ill intentions when Mrs. Bellows regains our attention, "This is important. Remember, all of this never happened. I do not exist, these men here do not exist, and what we all went through we never went through. And if it does not exist then you cannot talk about it, post about it, or whatever other means you may be tempted to share. For your sake and ours, please do not. I wish you all quiet success." She hops in the passenger seat and rummages through the glove compartment.

Carter stands in front of everyone now, "Team, meet me at point Bravo Zulu. If I am not there before dawn, then get off the grid until I reach you. You other guys, I do not know who you work for but you are good in my book. Find your way back and keep quiet. And thank you for battling it out with us. As for you kids, find a hideout and stay there for at least a week. Check the net and see if there is any chatter out there. I may contact you." He turns around and gets behind the wheel. Just like Carter. For him it is never about this moment. It is always about the next moment. I guess that is how he keeps his edge.

I jump in as the van starts to slowly move. I stick my head out of the sliding door and wave to them all and leave them with "Nerds rule?" It is a great rhetorical question. I keep my eyes on them. Then they adjust their posture as if they are going to go into hand to hand combat. I smile. They start doing the Haka war dance. Koonzo hearing their grunting faintly joins in. My sensitive side wants to come out, but I want to remember what I am seeing just in case this is the last time I see them. They finally leave my line of sight. I close my eyes recording the moment hoping to recall it later on in my life. I can feel my hair whip around as I sense the van accelerate. The wind feels good for a brief moment. I shut the sliding door.

Koonzo looks at me as Carter does a fantastic job of hitting every pothole on the road. I ask Carter, "Where are we headed?"

"To our rendezvous point. We have a small medical staff there. Be there in ten miles."

I grab Koonzo's hand, "Hold on, please."

He asks me, "You know, it was funny when you said I am too lucky for you."

I laugh and tell him, "I did not say that. I said you are too hardheaded for me."

Koonzo laughs regardless of the pain his wound is causing him. It is a funny moment in an uncomfortable situation.

Mrs. Bellows speaks up, "Drop me off right next to that bar. I know the owner."

Carter pulls behind the bar. Mrs. Bellows opens the rickety door and tells Carter, "We shall meet up in 13-days." Her voice cracks fas if she had not spoken for a lengthy amount of time.

Carter nods as the blood on his face is still glistening. She looks at me. Her voice is deep yet dry, "Darling, you are one hell of a young lady. Whatever happens, do not turn out like me." For the first time, it is difficult for me to distinguish her English accent.

What does she mean by that?

She closes the door as Carter smashes the accelerator. I look back to see Mrs. Bellows. Headlights turn on and she enters a black sedan. I thought she was going inside the bar.

Chapter 34

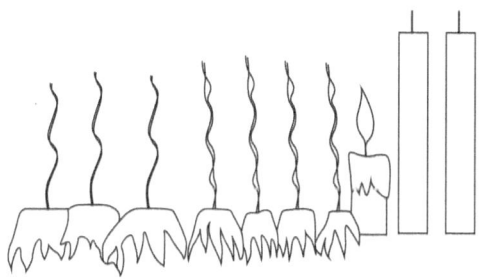

Monday early evening

We reach Carter's link up point and offload the wounded. It is a one-story luxury house in a gated community. The door opens but no one comes outside. The person waiting inside is an older Indian gentleman judging by his turban. He is wearing a teal surgical outfit who does not bother with any warm salutations. He must be a doctor. He points to the living room that has two tables and several chairs. Carter and I place Rilo and Koonzo on each table. He quickly looks over both. Carter gives him the rundown of each of their medical emergencies. After a quick examination of both, he tells Carter with a Hindu accent, "Your guy will need to go into surgery now. As for the kid, that poison is too far along. Plus, dealing with that piece of metal will only complicate things."

I object, "No! He is only a teenager! He has too much life left to die. You better help him!" I lunge at him, but Carter catches me.

Koonzo lays still listening to everyone talk about his terminal condition.

The doctor tries to explain it when Rilo interrupts with some exertion, "Do the kid, Doc. She is right. He has a lot more life to live for than the rest of us bums."

The doctor tells him, "The kid is beyond saving. I am sorry, Rilo. Young lady, I am sorry. There is nothing I can do."

I break out crying as I lay my head in Koonzo's chest. The doctor tells Carter, "We have to start now. I will need your help."

Carter follows the doctor into a set of double doors as he wheels Rilo. I stroke Koonzo's hair as he feathers through mine. He whispers in my ear, "It will be ok, Powa. But instead of sitting here watching me die, I need you to do something for me."

"Whatever you want Koonzo. What is it?"

He tells me, "I want my request to be special."

I wipe my tears away and say, "Every request is special."

But just like everybody else he says, "I want my request to be a live feed like your friend Nhim." That is no surprise for me. But I remain supportive, "Sure, let me find a camera." I head straight into the double doors. They have already begun cutting into Rilo. He is unconscious. I ask for a camera. The doctor points with his nose to a drawer. I grab it and head back out. Carter looks at me knowing what is about to happen. Both his hands are inside Rilo's stomach.

I return and tell Koonzo, "So what shall we talk about to pass the time?"

"I am scared, Powa. I am scared of dying."

"I am scared, too."

Koonzo adds, "But what will take away some of that fear is me knowing my request will be granted. Use the formula, Powa."

What formula? Wait. I completely forgot about 1X. The formula is with Rilo. I head back in through the double doors. They are having a hard time as the alarms on the machines keep Carter and the doctor busy as they work to keep Rilo alive. I do not bother asking them about the case. I see Rilo's bag on a chair. I find the case and run back into the other room.

I open it up. This cannot be happening. One of the vials is cracked and has spilled some of its contents throughout the inside. The other two vials look fine. I can work with that. I grab the formula page and unfold it. As I spread it on the table, I look it over. It looks undamaged. I unfold the second page. There seems to be a problem. The liquid that spilled inside the case has smudged a portion of the page, "It does not seem to be anything important. I got this. You ready?" He gives me a nod. I place the remaining syringe on the table. I grab the first serum, sodium thiopental. I put the syringe inside the vile. Several milliliters later, I move onto the…This is a bad problem.

I tell Koonzo, "The other two vials…their labels are smeared. They both have long scientific names. And to make things worse, they both start with the letter 'P.' What do I do, Koonzo?"

He does not reply. I stop looking at the vials and focus on him. His eyes are closed. He looks pale. No, am I too late? So soon? "Koonzo?!" I shake him hard.

He opens his heavy eyes, "I just want to take a little nap. I feel tired." I pinch him hard, "You stay awake because I am not going to be freaking out by myself."

His only reply, "Ouch! Okay, okay! Give me the juice!"

"Which one do I use?"

"Pick the one you would use on yourself." His voice begins to sound sleepy. I kick the table. His eyes shock themselves open.

I shake my head, "This does not help me, Koonzo!"

His voice sounding tired says, "You got this, Powa." I am going to lose him if I do not do something. My mind is freaking out. Okay, screw it. I grab the vial near me.

I add the required milliliters, "Okay Koonzo, I am going to stick you now. Just relax." I give him another hard pinch. He reacts with a squint but not as animated as before. Here I go. The vein in his left arm looks reassuring. I poke the vein, regardless of how shaky my hands are, and slide the needle in delicately. I push the plunger in slowly. I get lucky and the formula settles inside. Once the contents are emptied, I withdraw the syringe and place my hands around his face, "I did it, Koonzo! You are going to get your request, but you have to stay awake for me."

He opens his eyes with a smile, "Looks like it is showtime. Okay, so what do I do?"

"You just have to think about the camera. The cocktail will help make this process easier." I pick up the camera and after connecting it to the monitor I move it closer to us. I make a few selections on the menu and everything is in sync.

I tell Koonzo, "Look, I even have the monitor on to show you we are on live."

Koonzo's eyes open up even larger, "Oh my, how is my hair?" I go over to his head while looking through the camera and make a poor attempt at fixing his hair. Honestly, I made more of a mess. He laughs it up and fixes his own hair.

I ask Koonzo, "So what do you want to tell the world? Make it good, Koonzo."

He looks at the camera, "World, I am dying. I lived my life the way I believe I should live it. I wish I could have been a better person, but I think I did okay. For my friends, I will miss you guys. Sung-Suu, you are the second greatest nerd I know. Your chin is the first. Cliffster, you are a kind teddy bear with fabulous hair even though that chemical burn will make you bald when you get older. Noni, keep the chaos under control. And Goji, control the chaos. And both of you keep Scratch Cat going. Best videos on the web, except for this one." Koonzo struggles to do the conclusion beat. I laugh to reassure his effort to provide some humor.

He continues, "Shaboomba, you are one good looking nerd, but you cannot hold a candle to me...Pancake Hank. And then we have the final member of our clan. Powa, I had a crush on you in school. Now that I know you, my crush is even worse. It would have been fun, but it never would have lasted. I would eventually kick you out of my group for falling in love with a nerd."

He smiles, and I do my best to reciprocate. I turn the camera around, give a wave and kiss the top of the lens making sure I do not smudge it. I figured I would show the world a quick display of affection. If anything it will only make Koonzo's video go just as viral as Nhim's. But the emotion of the end comes over me. I can feel a tear tumble down my face. I use the camera to hide my emotion. He does not need to see that, and I wish he did not say that. But my tears begin to drain through my nose. I sniff them back inside.

Koonzo keeps looking into the camera. I can tell he wants to make a smart comment, but he decides not to. I am grateful for his thoughtfulness and say to myself, "Thanks, Koonzo." I have to grab a tissue and blow my nose before all anyone hears on this video is me snorting my boogers into my face. I place the camera on the table.

I turn away to wipe my face and clear my nose when his weak voice speaks, "It is from an anime movie." I stop wiping my nose for a quick second. He continues on, "When I introduced myself to you, you asked what kind of name is Koonzo. My mom is a fan of the anime movie 'Budacon.' The hero's name is…you guessed it. My mom is a nerd, a fantastic and beautiful nerd. She always told me to be proud of who I am whether it is a snail, tortoise, or ostrich. They all have adapted, survived, and evolved."

I clear up my tears and grab the camera. I hold it back up to my face. As I focus back on Koonzo, his eyes are closed again. I get a bad feeling in my stomach. I hope I am wrong. I shake him to get a response. Nothing. I pinch him extremely hard. No response. I slap him with every emotion to wake him up. His head takes the strike. My eyes begin to water again. I try to compose myself. I bite my cheek and pinch myself but nothing is going to work. My friend is gone. Koonzo is gone. A friend that almost became more than a friend has left me in tears. His body is limp but looks like he could wake up any moment. His skin has lost some color which is disturbing. His eyes are thankfully closed. I want to grab his hand but am worried about how that would feel. The monitor is still streaming. Now is the waiting period. I put the camera down still focused on Koonzo. I go to his bedside and decide to hold his hand. It does not squeeze my hand back. Its warmth is no longer there. His friends do not even know he is gone. That is going to be very heartbreaking for them. I try not to think of any memories about Koonzo. It will only prolong the pain. All of a sudden, I realize I am pretty exhausted.

I close my eyes and try to clear my mind. For some unknown reason, I think of these strobing lights. That is weird.

Why would I think of that at a time like this? I open my eyes and realize I was not imagining those lights. The request has begun. To my surprise, although I should not be, Koonzo chooses the camera. Rings of light orbit the camera in multiple angles. Each ring strobes at a different tempo and at different levels of illumination. This light display from the camera is one of the most beautiful ones I have seen. Without thinking, I reach for the camera with my left hand. I do not understand why I did that, but the pain is real. It is very hot to the touch but just enough for me to push beyond my tolerance level. As each ring strobes until it no longer flashes, the rings slowly disappear. But the heat gradually increases. As a ring disappears, a portion of the camera vanishes with it. There is something else. A silhouette flashes from the center of this camera. I cannot describe what this is. The silhouette shrinks as each ring disappears. Once the last ring dissolves, the glow within the room disappears as well. The camera is gone.

As quickly as my hand got hot, I feel it becoming freezing cold. So cold in fact that my hand drops to the side of my body. I can feel my blood turn cold inside my arm as it pumps back towards my heart. I frantically rub my hands together for warmth.

I cradle my left hand as I kiss his forehead in hopes it will send his soul to a place where he will find a few nerd angels to keep him company.

Carter enters from the double doors, "Thank you, doctor."

The doctor holds up a brown paper bag, "Give him these for the pain. If the stitches break, call me. Other than that, his recovery will take about four weeks."

Carter looks worn down. The poor guy has been through a lot. He reminds me of a race car that finally finished a hard-fought race and the engine is about to finally be turned off.

Unfortunately for him, there is a knock on the door. Carter and the doctor lock eyes with questions. Carter pulls out his gun. The doctor shrugs his shoulders. Carter tilts his head telling him to head to the back. He finds me and looks over at Koonzo's body. He holsters his weapon, "If they are knocking then they probably have this place surrounded. Two magazines versus their firepower? Fight another day."

He heads to the front door and puts his hand on the door knob. He looks over at me and says, "You did good, kid. I hope you keep doing good. A lot of kids your age will lose themselves in all this. Be better than them. And then be thankful. Oh, and whatever happens after I open this door, make sure you look out for Mrs. Bellows and tell her what happened here." I do not know how to answer that. Do I say 'goodbye?' Do I say, 'thank you?' Do I go up there and give him a hug? Is this the last time I will ever see him? What do I do?

The door opens and a familiar face stares at Carter. This gentleman is about three inches shorter than Carter with a slightly slender build than him. But the face is what has me intrigued. Where have I seen that face? It hits me. He was on the monitor that popped down from Momma's belly. How did he find us? He introduces himself, "Mr. Carter, my name is Marcus Payne. I am with a certain agency and am inquiring about the events that took place at the HyphenDash complex."

Now I can put the voice to the face. It is not a rough masculine voice. His English is proper, and his words are well annunciated. He sounds like a well-educated person. Carter opens the door wider to allow Marcus inside. They both have a seat. Marcus notices Koonzo's body but does not ask any questions about it, in fact, it looks like seeing the dead body does not even bother him. He also glances at me. He points to one of the chairs and gestures me to join in their conversation.

Carter starts, "Look, all we did was go in there to get my boss out who was illegally detained."

Marcus holds his left hand up, "Mr. Carter, let me start. It will make this dialogue a bit smoother." I can tell Carter just wants to get out of there as he flexes his jaw muscles. Marcus continues, "My agency was on assignment. We were about to conduct a very complex raid on a terrorist cell. I get this red ring. That means an emergency call that I needed to answer no matter what the situation may be. I answer it and it is my supervisor. And guess what he tells me?" Carter gives no answer. He maintains his posture like a statue. Me, on the hand I am on the edge of my seat. I cannot wait to hear what this guy is about to say.

Marcus answers his own question, "He tells me to stop all operations. Then my boss orders me to move all my assets to another location, a warehouse. I was to raid that location. And to make it even worse, my team is only allowed to use non-lethal ammunition."

Carter arches his eyebrows as if saying, "Why are you telling me all of this? I got more important things to do."

Marcus keeps with the story, "Of course, now I am pissed off at him. I ask him, "What gives?" And he tells me a special directive has been passed down as severe and urgent. So, we raid the place and capture the bad guys. What do we find inside this warehouse? Two of the largest piles of money I have ever seen. Then a car comes creeping in. My first reaction is to ask how come my team did not bother to tell me I have a visitor? But now my focus is on the car. It cannot be bad guys because my team would have handled them already. The car parks and from the passenger side I see a lady get out. She is close to my height, very good build. I can tell she can hold her own. I can also tell she is some kind of a federal agent or something of that sort.

She walks up to me already knowing who I am and says, 'Agent Payne, thank you for responding efficiently.' I think to myself this is the person who blew off seven months of my operation. And I tell her that. I tell her a lot went into that busted operation. She informs me that what she had going on was critical and apologizes for the gross inconvenience. From what I remember, her explanation is that she intercepted a transmission from a source that is associated with HyphenDash. That was her only lead, so she went with it. Then she tells me to place my two Terradrones, the six-legged mechanical combat scorpions, inside the pallets of money and wrap them in Absorba sheets to conceal them from detection. In that transmission, she must have known a pick-up team would arrive for this money. She used one of her agents to make the drop with the HyphenDash pick up team. Of course, you guys know the rest."

Carter asks, "So were those guys at the warehouse HyphenDash?" "I doubt it. If not then the pickup team would have recognized them. I would guess they were a favor called in to guard the money. I could not tell you how the money got there or where they got it from."

I chime in, "We noticed that your Terradrones were not attacking effectively."

Marcus retorts, "Let me stop you there, little lady. The complex you were in was not made out of paper. Getting reception was difficult. We were dealing with connectivity issues. Even our video feed was lagging. One moment we were good, and the next video feed had parts of our sensors blown off. At that point, I put them on autonomous mode while we worked on connectivity."

Now it makes sense why Momma and Poppa were having a hard time attacking. Then I made the comment, "So once you established connection, you were able to lower the underbelly and help us out."

Marcus comes back with, "Yes, the agent placed some gear in there for you guys to use."

"Well if this agent knew where we were and what was going on then why did she not use her own resources?" I had to ask because it makes no sense for them to use Marcus' resources.

He replies, "Do you think I did not ask that? She told me it was because the situation was urgent and secret, and she could not amass her own resources in such a short amount of time. She also said because of our inconvenience my agency would be compensated handsomely as well as my entire team. Of course, I do not put too much faith in that statement. But just to let you know, she was not lying. They paid my agency a big incentive as well as funded our accounts to acquire three new Terradrones vice two. I never figured the government to move quickly when it comes to paying anyone.

Carter breaks his silence, "So what do you want from us?"

"I just want to know what the big deal is? I mean I was about to take down a very complex terrorist attack and whatever you had going on is more important than that? I see you got a dead body over there, so it must be something serious. But what is more serious than terrorism these days?"

My eyes start to swell with tears again. I am reminded of my mother and Koonzo. Are they more serious than terrorism? Maybe not but they are serious for me. Carter observes my reaction to the question.

He asks Marcus, "What happened with your operation?"

Marcus looks down at his hands, "Fortunately, nothing has happened. The threat is real, though. We were anticipating the attack to take place two days ago. We stuck around just in case they were behind schedule. Things went cold yesterday.

That is normally when they set in their positions. But something must have gone wrong. These guys generally stick with their original schedules because their hierarchy on the Ivory Coast are waiting and watching them."

As Marcus continues, I view the monitor and realize people are posting on Koonzo's request. I begin to get excited as I look over at Carter with a small hint of a smile. I can tell he has been looking at me while engaging with Marcus. He gives me this look to cover up my sign of joy. Carter pats his left hand on the table. I take that as an added signal to calm myself. Possibly, he does not want me to give Marcus any other reason to stay longer.

I put my hands over my face. I want to read those posts and see how much they appreciate Koonzo's last gift to the world. Carter glances at me and then looks at Marcus, "Hey look, can we do this another time? We have been through a lot. Not to take anything away from what you have been through, but we really need to decompress."

Marcus replies with an understanding tone, "Yes, sir. I completely get it. I will get back with you in three days." They both get up and push their chairs in. Carter leads Marcus to the door. As Marcus exits, he turns around and asks, "One quick question, Carter. How did you manage to work for Mrs. Bellows?"

To me, this is an odd question to ask just before departing. Surely, he has done his research and knows of Mrs. Bellows. But what relevance does that have with any of this? I look over at Carter. His face gives no clues as to what he is thinking. I bet he is an excellent poker player. The longer they stare at each other the more uncomfortable and tense the room feels. It is like a fight is about to break out but neither one of them wants to be blamed for jumping to conclusions.

Carter opens his mouth preparing to say something when the house begins to shudder. The dishes in the kitchen clatter as everything on a shelf falls down. Could it be that HyphenDash has found us?! There is no way this is an earthquake. We all adjust our posture to keep from falling. The quake only lasts for about three seconds. Several short seconds later, the sound of an explosion takes place behind the house.

Are we under attack?! I look at Marcus, "Did you do all this so you could capture us?!"

Marcus' eyes tell me the truth. He is just as surprised as I am about what is going on. Then two more large tremors shake all the loose items in the house again. That is followed by the sound of two slightly smaller explosions. We can hear the car alarms going off.

From the double doors, the doctor comes yelling out, "We are under attack!" Carter pulls out his weapon. Marcus dittos the motion. The doctor runs to the far wall and pushes a button. The wall turns into panes of glass. Beyond the window pane is a pleasant view of a well-groomed backyard and a vanishing pool that faces the city. No bad guys are seen trying to infiltrate the house. The doctor opens one of the window panes which happens to be a sliding door, "Come here! Look for yourselves!" He runs to the far edge of the yard and points. The suspense is driving me nuts. I run out there as well. What I see is a disaster zone. The four columns of smoke begin to tower over the skyscrapers. The city has just been attacked. We are not far from the scene. I would say we are about ten-miles away. But then again, I am a poor judge of distance. This house is perched perfectly so we can see the majority of the action. But still the doctor brings out a set of binoculars and a telescope. He hands me the binoculars. I peek through and notice one of the navy ships is on fire. The hull of the navy ship next to it has flames protruding from a large hole near the back. I look for the second plume of smoke. Oh no, the convention center has been hit. Two bombs have gone off there as there are two columns of smoke on both ends.

Carter speaks, and it briefly startles me, "Do you think these are your bad guys, Marcus?" Then we see a bright flash. We cover our eyes as the concussion of the blast reaches us seconds later. As I search for the point of origin, this bad feeling enters the pit of my gut. I see it and yell, "They got the aircraft carrier!"

The doctor adds, "It is the USS Midway. It is a floating museum."

Carter grabs the binoculars from me, "It is not going to be floating for long. The hull has been breached. The ship is taking on water." The body count is going to be high. I can see the requests lighting up all over the place down there."

As he keeps looking, Carter asks Marcus again, "These have to be the terrorists you were eyeballing, right?"

Marcus gives no answer. I look around and he is not even outside with us. Carter keeps the binoculars to his face. Knowing that Marcus is not here, he tells me, "Go inside and see if he is making a call or checking the net."

I leave Carter and the doctor to themselves. I begin to search inside. I check out the other rooms. Nothing. And to make things weird, Koonzo's body is not here. I yell out, "Carter, Koonzo's body is gone! Why would Marcus take Koonzo's body?!"

Carter does not answer. I check everywhere again. No way did he come back to life. No way did he disappear like the request. No way, am I losing my mind? As I continue my search, the computer screen catches my attention. The posts are scrolling through. They must be talking about the San Diego attack. Maybe I can get some more information. I begin to read them. They are not discussing the attack. They are discussing Koonzo's request. I scroll back to see if this is true. Yes, all these posts are about Koonzo. The live feed is still on. My goodness, Koonzo managed to be the internet sensation he aspired to be even above the terror attacks. Some of the posts read, 'What am I looking at?! Totally fake. Is this real? CGI. Is this the same as the little kid's video?'

I am confused as to how I should feel. I am happy for Koonzo and this great accomplishment. But a city is bleeding out and people are not talking about it. Is this request more important than terrorism? I head back out to see what Carter and the doctor are doing. I do not get a chance to ask what they are going to do. My eyes control my body. I am paralyzed. My jaw drops. I look back at the destruction and witness a city full of requests. The glow from them are still bright enough to pierce through the black smoke. It is a beautiful tragedy that I allow to burn into my mind as tears run down my face. I am confused, though. Are these tears for those that perished or for this unique sight hopefully not everyone should ever observe again?

Carter breaks my concentration as he places his hand on my shoulder, "Time to go, kid. You rolling with us or you going at it alone?"

Chapter 35

Sunday	Monday	Tuesday	Wednesday	Thursday	Friday	Saturday		
Jeden	Dva	Trois	Pedwar	Fem	Hex	Set	Octo	Nava (New Sunday)

The devil's hour

In a facility on a different continent, a technician informs his supervisor of a discovery. Technician says, "Ma'am, we have found something."

The Supervisor replies, "Show me." Her voice is raspy and harsh. The technician pulls up an image of the night sky on a large touchscreen monitor. Then he magnifies an area. He continues to magnify it until he stops. He punches a button and draws a red circle in space.

The supervisor asks, "Ok, we are in space. You want to enlighten me on the mystery?"

"There is a frequency that is similar to one of the rays of light we captured a few days ago."

The supervisor replies, "If it is a frequency like the ray of light then we should be seeing light coming from that area."

The technician does his best to maintain his excitement, "You are correct. But for some reason we are not seeing it. I do not understand it myself. But the most interesting thing is that the frequency is not emitting from that area. It is entering into that void."

The supervisor pauses briefly. Then she says, "Well it looks like we have some investigating to do. Give me details as soon as possible. The attack on San Diego is going to take up a lot of resources right now."

The technician replies, "I will direct several of our satellites to focus in that direction."

The supervisor replies, "Looks like this will be the moment of truth for HyphenDash."

The technician replies, "That reminds me. Here is the report on that infiltration event. Also, the agency involved received the transfer of funds that includes Agent Payne and his team's incentive boost. Also, the detained HyphenDash guards are currently undergoing interrogations. We are still waiting on your green light to bring in the escapees. Is there anything else Madam Everest?"

Everest replies, "Yes, keep an eye out for Ms. Powa. We may need her again."